The shining sp...
cover of this boo...
story inside. Loo...
buy a historical r...
the very best in q...

A CAPTIVE'S DESIRE

"Sierra?" he whispered.

She didn't answer, knowing what he was asking. It wasn't like him to ask, she thought. He was a man who took what he wanted, and besides, she wasn't certain what her answer should be.

His lips brushed along her jawbone, his breath almost featherlike on her skin. "Sierra? Are you awake?"

She closed her eyes, pretending to be asleep. Her pulse began to race, but she must not give him what he sought. She must not. . . .

It was hard to remember why, for her emotions raced as his hands stroked her flesh. She gasped at the sensations he aroused.

"Just what I thought," Cholla murmured. And his mouth came down to cover hers very gently.

She tried to remember that she must not let herself enjoy this newfound sensuality he had taught her. She must resist or lose her dignity as a captive. She moaned as he continued to caress her. Didn't she want to stop him? What an insane question, she thought indignantly, even as she pulled him closer. . . .

"APACHE CARESS is emotionally charged, historically accurate and smoldering with sensuality . . . an absorbing, compelling read for every Western romance fan."

—Kathe Robin, *Romantic Times*

SURRENDER TO THE PASSION

LOVE'S SWEET BOUNTY   (3313, $4.50)
by Colleen Faulkner

Jessica Landon swore revenge of the masked bandits who robbed the train and stole all the money she had in the world. She set out after the thieves without consulting the handsome railroad detective, Adam Stern. When he finally caught up with her, she admitted she needed his assistance. She never imagined that she would also begin to need his scorching kisses and tender caresses.

WILD WESTERN BRIDE   (3140, $4.50)
by Rosalyn Alsobrook

Anna Thomas loved riding the Orphan Train and finding loving homes for her young charges. But when a judge tried to separate two brothers, the dedicated beauty went beyond the call of duty. She proposed to the handsome, blue-eyed Mark Gates, planning to adopt the boys herself! Of course the marriage would be in name only, but yet as time went on, Anna found herself dreaming of being a loving wife in every sense of the word . . .

QUICKSILVER PASSION   (3117, $4.50)
by Georgina Gentry

Beautiful Silver Jones had been called every name in the book, and now that she owned her own tavern in Buckskin Joe, Colorado, the independent didn't care what the townsfolk thought of her. She never let a man touch her and she earned her money fair and square. Then one night handsome Cherokee Evans swaggered up to her bar and destroyed the peace she'd made with herself. For the irresistible miner made her yearn for the melting kisses and satin caresses she had sworn she could live without!

MISSISSIPPI MISTRESS   (3118, $4.50)
by Gina Robins

Cori Pierce was outraged at her father's murder and the loss of her inheritance. She swore revenge and vowed to get her independence back, even if it meant singing as an entertainer on a Mississippi steamboat. But she hadn't reckoned on the swarthy giant in tight buckskins who turned out to be her boss. Jacob Wolf was, after all, the giant of the man Cori vowed to destroy. Though she swore not to forget her mission for even a moment, she was powerfully tempted to submit to Jake's fiery caresses and have one night of passion in his irresistible embrace.

Available wherever paperbacks are sold, or order direct from the Publisher. Send cover price plus 50¢ per copy for mailing and handling to Zebra Books, Dept. 3560, 475 Park Avenue South, New York, N.Y. 10016. Residents of New York, New Jersey and Pennsylvania must include sales tax. DO NOT SEND CASH.

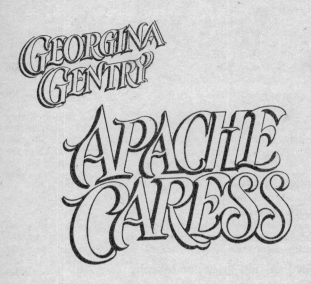

GEORGINA GENTRY

APACHE CARESS

ZEBRA BOOKS
KENSINGTON PUBLISHING CORP.

ZEBRA BOOKS

are published by

Kensington Publishing Corp.
475 Park Avenue South
New York, NY 10016

Copyright © 1991 by Lynne Murphy

All rights reserved. No part of this book may be repro-
duced in any form or by any means without the prior written consent of the Publisher, excepting brief quotes used in
reviews.

If you purchased this book without a cover you should be
aware that this book is stolen property. It was reported as
"unsold and destroyed" to the Publisher and neither the
Author nor the Publisher has received any payment for this
"stripped book."

First printing: October, 1991

Printed in the United States of America

Civilization prefers people who conform. Its motto might well be: *The nail that sticks up will be hammered down*. Occasionally a rugged individualist comes along who is molded of such fiery steel that he will not bend or be driven; he tries instead to break the hammer. One such man became a Western legend, to his Apache people and to those he fought. This novel is dedicated to him.

In Memory of Massai

and all the other valiant Native Americans who suffered or died because they refused to be hammered down.

Prologue

Picture this: an Arizona Apache warrior loose on the outskirts of the city of St. Louis, Missouri. Yes, it actually happened during September, 1886, in one of those strange and little-known true episodes of American history.

Like all great adventures that have been told and retold, even the Apache can no longer discern what is fact and what is legend about this warrior's escape from a train carrying his people to a Florida prison after Geronimo's final surrender.

So some of the story you are about to read is true. Some of it is what might have happened. There is no question that 1,500 miles of hostile terrain, armed settlers, and determined soldiers stood between him and his impossible goal. Or that, against overwhelming odds, he determined to return to his beloved homeland.

And maybe, in sheer desperation, he took a white hostage, like Sierra, who had good reason to hate the Apache. . . .

Chapter One

September, 1886
Near East St. Louis

Now that she was widowed, all alone in the world and losing the farm to the bank, where would she go and what would she do?

Sierra thought about it again as she carried a box of dishes out the door and lifted it into the wagon. At least there wasn't much to pack and load. She squinted at the late afternoon sun. By tomorrow morning, she who had never been allowed to make decisions, had to decide what to do with the rest of her life.

With a sigh, she brushed a wisp of black hair back into its bun and leaned against the wagon, listening to the lonely whistle of an approaching train. It sounded as forlorn as she felt. She looked toward the track running just past her fence a hundred yards away. How she envied the passengers as she watched the engine puff toward her from the west. At least some people in this world were safe and secure and knew where they were going.

9

Sierra wished she could say the same. Reared by a stern, protective grandfather, then married last spring to a dominating cavalry officer, Sierra had resisted her rebellious impulses and done as she was told. Now, with both of them dead, she felt like a small bird thrown out of its cage into a hostile world it was unprepared to deal with.

The train chugged toward her, black smoke drifting on the warm September air. Sierra wondered where it had come from and where it was going? Only a few miles behind that train lay the wide Mississippi. She had never even been west of that river, much less far away to the mountains she was named for.

A cinder blew from the smokestack onto the sleeve of her plain black dress, and she brushed it away. The train was abreast of her now, and Sierra stared at the vague outlines of people in the coach windows, wondering who they were and where they had come from. Her wild, reckless young mother had longed to go West and had never fulfilled that dream.

The train whistled again. Two men came out of one of the passenger cars, moving across the connection toward the baggage car behind. They paused on the swaying platform. The second man wore a blue uniform, but Sierra hardly saw him, her attention being centered on the big, wide-shouldered one. *Merciful heavens, an Indian. A red-skinned savage.* Sierra recoiled at the thought, staring at the dark-skinned man. Naked to the waist, the silver conchos of his tall moccasins reflecting the late afternoon sun, he stared back at her with moody eyes as dark as her own. He wore buckskin pants and a red headband that held straight black hair back from his ruggedly handsome face.

The way he looked at her compelled Sierra to touch the throat of her prim widow's dress to make sure it was buttoned. Wild and male as some range stallion, Sierra thought, and noted with relief that he wore shackles.

Indians. It was because of them that Robert lay dead in a hero's grave far away in Arizona and she was alone in the world. She glared at the savage, hoping that the Army was taking him somewhere to be hanged.

Cholla paused on the swaying platform, watching the white girl standing by the small, canvas-covered wagon. Why was she glaring at him as if she hated him? It made no sense, but then who could understand the thinking of whites? Cholla had scouted for the Army against renegades like Geronimo, yet the Apache scouts were now being shipped to that same Florida prison as the hostiles.

Anger at the injustice and the betrayal smoldered in his soul, fueled by the way the dark-haired girl put her hand to her throat as if she feared even his gaze.

Lieutenant Gillen pushed him roughly. "Blast it all! Get on in that baggage car!"

Cholla half turned, ready to strike out at his captor, then realized this wasn't a good time or place to attempt to escape. And he intended to escape . . . or die trying.

He let Gillen shove him into the baggage car, thinking he had not lain with a woman in many weeks.

But it was not an Apache woman or even a Mexican *cantina* girl he thought of now. In his mind, he imagined that white woman shaking her long hair loose from its pins so it blew wild and free about her naked, pale shoulders as she slowly peeled off the black dress. Her

11

face had been brown as any Apache's from the sun, but under the black fabric, her breasts and thighs and belly were surely as pale as the mountain snows of the high country.

Gillen slammed him up against a stack of crates in the swaying baggage car. "You damned Injun! I saw the way you looked at the white girl! Got rape on your mind, do ya?" He tried to kick Cholla between the thighs, but the Apache managed to protect himself.

"You're voicing your own thoughts." Cholla glared at him. "If you weren't armed, and I weren't chained hand and foot, you wouldn't be so brave."

The officer laughed and hefted the rifle in his hands. "You're smart, Cholla, too damned smart! You know I'm looking for any excuse to kill you before I finally have to unload this train at Fort Marion."

"Just remember"—Cholla smiled without mirth—"if you kill me, you'll never find out what you want to know."

Gillen pushed his hat back on his brown, curly hair and swore softly. "You red bastard, there's *two* things I aim to find out!"

Cholla looked at the shorter man. "You're running out of time, Lieutenant."

Gillen took a paper bag full of candy from his jacket, popped a piece in his mouth. Even from where he was, Cholla could smell peppermint on the lieutenant's breath. "Blast it all, why do you think I brought you back here away from the other prisoners? I intend to beat it outa you!"

Cholla wished he could get his hands on that rifle. "All I've got to do is yell, and the other soldiers will come running."

"After serving with you, Cholla, I figure I know you pretty damned well. You're too proud to scream for help." Gillen leaned against the small window. "Tell me what *really* happened that day to Forester, and tell me about the gold."

Cholla shrugged, watching for an opening. "It was all in Sergeant Mooney's report; you read it. As for the gold, you know the Apache god, Usen, forbids us to dig for it."

"But you all know where's it's likely to be found," the lieutenant insisted.

Cholla's skin felt raw from the iron fetters. He rubbed at his wrists, and the chains rattled. "If you say so. I'm just a scout."

"Blast it all! Don't be so damned calm and superior with me, you damned Injun!" Gillen rolled the candy around in his mouth, hefted the rifle.

"Why hurt the innocent with the truth?"

"God damn it! The truth is what I want to know!" Lieutenant Gillen advanced on him.

"The men who survived that ambush know; no one else ever will." Cholla forced himself to control his temper. He must not attack the officer. That was what Gillen was after, an excuse to beat him senseless or kill him.

"You blasted red bastard! I'm gonna kick you bloody! You'll tell me everything before I finish with you!" He brought his rifle back, slammed the butt hard against Cholla's ribs.

The pain was worse than the Apache had expected. He went for Gillen's throat, mindless, enraged. As he attacked, the officer swung the rifle again, catching Cholla across the ribs, knocking him back against a

13

stack of boxes in the swaying, noisy car. The boxes fell with a crash, but Cholla managed to keep his footing, even though the breath had been knocked out of him. All he could do was double over, gasping for air, stalling for time as the officer advanced on him.

Gillen smiled slowly. "You attacked me, scout. That's all the excuse I need. When I get through slamming you between the legs with this rifle butt, you'll never top another woman, much less look at a white one!"

His flesh seemed afire with bruises, but Cholla feigned even more pain than he felt. Under his feet, the train swayed into a curve, beginning to slow its speed. If he could get that rifle, he would kill Gillen. After that, he didn't care what the Army did to him. Even hanging was better than life in a cage thousands of miles from home. He didn't straighten up. "Please," he gasped. "I'm hurt . . . don't hit me again. I . . . I'll tell you what you want to know."

The officer hesitated. "Didn't think it would be this easy, you lousy redskin. Maybe you're not as tough as you —"

Cholla dived for his legs. Even though the train seemed to slow as it went into a wide curve, the momentum and the swaying caused them both to hit the floor hard. They rolled over and over in dust and a tangle of chains, the clatter and the puffing drowning out the desperate sounds of their life-and-death fight.

The chains hampered Cholla. Gillen managed to stumble to his feet, a triumphant gleam in his eye as he cocked the rifle. Recklessly, Cholla charged him again. Gillen would kill him anyway, he might as well take the white man with him.

They meshed and fell against a stack of heavy crates

14

that swayed dangerously. Now Cholla slammed Gillen up against the small window, and it shattered as they fought for the gun. If he could just cut the white man to pieces against the jagged glass . . .

But Gillen seemed to sense Cholla's thought as he, too, twisted to throw the Apache scout's arm against the knifelike shards. Cholla's warm red blood smeared them both as the train slowed to a crawl in its curve.

By Usen, he had to get that rifle. Oblivious to pain, Cholla fought with desperation, slammed Gillen hard against the wall. With an agonized cry, the white fell, and the rifle flew out of his hands just as the crates crashed down.

Fettered as he was, Cholla just barely jumped out of the way. Gasping for breath, he managed to keep his balance, his body one aching mass. Gillen lay covered with blood, motionless near the crates. Dead, Cholla thought with relief, and he turned his attention to the rifle wedged under the fallen boxes. He needed that weapon. At any minute, another soldier might come back to investigate why they had been gone so long.

Cholla looked out the shattered window. Late afternoon, thousands of miles from home. If he had the rifle, he might have a chance. The train gradually slowed to a crawl.

With superhuman effort, he put his wide shoulder against the crates, trying to move them. He felt the veins in his massive body bulge. Sweat stood out on his bloody, naked skin as he threw his strength into the effort. Whatever was in the crates, it would take more than one man, no matter how strong, to move them. And the rifle was under them.

Beneath his feet, Cholla felt the swaying train begin

15

to pick up speed as it came out of the curve. He knew he had to make a choice. Soon it would be hurtling down straight track and jumping would mean certain death. Yet how could he survive in this white man's country without a weapon?

He struggled again to move the crates, groaning with the effort. The train whistled as it picked up speed, clacking over the tracks. In another minute, it would be moving too fast to jump, but staying meant he'd be hanged when the soldiers found Gillen's body.

Cholla didn't have much choice. However slim his chances were in this strange country far from home, he would have to try to escape. He had lived most of his thirty years on the edge, always taking risks. To do otherwise was not living but existing like a bird in a cage; the same kind of cage that had awaited him in Florida. Captive security against dangerous freedom. Better to take his chances jumping.

The chains clanged as he stumbled out onto the swaying platform between the cars. Cinders blew past him in a cloud of smelly smoke. By leaning out, he could see a downhill slope ahead. The train would be picking up speed, hurtling down the hill in only seconds more. To leap then was to die. Remaining, he'd be hanged when the soldiers found the body.

Cholla took a deep breath, said a prayer to Usen and jumped as far as he could, hoping to clear the hurtling cars. For what seemed eternity, he hung in midair. If his chains caught on anything, he would be dragged under the giant wheels and killed. Or worse yet, maimed.

He hit the ground hard and rolled. Cholla remembered the smell of crushed weeds, the numbness of his flesh, the taste of blood from his cut lip. He told himself to get up. They would be looking for him. But he could not force his muscles to respond.

Dimly, he heard the distant whistle, the far-off chugging of the train. He lay there, listening to the fading sound, expecting to hear the shrieking squeal of brakes as someone found the dead man, pulled the emergency cord. Cholla struggled to sit up in the patch of tall weeds. Through them, he saw the train still moving away, swaying and puffing as its speed increased.

He must leave this place. Very soon someone would find Gillen and the train would back up, the soldiers looking for him along the tracks. He needed to get far away before that happened. Uncertainly, he got to his feet and assessed his injuries; weary, dirty, and bloody from the glass cuts — but no broken bones.

Cholla glanced toward the late afternoon sun. Under cover of darkness, he had a better chance. *Chance of what?* The chains rattled as he moved. No weapon, no food, no one to help him. At least fifteen hundred miles from familiar territory. In the distance, the train disappeared over the rise, but its whistle echoed and its smoke hung on the pale blue horizon. He began to work his way through the tall weeds.

When he found a small creek, he walked down it to confuse the tracker dogs the Army might bring in. Then afraid of being seen, he drank his fill and lay in the shelter of some bushes, waiting for darkness to fall.

What was he going to do? Up until now, he had thought only of surviving minute to minute, but he was a seasoned warrior, used to danger and hardship. Coolly, he began to think and make plans.

If only his friend, Tom Mooney, were here. *Sikis*—

brother, he thought. But Tom had been left behind at the Arizona station, arguing with his superiors and risking court-martial by trying to prevent Cholla and the other loyal Apache scouts from being forced on that train. Cholla didn't even want to think about what had happened to his horse and his dog. They were no doubt dead, as was beautiful young Delzhinne, and as he himself soon would be.

One thing was certain, he would not go to his grave without a fight. Deep in his heart, he knew he had no chance of making it all the way back to the West. Only a few miles from here lay that big river, the Mississippi, and it was too wide to swim. By Usen, he could not win, but he would not quit. When they killed him, he would go down fighting. That was what made the whites hate him so; he wouldn't conform. He wouldn't bend, and they couldn't break him. Cholla, like the desert cactus he was named for, was tough, dangerous to tangle with.

He rested until dark and then began to travel. Tired and hungry as his brawny body was, his mind was clear. Many times he had been in bad situations, but his level head and bravery had saved him. Not only the Army but armed citizens would be searching for him, eager to kill. If he were to have any chance at all, he had to get the chains off. But to do that, he needed tools; blacksmith's tools or maybe an axe. Where were such tools found?

Farms. Cholla looked down at the chains on his wrists and ankles. He must find a farm where there were no dogs to scent him and give the alarm. Most whites owned dogs. When the creatures barked, men came out with guns.

He tried to maintain a slow trot, the chains jangling as he moved. Lithe as a puma, though a big man, Cholla concentrated on putting distance between him and where he had jumped from the train. And then what? he thought ruefully. If he managed to travel all those miles back to the big river, how would he get across? He could hardly walk across that giant bridge. Maybe he could sneak aboard a freight train headed west across it.

With that thought, he paused when he saw the rails gleaming in the moonlight. Yes, maybe he could follow the tracks back, almost to the giant river, and sneak aboard a train. It might take the white men several days to get tracker dogs. Right now, his first priority was getting the chains off.

He walked along the tracks, headed west. Several times he stopped and scouted out a farm, hoping to find tools and food. But always the distant barking of dogs or the sight of men in farmhouse windows, made him decide to move on, seek an easier target. One thing was certain, he needed to be unfettered and on his way before daylight.

His belly growled, and his body ached. Dried blood stained his headband. But Cholla was used to hardship. His father had been killed by drunken warriors in a raid, and he, Delzhinne, and Mother had nearly starved before Mother began to clean and cook at the white soldiers' fort. Cholla had grown up among whites. The last several years, he had scouted for the Army because he knew that leaders like Geronimo would only prolong his peoples' ordeal. General Crook had given his word that they could stay in their beloved country.

However, General Miles had taken over and the promises Gray Fox Crook had made were no good. All the Apaches had been betrayed and gathered up to be shipped away to prison, even those who had served as Army scouts. Anger at the injustice burned deep in Cholla's heart as he moved across the dark countryside. Never again would he trust the whites. He who had been lied to, mistreated, and shown no mercy would respond in kind.

Around him, crickets chirped in the dark night and somewhere a dog howled. The lonely sound echoed through the stillness, making him think of his own dog, Ke'jaa. Cholla winced when he remembered the chaotic scene at the railroad station as the Apaches were forced on board the train. Hundreds of the Indians' dogs had run about in the confusion, barking and whimpering, trying to follow their masters onto the train. They had been beaten back by the soldiers.

Cholla had put his face against the window as the train pulled away. His friend, Sergeant Mooney, stood forlornly on the platform, the dogs barking and milling about, running after the departing cars. Ke'jaa. The name meant "dog" in his language. Big and half-coyote, his pet had run alongside the train for miles, trying vainly to keep up with Cholla while Lieutenant Gillen had laughed about the fate of the Apaches' dogs once the train was gone. No doubt Ke'jaa had been shot along with hundreds of other dogs.

At least Gillen wouldn't be riding Cholla's fine stallion now. The Apache took some satisfaction in that thought as he paused and caught his breath. In the moonlight, he tried to get his bearings. Where was he and how far had he come?

Up ahead lay a farm. He could see faint light streaming through the windows of the small house near the train tracks. *Were there dogs?* If not, maybe he could steal some tools from the barn, or even a horse. If he were lucky, there might be a smokehouse with some ham or bacon. Though Apaches weren't fond of pork, Cholla had lived too long with the whites to like mule meat and some of the other delicacies the wild Apaches relished.

Cautiously, Cholla slipped closer to the house. Out front was a small, canvas-covered wagon, the type a peddler might use. There was something familiar about this place, but he had passed a hundred such scrabble-poor farms on the long train trip.

He moved along, silent as a shadow, listening for a dog or maybe a man's voice drifting through the open windows. *Nothing.* Out behind the house, a small barn stood silhouetted against the moon. He remembered then why the place looked familiar to him.

In his mind, he stood on the swaying train platform again, returning the stare of an ebony-haired girl in a black dress. She had glared at him, curious and yet hostile. Cholla remembered the hatred in her tanned face and wondered about it. It had been a long time since he had lain with a woman. But Apaches had a taboo against rape. They were afraid that evil spirits would haunt them for taking an unwilling woman. Still, the thought of the girl drew him slowly toward the small house.

I need to see if there are men on this place who might come out to the barn if they hear a noise, he told himself. Then he remembered that the woman had worn a black dress, the sign of a widow. Still there might be brothers or a father or some other male relatives who would shoot at him. He had better investigate the scene before he tried to take tools or food.

Cholla went to the window and looked in. The woman stood within, clad in a flimsy white garment, a photo in her hand. As he watched, she bent over a trunk, put the small framed photo inside, took out a hairbrush, and straightened. On the table were an oil lamp and one lone plate and cup. The scent of frying bacon and hot bread drifted from the stone fireplace through the open windows.

His heart pounded harder. The woman was alone. The one plate told him that. Alone and defenseless. His gaze swept the room looking for weapons. He saw none. Besides the trunk, there were boxes stacked about as if she were packing to leave.

His attention returned to the woman. The chemise was so sheer, Cholla saw the dark circles of her nipples through the fabric. Her skin was tan except where dresses protected it, and her pale breasts swelled beneath the white underthing. While he watched, she took the pins from her ebony hair, shook the locks out, and began to brush them.

Cholla watched the light reflect on her hair as she brushed, her breasts moving with each stroke. He had a sudden vision of her lying on the small rug before the fire, the thin chemise pulled up around her hips, her long black hair spread under her. Her mouth looked as soft and full as her breasts. He saw himself walking toward her as she smiled and reached up to him, spreading her thighs. He would lie down on her, covering her small, pale body with his big dark one. He would tan-

22

gle one hand in her hair and lift her face up to his while his other hand pushed down the chemise. As he had thought, her breasts and belly were milky white where the sun had not touched her skin.

Cholla took a breath and then sighed, feeling his manhood hard and aching, wanting the relief the girl's body could offer. She turned suddenly and stared toward the window as if she had heard the sound. He held his breath and did not move. Then she shrugged, as if convincing herself that it was only her imagination, and resumed brushing her hair. With each stroke her breasts moved, and Cholla imagined how they would feel when he closed his big, callused hands over them, the nipples erect against his palms.

He looked down at the fetters on his wrists and ankles. His very life and freedom were at stake; he had no time to think of women. His arm was bleeding again, but he couldn't do anything about that right now. He moved as carefully as he could to keep from rattling the chains.

Turning, he crept toward the barn. Maybe he would find some blacksmith's tools or at least an axe there. There must also be a horse, or the wagon wouldn't be out front. It looked as if she was loading it to leave on the morrow. When he had first seen her from the train, the pure hatred in her stare had mystified him. She'd be even angrier tomorrow when she found a horse and some meat from the smokehouse missing. He could travel many miles before the widow found that someone had been about in the night.

Cholla paused at the open barn door, breathing in the scent of sweet hay and leather harness. An animal snorted and stamped its hooves in a shadowy stall as he

23

crept toward it. He put his hand on the top rail, guiding himself through the darkness. As a scout, Cholla had had a lot of experience with cavalry mounts.

The animal snorted again. "Easy, boy," he soothed. "Be still. Once I get these chains off, we're leaving."

Then Cholla brushed against something on the top rail, something fluffy and feathered that set up a terrible, loud squawking and wing-flapping.

A chicken. He had awakened a stray barnyard hen perched on the rail, and she'd set up a racket as if a fox were after her. As Cholla paused, uncertain what to do, the chicken squawked and flapped, further exciting the creature that was snorting, maybe at scenting the fresh blood on Cholla. The animal now began an ungodly heehawing.

By Usen, a mule. A damned mule. That creature and the noisy hen were making enough racket to be heard for miles.

What to do now? Cholla looked toward the house. Would the woman come out to investigate the racket? Maybe she hadn't heard it.

She came to the window, peered out uncertainly. Cholla watched her, hoping she would stay inside. Even though she had looked at him earlier with eyes full of hatred, he didn't want to kill her. He glanced at the chains on his wrists. By looping them over her head, he could break her neck before she had any chance to cry out.

In the darkness Cholla pressed his back up against the wall and held his breath. He heard a sound and twisted his head to look. The woman stood in the doorway of the small house. She held a rifle and a lamp. For a long moment, she hesitated as if afraid, then started toward the barn.

Cursing silently, Cholla pressed himself against the inside wall, listening to her footsteps coming closer. He had never hurt a woman, but there was no way out of it now. To insure his own safety, he would have to kill the one with the hate-filled eyes.

Chapter Two

Sierra stood by the trunk in her chemise, holding the small photo and staring at Robert's handsome face. It had been a whirlwind courtship and such a brief marriage before the dashing lieutenant was sent to Arizona Territory. Robert. He wasn't the type to be called Bob. Under the shock of blondish hair, his almost turquoise-colored eyes stared back at her as cold and remote as his personality.

They had both had their pictures made that day. She wondered idly what he had done with hers? It hadn't been among the little package of personal items included with the medals and the letter of condolence from his commanding officer.

Was there a chance he might have been carrying it with him so it had been buried with his body? She could only hope he cared that much, but in reality she knew better.

She was a widow because of a bunch of bloodthirsty Apaches. It was ironic somehow. At her stern grandfather's urging, she had married Robert, though with misgivings. Now both men were dead, and she faced the world alone.

With a tired sigh, Sierra bent over the small trunk and tucked the photo in the tray next to Robert's medals and her hairbrush. At least Robert hadn't shirked his duty. Somehow Sierra had figured him for a coward. She felt guilty about that. She had hoped she and Robert could be reconciled, but now that would never be.

Sierra took the hairbrush out of the tray and pulled hairpins out, shaking her long ebony hair down to brush it. So few things to take, really: personal items, clothes, scissors and sewing notions tucked deep in the trunk, a few household items. The furnishings would stay with the house when banker Toombs and the sheriff came to put her out tomorrow. She intended to be gone before they got here. She brushed her hair with angry strokes.

Abruptly, Sierra had the eeriest feeling that she was being watched. She paused, looked around, realizing that she stood in a skimpy chemise near an open window.

Then she chided herself for being a fool and reminded herself that Grandfather's old rifle was in the cupboard. She could shoot fairly well for a woman, so she hadn't been afraid to live alone this past summer. Besides, in all these years there had never been any trouble or thievery in this peaceful farming area.

Again, she seemed to feel someone watching her. It was almost as if a man's big hands reached out and stroked her bare shoulders, gradually pulled the thin chemise down to expose her breasts.

Sierra, you ninny! Why are you having crazy thoughts like this? Then she remembered the savage on the train late in the afternoon. He had stared at her in a way that

27

made her feel as if he would like to put his hands all over her. . . .

She tossed the hairbrush into the trunk, closed it. Men. She supposed whatever their color, they were all alike. She had had such storybook ideas about marriage before Robert had deflowered her quickly and mechanically on their wedding night, then rolled over and gone to sleep.

She heard a sudden, surprised, squawk from the direction of the barn and ran to the window. Merciful heavens! Was there a varmint after her few remaining hens?

The mule brayed long and loud. Sierra hurried to get the rifle, checked to make sure it was loaded. The hens she could spare, but if the varmint was something big, like a bobcat, she was worried about the mule. She'd need that mule tomorrow. How she missed her old dog. She'd felt safe with Rex guarding the place, but he was dead now, too.

Still clutching the rifle, Sierra slipped on her shoes and reached for the kerosene lamp. She hesitated in the doorway, remembering the eerie feeling she'd had only moments before, and holding the lamp high, peered out toward the barn. Never had the night looked so black and ominous. The flickering lamp threw such a dim, small circle of light into the shadows.

When I get to the barn, she told herself, I'm going to find a possum or maybe a stray cat. Mercy, she was making too big a thing of this. Taking a deep breath for courage, Sierra checked the rifle again to make certain it was loaded, held her lamp high, and started forth.

Cholla looked around the edge of the barn door. By Usen, she had more courage than most women, she was coming out to investigate, and she carried a rifle. That made her dangerous.

He watched her walk toward the barn, her lamp a little flicker of light in the darkness. She must not see him yet. He had no desire to hurt a woman, but he might have to kill this one to keep her from killing him. Certainly he couldn't let her see him and then escape to spread the alarm. Maybe she would only glance inside and then go back to the house. If so, he would steal some tools and the mule, and slip away in the night, even though he needed that rifle to survive.

Cholla flattened himself against the inner wall. His wounds were sore and caked with dried blood, and his belly again reminded him that he'd had no food, but he was used to hardship, hunger, and even burning thirst. Determined to survive against hostile conditions and varied enemies, he had lived on the edge, taking one risk after another. Tonight was no different. He held his breath, his muscles tense as he waited.

Cautiously, Sierra crept toward the barn, rifle at the ready. Her heart beat harder, even though she knew a possum or a small fox was no real danger except to stray hens. She paused in the doorway of the barn, holding her lamp high. The reassuring scent of hay drifted on the warm night air.

What was that dark, shiny spot on the barn floor, blackly scarlet against the yellow straw? She stared down at it a long moment A chill ran up and down her back like the stroking of a skeleton's bony fingers. Blood. That was what it was; blood.

Oh, Lord, the possum had gotten the chicken after all. That was why the thing had squawked. The mule snorted at her from his stall, and Sierra sighed with relief. Well, it was too bad about the old hen, but probably the varmint had fled. She set the lamp on a box and looked around. The interior, except for her small circle of light, seemed as black as a witch's soul.

The mule snorted and stamped its hooves again.

"It's all right, boy," she said reassuringly. Cradling the rifle in the crook of her arm, she started across the barn to the stall.

She heard a sudden rattle of metal as if someone had dropped a bucket of horseshoes, and then something reached out of the shadows and grabbed her, yanking her through the darkness, the rifle clattering from her grasp.

In terror, Sierra tried to scream, but a hand went over her mouth and an arm yanked her back against a big body that felt hot against her almost naked skin. She even felt his heart beating against her as she struggled in the maze of chains wrapped around her.

"Stop it!" A deep voice ordered sternly. "Stop fighting, or I'll kill you!"

Sierra obeyed numbly. It was like a nightmare; this faceless man with chains jangling pulled her slim body hard up against his almost naked one. One of his hands was clamped over her mouth, the other encircled her just under her breasts, holding her tightly.

An escaped convict. Yes. With the chains, that's what he was. She didn't doubt he would make good his threat. Pulled up against him, she felt his rippling muscles, even his virile manhood.

She couldn't see him, but his warm breath stirred her hair as he put his mouth close to her ear. "We're going back to the house. You got food in there?"

Sierra nodded awkwardly, acutely aware of the heat of the arm pressing up under her breasts. She trembled in spite of herself.

"I won't hurt you," he whispered. "I watched you through the window for a while."

The aroused tone of his voice left no doubt in her mind. He was going to do more than kill her. First he would rape her.

"Now, Dark Eyes, I'm going to take my hand away. If you scream, you'll be sorry. Understand?"

Sierra nodded, too terrified even to think. He sounded desperate. What was he wanted for? Murder? If so, he wouldn't hesitate to do it again.

Very slowly, he took his hand away from her mouth, but the one around her middle remained in place. The chains rattled as he moved.

"P-please don't hurt me," Sierra gasped, "take the gun, or the mule, anything; just don't hurt me."

"By Usen, I meant to throttle you with my chains; don't know why I hesitated. Now what will I do with you?" His breath felt warm on her bare shoulder.

Sierra didn't dare move or look back at him as he kept her pulled up against him. *Rape.* Yes, of course he would rape her. "My—my husband and six brothers will be home in a few minutes. You'd better go while you can."

He didn't let go of her, but his other hand grasped her bare shoulder. "You're lying, Dark Eyes. You're here alone; I know that."

He sounded angry and exhausted. She must not cry

31

or panic or take any unnecessary risks. But her throat felt so dry, she wasn't sure she could get any words out. "Who . . . who are you?"

"What difference does it make? They call me Cholla."

She repeated the word in her mind, the same way he'd pronounced it; *Chaw-yuh*. She couldn't even guess what language it was.

He spun her around to face him, and the chains rattled again.

The moon came out and shone through the open barn door as Sierra looked up at him. Shadows hid his face, but he was almost a giant of a man with the widest pair of shoulders Sierra had ever seen. And he was naked from the waist up.

"Do you have an axe or some blacksmith tools out here?"

He meant to kill her. "P-please," she managed to say, "take the rifle and whatever else you want; just let me go."

"The axe," he insisted, his face still hidden by shadow. "I want to get these chains off."

She almost gasped with relief. "There's one by the woodpile next to the house."

"Good. You lead the way."

As Sierra watched, trembling with fear, he leaned over, grabbed up the rifle, caught her arm. "Okay, you pick up the lamp and let's go."

He held her so close against him, she could feel the heat of his bare skin as they started back up the path. Once she stumbled, and the sheer strength of the man kept her from falling.

Strong. Big. Dangerous. What had he been thinking as he watched her through the window? Sierra tried to block that from her mind. If this escaped convict would only let her live, she would submit to him.

When she pointed out the woodpile, he insisted on carrying the axe along with the rifle.

They went inside.

"Set the lamp on the table," he ordered. He sounded weary and desperate.

Gingerly, Sierra did as she was told. He let go of her arm, and she whirled away, cringing against a wall as she saw his face in the light. A savage. He was a half-naked redskin!

Her horror and fear must have shown in her face because he smiled without mirth. "Every white woman's worst nightmare, right?"

She was too afraid to answer or even move.

"I saw you from the train," he said softly. When he laid the axe and the rifle on the table, the chains rattled.

The train. In her mind, she stood by the wagon in the late afternoon, staring back at a handsome, half-naked man. How had he managed to get off that train? Every white woman's worst nightmare? She doubted it, but she now had to face the reality of being raped *and* killed.

She took a good look at his massive body and saw the blood on his arm. "You're hurt."

He shrugged and slumped down on a chair. "I'm the winner. You should see the loser."

Merciful heavens, he had killed somebody. That was how he had escaped. He had killed a guard and had nothing to lose by killing again.

A frown crossed his dark, high-cheekboned face. "Stop glaring at me. I could use some food."

"Yes . . . of course," Sierra stammered. She could

stall the inevitable by feeding him. "I don't have much; some bacon and leftover biscuits."

"Sounds good compared to Army grub." His moody gaze swept up and down her body.

She glanced down, realized all she wore was the flimsy, sheer chemise, and crossed her arms over her breasts to protect them from his stare. "Y-yes, I'll get you some food." She started across the room toward the fireplace. "You speak awfully good English for a . . . for a—"

"Savage?" he filled in with a derisive snort. "I was raised around soldiers. My mother washed clothes at the fort after my father was killed."

She picked up a butcher knife, began to slice bacon. She glanced at the axe and rifle next to his hand. If he relaxed enough to let down his guard, could she possibly. . . ?

"Don't even think it," he said from his chair.

"You haven't a chance," she blurted out without thinking, surprised at her own daring. "You ought to turn yourself in."

He rubbed the back of his neck. "So the soldiers can kill me? I tried to play it their way, conform, do what I was told. This is what it got me. Renegades like Geronimo were right, after all." He sounded angry, bitter.

He looked more like a renegade than a conformist. Those who did as they were told didn't make waves; they stayed out of trouble. *The nail that stands up will be hammered down.* It was one of her immigrant grandfather's favorite proverbs.

Sierra said nothing as she poked up the fire, put the skillet full of bacon on the coals.

"Smells good. You got any whiskey?"

Sierra hesitated. Robert had been brutal and a little crazy when he drank. She'd heard tales of how whiskey affected Indians. "No." She didn't look at him as she busied herself with the bacon.

"Like most whites, you're a liar. Get it for me!" His tone left her no choice.

Sierra got the bottle out of the cupboard, brought it over. He stared up at her a long moment, looking utterly drained, his dark, rugged face lined with pain and fatigue. When he reached for the bottle, their hands touched, and she was acutely aware of the heat and the size and the power of this half-naked savage.

He took a small drink right from the bottle. "What's your name?"

"Sierra."

"Sierra." He said it slowly as if savoring it. "Like the mountains?"

"My mother wanted to go West, but never got to." Zanna. Sierra barely remembered her mother. Grandfather Kovats had taken his unmarried but pregnant daughter away from Hungary to avoid disgrace, but he had never really adjusted to America.

"Here, Sierra," the Indian said, "see what you can do about my arm."

"I don't have any bandages."

"Then rip up part of your petticoat and do the best you can." He gestured with the bottle and the chains rattled.

Sierra tore off a scrap of her chemise. It meant that even more of her bare legs showed, but since her breasts were clearly outlined even to the dark nipples under the sheer fabric, she was almost naked already. The way he watched her as she knelt by him left no doubt as to what he was thinking.

He handed her the bottle. "Pour some of this on it, then wrap it."

"It may hurt."

"I'm no stranger to pain. Just do it and get it over with."

Sierra took a good, long look at the big man. His lithe, sinewy body had numerous scars. A warrior. Here was a man who made the world meet him on his own terms. The kind of a man she had hoped Robert would be.

"What are you waiting for?"

"If I hurt you . . ." She didn't finish. If she hurt him, would he turn his strength and fury against her? Robert had had a foul temper. "If I hurt you," she began again, "it . . . it isn't because I mean to."

His expression was cold. "You'd cut my throat if you got the chance. I saw the way you glared at me when I was on the train."

Damn him anyway. With relish, Sierra took a deep breath and sloshed raw whiskey over the wound.

He gasped and closed his eyes briefly, gritted his teeth. Sweat broke out on his face, but he made no cry, not even a whimper. He has courage, she thought grudgingly. He may be a damned redskin, but he's brave.

His fingers trembled a little as he took the bottle from her hand and drank from it. "All right. Now wrap it up."

She had to touch his bare flesh to do that. His brown skin felt warm, and powerful muscles rippled beneath it. Robert had been puny by comparison, she decided. Then, shocked that she had had such a thought, she blushed.

"What's the matter?" He looked at her keenly.

"Nothing. The bacon's burning." She jumped up, went to the fire, pulled the skillet off the coals. Sierra avoided his eyes while she got him some biscuits, filled a tin plate, put it before him. Her hand shook as she set the plate down, knowing what was bound to happen to her after he got his fill of food and liquor.

But he set the whiskey aside and grabbed the food.

She watched him wolf it down. "Didn't they feed you on that train?"

"Not much." He wiped up some of the grease with a bit of biscuit. "The fewer Apaches alive by the time they reach Florida, the better the Army will like it."

Apaches. The same tribe that had killed her husband. Why, this very warrior might have been the one . . . She didn't even want to think about it.

"I saw you loading the wagon," he said. "Where are you going?"

"A bunch of people are coming for me at dawn—a wagon train. If you're smart, clear out of here as soon as you eat."

"Your's looks more like a peddler's wagon."

He was smarter than she'd thought. Janos Kovats and his granddaughter had raised vegetables and sold them off the back of that wagon. Early last spring, they had been in town to buy seed, and that was how she'd met Robert.

She didn't like the way the Apache was looking at her now.

"I know you're wanting to get going," she said, reaching to gather up the leftover biscuits, "so I'll pack you some food—"

"And you think I'll leave you behind to alert the whole countryside?"

Her blood almost froze in her veins. "Don't kill me!" she blurted out. "I won't tell anyone I saw you. I swear I won't!"

He pushed his empty plate back, smiled. But there was no mirth in his cold, dark eyes. "Do you think me a fool or just a simple savage? I wouldn't be out of sight before you'd be running to the next farm to spread the alarm."

That leaves only one option, Sierra thought. He was going to kill her. The only question was whether he would rape her first. She watched his supple hands as he took off the bloodstained scarlet headband, tossed it on the table. He wouldn't even need a weapon. Big as he was, the Apache could break her back across his knee, snap her neck with those powerful fingers.

The chains on the Indian's wrists rattled. "By Usen, I'm not sure what to do about you. I sure can't turn you loose."

I will do anything to stay alive, she thought, to give myself a chance to escape. "Don't kill me," she said again, hating him. "Don't. I . . . I'll do whatever you want, just don't kill me."

"If you're offering me your body, I can take that anyway. There's no one to stop me."

There was no arguing with that logic. Sierra didn't meet his gaze. He was playing with her, taunting her. He would rape her and then kill her.

"Dark Eyes," he said, "you've added a complication I didn't count on. But right now, I need you."

He picked up the axe.

"Oh dear God, no! Please!" She fell on her knees before his chair. Tears came to her eyes and ran down her face.

With a clatter of chains, he reached out and caught a lock of her hair, fingered it. "I have hated the whites for betraying my people," he said softly. "Sometimes at night, I dreamed of having one of their women naked and on her knees before me, begging, willing to do anything I wanted her to do."

"I will!" Sierra said. "Anything!" Her breasts were almost brushing his buckskin-clad knees.

"Then help me get these chains off." He held out the axe.

"What?" She was taken aback.

"You heard me." He stood up, pulled her to her feet. "This axe will break the links if you swing it hard enough."

He picked up the rifle also, led her over to the fireplace, reached for a sturdy log, and laid it on the hearth. Then he looked at her a long moment and again offered her the axe, motioning with the rifle. "Just remember, if you try to kill me and don't get me the first time, an Apache knows how to make a person long for death."

An Apache. He isn't just an Indian, she reminded herself, he's an Apache; a member of the tribe that left me adrift in a hard world. She hated him more than she'd ever dreamed she could hate a man.

He frowned. "What's the matter?"

"Nothing." Keeping her features immobile, she accepted the axe. She would swing it hard and cleave his skull in half. He'd be dead even as he hit the floor.

The Indian knelt and spread his chains over the log. "Hit it hard and square." He looked up at her as if read-

39

ing her thoughts. "You haven't got the guts to take the chance."

Was he right? Or was it that she couldn't cut another human being in half, even a hated savage? Sierra felt angry at him and at herself. For a long moment she paused. Either way, she couldn't do it. She swung the axe. Sparks flew and metal rang as she hit the link.

"Again and harder!" He commanded. She swung it again, and the link snapped. "Good!" he said. "Maybe somewhere down the line, I'll find a blacksmith shop that has the tools to take the cuffs off. Now my feet."

He kept the rifle leveled on her as she chopped those chains in two. Then he reached out and took the axe out of her hands.

Her one chance — and she hadn't taken it.

He sighed heavily and rubbed the back of his neck. "I've got to have some rest, but what am I to do with you?"

Sierra was afraid to answer. He did look weary and spent. Maybe he'd drop off to sleep and she could run for help, although the next farm was a mile away.

He got up, rummaged around in a box of things in the corner, came up with the rope she had been using to tie up boxes. "I think I won't be able to sleep unless I know you aren't going anywhere."

She knew better than to argue with him. At least he wasn't going to rape her — yet. She watched him walk over, pick up the knife she'd used on the bacon, put it by the rifle and axe.

The scissors. She thought about the pair of scissors in the trunk. Not much, but better than nothing. She couldn't get them now without arousing suspicion, but maybe later . . . if he didn't kill her first.

40

He piled the weapons up on the table and went over to the small rug in front of the fire. "Come here."

She didn't know what else to do but obey him. She had a feeling that he had always been one who took command.

He stood, towering over her, so close that when she breathed her nipples almost brushed against his massive chest. "Put your hands behind your back."

She obeyed. Without saying anything, he reached around her with both arms, tying her hands behind her. For a long, heart-stopping moment, she was in his embrace, his hard chest rubbing against her breasts as he tied her hands. She felt his body all the way down hers; even his manhood through their clothing.

She must have made a small sound of dismay, for he stopped suddenly and looked down into her eyes. His breath was warm on her cheek, and his manhood went rigid against her. Very slowly, he pulled the straps of her chemise off her shoulders, pushed the lace bodice down so that her breasts were bare.

He looked her up and down a long moment and Sierra felt like a slave girl on an auction block. She dared not protest or do anything to anger him, trussed and helpless as she was.

"I always wondered what it would be like with a white woman," he whispered. "White soldiers make whores of our women, but they would kill me for even doing this." Cholla reached out, cupped her left breast in his big hand, ran his thumb across the nipple. Abruptly he slipped an arm around her bare shoulders, pulled her up against him and kissed her hard, forcing his tongue between her lips, his hand still squeezing her breast.

Sierra closed her eyes, unwilling to look at him as he

41

handled her, ran his tongue deep in her mouth. She felt his hard manhood throbbing against her as he stroked her nipple.

He pulled away from her with a shuddering sigh. "Lie down on the rug, white woman."

With her hands bound behind her, and her chemise down to her waist, she did as he ordered.

He knelt on one knee and looked down at her. She saw the hard bulge of his manhood throbbing against the tight buckskin. He was finished playing with her. He would do it now.

He ran his dark hand across her white breasts and down her belly. She felt the heat of it through the thin fabric. Then his hand trailed slowly down her bare thigh. His fingers were hot, but their heat was not as intense as that in his dark eyes. Very slowly his hand traveled down her leg, and then he caught her trim ankles in it and reached for another piece of rope.

He wasn't going to . . . ?

Her expression must have mirrored her surprise and disbelief because he paused. "I said I'd *imagined* what it would be like." The savage looked at her with an intense hunger that she had never seen in Robert's eyes.

Then he sighed and lay down next to her on the rug. "I'm sure there's a bed, but I'm used to nothing more than a blanket before a campfire."

Of course, she thought with relief, he is exhausted. She wouldn't even think about what would happen after he had some rest. He dropped off to sleep almost immediately.

But Sierra did not. She lay there, his half-naked body against hers, remembering the feel of his thumb stroking her nipple, the heat of his hand moving down her bare leg to her ankle. Trussed up and awaiting his next whim, she felt like some kind of ritual sacrifice. She had no doubt that when he awoke refreshed, before he killed her and fled, he'd use her right there on the rug before the fire.

In spite of herself, exhaustion eventually overcame her and she dozed off. When she awakened just before dawn, he was resting on one elbow staring down into her face.

Now, she thought, now is when he takes me.

Chapter Three

Sierra rolled away from him with difficulty, sat up. "Why don't you just steal what you want and go?"

He sat up, too, felt his bandaged arm tentatively. "I've thought of a better idea."

The look he gave her told Sierra she wasn't going to like this. Her arms and legs were cramped from her bonds. "How about untying me? I don't think I have any circulation left."

He grunted and reached to untie her wrists and then her ankles. He had such brown, callused hands, and they were warm on her bare flesh.

Sierra rubbed first one wrist and then the other. It must be almost dawn. Surely there was a posse or Army patrol scouring the countryside this morning looking for the fugitive. There might even be a reward.

A reward. Money to pay the bank. Maybe the stranger was going to provide the answer to saving her farm. Banker Toombs and Sheriff Lassiter were due here to serve the papers on her in a couple of hours. If she could just delay the savage . . .

Sierra shook her hair back. "I . . . I need to relieve myself."

"Go on outside. But don't try to get away, I'll keep an eye out. We'll gather up what we need and get out of here."

"*We?*"

"You heard me. I need a hostage; at least for a while."

Merciful heavens. He intends to leave no witnesses, Sierra thought with a shudder. When he doesn't need me any longer, he'll kill me and hide my body.

She trembled as she stood up. Could she stall him 'til the sheriff came? Or maybe she might slip away and run to the nearest neighbor. No, that family had small children. If Cholla followed her, she would be putting them in danger. A farm where there were grown men was almost two miles away. When she looked at him, the savage was staring at her slim form as if he could see through the thin chemise. She was aware that blood rushed to her face. "I'll get dressed."

The savage's dark eyes swept over her again, and she felt naked and vulnerable.

"All right," he agreed, "we've got to get moving."

She took her time about putting on the plain black dress over the chemise, having a little difficulty with the buttons down the back since her arms were so stiff from being tied.

"You need some help?"

"No, I . . . I'll manage." She didn't want him putting his hands on her. Sierra slipped into her shoes and reached for the hairbrush.

"Look," he snapped, "you aren't going to a party. Forget your hair for now."

She must not anger him. "All right. I'm going outside to . . . well, you know. Then I'll search the barn to see if those old hens laid any eggs yesterday."

"No"—he shook his head—"we've got to leave."

"We'll have to eat sometime," she argued, "and I've got bacon and some homemade bread already baked."

He merely grunted as if giving grudging approval. "I'll look around, see what else we might be able to use."

"How far do you intend to take me?" She felt her heart begin to beat in apprehension. Only as far as a likely place to hide a body, she thought.

"Haven't decided yet. Now hurry. And don't try any tricks. I'll keep an eye on you."

"I'm not a person to take chances. I always play it safe. My grandfather set great store on conforming; fear from the Old Country."

"And I'm just the opposite." The Apache frowned down at her. "Life was meant to be lived to the fullest, not cowering in fear."

"You'll live longer my way."

He frowned. "No, it'll just *seem* longer. I want to live, not exist."

"Is this living? On the run and hiding out?" She flung the words at him and then was shocked by her own bravado.

He grabbed her shoulder so hard, his fingers bit into her flesh. "I'm in this spot because white soldiers convinced me it was better for my people if they conformed. What a trusting fool I was!"

46

Sierra pulled out of his grasp and slammed out the door without another word. She felt him watching her as she headed toward the outhouse.

When she came out, he was still standing by the window. Sierra proceeded to make an elaborate show of searching around in the weeds for hen's nests, then went into the barn. What was she to do now? If only her mule had been broken to ride. But the stubborn old thing had only pulled plows and wagons in all his years on this farm.

Sierra ran to the rear of the barn, paused by the back door, thinking fast. If he thought she was searching the barn for eggs, she would have a few minutes to get away. Only a few hundred yards behind the barn was a thicket where she might lose herself from view. She would have the advantage because she knew the countryside, had played in the woods all her life. There was just a slim chance that she might manage to get away and make it to the Miller farm so they could alert the authorities.

Merciful heavens. If he caught her trying to escape, he'd kill her. But wasn't he going to kill her anyway? She who had never taken chances was being forced to now by desperate circumstances. Looking behind her to make sure he had not followed, Sierra slipped out the back door of the barn. She only took two steps before colliding with the big Indian.

She screamed and tried to run past him, but he caught her and they struggled. "Let me go, you murdering savage!"

"You lying white bitch! I knew better than to trust you!" He tried to pick her up, but she fought and scratched and bit in sheer desperation. She had nothing to lose if he was going to kill her anyway.

In the scramble of arms and legs, Sierra tripped and they both went down, struggling in the straw.

Her skirts worked up around her thighs as they rolled and fought, but he managed to grab both her wrists. Sierra was no match for his strength. He lay half on top of her, pinning her down by sheer weight while she gulped for air.

"You conniving white tart!" he snarled, "I ought to—"

"I was afraid!" She struggled to get out from under him, very aware of his weight across her, the feel of his sinewy thighs and of his manhood. She could actually feel his heart beating against her breast, the warmth of his skin on hers. He held her wrists pinned against the ground above her head which arched her breasts up against him.

He, too, breathed heavily from the exertion. Sierra felt his breath hot on her cheek. Every time either of them breathed, his massive chest pushed against her nipples.

For a long moment, they lay there with him looking down into her face. One of his legs lay between her thighs and his manhood gradually went rigid as iron against her body. "If I had the time," he said slowly, "I'd do what you keep expecting." He stood up, yanked her to her feet. "I'll help you find those eggs. I'm hungry."

He hadn't killed her yet because he needed her to

48

help him escape. That was the only reason she was still alive. But when he had no further use for her . . . She shuddered. If she didn't outwit him or escape, she wouldn't see tomorrow morning. Brushing the straw off her dress, Sierra led the way into the barn. She noticed the Apache had lost one of the bright silver conchos off his tall moccasins. She couldn't remember if it had been missing last night, but it didn't matter.

While she searched for eggs, he found some tools in the barn, managed to break the steel cuffs off his wrists and ankles, hid the chains. Dawn had turned from gray to pink when they returned to the house with the eggs.

Cholla picked up the butcher knife. "I'll slice the bacon this time," he said pointedly.

Sierra fixed breakfast as slowly as she could, ignoring his attempts to hurry her. She needed time to think or at least stall him until banker Toombs and the sheriff turned up. They finished eating.

"Now"—he thought aloud—"I need some clothes."

She looked him up and down. "Maybe some of my husband's clothes might fit you."

He frowned in evident disapproval. "Apaches don't keep dead relative's things, they give them away."

"Well, if you're too superstitious to wear them—"

"How long's he been dead?"

"Since July." Funny, she felt no pang of loss, only guilt. The brief marriage had been a failure. Sierra had really tried, but in a few weeks, she had realized that Robert had never loved her.

49

"What happened to him?" The Indian stared at her curiously.

It would surely enrage this savage to hear her husband had been a cavalry officer killed in action against the Apache. Robert might even have fought against this man; killed some of his relatives. This warrior might even be the one who widowed her.

"He . . . went off looking for gold in the West and got shot." It was the truth. It had hurt Sierra when she'd finally realized Robert must have asked to be assigned to Arizona Territory, both to escape the marriage and because of the gold rumors.

The Indian sat down on a chair, pulled off his moccasins and then his buckskin breeches. He wore only the briefest loincloth under them. "Gold. It is forbidden for Apaches to dig for Usen's own sacred metal. But the soldiers wanted it, and thought we all might know where to find it."

He was all but naked, hard muscles rippling beneath scarred brown skin. Sierra tried not to look at him as she got up, went to the big walnut wardrobe, took out some of Robert's pants and shirts. She looked at the Indian's feet. "I'm afraid my husband had bigger feet than yours."

"Never mind, I like my moccasins better anyhow. Finish packing whatever you need. I'll hitch up the mule." He took the clothes from her, and she watched the way his massive chest breathed as he put the shirt on, buttoned it.

His legs were strong and bare, the brief loincloth revealing the large bulge of his manhood as he put on the pants and the tall moccasins. Yes, he was bigger

50

than Robert in at least one place.

Her gaze went to the old rifle, the axe, and the butcher knife, but he walked over, picked them up.

The scissors. The only thing left she might use for a weapon. Sierra gestured toward the small trunk. "I want to take that."

He nodded, picked it up easily and carried it out the door to the wagon. "Hurry up. I'll get the mule."

Sierra watched him put the trunk in the wagon, walk toward the barn, his muscular hips lean in the tight pants. She gripped the door a long moment and sighed. In less than twelve hours, she'd taken more risks than she had in a whole lifetime, but she had a sinking feeling she was only delaying the inevitable. At least she was still alive. If she could only stall him a little longer, banker Toombs and Sheriff Lassiter might get here. What was the best way to get his mind off leaving in such a rush?

Sierra shook her hair back, remembering the way his maleness had hardened against her body, the way he had looked at her, as if he would like to rip her dress away and take her right there on the rug like a common whore. Was she desperate enough to let him do it?

With a shudder, she decided she was. It was better than dying, but not much. She hated him so much that for a moment, she wanted to run out and attack him with her fists; then she managed to control herself. Anything to delay him. She took her own sweet time gathering up a skillet, a side of bacon, some foodstuff. Put all of the things in a box. Struggled to carry it out to the wagon and lift it up in the back.

51

The Indian came up just then, leading the mule.

"Why didn't you ask?" he said. "I would have carried that. It's too heavy for you."

She sneered. "I've been running this farm alone since late spring so I can manage without any help from you." She would have been embarrassed if he knew that she also did it while Robert was there. Grandfather had always helped, but then he'd fallen out of the loft and onto the sharp plow a couple of weeks after her marriage.

"Suit yourself." The Indian only shrugged and began to hitch up the mule. "That's what big men are for."

"Is that all they're for?" She said it archly, her heart beating with apprehension. She didn't really know how to flirt. Shy and isolated from most people who thought the immigrant and his granddaughter a little peculiar, Sierra had married the only man who had ever kissed her.

"What's that supposed to mean?" The savage looked over his shoulder at her as he finished with the harness.

She must do whatever she could to delay him until the sheriff arrived. "I . . . I've been without a man a long time. . . ." At that point, she lost her nerve. "There's other things in the house. I'll get them." She fled inside.

He followed her in. She went and stood in front of the fireplace, staring at the dead ashes.

He came up behind her. "Are you offering yourself to me, a dirty savage? Why?"

"In exchange for letting me go!" She whirled

around, shaking now.

He raised one eyebrow at her. "If I wasn't in a hurry and didn't need a hostage, I'd be tempted. But I like my women eager, and I'll bet you're as cold as your eyes."

Cold. That was what Robert had called her. But then he was always in such a hurry to be done . . .

The Apache laughed. "Go get in the wagon, Dark Eyes." He went outside.

Her face burned with humiliation. The Apache wasn't interested in her body, despite the way he had acted last night—or had he seen through her ploy? Sierra hesitated. Should she try to leave a message in case they didn't meet a posse or the sheriff along the road? No, her captor was too smart for that. He'd look around inside before they left. It seemed hopeless.

She went out to the wagon, aware that sometime this very morning she was going to have her throat cut by a savage with a strange name. Without thinking, she asked, "What does it mean—Cholla?"

"It's a type of thorny cactus, not something to be messed with or you'll be sorry."

"Very appropriate, I'm sure," Sierra said.

"There's some as think so." He grabbed her by the waist before she could object and lifted her up onto the wagon seat. His big hands had almost spanned her slim waist, and she could still feel the heat from his fingers. "You should brush your hair. Anyone who sees you might wonder why it's so tangled. I'll get your brush—"

"Never mind, I can get it myself." She turned

53

around and saw he had put the trunk directly behind the driver's seat. She didn't want him digging around in there and finding the scissors.

While she hurriedly brushed her hair and tied it in a bun at the back of her neck, he went inside, probably to make sure she hadn't left any notes and maybe to pick up whatever he thought might be of use later. Then he came out with the rifle, the axe, and the butcher knife; climbed up in the back of the wagon and positioned himself behind the trunk, under the canvas cover. "Now, Dark Eyes, you are going to drive. No one will even know I'm back here. You can handle a mule, can't you?"

"Yes." She picked up the reins. Although he was squatted behind the trunk, he was close enough to touch. She felt his hand hot on her back and then the sharp blade of the knife against her flesh.

"Just to remind you, not to give any signals to anyone you pass. If there's trouble, you'll be the first one to die."

His tone left no doubt in her mind that he'd kill her. "Cholla, if I help you escape, will you free me somewhere?"

"Get moving," he said. "You aren't in any position to bargain."

That was certainly true. She had delayed him as long as she could. There was nothing to do now but slap the old mule across the rump with the reins and start off down the road. "Where do you want me to head?"

Through the black fabric, she felt his fingers stroke

up and down her back. "You know where the big bridge that crosses the river is?"

"Yes." The feel of his hand unnerved her. She'd been under stress for too many hours, waiting for him to rape and kill her. Sierra watched the mule's rump as it plodded along pulling the wagon. "You want me to drive to Ead's Bridge?"

"If that's what they call it."

"But there'll be a lot of traffic; people."

"Is there another bridge?" He sounded as tense as she felt.

"No, not for miles." Sierra smiled to herself. He really was trapped on the east side of the Mississippi unless he could find another way. "There might be a ferry boat somewhere, but I don't know of one. Or you might try swimming it."

"No one could swim that. We'll have to try getting across the bridge. Do you know how to get there?"

"Yes. Grandfather and I used to go into East Saint Louis on Saturdays in the summer. We sold vegetables from the back of the wagon there."

They were driving past his grave now. What was it Grandfather had tried to tell her when he had been dying in her arms? Robert's screams at finding him had brought her running to the barn. They had buried Grandfather next to her mother under the apple tree. Then Sierra had been all alone in the world except for her dog and her husband.

Merciful heavens, she was saved! Over the rise in the road, riding toward them, were the banker and the sheriff. Behind her, her captor cursed softly. "You vixen, now I know why you were trying to delay me!"

She felt the blade of the knife and the heat of his hand on her back and glanced over her shoulder. The Apache hid behind the trunk, an old quilt over him so he couldn't be seen.

He poked her with the knife again. "Remember I've also got the rifle," he growled. "I can kill all three of you if I have to!"

Sierra had no doubt of that. She reined in as the two men hailed her and rode closer. How could she let them know about the renegade hiding in her wagon without getting all three of them killed?

The two reined in and sat their horses, looking down at her. The old sheriff pushed his hat back and looked embarrassed. Otto Toombs smiled, the sunlight reflecting off his bald, freckled head. "Morning, ma'am."

"There's not much good in it," Sierra snapped, "with you taking a poor widow woman's farm—"

"It's legal." Toombs smiled thinly. "Your husband should have thought of this before he mortgaged the place and gambled and drank up the money."

Sheriff Lassiter fidgeted and pulled at his mustache. "Doggone it, Mr. Toombs, this don't seem right somehow; not with her husband bein' a hero and all."

"Medals and pictures in the newspaper don't answer to my father-in-law, and you know it," the paunchy banker retorted.

Sierra only glared at him. Rumors were his grouchy old father-in-law made Otto's life miserable. Otto had brought new capital to the troubled bank, but Sierra couldn't imagine why old Griswold had pushed his elegant daughter, Julia, to marry the rich bumpkin.

The sheriff shifted his weight in the saddle. "Maybe you could work something out—"

"I offered her a job as a cleaning girl at the bank," Toombs huffed. "I'm not a hardhearted man."

Sierra only looked at him, remembering her trip into town a few days ago to beg for an extension on the mortgage. Otto Toombs had taken her into his office, then had closed the door and had tried to unbutton her dress.

"Miss Sierra"—the paunchy banker smiled—"that job offer is still open. Maybe I could even talk my father-in-law into letting you stay on this place."

"I'd rather be out in the street."

The sheriff sighed. "I really hate bein' a part of this, ma'am."

"I know you do, Hank." She tried to think of some way to signal the lawman that there was a fugitive in the wagon. The knife pressed into her back warningly. Hank Lassiter had a sick wife. Sierra didn't want him to get hurt.

The banker took out a cigar, stuck it in his fat mouth. "You'd better think again about my offer, Miss Sierra. Do you have any place to go? Any relative?"

"I have some job prospects in Saint Louis," Sierra said. The memory of his pudgy fingers opening her dress, pulling at the front of her chemise sickened her. Before she had managed to get the desk between them, he had pulled her up against him and had kissed her, ramming his wet tongue between her lips.

Only her threat to scream and bring everyone running had made him turn her loose.

"Well, ma'am" — the sheriff took off his hat and fumbled with it — "I wish you luck, but be careful. Word's come there's a bloodthirsty Apache loose."

"Merciful heavens!" She felt the knife touch her back. "An Apache just outside Saint Louis?"

"It's true." Lassiter put his hat on. "They say he was one of Geronimo's men, being sent with the others to Florida when he overpowered an officer and escaped off the train. They're bringing in tracker dogs as soon as they can get them. That Injun's liable to be anywhere by now."

She almost screamed out then, knowing the lawman might get the first shot in and save her from being kidnapped. On the other hand . . . Sierra thought about that sick wife. "I . . . I'll be careful." What could she do? How could she let them know?

The banker lit his cigar, shook out the match. "If you change your mind, Sierra, about the job, you know where to find me. I'm a kind man."

"Kind!" Sierra snorted. "You'd steal the butter off a sick beggar's biscuit!"

Toombs turned an angry red. For a long moment, she thought he would dismount and confront her. With him standing between her and the sheriff, his fat body might get the first bullet if Sierra dived from the wagon, and maybe the sheriff could get the savage before he could reload.

The banker looked over at the sheriff's disapproving face and seemed to reconsider. "Now, Miss Sierra, I am sorry about all this. But business is business.

Sheriff, let's go inspect the property." He nudged his horse and started down the road toward the house.

Sheriff Lassiter opened his mouth as if to speak, seemed to think better of it, sighed, and then nudged his horse, too.

Sierra turned on the wagon seat and watched the pair ride away. If she screamed, she would be taking a big chance. On the other hand, she might not get another opportunity to escape. While she hesitated over her decision, the two rode on down the lane.

"Damn it, Dark Eyes," Cholla snarled, "you almost provoked that fat man into getting down. I thought you didn't take risks?"

"I do if I'm desperate."

"Get moving."

She couldn't think of any action to take. With a sigh, she turned around and slapped the mule with the reins. The wagon lurched forward. She felt his hand on her back and his breath close to her ear. Maybe there would be a posse or an Army patrol along the road toward town. "Why don't you just take the wagon and let me go?"

"Sure." He laughed thinly. "Do you think I'm loco? How far do you think I'd get? No one will stop a respectable white widow driving along."

"Then when are you going to free me?"

"When I don't need you anymore to help me escape."

"Do I have your promise that when you feel safe you'll let me go?"

"I don't imagine you'll believe my words anymore than I'd believe some white officer's."

59

"An officer is a gentleman." Sierra said it crisply, feeling somehow that she had come to the defense of the whole United States Army. However, if all soldiers treated women like Robert had when he was drunk . . .

"I knew several who weren't," Cholla snapped. "And Gillen was out to kill me since we got on the train. I just got him first."

She shivered at the thought, even though the mid-morning sun felt warm on her. He had killed men— the last one only yesterday. She was going to have to accept the word of a killer because she had no other choice. Still it was the only hope she had to cling to. If she could just get him across the river, maybe he would slip away and she could get on with her original problems. Funny how not having a job or a roof over her head seemed so unimportant when she was staring death in the face. If she could deal with this and survive, she might not ever be afraid again.

"What are you thinking about?" he asked, behind her, as his hand touched her shoulder.

"Nothing," she lied. Sierra watched the road and kept driving. The wheels creaked in the stillness as they approached the outskirts of East St. Louis. Here and there were houses, sheds, small businesses. Women stood on the streets visiting with each other as men drove laden wagons by. The elegant Griswold carriage, drawn by two fine black horses, passed by, and Sierra recognized Toombs's snooty wife and her stingy old father inside.

A lot of foot traffic and many horse-drawn vehicles clogged the street approaching the big bridge. Sierra sighed, remembering when she and Grandfather had parked their wagon in the shade of that elm up ahead and had sold vegetables to the passersby. This section of town, near the bank, was old and full of warehouses, rundown hotels, and freight yards. It smelled almost as bad as it looked. Sometimes men came out of the hotels, looking both ways before they hurried down the street. Occasionally, she saw women wearing face paint and once she even saw one with a cigarette in her mouth!

She felt her captor's big hand on her back again. "Is the bridge up ahead?"

"Yes." She nodded. "But I've never been on the other side of the river—"

"You let me worry about that. Your job is to get me across. The army'll never think I can cross it."

Sierra looked at the giant Ead's bridge as her mule moved slowly toward it. She studied the wagons and carriages pulled to a stop up ahead, the trains moving across the lower level of the bridge. She saw them then—her rescuers, all dressed in blue uniforms. She laughed out loud without thinking.

"What's the matter?" Cholla whispered behind her.

"Merciful heavens, an Army patrol," Sierra said triumphantly. "You can't cross the river here. Soldiers are searching every wagon!"

Chapter Four

Lieutenant Quimby Gillen stood at the street corner, thinking he probably shouldn't have left the bridge patrol unsupervised. But, blast it all, didn't he deserve a little rest and relaxation after that damned Cholla had almost killed him?

Gingerly, Gill touched his bandaged head and looked up at the afternoon sun. Blast, but it was hot for September! Everything his friend, Forester, had told him about East St. Louis must be true.

Gill paused on the curb, ready to cross. He clutched the sack of bottles closer, wondering if he were in the right neighborhood? His teeth were bothering him again, but he wasn't going to give up the candy. The toothaches, combined with the bruises and cuts from the fight that had left him unconscious in the baggage car, put him in a foul mood.

A canvas-covered wagon, the kind Gypsies might drive, passed him. An elderly mule pulled it slowly toward the big bridge at the end of the street. The dark, rather shy-looking woman driving the mule glanced at him and Gill suddenly thought she seemed exotic and mysterious. Maybe it was the magnetism of her eyes. At the very least, he felt a sudden recognition as if he knew her.

Gill thought about that for a minute, searching his memory as he shifted the sack to his other arm, reached in his uniform jacket for the little bag of hard candy he always carried, popped a lemon drop in his mouth. No, he had never met her before, because he had only been through this area on the train. *Then why did she look familiar to him?*

Hair as black as a crow's wing, and somewhere in her middle twenties. Not a great beauty by Gill's standards; not flashy enough, still there was something almost haunting about those big, dark eyes. He knew suddenly what it was; her eyes reminded him of that Apache girl's.

Gill crossed the street, staring after the little covered wagon as it approached the bridge patrol. At noon there was a jam, for Corporal Finney stopped each and every wagon and carriage for inspection just as he'd been ordered. Gill snorted. That damned Cholla wouldn't be stupid enough to try to cross the Mississippi here; that would be foolhardy even for the Army's best Apache scout. When the tracker dogs arrived tomorrow and picked up his trail along the railroad tracks, they'd run him down soon enough.

Blast it all, what had he done with the address? Gill fumbled in his pocket for the scrap of paper, remembering his late friend's words: *If you're ever in the area, go see Trixie. She'll give you a time you won't forget. Just remember to bring plenty of that patent medicine.*

He had that, all right. Gill clutched the big sack full of bottles and went up the creaking stairs of the rundown hotel. Since Trixie lived so close to the bridge, it wouldn't hurt if he took just a few minutes off and left young Finney in charge. They'd catch that Apache bastard, all right, but it wouldn't be here. More than likely, Cholla was dozens of miles downriver by now, still trying to find a narrow place to cross. Like any wild beast, he would try to head back to familiar haunts; too naive to realize how hopeless it was for a man alone to go that far. *Dead or alive.* That was what the brass had said. Gill hoped it was dead. And he wanted to be the one who fired that shot. After all, it was his Army career that was in jeopardy because of the Apache's escape.

Checking the scrap of paper again, he paused before a numbered door, rapped sharply. A frowsy woman with unusually large breasts, wearing a soiled green satin robe, opened it, still pushing her dyed black hair out of her eyes. "Yeah?"

Was it dyed to hide the gray? She was pretty in a flashy way, but she wasn't all that young, or maybe she had just lived hard and fast.

"Miss La Femme, you don't know me, but I'm Lieutenant Gillen. We share a mutual friend; he told me to look you up if I was ever in this area."

"Yeah? Who's the friend?" Her heavily painted mouth smiled suspiciously as she looked him up and down.

He wondered if she was as good in bed as his buddy had bragged? "I should have said *late* friend, I guess." Gill gave her his friendliest, warmest smile. "Lieutenant Forester. Lieutenant Robert Forester."

Sierra drove the mule toward the bridge. "What should I do?" she whispered. "There're soldiers on the bridge!"

"Keep your eyes straight ahead." The Indian put his hand on her back again. She felt the heat of his fingers through the black fabric. "Let me think a minute."

A cavalry lieutenant about her own age, with a mouthful of something and a sack held in one arm, stared at her from the curb. His head was bandaged, and he wore a scowl.

"By Usen," she heard the Indian behind her mutter, "Gillen! I thought the sonovabitch was dead. I ought to—"

The lieutenant crossed the street and headed for a seedy-looking hotel.

"Nothing I can do about it now," Cholla said. His tone matched Sierra's murderous anger at the savage who had invaded her life, added to her problems.

She looked at the bridge ahead. "Why don't you just surrender? Aren't you tired of taking chances when you know you can't win?" She hated him, but she couldn't help but admire his nerve and determination. People must conform to survive; hadn't Grandfather drilled that into her head?

"Surrender?" The Indian sneered. "I'd rather die trying to escape."

"Maybe I should turn around and go back," Sierra said, staring straight ahead, "We haven't a chance of getting across here."

"Maybe crossing here is the smart thing to do because Gillen won't think I have the guts, or that I'm stupid enough, to try it. I'm going to hide under this old quilt. You think of something; anything to keep them from checking your wagon."

"What! How can I do that?" She knew both panic and fear as the knife pressed into her back again.

"That's your problem," the muffled voice warned her. "Just remember, if I'm discovered, you'll be the first to die, and I intend to take as many people with me as possible."

Risks. She was being forced to take life and death chances, when all she wanted to do was conform and blend in. But she kept driving. Oh, mercy, the whole town must be full of soldiers looking for the escaped Apache.

Ahead of was a hopeless snarl of carriages and wagons. A very flustered young corporal appeared confused and under pressure as he tried to keep order. Behind Sierra, drivers shouted curses at the delay. With wagons and carriages now hemming her into the slow lineup, there was nothing she could do but inch the old mule forward. She watched the soldiers examine drays loaded with crates and order people out of carriages.

Her hands became sweaty with fear. When the soldiers discovered the man hiding in her wagon, there was going to be shooting because he had said he wouldn't be taken alive. Some of the people in this crowd would be killed. Surely the first one would be Sierra Forester. Her mouth felt so dry she couldn't swallow as the soldiers checked out the wagon ahead of hers and waved it on through.

Heavens. It was her turn. She took a deep breath as the boyish corporal approached. He had sandy-colored hair with a lock that hung over one eye, and sweat ran down his reddish neck into the tight collar of the blue uniform.

"Ma'am, I'm sorry." His Kansas twang was apologetic. "I'll have to ask you to get out so we can inspect all those big boxes and trunks."

Sierra felt her captor's hand nudge her in warning. All she had to do was take a chance; jump from the seat, shout, He's here, all right, hiding under that quilt!

She couldn't bring herself to take the risk. Besides herself, this very young man would die—and who knew how many others?—before the soldiers killed the fugitive.

Sierra didn't move to descend, but she did give the corporal her most beseeching smile. "Oh, must I? I've got a long way to go before dark."

He hesitated, looking at her black dress that told the world she was widowed. "I . . . I . . . I'm ordered, ma'am, to check out every vehicle. We're looking for an escaped Indian."

Sierra felt the knife press against her back, and fear made perspiration run down between her breasts.

"An Indian? Here in East Saint Louis? Surely you joke!"

He shook his head, while the noise around them grew as the traffic worsened. "Afraid not, ma'am. An Apache scout being shipped to Florida managed to get off the prison train. Almost killed an officer doing it."

"A scout?"

"Yes, ma'am. He scouted for the Army."

That didn't make any sense to her. "If he worked for the Army, he must have done something terrible to get imprisoned."

He shook his head. "I don't know, ma'am. There was orders to send them all, but he got away. Look, ma'am, I can see you're a widow and all, but I do have my orders—"

"An *officer's* widow," Sierra said gently, and she looked at him sweetly. "Killed in action just a few weeks ago. Now I've lost my farm."

"Oh, Lord, I'm sorry, ma'am. I didn't realize. . . ."

"Corporal, do you really think a helpless widow would have any reason to try to smuggle a blood-thirsty redskin across the Mississippi?"

"Well, no ma'am, but—"

"And, Corporal, some of these people you're holding up"—she gestured with her head toward all the ranting, shouting men hanging out of carriages and wagons—"some of these people are probably going to call the mayor and friends at the state capitol before the day's out."

The boy brushed his hair back with a gesture of

defeat and frustration. "I just don't know what to do! The lieutenant left strict orders before he went off, and he hasn't come back—"

"Then why don't you just take charge and make things happen?" Sierra managed a sweet smile again and fixed her most haunting gaze on him. "Let a few wagons and carriages through until the traffic lessens. After all, you don't really expect to find this savage riding across the Mississippi into Saint Louis in some lady's carriage, do you?"

The boy laughed with her at the silliness of the idea. "That's what the lieutenant says, but the higher-ups. . . ."

Behind them, the line of waiting vehicles grew longer. Sierra fidgeted, feeling the knife point in her back. The savage was right; she'd be the first to die.

"Please, Corporal," she beseeched, "if we all have to wait, I'll be out on the road alone in the dark, trying to find my way. Who knows what will happen to a poor widow after dark on the streets of Saint Louis?"

The whole thing was obviously too much for the young man to deal with. He threw up his hands in a gesture of defeat, turned and shouted at the patrol, "All right, men, let's allow a few vehicles through until we get rid of this jam! We just won't tell the lieutenant."

Sierra breathed a sigh of relief at the nods of agreement. The missing officer must not be too popular with his men. Lucky for her. The soldiers moved out of the way, waving her wagon through.

It seemed to her as if it were a million miles across

that bridge as the mule clopped along. Below her, a river boat moved slowly past, churning up frothy white foam on the brown water. She heard the hidden man sigh, knew he was tense too. Somewhere on the other side, he would release her. At least he had said he would. Suppose he didn't?

Craning her neck, she looked toward the water far below. For a split second, Sierra toyed with the idea of jumping from the wagon seat, diving over the side. No, that was suicide, since she couldn't swim. It was a long way down and her full skirts would drag her under. She'd either have to trust Cholla for the time being or hope for another chance at rescue in the big city across the bridge. Merciful heavens, at least she was still alive.

She reached the other side of the bridge with a sigh of relief. "Okay, I've done what I was supposed to do," she said over her shoulder. "Somewhere on one of these side streets, I'll let you out, and—"

"How the hell do you expect me to find my way about in this maze? I came through this city on a train."

"You said you would let me go once you were out of danger," Sierra reminded him as she brushed a wisp of black hair back into her bun. "Suppose I get you to a train yard so you can sneak aboard a freight train headed west?"

For a long moment, she didn't think he would answer her. The wagon moved slowly along a street in the shabby warehouse district.

If he would just get on a train and let me go! Even finding a job and a place to live didn't seem like such a terrifying challenge anymore, not after what she'd dealt with these past few hours.

The man behind her put his hand on her shoulder, squeezed gently. "Let me think about it while you keep driving. Somehow I think that's what Gill would expect me to do, try to hop a train. If so, they'll be checking every freight car that leaves St. Louis."

"Uh-oh," Sierra said suddenly, looking at the snarl of wagons on the road ahead.

"What's the matter?"

"There's a beer wagon overturned, barrels scattered everywhere. Police are trying to straighten things out."

"Get us through it," he whispered, and once again she felt the knife against her back.

A big Irish policeman on a bay horse rode up, reined in. "Dear lady, you'll have to take your wagon another way."

Sierra looked up at him, her heart beating hard. The man wore a pistol. She had reached a point of desperation and exhaustion. *If I shout and leap from the wagon seat at the same time, what can my captor do?* Let the policeman and the savage shoot it out. Sierra tensed and got ready to jump.

Lieutenant Gillen leaned back against the sofa cushions and smiled as he accepted a smudged glass of beer from the painted brunette. His teeth were hurting again, but he was in a better than average humor. *Trixie*. Sounded like a name for a pet dog. At first he had been afraid she wouldn't let him in, but at mention of Forester's name, the door had swung wide.

Now he'd been here fifteen minutes and already she was sitting down next to him, sipping out of that patent medicine bottle and leaning forward to catch every word. That gave him a good view of her big breasts.

"Yes," he said and wiped the foam from his lip, "I told Robert just a few days before he was killed fighting Apaches that if I was ever in East Saint Louis, I'd look you up and pay my respects."

"Ain't that sweet of you, Lieutenant."

He smiled warmly at her and reached for the bag of hard candy in his jacket, remembering some of the bawdy tales Forester had told of his adventures in Trixie's bed.

Trixie wiped her eyes and held the medicine bottle close to her bosom before taking a big gulp. "Robert and I was old friends. "We're both Texans, you know."

Gill nodded with warm sympathy. "Robert told me about your . . . nervous condition. That's the reason I brought the medicine with me." He glanced at the label: Doctor Zorenoff's Secret Tonic and Elixir. Good for Every Ailment of Man and Beast. Almost twenty-five percent alcohol, Gill noted and a big shot of that newest wonder drug, cocaine.

A couple of bottles of this and the broad is yours. Robert had laughed. *She's a talented bitch, but not the way she thinks.*

72

"I'm a singer," Trixie offered, "just waitin' for a lucky break. That's how I ended up here; a banker fella told me he had connections, but it hasn't amounted to nothin'." She stood up, began to crank the phonograph on the table next to the sofa. It creaked out a thin, reedy melody as she cleared her throat and began to sing: " 'I'll take you home again, Kathleen. . .' "

Gill winced. Robert was right; Trixie couldn't carry a tune in a bucket. He managed to keep a straight face while she wailed the words in a slightly off-key voice, rolling the peppermint around in his mouth, a smile frozen on his face. He hadn't heard such screeching since Pa had rocked on an old cat's tail.

Finally, she finished. "Would you like to hear more? I do 'Last Rose of Summer,' and 'Lorena,' and—"

"No, no, Miss La Femme." He raised a hand in protest. "With such a wonderfully delicate voice, you must not waste it on me; save it for your next performance."

She beamed at him, flopped down, leaned against the sofa cushions, put the bottle on the lamp table, and reached for a pack of cigarettes. "Robert always said I looked just like the Cameo girl, do you think so?"

What in the blasted hell was the Cameo girl? "Now that you mention it, I think so too, only you're prettier and certainly more talented."

He watched as she took out a cigarette, lit it. Gill had never seen a woman smoke before. For the first time, he noticed the cigarette pack. Cameo Cigarettes, the label read. A picture of a beautiful, dark-haired girl in a big hat decorated the box.

She blew a smoke ring. "I'll reckon you couldn't guess Trixie ain't my real name. I'm really Thelma Blogdett."

"Really? Trixie La Femme just . . . just fits you somehow."

The girl beamed at him. "Did you know Robert long? Me and him was old friends from years ago when I worked at Miss Fancy's in San Antone."

"No, not long, but he reminded me so much of my brother Harold." His brother had always looked after him, slipped candy out of the store for Gill. But Harold was dead of typhoid, and Robert Forester had taken his place as Gill's friend. Now Robert was dead too, and under suspicious circumstances. . . .

Trixie leaned closer. "You know Robert really was from a fancy Austin family, but he was wild as a colt grazed on loco weed. His mama disowned him, cut his inheritance off, so he joined the service."

"How'd he end up here?"

"The Army sent in a few troops last March when that big railroad strike tied up all the freight trains and got some people killed."

"I wondered what he was doing up north. When I met him at Fort Bowie late last spring, Robert said he was running away from a wife he didn't want."

Trixie threw back her head and giggled. "Did he tell you I found that wife for him?"

"No." Gill touched his bandaged head with his free hand, then let it drop carelessly onto her knee.

74

"She's one of them foreigners, even though she was born in America," Trixie said with a disdainful wave of her cigarette. "At least her grandpa could hardly speak English; funny old man with a long beard. I only knew of the two, but I hear the girl's mother died when she was little. Sierra's a woods' colt; gossip says."

Gill looked at her blankly. "A what?"

"You know, a bastard." Trixie took another sip of tonic. She was beginning to look a little drunk. "I suppose that's why the old man brought them to America, trying to escape the disgrace."

"Sierra. Yeah, I remember Robert mentioning the name." He wasn't really interested in meeting some virtuous little wife. Gill moved his fingers ever so slightly on Trixie's knee, waiting for her to protest. She didn't.

Trixie shrugged. "I ain't been here long enough to know all the gossip. She and her grandpa didn't mix much with anyone; locals are mighty suspicious of foreigners. They used to come into town once a week and sell vegetables out of the back of their wagon right out here on the street near my window." She motioned with her cigarette.

Gill moved his fingers on her knee until they were under the soiled green satin and on bare flesh. "Why would Robert want some little mouse like that if he could have a beauty like you?"

Trixie giggled again. "Actually he had us both! Gossip was the old man had money hidden on that farm, that they lived so poorly because he was eccentric and buried all the gold they must have brought from Europe." She spread her knees ever so slightly and Gill took it as an invitation. "When I told Robert that, he arranged to bump into the girl, see if he could charm her into telling where it was buried."

"I presume he didn't find out?" Gill stroked her bare thigh and moved his fingers upward.

"Naw." She shook her head. "Even after he married her, he didn't learn nothin'. He finally decided there wasn't no treasure. Then Grandpa got killed in an accident. I could tell you something about that. . . ." Trixie seemed to reconsider, and her voice trailed off for a moment. "Anyways, Robert talked his wife into signing papers so he could borrow against the farm; I don't think she even knew what she signed."

"And when the money was gone, Robert was too?"

Trixie laughed. "We had us a good time while it lasted!" She blew smoke toward the ceiling. "His mousy little wife once came to me and begged me to give him up, said she was tryin' to save the marriage. I just sneered at her and told her he didn't care nothin' about her."

"But by then Robert had gone off to Arizona looking for gold?" Gill guessed.

She took another swig of medicine. "He was gonna send for me if he ever found any of that gold them Apaches are supposed to know about; we was going to 'Frisco where I could be a star."

"And blast it all, now he's dead and he never found the gold." Gill sighed.

She looked at him with sudden interest. "Did Robert ever talk about me?"

"Miss La Femme, you just can't imagine how he talked about your talent." Gill slowly ran his hand up to where her thighs joined, remembering the plans Robert had had for this stupid whore. He'd planned to sell her to one of the bordellos on the Barbary Coast. It suddenly occurred to Gill that Trixie would be worth even more in some godforsaken desert hellhole like Bowie Station or Tombstone.

"Was you there when he was killed?" Trixie took a deep drag on the cigarette. "The local papers said he was a hero, medals and all. Funny, that didn't sound like Robert to me. I always figured he'd turn and run when it came right down to facin' Apaches."

That was exactly what Gill suspected, but he didn't say so. He shook his head. "We heard the gunfire. It was too late by the time my patrol arrived. His men said Robert had died in a vain attempt to save them. All but a handful was killed by the savages." He leaned toward her, kissed her. Maybe later he'd tell her about Robert's wound.

"Ain't you the sweet one, though?" The girl moved closer, smoke trailing from her nostrils, and snubbed the cigarette out in the ashtray on the lamp table. She smiled up at him and didn't move away. Her robe had fallen open, revealing a generous expanse of freckled breasts.

Gill felt his manhood go hard, and he reached out, pushed the robe off her shoulder, and stroked the freckled skin. "That's why I came, Trixie. Robert

77

knew we were both in constant danger. He said if anything should happen to him, I was to come see you and tell you how much he cared."

"Oh, it's so sad!" The girl was in his arms now, weeping sloppily on his chest. "And to think they sent his medals to that little chit of a wife instead of me! You been to see her?"

"No." As a matter of fact, Gill thought, I almost forgot about the wife. Only three things occupied his mind: finding that Apache gold, killing Cholla, and bedding Robert's favorite whore. "Trixie, maybe we need to comfort each other; you know, Robert's best friend and his girl."

She nodded ever so slightly as she leaned her big breasts against his arm and lit another cigarette. "Gill, do you know any people who could help me with my career?"

"I sure might, honey. Why I know lots of rich and important people. My old man owned a chain of stores."

Actually it was one run-down general store in an Indiana town of two hundred people. The family just barely scratched out a living, and his pa was so tight, he would never let either of his two sons have a piece of candy from the big jars on the counter, though they worked without wages.

Gill kissed her. Her mouth was hot and wet and eager. A tart like this one would look good to those soldiers back in Arizona. They seldom saw anything but Injun women. He'd set her up as a whore and keep most of the money just as Robert had planned

78

to do. Trixie had talent, all right, but it was all between her legs.

He ran his hand down, cupped one big, freckled
breast, and pulled her to him.

Trixie inhaled a deep puff of smoke, leaned over,
blew it into his open mouth. Gill took a deep breath,
his giddy excitement mounting. "Oh, honey, I never
smoked like that before!"

It seemed so erotic, breathing the smoke from her
ripe mouth, breathing it back deep into her throat.
"Blast it all, Trixie," he murmured, "I've been looking
for a girl like you all my life."

She trailed smoke into his mouth. "You'll help me
with my career?"

"Yes, oh, yes!" He would have promised anything
at that moment just to get her robe off.

She smiled at him, then opened her robe, slowly,
tantalizingly. She crushed the cigarette out. "I got another patron right now, but I don't seem to be gettin'
nowhere in show business."

"With all your talent? Impossible!" He was half on
top of her, her big breasts filling both his hands.
There was no limit to what he could earn pimping
this tart or selling her to one of those rich Mexicans
south of the border. Once Trixie was in Mexico, she'd
never be heard of again and the government wouldn't
take action over a missing whore.

"My patron's a banker." Trixie pouted against
Gill's open mouth. "Promised he'd introduce me
to important people in New York theater, but
all I've had so far is two short stints in second-

rate dives in the worst part of Saint Louis."

"Not nearly good enough for a star like you, honey," Gill said as he fumbled feverishly with his buttons. "You be friendly to me and I'll take you to the West Coast." Or at least as far as Fort Bowie, Arizona Territory, he promised himself as he ran his tongue over her nipples.

She spread her thighs, and he slid slowly into the hot wetness of her. "Umm, just like warm honey," he breathed. "Oh, Trixie, you really are something special."

"So are you, Gill." She giggled. "I'm so glad Robert sent you. . . ." She slipped her tongue into his mouth and locked her legs around his hips.

It was awkward on the sofa, Gill thought, but he didn't dare suggest they move to the bedroom. He'd better take whatever the dumb tart offered while the getting was good. She had talent, all right. Her body seemed to be literally sucking the juice right out of him, her long nails digging into his back through the blue uniform.

I need to get back to the bridge, he thought. But at this instant, passion overruled duty or hatred. Coupling with this hot bitch was more important than catching or killing that Apache. He quickened his thrusting while her mouth explored his. Then all he could think of was pouring his seed deep into her.

Gill's last conscious thought was how much fun he and Robert would have had taking turns on Trixie just as they had done with that other girl. . . . He dozed off to sleep, his bandaged head resting on her freckled, sweaty breasts.

Sierra had had second thoughts about alerting the Irish policeman when Cholla held onto the back of her dress. The man couldn't see him hiding there, of course, but she knew it would be almost impossible for her to escape without getting knifed. So she had merely asked how to get out of town and had followed the big man's instructions.

Her old mule was nervous in the traffic, so it took most of the afternoon; but at dusk the wagons had passed the outskirts of town and was headed down a country road where houses were fewer and farther between. On a long, empty stretch, Sierra reined the mule to a halt and turned to face her captor. "All right, I got you out. Now you keep your promise."

"I said when I was safe," he retorted. "What am I supposed to do, drive this wagon through the countryside myself? The first farmer who sees me will call the law!"

"That's not my problem."

He looked at her with dark, smoldering eyes. "I didn't hear everything that was said back there, but I did hear you tell that corporal your husband was an officer killed on duty."

"I told him whatever I thought it would take to get us through that road block." Sierra looked away, feeling her heart lurch. What would this savage do if he knew her husband had been killed heroically fighting Apaches?

81

He leaned over her shoulder. "It'll be dark soon. There's a grove of trees up ahead. We'll camp there while I decide what to do."

"That wasn't part of the deal."

"By Usen, for a woman who says she never takes chances, you goad me to anger!"

"Sheer desperation," Sierra snapped, as she brushed a loose wisp of hair back into her bun. "If you weren't such a liar—"

"I didn't say exactly where I'd free you," he countered. "I'm still too close to Saint Louis to feel safe."

Sierra thought about the scissors in her small trunk. Sooner or later she was going to have to risk trying to kill him. She didn't believe he intended to let her go. If he were going to murder her anyway, she had better try to get him first. "Okay, we'll camp." She nodded and looked at his shoulder. "While we're at it, I'd better see about rebandaging that wound."

He shrugged. "I've had worse than this; forget it."

She wasn't about to do that. She needed an excuse to get in that trunk. She slapped the mule with the reins and headed the wagon down the road at a brisk trot. "Do you have a wife waiting for you in Arizona?"

For a moment, there was no answer, and she had almost decided Cholla had not heard the question when he finally shook his head. "With Delzhinne dead . . ." He frowned suddenly. "Don't ask more. You have caused me to speak the name of the dead, which is taboo among the Apaches. It calls them back from the Spirit World."

When she glanced back over her shoulder at him in the twilight, his expression mirrored tragedy. His lonely, forbidding face said he was as alone in the world as she was.

Sierra felt uneasy as she pulled into the grove of trees and reined in. She hadn't thought of him as a human being, she had considered him a dangerous animal.

Merciful heavens, if she began to think of him as a person, she might not be able to concentrate on killing him.

Look out for yourself, Sierra, just like he's doing. If you can get him to let down his guard so you can get your hands on a weapon, kill him without a flicker of conscience, as if he were a mad dog, dangerous to civilized society.

But how was she to get him to let down his guard? Other women used the lure of their bodies to charm men into obliging. Sierra was no good at the sex thing. Hadn't Robert told her enough times that she was too cold and inept for any man? At least that was the excuse he'd always used when he'd been delayed in town, which was often.

There had been another woman in Robert's life. He had taunted her with descriptions of the big-breasted tart, and once Sierra had seen him with her on the street. She had been too timid and unsure to know what to do. Her old-fashioned upbringing had made her try to save the brief marriage, even though there was no love, no tenderness, between them. She had even hunted up Miss Trixie La Femme and begged her to stay away from her

83

husband. The woman had laughed in her face.

By then Robert had gotten himself transferred to Arizona. It was only later that Sierra realized the paper he had bullied her into signing was a mortgage. . . .

Slowly, Sierra climbed down from the wagon seat and shook the wrinkles out of her dress.

The Indian climbed out too, looked around. "Seems safe enough to camp here."

He reached out, caught her shoulder, stood looking down at her. His big frame was close enough so that her breasts almost touched his chest when she breathed. Alarmed, she took a step backward, but he didn't let go of her shoulder. The way he looked at her made her heart pound in sudden excitement and apprehension. It left no doubt as to what he was thinking.

Merciful heavens, now that he felt safe from immediate pursuit, he had something else on his mind. Out here in a lonely woods, far from anyone who could stop him, the virile Apache intended to rape her!

Chapter Five

Sierra looked up at him, seeing the desire in his dark eyes. She pulled out of his grasp. "I imagine that bandage needs changing. I'll get some cloth from my trunk—"

"I'll do it," he snapped and wearily ran a hand across his forehead, then cursed. "My headband. Where's my headband?"

They looked at each other, and she remembered the bloody red rag. "Don't you remember? You took it off last night and threw it on my kitchen table."

"By Usen, I hope it isn't found by someone who knows what it is."

Sierra hoped fervently that it was, but she realized that chances were slim. "I'll get the cloth—"

"Fix us some food." He rubbed the back of his neck as if his head hurt. "I'll get that."

Sierra started to protest, realized that would make him suspicious. She could only hope he wouldn't find the scissors. "Suit yourself." She shrugged and began to build a small fire.

* * *

Cholla unhitched the mule and hobbled it near the creek so it could graze, thinking about the girl as he did so. There had to be a reason she seemed so eager to help him. With the hatred he'd seen in those dark eyes, it wasn't because she was worried about his wound. No, there was something in that trunk Sierra didn't want him to find. What was it?

He felt her watching him as he climbed up in the wagon, dug around in the trunk. The last rays of daylight reflected off a small frame. Cholla turned the photograph over. A familiar face stared up at him. For a moment, he felt such shock that he could only stare at the handsome, smiling face of the white officer he hated most in this world. *Robert Forester.* This was what Sierra had hidden, not wanting Cholla to find it. Was the dead officer her brother . . . or her husband?

Cholla put the photo back in the trunk, managed to still his shaking hand. He would not let her know he had found it . . . not yet. Gathering up some cloth from the trunk, he closed the lid and went back to the fire.

Sierra looked up at him curiously, but he kept his face expressionless. How ironic it was that Fate or Usen had thrown this particular woman into his power. It was too convenient to be coincidence. Someone had planned their meeting so that Cholla might finally get what was due him.

"What's the matter?" she asked.

"Nothing." He sat down on a rock and watched her

lay out the bread. He had really intended to let her go unharmed as soon as he got safely away from St. Louis. Now he was not sure what he would do with her. Cholla tried to think of some appropriate vengeance. Whatever he had promised Sierra meant nothing to him now that he knew there was some connection between the black-haired girl and his most hated enemy, Lieutenant Robert Forester, the officer who had almost gotten his patrol wiped out in that arroyo. But of course there was more to it than that — much more.

Revenge, though he thirsted for it, must be put aside, Cholla thought with a regretful sigh. His immediate concern must be getting out of the area where the Army would be searching. After that, he had plenty of time to decide what to do about the white girl. One thing was certain; everything was changed now that he knew her secret.

Sierra kept her eyes on the frying pan as the big savage returned from the wagon with some cloth in his hand.

She glanced up at him. His expression had changed somehow, but he didn't have the scissors in his hand. Had he not found them, or was he only playing cat and mouse with her? He sat down on a rock, and though he said nothing, she felt him staring at her.

"We'll eat first," she said, licking her dry lips, "then I'll rebandage that wound."

"All right." His gaze seemed cold and hard.

Sierra watched him out of the corner of her eye as

she fried bacon. His wide shoulders looked as if they would split Robert's shirt, and his sinewy thighs strained against the cloth of the pants. The conchos shining in the firelight caught her attention, and she remembered one was missing. Had it been missing when he had first shown up at her farm? Sierra couldn't remember. For the thousandth time, she wished she had managed to leave some kind of note for Otto Toombs and the sheriff to find, but it would have been a foolhardy risk.

The way he kept looking at her made her shiver as if he'd put his hands all over her naked body. She couldn't meet his hostile gaze. Hurriedly, Sierra took a couple of tin plates from a box and tore off some hunks of her homemade bread. "This stuff won't last forever," she said as she handed him a plate, poured him some coffee.

He put the plate down, wrapped his hands around the cup as if seeking comfort from its warmth. "I'm a good hunter," he said softly, looking at her. "We won't go hungry."

She didn't like the possessive look he gave her. Sierra remembered with a shiver that he could take her any time he wanted. They seemed a long way from anyone who could stop him. "If you shoot that gun around here, it might bring someone running. There're probably people close by."

If he caught the desperation in her tone, he gave no sign. The Apache shrugged and dug into the food. "I'll make some snares for rabbits, maybe make myself a bow. Roasted rabbit sound good to you?"

"What sounds good to me is being told you're going to set me free like you promised." Sierra said it with a spirit that surprised her.

He chuckled. "So the kitten can show its claws and turn into a bobcat after all!"

She wasn't sure by his tone whether he was pleased or merely amused by her rejoinder. "You can travel faster alone," she said.

"Except in white areas." He paused as he ate. "The sight of my face would set a hue and cry after me."

The tension of the past several days was getting to Sierra. He didn't intend to free her; he'd only been playing with her. In her desperation, she'd believed him, just as she had tried to believe that Robert really loved her. "If you'd give up, at least you wouldn't be hunted down and killed like a fox with the hounds after it."

He gave her a long look, set his plate down. "Life is full of risks," he said softly. "People who want security—a guaranteed, safe existence—deserve to be stuck in some cage. I'm not willing to trade freedom for three meals a day, and be in a pen for whites to taunt and stare at."

"You'd at least be alive."

His mouth curled into a mirthless grin. "You call that living? I'd rather take my chances."

"But you don't have a chance—not one! Don't you understand that?" she screamed at him. "It's crazy to think you can get all the way back to Arizona! And even if you do, won't the Army be waiting to grab you there?"

"A slight chance is all the odds I ask," he said, "and as for the Army, well, Sergeant Mooney is trying to contact Nantan Crook to help the Apaches. Crook is a hard but a fair man. Maybe he will talk to the White Father in Washington. If that doesn't work, perhaps I can get across the border and lose myself in the Sierra Madres."

"The Sierra Madres." She stared into the fire, remembering. "My mother was his love with the West and its mountains; so romantic, such an impossible dream."

He looked intrigued. "What happened to her?"

Sierra shrugged. "My grandfather was afraid to take chances, so they never went farther west than our little farm. I think the biggest, bravest thing Janos Kovats ever did was come to America. I doubt he would have done that if my mother hadn't disgraced him. I think facing the people in his village with an unmarried, pregnant daughter was more than he could stand."

"And your father?"

"Who knows? The subject was never discussed, although I wondered." She sighed. "I don't know whether he was a charming Gypsy or a Hungarian nobleman who amused himself by dallying with a pretty peasant girl. The only clue I have is the word 'Tokay.' "

"Was that his name?"

"I don't know. Maybe it's a place."

"You have no brothers or sisters?"

"I have no one," Sierra said with a shake of her

head. "I miss Mother most of all, although I barely remember her. Zanna was the type of free spirit who caused gossip by swimming naked, going barefoot, and letting her hair blow wild and free as any savage's." She looked up at him suddenly, realizing what she had just said. "I didn't mean . . ."

"I know what you meant," Cholla said, and he didn't smile.

"Zanna wanted to go West," Sierra explained hurriedly, brushing a lock of hair back into her prim bun. "Somehow she thought we would have a whole new start there, but Grandfather was afraid; always afraid to face life, take risks. He said, 'The nail that stands up will be hammered down'; his European background made him always fearful."

"Are you your mother's child or more like your grandfather?"

It was a challenge, the way he said it, and at first she didn't know the answer. Then she did. That was why she had let herself be swept into marriage when she'd had such doubts about Robert. She had opted for security, knowing her grandfather was old and needed help on the small farm.

The Apache interrupted her thoughts. "It's late. You want to see what you can do with this shoulder?"

Of course she couldn't say no, or that she hoped the wound got infected and killed him. But she could try to get her hands on those scissors, even though she wasn't sure she would have the nerve to stab him. The way he glared at her unnerved her. "Take your shirt off, and I'll see what I can do."

91

As the big savage obeyed, she marveled again at the size and strength of him, the way his muscles rippled under his brown skin as he took off the shirt and handed her the cloth he had taken from the trunk. She would have to touch him to change the bandage. Well, that couldn't be helped. Sierra unwrapped the old strips of cloth and frowned. "If you were any other man, you'd probably already have a bad infection."

"I've survived worse."

"No doubt you have." He reminds me of a stallion, she thought as she got up, dug around in the box of supplies, found the whiskey. "The wound looks a little better than it did yesterday."

He flinched when she poured alcohol over it, but he made no sound. Robert had been such a whiner over any little thing, from a blister to a splinter in his finger. For the life of her, she couldn't imagine her husband doing all those brave things and dying a hero. If Cholla had been a scout, they might have known each other, but she was afraid to ask.

Gently, Sierra wiped the wound and then rebandaged it. His skin was warm under her fingers. "I'm sorry I had to hurt you," she said softly, and was surprised to find she almost meant it.

"If you're trying to soften me up, thinking I'll let you go—"

"I only expect you to do what you said you would," Sierra snapped.

"I expected the same from whites. You see what I got."

"Does that mean you aren't going to let me go?"

"Stop badgering me," he answered and looked away. Something seemed to be smoldering in him—an anger.

His toying with her was more than her frayed nerves could stand. She couldn't hold back the tears. "What is it you want from me? I've done everything you've demanded, yet you still hold me prisoner. I must be more trouble to drag along than I'm worth to you! Why do you do it?"

"That's what I keep asking myself. It would be easier to just kill you and be done with it, but . . ." Suddenly his strong arms came up, pulled her hard against him; and his mouth claimed hers, roughly, possessively.

Frightened, Sierra pulled away. She had never been kissed like that. It called out to something wild and untamed in her own nature, unnerved her. Maybe she was really like her passionate, reckless mother after all, the way this stranger's kiss affected her, aroused something inside her she had never known was there. They stared into each other's eyes, only inches apart.

"You're my prisoner, my captive," he whispered urgently, "I can do anything I want with you and there's no one to stop me."

She looked at him. "You're bigger than I am; we both know you can force me anytime you decide to."

For a long moment, the only sound was a cricket in the grass and the crackle of the small fire. She looked at the tortured dark face and saw her abductor almost

93

as a human being, not some dangerous animal who deserved life in a cage. Then she thought of Robert again and hated the Apache for the cruel turn her life had taken.

"It's late," she said softly. "Why don't we get some sleep?" She felt exhausted and confused, remembering the taste of his mouth, the heat of his body against hers. And she was shocked and annoyed that this primitive male had managed to arouse her in a way her own husband had not.

"You're right." But he didn't move. He kept glaring at her. Then he shrugged, got up to go to the wagon, came back with ropes.

"Oh, no," Sierra jumped up and began to back away. "Please don't!"

"Sorry, I don't want to do this. But I can't take a chance on you slipping away in the night." He caught her, twisted her hands behind her back. As he reached around her to tie her hands, his hard, naked chest brushed against her breasts, arousing confused feelings all over again.

She looked into his dark eyes as he stood there staring down at her, his face only inches from hers. For a moment, she thought he would kiss her. Her body was pressed against his all the way down their legs, and she felt his manhood gradually go hard against her belly.

With an abrupt curse, he swung her up into his arms, carried her back to the fire. "You're right; I don't know why I don't let you go or kill you. You are more trouble than you're worth!"

Sierra felt her heart squeeze with fear, but she managed to keep silent. Maybe he wanted her to beg for mercy. She was just stubborn enough to decide she wouldn't. Maybe she wasn't a mild little mouse after all.

He set her down on a blanket near the fire, tied her ankles together. His hands felt hot on her bare skin. Then he took a deep breath and stood up, looking down at her. She had a feeling he was fighting an urge to throw himself down on her and use her body until he was sated. Finally he tossed a blanket over her and lay down next to her on another.

"With autumn coming on, it may get chilly tonight," Sierra said, dreading the cold, long night.

"In that case, you're welcome to share my blanket," he barked and turned his back to her.

As Sierra tried to get comfortable with her hands bound behind her, she stared at his powerful back. Even under the shirt, the ropy muscles were evident. She'd seen old scars. No doubt he had survived many a fight. At least she hadn't been raped . . . yet. He didn't intend to let her go; she could sense the change in him just since they had camped.

It must have been nearly dawn when Sierra half awakened, shivering in the chill air. She felt heat radiating near her and snuggled closer to it. As she drifted back off to sleep, she was only dimly aware that strength enveloped her and pulled her into a circle of warmth. Feeling oddly safe and secure, she drifted back to sleep.

95

* * *

Lieutenant Quimby Gillen awakened just before dawn, stretched and wondered where he was.

Oh, yeah. Trixie's bed. With a grin, he rolled over and rising up on one elbow, looked down at the sleeping, naked girl. The tart wasn't half bad. Too bad Robert wasn't here so they could enjoy her together like they'd done that Apache girl.

Gill lay on his back, listening to Trixie snore and remembering that night last summer. For the next weeks, both officers had almost gone crazy, listening for a footstep behind them. Maybe Cholla didn't know, but on the other hand, their nerves were raw, thinking he might be stalking them, just waiting for the right time to make his move. . . .

"Blast!" Gillen rattled the little paper bag as he took out a lemon drop. He crunched down on the candy. "This is about to drive me loco, wonderin' if Cholla knows and if he's just waitin' for the right time to take revenge."

"Maybe he's not as smart as you give him credit for." Robert shook his head and sipped his whiskey. "Even so, we go on lots of dangerous patrols. Maybe on one of them our Injun scout is liable to get shot and killed, and who's to say the hostiles didn't do it?"

"Sergeant Mooney would never let you get away with it."

"That damned Injun lover!" Robert gulped his

drink, wiped his mouth. "He and that Lieutenant Gatewood are loyal to General Crook. I won't feel safe 'til both of them get transferred out of Arizona." His pale turquoise-colored eyes gleamed. "Besides, it's only fair. My big sister Emily was raped by Injuns more than twenty years ago, and she's been crazy as a loco weed-eating horse ever since."

"Was they Apaches?"

"Naw, Comanches. But Injuns are Injuns." Robert brushed the shock of blondish hair back. "Emily was ugly as a mud fence anyway—and fat too. No man in Austin would have married her, even with all our family's money."

Robert Forester had everything Gill envied; money, family, connections. And he looked out for Gill, too, just like Gill's brother had.

Gill offered the bag of candy to the Texan, but Robert shook his head. "How can you eat that damned stuff continually?"

"My old man owned a store and never let me have any out of the jars on the shelves. I always said when I had my own money, I'd buy all I wanted."

"The height of ambition," the elegant officer commented, and Gill wondered if he was being laughed at.

"If we ever find that Apache gold, Robert, we'll have all the women and liquor and candy we want."

"If Cholla doesn't get us before we get him first!"

"Gill honey? You're talkin' in your sleep."

97

With a start, Gill sat straight up in Trixie's bed, looked around. Bright sunshine streamed in the window and across the stained wallpaper. "Oh, blast. I must have dozed off. I've got to get back to the bridge." He gave her a long, searching look. "Did I say anything?"

"About what?"

"Never mind. I got to go see what's happening."

"It ain't that late, and you checked with the corporal at midnight. There wasn't nothin' happenin'."

"That's probably true. Cholla ain't loco enough to try to get across the river at the biggest city on this end of the river." Trixie was right. If anyone spotted the Injun, someone would come to tell him. And the tracker dogs would be here late tomorrow. Then the Army would start looking in earnest. So far, the government had managed to keep it out of the newspapers, so the citizens wouldn't panic.

He got up and dressed hurriedly. "I'll be back."

Trixie beamed at him from the rumpled bed. "I just knew you was the right one, Gill. I'm gonna tell my other patron today that I'm finished with him and all his big talk about gettin' me into show business. I'm gonna end up singin' in San Francisco, right?"

"Sure, honey, sure." He reached for his hat, made sure he had a little bag of candy in his jacket. Singing. He had better uses for that talented little mouth — and so would that bunch of eager troopers around the fort.

* * *

Gill found himself actually whistling as he went down the stairs. Blast, he would have a hard time paying for her train ticket, but he could consider it an investment, just like any businessman. Once he got Trixie out to Arizona, he'd keep her on her back, working until she had calluses there. What Robert hadn't lived to do, his buddy would do. At least that thought kept him from worrying about what was gonna happen to his Army career over that damned Apache's escape.

Gill yawned as he approached the patrol. "Anything new, Corporal?"

Young Finney looked exhausted as he saluted. "Nothing at all, sir. The men are tired of this duty."

"Can't blame them for that." Gill flagged down a carriage and waved the occupants out. He loved annoying and inconveniencing his betters. "Maybe when the dogs get here they'll scent out where that Injun jumped from the train. At any rate, maybe the brass will send us somewhere to look besides this damned bridge!"

Trixie spent the day practicing her scales and sipping patent medicine. She liked the feeling of well-being she got from the stuff; it was better than getting drunk. Besides, she had promised her preacher father that she would not touch whiskey. Medicine was not the same thing.

She was excited about going West. She'd sensed that her present gentleman was growing weary of her and now sometimes made excuses not to see her. Besides that, he was always afraid to take Trixie anyplace, afraid his wife might see them together and his powerful father-in-law would come down on him with a vengeance. Trixie knew more about the family than her patron did. Some of it she was sure would shock him. Anyway, her gentleman friend wasn't doing anything to help Trixie's career. Just like in bed, he promised more than he delivered.

Trixie waited until late afternoon, almost time for the business to close. She got dressed up, complete with a big picture hat. Looking in the mirror, she knew she looked just like the Cameo girl. She took a big swig of patent medicine, went downstairs and out onto the street.

In the distance, she could see the patrol still stopping traffic on the bridge. This evening Gill might come by, and she wanted to be able to tell him she had made a clean break with her other patron and was free to go West.

Trixie went around to the building's side entrance and walked down the hall unnoticed. A few minutes 'til three o'clock, almost closing time, and not many people around. She opened the door of his private office. "Hello, sweet."

Otto Toombs looked up from the pile of mail before him, frowned, and resumed slitting a letter with a brass opener. "I've told you before not to come to the bank. Suppose my wife should happen in or one of my worthless brother-in-laws — or my father-in-law decides he needs to go over some figures with me?"

Trixie thought about it a minute, decided there was no point in telling Otto that several other members of Otto's family still paid for the pleasure of her company now and then. "I just needed to see you, Otto. Don't worry, there ain't hardly nobody in the bank, and nobody seen me come in; I made sure of that."

"Trixie, if you are ever going to make it as a big time entertainer, you need to improve your grammar." He frowned and pushed back his chair, stood up.

"I can remember when you didn't pay no attention to the way I talked." She batted her eyes at him, came around the desk. While she was here, maybe she could get a little traveling money.

The paunchy man laughed. "You hot little bitch! I sometimes forget between-times how talented you are!"

Somewhat mollified, she went into his arms, looked down at the things on his desk. "What's that?"

"Oh, this?" He picked up the bloody, dirty, red rag. "Damned if I know. Something I picked up off the table at the Forester place when I was out there yesterday." He tossed it back on the desk.

Trixie pressed her generous breasts against his vest. "I could use a little money, Otto."

"You've been hitting that cocaine stuff again, haven't you? Trixie, I told you that stuff'll kill you, I don't care if everyone is singing its praises."

She sulked as she sat down on the edge of his desk. "Does that mean old Hiram won't give you no pocket money?"

His florid face turned a shade darker and he

101

scowled at her. "Don't rub that in, Trixie. Someday you'll go too far. Here." He took a silver circle out of his pocket, tossed it to her.

"What's this?" Trixie turned it over in her hand, examining it before tucking it safely in her purse.

"I'm not sure what it is." The banker shrugged. "Looks like a piece of jewelry or something. Something else I picked up out of the dirt behind the barn at the Forester place; looks like there was some kind of scuffle there. Maybe it's an old Spanish coin or something. There's always been tales about that crazy old Hungarian hiding money on the farm. That's one of the reasons I didn't give the widow an extension on the note; I aim to find out."

She grinned at him and lit a cigarette. "Why did I think it was because you was tryin' to put that girl in a spot where she needed money bad enough to do *anything* for it?"

"Now, Trixie, she's a hero's widow." He fingered the diamond stickpin in his tie. "I'll admit I offered her a job cleaning around the bank offices."

She laughed coldly. "Otto, you're all heart."

He pulled her to him, put his hand on the swell of her breast. "Since you're here, Trixie . . ." His voice trailed off as he put his mouth over hers, pushed his tongue in deep. "You got time . . . you know what I like. . . ."

She knew what he liked, all right. When he was in Trixie's bed, he liked to pretend Trixie was the elegant Julia Griswold Toombs. Then he did things to

Trixie he would no doubt like to do to his wife and didn't dare.

"Trixie, please, you know how cold my wife is—"

"Is she?" She was baiting him.

"I've told you enough times. She never lets me touch her; cold as a corpse, that one."

She pulled away from him. "I've often wondered why that elegant beauty agreed to marry you."

"Her father hurried her into it." He looked at the pile of mail on his desk and sighed. "I wasn't naive enough to believe the fancy Griswolds would want a man who made his money off slaughterhouses in their blue-blooded family."

"Aren't they originally from Philadelphia?" She smoked and thought about the elegant Julia. "I see her going by with her old man or brothers every once in a while, in that fancy carriage with the matched black horses."

Otto nodded and pursed his mouth. "At first, I thought there was some scandal attached to her, like maybe she was expecting a baby, but she'd never let a man do enough to get her in a family way. Would you believe I had to rape her on our wedding night? I told her I had a legal right to her body and she spat in my face."

"If she's straitlaced, everyone says her old man and her brothers sure make up for it." Trixie wondered if Otto knew that before she was his mistress, old Hiram Griswold and then one of the sons had been her patrons? She reached out to toss the cigarette into the spittoon.

"Trixie, please . . . Do it. . . ." He put his sloppy wet mouth over hers again, one hand reaching to squeeze her breast, the other going to unbutton his pants.

"I need a little money, Otto."

"Please . . . You'll get it."

She slid down his body until she was on her knees before him, doing what she'd done for him many times before. Then, suddenly she stopped and stood up.

"What the hell's the matter?" Big beads of sweat stood out on Otto's bald head, "God, don't quit now. I was just about to —"

"I got no time." Trixie smiled at his discomfort. "I'm leaving town, Otto. That's what I came to tell you."

"What? You can't go now." He tried to force her back down on her knees before him, but Trixie stumbled back against the desk. "I don't want to lose you, Trixie. Remember, I told you I had big plans for your theatrical future —"

"All the future I got with you is calluses on my knees and rope burns on my wrists from being tied to bed posts so you can act out your sick —"

"It's money you want, isn't it, you little tart? I'll give you money, just finish —"

"Your old lady would give me more, I'll bet, to hear about your cheatin'." Trixie taunted. "I'll bet she'd love to have enough evidence to tell Papa."

With a muttered curse, Otto grabbed her and they struggled by the desk as he tried to force her to her knees. Trixie lost her balance, and they fell backward on top of the pile of mail.

"So it's blackmail, is it?" He had her down on the desktop, struggling to get his hands up under her skirt. "Okay, you little whore, I'm through fooling with you! I'm gonna take what I want right now and then kick you outa here! I doubt Julia cares whose bed I'm in, as long as it's not hers!"

Isn't that the truth? "Otto, you're hurting me!"

"I'll show you 'hurt,' you clever little whore!" He was lying half on top of her now, his hand ripping her bodice, pulling at her breasts. "All the talent you got is between your legs, Trixie! You think you're smart, don't you? Getting me worked up and then laughing! You aren't going anywhere until I say you can!"

"Otto, stop. You'll regret this." She looked up into his sweating face as he pulled at her breasts, forced himself between her legs. His eyes gleamed with an almost insane lust. When Otto Toombs came back to his senses, he would be afraid and regretful, and there was no telling what he would do to protect himself and his reputation. She had to make him stop. He was ramming and ramming into her, his slobbering mouth all over her nipples, as she lay helpless across the desktop.

She reached up and slapped him hard. "You old fool! Get off of me before I scream and bring everyone running!"

She saw the sudden gleam in his hand as he grabbed the sharp letter opener. "You tart, how dare you threaten me? Maybe I'll kill you. Does that scare you, Trixie? Maybe I'll just carve my initials—"

"No, Otto. I was just kiddin,' honest!" Really scared, Trixie struggled to get away from him. He looked a little crazy. She had pushed and taunted him too far.

She suddenly dodged out from under him. He fell across the desk as she stood up, panting. "Now, Otto, quit acting crazy." Trixie tried to straighten her torn bodice. "I won't tell your old lady, I just need money, that's all."

Otto made a choking sound and struggled to his feet, his back still toward her.

"Otto?"

He turned around, gesturing wildly, gasping. Bloody foam covered his lips, and his shirt front was sticky with warm, scarlet blood.

"Oh, my God, Otto!"

The late afternoon sunlight streaming through the dark velvet drapes reflected off the handle of the small brass letter opener stuck at an angle in the banker's thick neck. When he tried to make a sound, only scarlet froth bubbled from his lips as his own blood drowned his vain attempts to cry out. Trixie put her hand over her mouth to hold back a scream. Then she backed toward the door as Otto Toombs fell across his desk, leaving a river of red across the snowy white envelopes and papers piled there.

Chapter Six

Trixie hurried out the side door of the bank. She started to run, then realized she must be calm or she would attract attention. In a few minutes, someone would find Otto Toomb's still-warm body. No one would believe it had been an accident. It was important to old Hiram Griswold that he maintain a clean and scandal-free appearance, for both the bank and his family; never mind what went on behind closed doors. He was powerful enough to make Trixie simply disappear if this created a scandal, and a death in the office of the vice president of the bank would certainly raise some eyebrows. Other members of Griswold's family wouldn't want Papa Hiram digging around too deeply in Trixie's secret involvements. She paused, collected her wits, straightened her mussed clothing, and walked down the deserted street without looking back.

They would find Otto soon enough when the bank closed. And if anyone had seen her leaving, she would deny everything. She forced herself to walk instead of run. It seemed like a hundred miles back to her hotel.

As she started for the stairs, she looked down the street, saw the patrol still on the bridge and began to tremble. *Gill.* Maybe Gill would know what to do.

Trixie went to the bridge. "Gill, I need to see you."

"Blast it, can't it wait? I'll be off duty soon."

"No, it really can't." She managed to hold back her hysteria. What she needed was a big slug of that cocaine syrup and a cigarette.

He started to argue with her, then took a look at her face and threw up his hands. "Okay, boys, I'll leave you with it. We're being transferred out in the morning anyhow. I told you looking for that Injun here was pointless."

He took Trixie's elbow, and she let him guide her around the corner of a building. "Now, blast it all, what is it that's so damned important it can't wait?"

She hadn't expected him to be so hard and unsympathetic. "Oh, Gill . . . honey . . . don't use that tone of voice. I thought you loved me." She dug around in her purse for a handkerchief, and when she retrieved it, the silver medallion Otto had given her came out too and hit the paving stones with a sharp, ringing sound.

Gill leaned over slowly and picked the silver thing up, whistled low. "Where in the hell did you get this?"

"Gill honey, ain't you listening to me?" Trixie sobbed and wiped her eyes. "I think I'm in trouble—"

"Well, that ain't my problem, sister. I haven't been in town long enough!" He caught her arm, shook her. "Tell me where you got this."

"In Otto's office," she sobbed. "He gave it to me and he had that red headband, too."

"What? Who the hell is Otto?"

108

"I been tryin' to tell you." Trixie gulped, then quickly filled him in on the details.

Gill didn't say anything for a moment. He just stood there, turning the silver thing over and over in his hand.

"Gill honey, don't you understand? He's dead, and by now they've probably found him. You was goin' to take me away, and now it's real important —"

"I just can't quite put the pieces together," Gill mused as if he hadn't heard her. "What was the banker doing with this thing!"

"Who gives a damn?" Trixie had lost her patience. "It ain't important —"

"Yes, it is, Trixie." He grabbed her shoulders and shook her. "Tell me how he got it. Believe me, it's important."

She hesitated, baffled by his interest.

"Look, Trixie, this belongs to the man I'm hunting," he explained patiently as if dealing with a child. "If I catch the man, I may get a promotion and the brass may overlook the fact that I let him get away in the first place. Besides, there might be a reward . . . especially since he just killed a leading citizen like Otto Tombs."

"But he didn't kill Otto. That was an accident. I told you about him and me strugglin' and how he fell on the letter opener. . . . Reward?" Gill's last words got through to her. A reward meant money.

"Yes, sweet, a reward." Gill patted her rear. "Think of money, a lot of money that the bank might put up to catch this killer. Now tell me the whole thing again right quick so I can get over to the bank."

"Bank?" Trixie lit a cigarette with shaky hands. "Why

109

do you want to go to the bank? You gonna turn me in?"

"Blast it all, Trixie, don't you understand? The Injun sneaked in there and tried to rob the banker. In the struggle before Cholla stabbed him, Toombs managed to pull the headband off him. That's a distinctive headband. All the Army's Apache scouts wear them so the soldiers can tell 'em from the hostiles and not shoot one of ours accidentally during a battle."

"Oh, now I see. Gill honey, you're wonderful!" She tried to kiss him, but he brushed her aside.

"Go back to your place and wait. I got to get to the bank and drop off this silver concho from Cholla's moccasin. Then I got to make sure the policemen find the things and know what they are. Whatever the reward for that escaped Apache is now, it ought to be double by tomorrow!"

When Gill returned to Trixie's room, he was so happy, he was whistling. In fact, he was in such good spirits, he stopped on the way and bought a big bottle of patent medicine for her and a bag of cinnamon drops for himself. That dumb tart had dropped a windfall into his lap.

"Trixie gal, how would you like to be seen on the arm of *Captain* Gillen?" He set the bottles on the table, picked her up and whirled her around.

"What?" she blinked at him.

"You heard me!" He set her on her feet, plopped down on the sofa, put his boots up on the arm. "I also leaked it to a reporter who showed up. By tomorrow, all the newspapers and the citizens will be outraged over that savage killin' a leading, upstanding citizen. They're talking reward. Word has gone out on all the telegraph wires. Cholla is big news."

"So now what?" She sat down on the sofa, took his head in her lap.

It had been a long time since he had been in such a good mood. Gillen reached up and opened Trixie's robe, stroked her freckled breasts. "So the Army's assigning me to track him down, no matter where the trail leads. I'll leave you some money, and you meet me out in Arizona in time for the holidays."

"Oh, ain't that grand!" Trixie lit a cigarette, giggled, then sobered. "But what was the Injun doin' at the farm?"

"Good point, Trixie." Gill stroked Trixie's breasts absently while he considered. "If Cholla was on Forester's place, do you suppose he went there lookin' for revenge?" The next thought that occurred to him made him sit bolt upright. "Or is there a chance that in that arroyo at the last minute, Robert told that damned scout something he didn't tell me? Could that lying Robert have known where the money was buried on that farm all along?"

"Then why did he ask to be transferred to Arizona?" Trixie trailed blue smoke from her nostrils, like a lazy dragon.

Gill thought about it a minute. "Makes sense. But he got a couple of letters from his wife he never bothered to answer. He just tore them up. Maybe she told him in a letter, trying to get him to come back to her."

Trixie giggled. "Fat chance! She was the shy and mousy type."

111

What type was Mrs. Robert Forester? Gill had never met her. He searched his memory for an image of the woman they were discussing. In his mind's eye, he saw the photo thrown carelessly in Robert's top drawer in their quarters at Fort Bowie. A man who was in love with a woman carried her photo on his person.

For a long moment, Gill stroked Trixie's freckled breasts as he wondered what had happened to the photo. No doubt Sergeant Mooney had gathered it up along with the rest of Robert's personal things and had returned it to his widow along with the medals and letters of commendation.

In his mind, Gillen saw the photo again: the ebony hair in a prim bun, the dark eyes, the exotic look of the Hungarian face. "I'll be goddamned!" he sat up with a groan.

"What's the matter, Gill honey?"

"No wonder that girl looked so familiar to me."

"What girl?"

"The girl driving the wagon toward the bridge. I didn't realize who she was but I should have since I had seen the photo." He stood up.

"Gill, would you please talk sense!" She rose, reached for her bottle of medicine, took a big swig.

Gill swore and paced the floor. "Blast it all! Escaped right under our noses, I'll wager! Who would suspect a widow in a little wagon? From what Robert said of her, she ain't the type to get mixed up with a wild stud like that one; no, he must be holding her captive. Yeah, that's it; he's using her for a hostage . . . or for revenge."

"What the hell you talkin' about, Gill?"

"And while we look on this side of the river, they've

crossed and he's maybe killed her by now; drove that wagon off in the Mississippi. That bastard is probably already on a train across Kansas, laughing his fool head off at how stupid we are!"

Gill ran for the door and took off down the stairs.

Cholla came awake suddenly in the early dawn. Although the morning air was chill, his shirt was soaked with sweat. He still dreamed of that fateful July day. He wondered if the other survivors had nightmares too? But it had been Cholla who had made the other four agree to remain silent about the events. Considering what had happened, there was nothing else he could have done. Tom, old traditional Army man that he was, was the only one who had hesitated about going along, but the scout had made the sergeant see the sense of it.

Cholla looked around. For a split second, he wasn't sure where he was or why. A woman lay curled against the warmth of his chest. For a second, he blinked at the sleeping, dark-haired white girl whose hands were tied behind her back, and then everything that had happened in the last several days came back to him. Reality was as horrible as his nightmare had been. It was both ironic and insane that Cholla was using Robert Forester's widow as a hostage. Cholla was living on borrowed time, he knew that. The girl was right, he had no chance of betting back to the wild, desolate country that he loved. And yet he must try. Freedom meant more to him than life itself.

Revenge. At least he would have his revenge. No

wonder she had tried to keep him out of that trunk so he wouldn't find the photo. What would be the perfect vengeance? To kill her? No, that was too simple.

Delzhinne. The beautiful Apache girl who had meant more to Cholla than life itself had been raped and then shot between the eyes. Tom had found her and had taken his friend out to the spot where she lay. Yes, he should pay Robert Forester back in his own coin. Cholla frowned. He had no stomach for killing women. He smiled to himself, thinking he knew of an even better revenge. He considered it only just that he put his baby in the lieutenant's woman.

Yet there was an old Apache taboo against rape. He must seduce Forester's woman, make her want him enough to surrender to him. Then when her belly swelled with his child, he would dump her off at some white fort to live disgraced by the brown baby sucking at her breast. Maybe he would even try to take her to Austin, to Forester's haughty mother, and leave her there. If the Foresters were as important and rich as the lieutenant boasted, the disgrace would be complete.

Gently, Cholla brushed Sierra's hair away from her face. "Are you awake?"

Sierra woke with a start, looked up into her captor's dark eyes. There was no mistaking the desire she saw reflected there. For a moment, she almost pulled away. Then it occurred to her that as long as she exhibited fear and distrust of him, he would never let down his guard. To escape—or kill him—Sierra needed to be trusted so he no longer guarded her closely, tied her at

114

night. For her purposes, she was going to have to make him want her even more. She would have to seduce him.

She hesitated only a moment. How different could it be with him from what it had been with Robert? If she closed her eyes . . .

Taking a deep breath for courage, she opened her lips slightly, looking up at him. He paused as if unsure whether she was offering them to him, and then he bent his head and brushed his lips across hers.

Robert had never kissed her that tenderly. The Apache's gentleness surprised her. After all, she lay bound and helpless, he could use her body for his needs as hurriedly and roughly as Robert had done.

She willed herself not to pull away as warm lips caressed hers and hands went to her shoulders, drawing her up to his mouth. His tongue felt like a flame as it flickered across her lips, and when she opened them, it slipped inside.

She felt an unaccustomed warmth stirring deep in her. Robert had never aroused her so. But then Robert's kisses had been quick; with him, everything about the act had been rushed as if he couldn't wait to finish with her. In contrast, Cholla kissed her so leisurely it seemed he planned to spend hours doing nothing else. Sierra suddenly felt guilty. Her husband had only been dead a few weeks, yet here she was letting one of the tribe that had killed him put dark hands on her. The end justifies the means, she told herself. She would have to endure this until she could kill him or escape.

His arms went around her, and she felt him fumbling

with the ropes that bound her. "I like a woman to hold me when I make love to her," he whispered.

Her arms were cramped, but when he freed them, she dutifully slipped them around his neck, in awe of the powerful, corded muscles there. At any moment, he would untie her ankles, rip away her lace drawers, and ram into her, coming in a quick, hot rush as her husband had always done.

But the Indian made no move to untie her legs. They lay there in the gray dawn on the blanket, with him stroking and kissing her.

I must not know the proper things to do, Sierra thought. Robert had always said she was lousy in bed when he'd taunted her with his whore. When Sierra had responded that all she knew was what her husband had taught her since he'd been her only man, he had slapped her.

She must make this savage desire her enough to let down his guard. How else could she kill him or escape?

Shyly, Sierra slipped her tongue between his lips, probing deeply as she clung to him, pulling his bare chest to her. Even though the cloth of her prim dress was between them, she rubbed her nipples up against him. She felt his sharp intake of breath, and for a long moment, he kissed her with abandon, his hands on her shoulders, drawing her to him.

Then he seemed to come to his senses. He let go of her and sat up. He looked as surprised and unnerved as Sierra felt.

"We've got to get going," he said, and reached down to untie her ankles.

His big hands felt warm on her bare flesh, and they

116

seemed to linger on her ankles. She lay looking up at him, waiting for him to roll over on her and finish, but instead he got up. She watched him walk over, begin to put on his shirt.

Robert had been right. She wasn't desirable or knowledgeable enough to charm even a savage. And she had been worried about Cholla being so wild with passion that he would rape her. She felt a little chagrined, as well as relieved, at his lack of interest. Still she would have to keep trying. If she couldn't charm him into caring for her, sometime soon, he might just cut her throat and throw her in a weed patch, and no one would ever know what had happened to her.

Without another word, Sierra got up, went into the bushes to relieve herself, washed up in the creek, and fixed breakfast.

As he ate the Apache stared at her thoughtfully. She wished she knew what he was thinking.

"What happens now?" she asked as she finished her coffee.

He looked at her as if seeing her for the first time.

She asked again, and he started as if he hadn't been listening. "What? Oh, the trip."

Sierra was puzzled. "Yes, we're on the run, remember? The Army is looking for you, probably dead or alive."

He raised one eyebrow at her. "You could use that reward, I'll wager. That would help a poor widow a lot, wouldn't it?"

She didn't know what answer he expected, so she said nothing. Tonight, she thought, if I'm lucky enough to get through today alive, I'll try again to charm him.

117

Cholla finished his food, leaned against a tree, obviously deep in thought. Finally he said, "I think the Army will expect me to try to return the way I came . . . if they finally figure out I managed to get across the Mississippi."

"How did you come?" She got up, began to collect the dishes, kicked dirt over the fire.

"The train from Bowie Station ran east to Albuquerque, then north along the mountains. When we reached what Gillen said was Colorado, we turned and went due east across Kansas." The Apache looked sad, thoughtful. "Once that was all buffalo country; now everywhere I looked across those flat plains there were farmhouses."

Cholla rubbed the back of his neck thoughtfully. "If the Army expects me to try to follow those same tracks or hide on one of those Kansas trains, I'll do something else."

"Like what?" Sierra took the pins from her hair, began to brush it. She felt him watching her.

"I think I'll do what the Army doesn't expect, which is turn south now and go through the hills, maybe catch a freight train through eastern Indian Territory."

"What about the wagon and the mule?" Maybe he was going to say he was giving them to her, and she could turn around and go back.

"I haven't decided," he said, running his tongue over his lip. "But then, I don't know if there's a train through the Indian Nations yet."

Sierra didn't ask any more questions. At least he had made it clear he wasn't releasing her today, but he hadn't said "we" when talking about catching the train.

She packed up their things. Before the sun was above the eastern horizon, they were headed across Missouri toward the Ozarks.

Days passed. He never touched her again. Sometimes he scouted the terrain, sometimes he rode on the seat next to her. They fell into a kind of routine, and she stopped asking when he was going to release her. She would either have to kill him when she got the chance or escape. Sierra bided her time.

She tried to look ahead and mind her driving, but his arm and body brushed against her occasionally, warm and strong. It made her think of his hands on her shoulders, his lips trailing across hers. In her mind, she saw those callused, dark hands pulling away the fabric of her dress so they could cup her white breasts.

Nervously, she glanced over at the strong hands resting on his knees and imagined them on her own knees, gradually pushing her skirt up as his fingers worked their way along her creamy thighs, spread her, and pulled her toward him. . . .

The thought sent shivers down her back. He was going to do it sooner or later, when he was sure he was safe from hot pursuit. If she looked up suddenly, Sierra sometimes caught him watching her, and she wondered whether he was planning her rape . . . or her murder?

As days passed, they moved along seldom traveled roads, stopping only a few minutes at a time to rest. She lost track of time or distance. They were almost out of coffee and most of the other supplies she had packed, but she hadn't found a way to get her hands on a weapon or to escape.

It was late afternoon, they had traveled what seemed to Sierra a long way.

Cholla looked up at the sun. "We'll travel until dusk and then stop for the night. Maybe I can snare us a couple of rabbits."

"If we cross a creek, we might try catching a few fish," Sierra suggested, pushing a wisp of hair back into her bun.

A frown crossed his rugged face. "Apaches don't eat fish or anything else that lives in water."

"You've spent a lot of time among the whites," Sierra said with a shrug, "you could learn. Fried catfish and hush puppies are really good, and I've got some corn-meal."

"We'll see." He stared at her.

She was suddenly aware of the heat of his body where it touched hers. Her heart beat unsteadily a moment, then righted itself. He was looking at her as if he had made a final decision. In a couple of hours, it would be dark. Sierra knew she had to decide whether it would really help her cause to seduce this man and whether she could stand to let a savage touch her. She who had always been afraid to take chances would be facing the biggest risk of her life.

The next couple of hours passed all too soon. Sierra was so nervous, her hands trembled as Cholla ordered a halt to the day's travel. They found a grove of trees with a spring, and the Indian set a snare out in the woods while Sierra made camp.

In less than an hour, he handed her a fat rabbit. "I told you I was a good hunter."

"It looks tasty after all that bacon." Sierra smiled at

him without meaning to, and then suddenly felt self-conscious. She had cornmeal, so she made some fried corn bread although there was no butter to go on it. She even found some late poke greens growing near the creek and boiled a pot of them.

Cholla accepted a plate with a murmur of appreciation.

She started to tell him that since she was a prisoner she had no choice but to please him, then remembered and only nodded. "After the first frost, persimmons will be ripe. They make good pies and —" She stopped in midsentence. She expected to be out of this mess or dead by the time of the first frost.

He didn't seem to notice that she hadn't finished what she was saying, but ate greedily. Robert had always picked around in his food, complaining about her cooking.

They were almost into the edges of the hills off to the the southwest. Maybe this was the night to try to escape. She would wait until he was asleep. The Apache began to tie her wrists and ankles. She complained, showed him the marks the ropes had left. "That hurt, tying me so tight."

"One thing I try not to do is hurt women . . . unlike some of the white men I've known." His tone was ironic, sarcastic, but she wasn't sure to what he referred.

Sierra waited until he was asleep and then began to struggle with her bonds. In a few minutes, she had worked her way out of the ropes. But she was afraid to move. Cholla seemed to have the hearing of a wild animal, coming awake at every sound. But tonight he slept heavily, as if exhausted.

Holding her breath, Sierra slipped away into the darkness. There is no moon tonight, she thought with relief. Maybe, just maybe, she had some chance of escaping. Hills stretched out ahead of her. *The Ozarks?* Surely somewhere up ahead, she'd stumble onto a cabin where someone would send for help, notify the Army, or send out a posse.

She was at least deep in the woods now and, with relief, she ran. She didn't even want to think about what he might do to her if he caught her. Her breath came faster, made her throat hurt as she hurried. He wasn't going to catch her; no, she'd hide in the brush if she didn't find help by daylight. Surely he wouldn't look for her if he realized she'd been gone for hours. He'd be afraid she might already have notified the authorities, so he'd hurry on, intent on saving his own neck. Of course he might take another hostage somewhere down the line. For a second, she almost felt guilty about that.

Then she shook her head stubbornly and kept running. An overhanging limb slapped her in the face. She rubbed her stinging cheek. No, he wouldn't take any more hostages because she would reach the Army or the law and he'd be captured, put where he belonged. Just where did he belong? On that prison train, of course, headed to the damp swamps of Florida. Now that she was almost safe, she could almost feel sorry for Cholla and the other Apaches who were being taken away from their beloved Arizona.

Was she mad? Feel sorry for those bloodthirsty savages who had murdered her husband? She must be too exhausted to think straight! Sierra tripped over a tree root and fell, lay there gasping for air. Suppose he was

122

right behind her? In a panic, she stumbled to her feet.

Think, Sierra, she chided herself. Don't panic, think! You keep crashing through the brush like a terrified deer and he'll surely hear you.

She forced herself to gather her wits about her, look around in the darkness. The leaves beneath her feet formed a soft cushion. The trees created a shelter above her. Somewhere a night bird called. She was on the edge of the hills. Where could she find help? Suppose by morning she was still wandering around in the woods and Cholla recaptured her? He would be angry, maybe as angry as Robert had been sometimes when he had come home drunk. She shuddered at the thought of Cholla doing to her what her husband had done.

You must be taught submission, dear wife, you must please me. He would slap her until she tasted her own blood. *A good wife is supposed to be obedient. Now lie down on your back and please me.*

Merciful heavens, suppose the Apache finally decided to use her as Robert had when he'd been angry? The image gave wings to her feet and desperation to her search. Somewhere nearby there had to be people who would help her. Sierra took a deep breath. Was that smoke she smelled? For a moment, she was glad. Smoke meant a stove somewhere. She was saved!

She stopped suddenly. Suppose she had gotten confused and had run in a circle? If she headed toward the scent would she find herself right back by Cholla's campfire? No. She shook her head, took a deep whiff. This was an unusual smell, a mixture of smoke and something cooking. It was a scent she didn't quite recognize, but she was sure it wasn't just a regular camp-fire.

She started running toward the scent, her heart beating harder. She didn't even care about the reward. The people she was about to meet could have the money, all she wanted was to get on with her life. Even facing an uncertain future in St. Louis with no money paled beside what she had been through. Maybe she wasn't such a gutless, conforming little mouse after all.

She topped a rise, and faintly, through the brush, she saw a distant fire and three men seated around it, leaning on their rifles.

Hunters. Oh, wonderful! She had found a party of armed hunters who would go back with her and capture that Apache. Her captor was about to become a prisoner. Sierra smiled with relief as she ran into the clearing. She could hardly wait to see the look on that big Apache's face when she came back accompanied by three armed men.

Well into the clearing, she came to an abrupt halt. What was that they were boiling?

The three whirled, bringing rifles to their shoulders even as Sierra stared in slow comprehension at the big boiler, the maze of copper tubing. Oh, Lord! It was too late to run away. Even as she began to back off, she knew she was in worse trouble now than before. She had stumbled onto an illegal still!

Chapter Seven

Sierra stared at the three rough, unshaven men. They whirled around, rifles at the ready.

"Zeke, who the hell is it?"

"Hell, Willie, it's a woman!"

"Gal, who are you and what're you doin' here?"

Sierra ran her tongue over dry lips as the men advanced on her. Three backwoods men. Zeke's teeth looked as snaggled as a broken picket fence, Willie's face was half-hidden by a tangled, dirty beard, and the last man seemed as big as a mountain and twice as dangerous.

"Hello." She tried to force herself to smile. She wouldn't be able to outrun them in the dark on terrain familiar to them but not to her. I . . . I'm lost and looking for help. There's a reward—"

"What'd you say about a reward, gal?"

"You hear her, Tiny? She must be goin' to report us to the law."

"No, I'm lost and I saw your fire." Her voice sounded so trembly in her own ears, she wondered if they heard her. "If you'll call the sheriff—"

Merciful heavens, that was the wrong thing to say. All three faces darkened. "I mean, the law is looking for me."

The bearded one gestured with his rifle. "And for us, too, gal. Now you come over here by the fire where we can see you, you hear?"

Should she obey? Those guns looked big as cannons. Old-fashioned, cap-and-ball guns, she noted. "If one of you would take me into the nearest town or would carry a message to a telegraph station—"

"You come over here, and we'll talk about it some more." The snaggled-toothed one gestured with his rifle again. "Ain't that right, boys?"

"Yep, Zeke, that's sure 'nuff right." The bearded one combed his filthy tangle with a grimy hand. "Are you comin', gal, or do we have to come get you?"

Sierra made a split-second decision. The gleam in their eyes warned her that she wouldn't be any safer with them than she had been with the Apache. And there were three of them. She whirled and took off, running back the way she had come.

"Get her, Zeke!"

"Shall I shoot?"

"Nah, if there's anyone with her, they'll hear the shots! Cut her off!"

There was nothing to do but run blindly through the woods, hearing the three fanning out around her. Sierra collided with a tree, fell, got up, and ran on. A bramble bush caught the fabric of her dress, and when she pulled free, part of the bodice tore, too, but she didn't care. All she could think about was escaping.

126

She was in more trouble now than she had been in dealing with just the Apache.

It seemed a giant fist had grasped her chest and was squeezing it. Winded, exhausted, but too terrified to stop running, she stumbled on — and ran right into the arms of the bearded one.

Sierra screamed long and loud, not caring anymore who heard her. Maybe if the Apache came, there would be a fight and she could get away while the moonshiners dealt with the savage.

"Shut up, gal!" A dirty hand was clamped over her mouth and she was dragged back along the path toward their camp.

"You get her, Willie?"

"Sure did!"

Sierra fought, but she wasn't strong enough to break free. He smelled of rancid grease and moonshine whiskey. The stench of him sickened her as she struggled, gasping for air.

She tried to get her mouth free so she could explain why she was there, tell them about the reward, but Willie kept his hand clamped over her mouth as he dragged her back into the clearing.

Tiny said, "Bring her over by the fire so's we can get a look at her."

Sierra stopped struggling as he dragged her into the light from the blaze, but he didn't take his dirty hand off her mouth.

"Whooee, look at her!" Zeke whistled through his snaggled teeth.

She looked down, saw that her torn dress revealed

one of her breasts. The three stared at her naked flesh.

"Wal, now we got her, what'll we do?" Willie asked.

The giant, Tiny, grinned, staring down at her. "With tits like those? I got me a good idea about what to do!"

"What if'n there's someone with her?" Willie asked.

"Like who?" Zeke spat tobacco juice through his gapped teeth. "Revenooers don't usually send women in to find a still."

Sierra tried to get her mouth free to tell them she hadn't been sent by the law, but the dirty hand stayed clamped over her lips.

"She must not have a man with her."

"Why'd you say that?" Willie scratched himself, holding her with one arm. She shuddered, wondered if he had lice.

"If you was a man with a woman like this 'un, would you let her go prowling around at night or would you have her spread out under you?" Zeke asked.

All three laughed.

"You're right," Tiny said. "She must be a runaway."

"Runnin' from what?" Willie demanded.

"Who cares? It just means that maybe nobody we know is gonna report her missin'."

Willie put his grimy face up close to Sierra's. "Does that mean we kin keep her?"

Zeke shrugged. "Reckon so. I got a woman at home and so do you, but we could use a spare; keep her out here near the still."

The big one snorted with laughter. "Then we kin share and share alike, right? Startin' right now!"

128

Determined she was not going to be raped by these three, Sierra bit down hard on the hand across her mouth.

Willie swore and slapped her. "Damned little bitch! Teeth as sharp as a fox!"

Stunned, Sierra tasted blood, but she tried to take in everything around her as she was dragged over by the fire and tossed down on a pile of leaves.

"Who gets her first?" Tiny said.

"I should because I caught her?" Tangled Beard argued.

"But I saw her first when she came out of the woods," Zeke said.

"Did not. I heard the footstep and turned around."

Maybe she could slip away while they argued. Sierra tried to sit up, but immediately, the men grabbed her. "Oh, no you don't gal."

Even as she struggled, Tiny and Willie pushed her back down, spread-eagled her.

Zeke said, "Let's see what we're gettin', boys." He reached down and ripped the top of her bodice away, revealing her breasts in the firelight.

"Let go of me!" She had thought she was afraid when the Indian grabbed her, but that was nothing compared to what she feared from these brutes. Sierra struggled anew, even though she was powerless against the three.

Zeke took an audible breath. "It does things to a man—don't it?—to see her half-naked, her skin all white as new cream. Hold her, boys!"

"Don't you touch me! I'll scream!" Her heart

pounded so hard, she was certain they would see it under her breast.

"Gal"—Zeke laughed—"I intend to do more than just touch you." He unbuttoned his pants.

"Hurry up, Zeke," Tiny spat tobacco juice to one side, "I want a turn and then we'll hold her for Willie."

Sierra struggled, but she realized it was only exciting these three animals. If she screamed, was there anyone to hear her?

But even as she considered the possibility, Zeke ripped away her drawers and her petticoat, stuffed the petticoat in her mouth.

She couldn't take her terrified gaze off his unbuttoned pants.

"Gal, you like what you see?" He threw back his head and guffawed.

"Git on with it," Tiny urged. "I'm hurtin' for my chance at her."

"No sooner said than done." Zeke grinned, leaning over her. Sierra began to struggle again as he came closer. Abruptly, she heard a clap of thunder. Zeke's mouth opened, and he grabbed for his chest. Warm, scarlet blood spurted from between his fingers and splashed across her bare thighs as he toppled sideways.

Tiny and Willie let go of her, cursing, and scrambled for their guns. "Where'd that shot come from? You see anybody?"

In the confusion, Sierra pushed the dead man away, stumbled to her feet, bolted for the edge of the clearing. Willie ran after her, grabbed her. "You ain't goin' anywhere, gal. You're the cause of this!

You—" He made a strange, choking noise.

"Willie, what's the matter?" Tiny demanded. "Willie?"

The bearded man stared down at Sierra, his eyes wide with surprised horror, then he toppled over like a falling tree, a butcher knife in his back. His falling body took Sierra to the ground.

She saw the blur as the bronzed form loomed up out of the shadows. Tiny managed to get off one shot, which went wild as the blur charged him.

Cholla. Cholla had found her. She must get away from both of them. Even as the two men meshed and fought, Sierra pushed Willie's body away, tried to stand up. Uncertainly, she watched them battle hand-to-hand like two giant stags or buffalo bulls fighting for a female's favors. If Tiny won, she'd be raped and possibly killed. Would she be any better off if the savage was the victor?

A rifle. If she could get one of the guns, she might kill both men and escape. Even as she thought it, Cholla twisted Tiny's arm and the big man screamed in pain. As Cholla stepped back, Tiny staggered off into the woods, his arm hanging uselessly. Cholla acted as if he might run after the big backwoodsman, instead, he turned back toward her.

A rifle lay on the ground between them. Sierra measured the distance to it with her eyes. Could she reach it?

Cholla was already striding over to pick it up. "He may be back," the Apache said, "and he'll bring others."

131

At that, her composure broke. It was too much to think about Tiny and his companions coming back to spread-eagle her, paw her, rape her. Sierra tried to hold the tears back, and failed. She ought to run, but she was exhausted, half-naked and she knew she had no chance of escaping from this man.

As if he was prolonging her anxiety over what he was going to do to her, Cholla walked over, pulled the butcher knife out of Willie's back, and wiped the blade on the man's filthy beard. Then he stuck the weapon in the waistband of his pants, picked up his rifle, looked at her.

Sierra buried her face in her hands and wept. She was too tired to resist or run away.

"Dark Eyes, are you all right?"

"What do you care?" she raged at him suddenly, finding a defiance in her soul she had not even known was there. "You got me into this spot."

"No, you got yourself into this spot," he said calmly, coming over to her. "You should have stayed with me." He looked at the two dead men. "The dirty bastards. Did they hurt you?"

"No. You interrupted them."

He reached down and she flinched, too weary to fight him anymore.

His hand cupped her small face. "Sierra, let me help you—"

"Don't touch me!" She tried to struggle to her feet, and he lifted her, swung her up in his arms. All she could do was weep in humiliating defeat against his shoulder as he held her.

"Sierra, we've got to get out of here," he murmured. "He'll probably return with some of his friends or maybe even go for the law."

The law she'd be glad to see, but she didn't want to end up raped by Tiny and his bunch. She hung onto Cholla's neck as he bent and gathered up the guns with one hand before swiftly moving through the woods, back to their camp.

When he stood her on her feet by the fire, she realized she was half-naked and smeared with blood. Her bare breasts brushed his rippling chest, and she stepped back. The way he looked at her, his deep breathing, the hard bulge of his pants told her what he must be thinking.

She crossed her arms over her breasts and glared at him. "I thought we had to hurry?"

"We do." He ran the tip of his tongue along his bottom lip very slowly, as if imagining it on her nipple. "Otherwise . . ." His voice broke off and squared his shoulders, turned to kick dirt over the fire. "We'll go as far as we can in the darkness and just hope Tiny thinks better of returning. Because of the still, he might be afraid to go for the law. We'll travel as fast and as far as we can before the mule tires out." He gestured. "Get in the wagon."

"I'm perfectly capable of walking alongside so the mule won't tire."

"Suit yourself." He shrugged and glared at her, began to load up the wagon.

Sierra didn't want to admit how weary she was, but it was hard to put one foot in front of the other as they

133

left the clearing and headed deeper into the hills. He hadn't given her time to change, so she stumbled along in the ragged and bloody dress, her breasts half-visible. When she looked up, she caught him staring at her.

Tired as she was, she began to lag behind.

"Sierra, if you think I won't notice if you fall behind and then try to bolt into the brush, think again."

She wasn't about to admit that she was too weary to keep up. She gritted her teeth and walked a little faster. She'd show this savage. It occurred to her that if she really became too tired to keep up, he might cut her throat and leave her on the trail. After all, he'd just killed two people without a moment's hesitation, why would he hesitate to kill her if she crossed him?

Finally, she just couldn't take another step, not on sore, blistered feet. She stumbled and fell to the ground.

"Sierra!" He strode over, lifted her up in his arms, looked down into her eyes.

She felt the heat of his skin against her bare breast, felt his heart beating strongly against her nipple.

"Damn you!" he muttered. "Damn you for being who you are!"

She didn't know what had angered him so, decided it was that she couldn't keep up. "Let me try again," she whispered. "I . . . maybe I can make it a few more miles."

"For a girl who tells me she never takes any chances, you're a stubborn little chit." He easily carried her toward the wagon, the sinewy muscles under his dark skin rippling. She looked down at her breast pressed against his bare chest and knew she should pull away, but she was too tired. With Tiny and other men possibly coming after them, she was at least safe from the Apache's advances for a while.

He reached up to settle her in the wagon, then went to walk alongside the mule. Sierra watched his back, the muscles rippling under the thin cotton shirt as he walked. His hips were small, and she wondered suddenly if they were as hard as the muscles of his chest. Then she remembered the heat of him against her breast.

Why am I thinking these thoughts? Because I have been expecting to be raped from the very first? No it was something more; something about the heat of his skin against hers, the strength of him. She had felt almost safe in his big arms as he had carried her back to camp after rescuing her from the three backwoodsmen.

The scissors. She still had those hidden in the trunk for use if she needed them. She closed her eyes and saw again the surprised look on Willie's face as the butcher knife burrowed into his back. Could she do something like that if need be? She tried to imagine stabbing Cholla with the scissors and winced. An Injun savage, she reminded herself, and my kidnapper. Yes, I could stab him if I got the chance. It was growing harder and harder to keep her eyes open as the wagon moved along, the wheels creaking rhythmically. Finally she slept.

It was daylight when the jolting of the wagon awakened her and she sat up, looked out. They were still traveling through the hills.

All day long they scarcely spoke, and they didn't stop except for necessities like grabbing a bite of dry bread and meat before he insisted on moving forward again. She was still bloody and dirty from last night, but he wouldn't stop long enough for her to wash up.

They kept moving until dark, when he seemed willing to camp.

"We've covered a lot of ground," he said. "If that *hombre* was coming after us or bringing the law, he'd have showed up by now."

She had had a forlorn hope that Tiny might have telegraphed the law or the soldiers, but maybe that was expecting too much.

As soon as they found a stream, they camped.

Sierra fixed food, and they ate in silence.

The night seemed as warm as a lover's breath on the skin. She finished eating and set the plate down. "Is it all right if I wash in the creek?"

He looked up from his plate. "Just let me hear you splashing. If it gets too quiet, I'll know you've sneaked away again."

"I'm more afraid of what might be out there in the dark than I am of you." She paused, surprised to realize this was not far from the truth.

He gave her a long, thoughtful look. Sierra felt the blood rush to her face at the desire she saw reflected in his eyes in the firelight.

Quickly, she stood up, got a towel, a clean black

dress, and a bar of homemade soap from her trunk. She thought about taking the scissors and tucking them into her clothing, then shook her head. No, for a little while, he'd be suspicious of her. She didn't want to take any chances on his suspecting anything. After all, he still had Grandfather's rifle, the axe, and the butcher knife. The backwoodsmen's guns had turned out to be old cap-and-ball types, not worth the trouble of taking along.

Hesitating at the creek bank before she took off her dress, Sierra wondered if Cholla would spy on her while she bathed, then decided she was past worrying about that.

The water was thigh-deep and warm, with the moon reflected in it. Sierra took the pins from her hair, waded over to put them with her things. She shook her hair down, letting it fall in a silken cascade around her shoulders and across her breasts. For a moment, she looked down at her reflection and saw herself as wild and free as her mother had been. She shook her head. No, she was too inhibited, too restrained.

Robert had complained about it, but it was ingrained in her. Grandfather had warned her repeatedly that only disaster awaited her if she turned out like her mother. *The nail that stands up will be hammered down. Conform. Blend in.* How many times had Grandfather said that? She must not take any chances, must not be a strong-willed individual trying to mold her own destiny.

Humming a little tune that Zanna had taught her,

137

Sierra washed her hair and pushed it back. Then she started to lather her body.

"Mind if I join you?"

Sierra looked up in alarm, crossed her arms over her breasts, still clutching the soap.

The big Apache stood there on the creek bank, watching her. Sierra reminded herself that sooner or later she must submit to him or she would never lull him into complacency so she might kill him or escape.

When she didn't answer, he slowly began to peel his clothes off, but his eyes never left hers.

Sierra knew she shouldn't look, but her gaze traveled down his dark, muscular body as he stripped. He was much bigger in that one place than Robert had been.

Sierra's heart pounded in apprehension, yet she forced herself to stand still in the water. Now the scout stood naked on the creek bank in the moonlight. It dawned on her that he was displaying himself proudly like a stud horse. Once at night, in a pasture, Sierra had seen a stallion about to mount a mare in heat, his iron bar of maleness almost beating against his belly as he circled the mare while she made soft noises deep in her throat. Then he had reared up and taken her, plunging hard. It had been savage and gentle, torrid and tender.

Slowly Sierra took her hands away from her breasts and let her arms fall to her sides. Bathed in moonlight, she knew she was about to become part of a primitive ritual that was as old as time itself.

Cholla never took his gaze off her as he stepped

slowly into the water. He stood so close that his shadow fell across her and, when she breathed, her nipples brushed against his brawny chest. But she did not retreat. She had set events in motion, and now there was no stopping them.

"I . . . I'm not afraid of you," she whispered.

"You have no reason to be." The Apache reached out for her, pulled her wet, naked body against his.

Chapter Eight

Sierra didn't cringe. She looked up at him boldly. "If you're expecting me to scream or swoon, I'm going to disappoint you."

He smiled. "You're full of surprises, Dark Eyes. You keep telling me what a faint-hearted mouse you are, reluctant to take chances, but I sense an outlaw streak trying to emerge."

Zanna, she thought with alarm. Underneath I'm much like my wild, tempestuous mother.

At all costs, she must learn to subdue that uninhibited spirit. *Those who conform, who don't stand out, stay out of trouble.* However, all that was uppermost in her mind right now was surviving. "Here." She handed him the soap. "You might as well wash my back."

He looked rather startled by her boldness, then chuckled. "By Usen, you do surprise me. Turn around."

Sierra obeyed, and he began to lather her back. She had to admit it felt good, his strong, supple hands massaging between her shoulder blades. Gradually his hands worked their way around her waist to her belly.

She stiffened for a moment, then relaxed and let him lather her there. If she let him make love to her, he might let down his guard.

His hands worked their way up her rib cage. Sierra gritted her teeth, knowing where they would probably go next. But they felt so good on her body.

Was she out of her mind? She was the widow of a cavalry officer who had been killed by Apaches. In that moment, she reminded herself how much she hated Cholla, but his fingers, stroking her skin, were sending little ripples of pleasure through her.

His hands went to her breasts. In that split second that passed before he cupped them in his big palms, she promised herself that when she stabbed him with the scissors, she would plunge them straight into his heart.

Sierra looked down. With almost detached interest, she watched his soapy hands caress and massage her breasts. She tried, but could not keep her nipples from swelling hard in response, jutting against his fingers, wanting still more. In rebellion, she closed her eyes so she couldn't see how traitorously her body responded to his touch.

His supple, gentle fingers worked their way across her shoulders and neck, sudsing there, then moved back down to caress her breasts. Sierra gasped at the unfamiliar responses his touch elicited from her as his hands moved down her rib cage again, stroking her belly through a silky layer of suds.

She almost cried out in protest when his hands went to her thighs, then remembered and clamped her lips shut. His breath was hot against her neck, his manhood hard and pulsating against her back. Would he take her right here in the water?

"Now," he whispered against her hair, "now you wash me."

She almost protested that she had never washed a man's body before, then decided she was being challenged. Almost defiantly, she turned in the water and looked up at him. Robert had never looked at her with the intense wanting and passion in those dark eyes.

Hesitantly she took the bar of soap from his hand. In the moonlight, she never took her gaze off his as she began to lather his brawny chest. Merciful heavens, he was big and powerful! She felt the hard strength under his dark skin as she ran her hands across his chest.

Without a word, he caught one of her hands in his own, made it linger on his nipples. They grew hard and swollen under her touch, but only his sharp intake of breath broke the silence between them. Somewhere a night bird called, and the water lapped softly against the bank.

How long could she prolong this ritual and what did he expect from her? For a moment, Sierra almost panicked in her uncertainty; then the look on his face told her that whatever she was doing, she was doing right, and she grew more bold.

Her hands went to his waist, then his belly. Hesitating, she grew brazen enough to reach around him and soap his hips. This movement put her soapy breasts against his wet body, and she felt his manhood strong and virile between them. She looked up at him.

Deep inside, she felt both excitement and fear at

this prolonged game. She was trembling as was he. Never had any of her sexual encounters with her husband lasted longer than a couple of minutes. By the time she had felt even the least stirring of interest, Robert had been finished and asleep.

Cholla still looked down into her eyes. Without a word, he reached back to take her hands in his, slowly bring them down between his thighs. "You know what I want," he whispered. "Touch me; touch me there."

Sierra was intensely aware of this moment in time: the sound of his breathing and the splashing of the creek; the feel of warm water like a man's wet kisses, on her thighs; the scents of soap and of his skin, of wildflowers somewhere in the nearby field.

The soap slipped from her nerveless fingers and she cupped her hands to receive his hot, pulsating manhood.

"Sierra . . . Dark Eyes . . ." He lifted her, sweeping her up in his arms in one gesture of strength, and then he stooped, plunging them both into the water to rinse away the soap. Coming up out of the water like some primitive sea god, he carried her to the moonlit bank and laid her down, half in, half out of the creek.

His mouth caressed her nipples until she gasped aloud at the unfamiliar pleasure, forgetting who he was, where they were. And furthermore, she didn't care. She arched up her body, letting it beg wordlessly for more of his touch.

Now his kisses slipped down her wet belly as he knelt in the shallows. Then he slowly spread her thighs. *Surely he wasn't going to . . . ?* Even her husband had never paid her that homage. Yet even

143

as she wondered, Cholla's lips caressed her there.

It was shameful to like it, not to try to stop what he was doing to her with his mouth, she thought. But she couldn't make herself protest. Then the hot blade of his tongue slipped inside her even as his big hands held her thighs captive. She was more than his hostage, she was a prisoner of pleasure—his . . . and hers. All that she could do was fear it might cease before she had had enough.

Waves of unaccustomed sensation began sweeping over her. Surprised and shocked by her own body's reactions, Sierra reminded herself that she must stop him, that she must not enjoy what he was doing to her. She reached down with both hands to push him away and found she was tangling her fingers in his ebony hair, pulling his mouth to her. Her thighs locked around him, willing him not to end this ecstasy he created for her, these shudders that generated in ripples from the font of her femininity.

The waves of sensation swept over her, and she became lost in the growing thrill of his caresses and the feel of his mouth, water lapping around her. Somewhere the night bird called again, and the scent of flowers and crushed grass drifted on the still air. A crescendo began to build deep within her. It took over her heart and her pulse and her soul, blocking out everything as it grew into something overpowering. Then it all came together in a dark rush that swept her into a crashing tide of emotion.

Sierra felt herself losing control, losing consciousness. For a split second, panic overtook her and she struggled against the black tide. Then his hands grasped her waist firmly and his mouth did forbidden, tantalizing things to her, and she surrendered herself to pleasure.

Gradually Sierra came back to her surroundings and wondered for a moment how long she had been unconscious. Then her eyes flickered open and she stared up at the dark savage looking down into her face. Without a word, he bent his head and kissed her lips, and she tasted the essence of her own body on his mouth. It excited her all over again. She seemed on fire with unfulfilled desire as she reached up to pull his brawny body to hers.

He hesitated only a moment, then he penetrated her but just barely. He was big, all right; she felt the hard steel of his maleness and wondered what it would be like when he went in to the hilt. In the silvery moonlight, he looked into her eyes, an unspoken question in his.

Would he pull back if she shook her head or managed to say the word 'no'? She didn't even seem able to breathe, much less say anything. And still he hesitated against her opening.

In answer, she locked her thighs around him and tilted her body up, her thighs pulling him toward her. He pushed slowly into her, all the way, into the deepest part of her, until she was impaled by him. Deep inside, she felt him throbbing with the seed he had brought to her, and once again, she remembered the virile stallion topping the mare in the mystery of creating life.

He pulled back until for a split second Sierra

thought he intended to withdraw, and then, very slowly, he thrust his sword into her velvet scabbard to the hilt. The sensation made her quiver all over. As he withdrew again, Sierra dug her nails into rippling broad shoulders, willing him to stay within her. Her sharp intake of breath seemed to excite him, and he began to ride her with a hard intensity, ramming harder and deeper each time.

Her body demanded that he give her what she craved, and her breath came in open-mouthed gasps as she coupled with him in an ever-increasing frenzy. His tongue went deep into her mouth even as he went deep inside her. It was all so new to her, she couldn't get enough of the pleasure he created.

At that instant he gasped deep into her throat and tensed, his lean hips thrusting into her at one moment and in the next frozen in quivering stillness against her.

Sierra felt him begin to give up his hot seed deep within her. Then she knew no more as her wanton body locked onto his so it could have what it craved. They were two wild, primitive things coupling in the moonlight.

Cholla gradually came back to consciousness, lying locked in the white girl's thighs. He had been a long time without a woman. That was the only reason this had been so intense a mating, he told himself. Grudgingly, he realized he had never experienced passion to equal what he had just found in the arms of Forester's woman. Maybe that was why it had been so wonderful — the added pleasure of revenge.

Sierra had belonged to his dead enemy. How furious Forester would be, if he were alive, to know an Apache was using his woman as a whore, as Forester had used the beautiful young Apache girl. *"An eye for an eye and a tooth for a tooth."* Wasn't that what the black-robed holy men of the whites taught at the mission school he had attended?

Yet she looked so vulnerable lying there beneath him. Sierra, he thought, prim and restrained, but locked deep inside her dwells a spirit as wild and un-tamed as the distant mountains. Without thinking, he bent and kissed her forehead. Her beautiful dark eyes flickered open and she looked up at him in confused wonder.

"It's all right," he assured her, and pushed her damp hair away from her face. "It's all right, Sierra." He must lull her into thinking that he was beginning to care about her. It would be convenient to have a woman to cook for him, warm his blankets when he needed her; and a hostage would come in handy if he was cornered by the law or the Army.

Besides, the search parties were looking for a man traveling alone, so he was much safer traveling with Sierra. Maybe he had promised to free her once he was out of danger, but he was the one to decide when that danger was past. Sierra Forester didn't know it, but that might be a long time off, and Cholla intended that much of their time together would be spent with her lying under his virile body. Wouldn't it be a grim joke if he put a baby in her belly?

Without another word, he disengaged from her, got up, went to get a blanket. With his strength, she was no weight at all to pick up. He wrapped her wet body

147

in the blanket, carried her back by the fire and lay down next to her. Sierra looked up at him as if to speak, but he shook his head. "It doesn't have to be any more than you want it to be, Sierra," he whispered. "We'll sort it out tomorrow."

She hesitated, her eyes full of conflict. Cholla gave her a reassuring look and she closed her eyes, and finally he heard her even breathing. But he couldn't sleep. *It doesn't have to be any more than you want it to be. We'll sort it out tomorrow.*

No, not tomorrow or any time, he promised himself as he looked at the sleeping girl. Cholla wasn't sure he wanted to delve too deeply into how much his enemy's woman had stirred him. He was a proud man and bent on revenge. It wouldn't do to let this woman become more than just an object to be used for his pleasure and his vengeance. When he deserted her with her belly swollen with his child, he would tell her about her chivalrous officer husband, about how Forester had raped and killed. . . .

He shuddered, remembering how Delzhinne had looked when he'd followed Tom out to the murder scene. There was something his friend wasn't telling him, he knew that from the way Tom's honest blue eyes wavered. Cholla felt too much anguish to press Tom for details.

Revenge, Cholla thought now as he looked down at Sierra Forester asleep in his arms. What he had only suspected about Delzhinne's death, he had found out in the arroyo that fateful summer day. Cholla would have his revenge on Forester by using his wife for his personal pleasure. If by the wildest chance, she should

148

come to care for him or become heavy with his child, it would make the vengeance even sweeter.

In the meantime, her body had just given him more pleasure than any other woman's had. That thought made him uneasy. Women were all very much alike, after all—breasts and soft bellies for a man to lie on, a warm velvet place for his thrusting, a hot mouth to tease and caress him into using her again. Still he had never experienced anything like the mating he had just had with Forester's woman. It had to be the irony of the situation, the thought of how the lieutenant would rage and curse if he were alive to know a brown savage he had hated was doing to Forester's woman what the lieutenant himself had done to Delzhinne. Cholla was both troubled and pleased with himself as he put his hand on her soft breasts, pulled her close against him and dropped off to sleep.

Sergeant Tom Mooney yawned as he awakened in the darkness of his sparse quarters at Fort Bowie. It would be dawn soon, yet his wiry body felt weary.

"Tom, you stubborn Irishman, why don't you admit you're too old for this and retire?" He sat up on the edge of his bunk and ran a hand through his thinning, reddish hair. His enlistment would be up the first of the year, and he still hadn't made up his mind.

The big dog in the corner raised its head and studied him.

"Yes, Ke'jaa, you half-coyote, it's time to get up." Tom felt around on the floor for his boots, wondering why he bothered with the ugly cur that would not even wag its tail when he spoke. Because it was his friend's

149

dog; that was why he had rescued it from the slaughter that commenced after the train pulled out.

But Cholla was gone, perhaps forever in spite of everything Mooney, Lieutenant Gatewood, and General Crook could do to help the Apache scouts. The scouts had helped end the bloodshed by renegades like Geronimo, and they had been rewarded by being gathered up at the last minute and loaded on a Florida bound train, too. It was neither fair nor just and Tom Mooney was both.

"You ugly sonovagun," he smiled at the dog and snapped his fingers at it, knowing the beast wouldn't come to him, "if your master wasn't my *compadre,* damned if I'd put up with your attitude. You're just like your master; independent, never doing what you're expected to do. Don't you know a dog is supposed to lick a man's hand when he feeds it and wag your tail once in awhile?"

The big yellow animal cocked its head to one side, listening, but it didn't move or show any sign of friendliness. It snarled at everyone who came close to it. At least Ke'jaa tolerated him because he was Cholla's friend. No, more than friend. Brother, *Sikis.* They had shared food and danger many times in the past several years. Once Cholla had saved Mooney's life. And then Tom had saved his.

The sergeant thought about the incident a moment, then stood up with a shrug, scratching his muscular chest with stubby, freckled fingers as he reached for his pants in the first rays of gray dawn.

Holy Saint Patrick, you're getting old, Tom, he said to himself as he looked in the small, cracked mirror on

150

the wall. You'll be forty-two next birthday, and what do you have to show for it? His parents were still alive, but feeble. They hoped he'd come home to take over the farm. Maybe it's time I gave it some thought, he decided, looking at the weathered face in the mirror.

Tom Mooney had been in the Army longer than some of the new recruits had lived, having joined up during the Civil War to follow George Armstrong Custer, hero of the Michigan troops.

Funny how things turned out. Custer had been dead ten years now this past June. Maybe it had been only luck that Tom hadn't been with him that fateful day at the Little Big Horn River. His deeply religious mother said he was being saved for some reason, something that God had scheduled for Tom in the future.

"You were right, Mother," he said, remembering the incident of this past July. Of course she would never know what had happened out there. He and Cholla and the three other men who'd survived knew, but it would be their secret forever. Cholla had insisted they all swear an oath.

Tom Mooney dressed quickly, considering retirement. Maybe he wouldn't mind returning to a Michigan farm if there was a woman to share his life there. Women had never paid him much attention. To begin with, he wasn't tall or handsome, and he was too shy to flirt or make clever conversation. Besides, for the past several months, he had been in love with another man's wife.

He reached for his hat, thinking about the woman, wondering if he could get up the nerve to go call on her if he retired. He imagined it in his head, even though he knew he would never do so. "Aw, Tom, don't kid yourself; you're no hand with the ladies or you'd have a wife by now." He paused at the door, turned to the dog. "Ke'jaa, I'm going to the stable, come along?"

The beast got to its feet, studied him a long moment.

"I know, I miss him, too. Maybe Lieutenant Gatewood has some good news for us. You know General Crook is doing his best to help, don't you? But there's politics involved, you see, and General Miles is in charge now. . . ." His voice trailed off as he realized he was carrying on a conversation with a dog. He cursed under his breath. Aye, he was a lonely man. He read poetry and took walks while other troopers went into town to drink and gamble and pleasure themselves.

Would she like poetry? Gently, he reached inside his jacket, took out the small photo. Such beautiful dark eyes she had, this black-haired woman he had never met. He felt a little guilty, knowing he had no right to keep this photo. Tom hadn't returned it with the officer's other personal effects. There was something about the woman's face that called out to his lonely heart.

"I wonder if she might be interested in a quiet Michigan farm?" he said aloud as he tucked the photo away inside his uniform. "All she can do is say no. Now what do you think of that, Ke'jaa? Should I write or go see her?"

The dog's red ribbon of tongue ran in and out over his great fangs.

"Sonovagun, are you laughing at me now? Maybe it is foolish, to think she might even consider a worn-out soldier, or even that I would ever get up the nerve to go see her. Still she looks like the kind of prim lady who might prefer the safe, secure life of a farmer's wife. Why there'd even be a place for you, dog."

The dog regarded him gravely. Mooney knew the half-coyote acknowledged only one master. The Apache scout had found the orphaned pup in a deserted den in the hills several years ago.

"At least I saved his dog," Mooney said to himself as the pair walked toward the stables in the gray light of dawn. In another thirty minutes, the brilliance of sunlight would reflect off the Arizona landscape, bathing the scene in color like a fiery painting, all scarlet and turquoise and golden. Here in the southeastern part of the Territory were the Chiricahua Mountains and old Cochise's stronghold in the hills. Beyond lay the desolate reaches and the wild Sierra Madre to the south of the border. A man could live there forever without getting caught. Hadn't Geronimo proved that?

Lieutenant Gatewood had been a brave man to go into Geronimo's camp, accompanied only by two Apaches scouts, and talk the old renegade into surrendering. Gatewood should get a medal and a promotion, Tom thought, but the officer was on the wrong side of the political maneuvering.

"Hey, hoss," he called out.

The fine paint stallion had already stuck its head out the stall door and now nickered at the sound of Mooney's approaching boots. Ke'jaa bounded ahead, sniffing the breeze eagerly, and stopped before the stall.

Mooney sighed and patted the black and white horse absently. "Sorry, you two, he's not with me, and he's not coming either. I know it's hard for you both to understand, but maybe General Crook will manage to talk President Cleveland into doing what's fair. Those Apaches, even Geronimo, trusted Crook to keep his word."

It hadn't been Crook's fault of course, and the general had resigned in a fury when the government reneged on the promises he'd made. Now Miles was enforcing the new edicts. Politics—all politics. It was more than a simple soldier could understand.

Tom stroked the stallion's mane, enjoying the scent of hay and horseflesh. The dog lay down patiently at his feet, but Mooney knew better than to pat it. The stallion had learned to accept Mooney because he was his master's friend. The dog had never even accepted her.

Delzhinne. It was an Apache word that meant 'dark-skinned.' Cholla had doted on her. Probably not more than sixteen years old and very beautiful. At least she *had* been. The sergeant winced at the memory, wondering again what he should have done when he'd found her body out in the brush. There had been a brass button clutched in her hand—a cavalry uniform button. Holy Saint Patrick. Could any soldier have dared to—? Sure and they'd all be too afraid of Cholla . . . unless the man was drunk.

What to do? He'd taken the button from her hand, put it in his pocket. A crumpled little paper sack lay on the ground nearby. He'd picked that up too, wondering if it had been dropped or had blown there from the fort? Then he had straightened her clothes to give her a little dignity, although it was all too apparent she had been violated. There wasn't anything he could do about the bullet hole between her eyes. Powder burns. She'd been shot at close range after her attacker had satisfied himself. Tom had spread his jacket over her face before he'd gone to get Cholla.

On the way, he passed Lieutenant Gillen, who looked a little the worse for wear, but there weren't any buttons missing from his uniform that Tom could see.

Tom told Cholla as gently as he could and led him out to the place. When Cholla pulled the jacket away, a fly lit on her open mouth. Cholla gagged and his shoulders shook. "Damn the renegade Apaches! They take revenge on a woman because I scout for the soldiers!"

In his pocket, Tom had a button and a crumpled sack that told a different story, but Tom Mooney made his decision in a heartbeat. His friend could only come to grief seeking revenge against a soldier. "Yes, that looks like what happened, doesn't it? The renegade Apache got her."

Later in the day, Tom spotted Forester, looking as if he'd just come off a long drunk, his uniform disheveled, with a button missing. Forester? Tom kept silent, uncertain what to do. His knowledge could only bring more trouble to his sorrowing friend.

If I had done things differently then, would it have changed what happened out at the arroyo that hot summer day only weeks later?

His thoughts were interrupted by the sound of boots, and Mooney turned toward the skinny corporal.

Schultz saluted. "Sir, Lieutenant Gatewood would like to see you."

Mooney gave him a half-hearted salute. "Johnny, we know each other too well for all this formality."

The man grinned, showing teeth stained by tobacco. "It's all this new spit and polish around here since General Miles took over. You never know who might put you on report."

"Well, sonovagun, you know it won't be me!"

They laughed in easy camaraderie. Schultz was a career man like himself. He and Allen and Taylor. The four of them and Cholla had survived that Apache ambush Forester had gotten his patrol into. Like Mooney himself, the other three owed their lives to Cholla's skillful scouting. They would have done anything for the scout—or their sergeant. Five men bound by friendship and a vow of silence about what had happened out there among the cactus and the chaparral of that sun-baked arroyo.

Schultz lit a cigar and shook his head. "I'm sorry we couldn't raise enough money to buy the stallion at the auction. I hate like hell to see Gillen end up with Cholla's horse."

"It couldn't be helped," Tom said, leaning against the stall door. "Gillen had left money to bid it in, probably made from crooked card games. Anyway maybe Cholla won't be coming back, so he won't know."

The corporal blew smoke. "It don't seem right,

the government selling the Apaches' horses."

"I reckon the President and the Army figure they won't ever need them again. They'll never get back from Florida."

The German frowned. "That don't sound like Cholla. He's as wild and free as this country of his; I can't imagine him living any other way."

"He won't bend, so they'll try to break him. Civilization doesn't like people who won't conform, and Cholla won't. They may kill him, but they won't cage him; he's proud, maybe too proud." Mooney flinched, thinking about his Indian friend and of what Cholla might be enduring at that very minute.

"At least you saved his dog."

Mooney turned to go. "Nobody wanted the Apache dogs; *everybody* wanted their horses." He walked briskly down the path, the mongrel dog trotting behind him.

Tom strode toward the lieutenant's office, the dog trotting at his heels. Mooney liked dogs, he did not like what had happened at the railroad station that day.

It had been sweltering hot, the alkali dust drifting on the stifling air as the Apaches' ponies trudged along the hundred-mile trip north from Fort Apache to the railroad station at Holbrook. Lieutenant Colonel James Wade, and his black Tenth Cavalry escorted the almost five hundred Indians.

Colonel Wade had told the warriors they were all making a trip to Washington to see the Great White Father. Tom and Cholla knew that surely couldn't be true, but they were sent along to assist because they both spoke the language. They didn't dare to voice their suspicions except to each other. Cholla said the government would see its mistake, would change the order before it shipped peaceful Apaches away. Each night, the Indians camped, stoically accepting their fate.

Cholla shook his head as he looked out at the hundred of campfires, red beacons in the dark. "I don't like it, Tom, this isn't what was promised when I went in and helped talk Geronimo into surrendering. In fact, the bunch we're herding toward the train station are peaceful people. There's been some mistake. Surely the government will have a wire waiting at the station to cancel the order."

Tom shook his head. "I feel for you, brother, having to help herd your own people to the train."

"You know I wouldn't be involved if I weren't sure this mistake would be corrected. Besides, I want to watch and make sure the women and children aren't mistreated."

"Do you suppose they'll have a band at the station?" It had seemed incredible to Tom that when they'd loaded Geronimo and his renegades into wagons for Captain Lawton to take to Bowie Station, the regimental band had played "Old Lang Syne."

"I hope not. At least the peaceful ones won't have to ride with the old renegade and his warriors. Geronimo's bunch are on another train through Texas."

"The white people of Arizona Territory have seen all they want of Apaches." Mooney squatted down before the fire, poured himself another cup of coffee, felt for the comfort of the photo and the book of poetry in his jacket.

Cholla only grunted.

In its place next to Cholla, the big, ugly dog raised its head and regarded Tom quietly.

Tom said, "They're raising hell in Washington, demanding we ship all of them out. I think they're afraid the Apaches'll go off the reservation again. You remember the torturings and killings Geronimo's bunch did when they'd get drunk and go riding off to Mexico."

Cholla patted the dog, and it licked his hand. "I have no love for the renegades. They killed my father, and have brought nothing but tragedy to my people. If it had not been for his death, I would not have been raised around the fort. Sometimes I begin to think like the whites, except they all conform like a bunch of ants. Even with that, I can still sympathize with the renegades. Apaches were meant to roam free, and that is all they ask, to live as they have always lived."

Tom Mooney sipped his coffee and listened. Somewhere a baby cried, and its mother soothed it with soft Apache words. Dogs barked, and the sounds echoed in the sultry Arizona night. Forester had admitted his guilt, but he had not mentioned any accomplice in those last minutes and Tom had never told Cholla about the paper candy sack. Suppose Gill was innocent and Cholla wouldn't listen to any explanation?

"Cholla, things are changing. You know that, and your people must change, too. That is why you ride with the Army. Outlaws like Geronimo will only get women and children on both sides killed by trying to return to the old ways that are no more."

Cholla shook his head. "Why is it we must conform, be just like whites or be considered worthless? Sometimes, late at night, I think of going across the border, into the mountains with my dog and my horse. That's wild country down there. A man could live out his lifetime in the Sierra Madres as wild and free as his ancestors. I could live off the land."

"It would be a lonely life," Tom said.

"Aren't we both lonely, brother?" Cholla's hand paused and trembled as he patted the dog. "Somewhere maybe there is a woman who would go with me and never look back."

"I hope you find her," Tom said, and threw the dregs of his coffee into the fire. "If she's out there, I hope you find her. If you do, see if she has a sister for me."

The Apache laughed. "Don't worry, if I ever find a woman I think is right for you, you can be sure I'll deliver her to you as a gift."

Tom grinned. "You do that."

Cholla stared into the fire, lost in his own thoughts and maybe bothered by the fact that he was part of this trek, no matter that he was under orders and that in the end it was for the best. The Apache were to be "civilized" and educated, taught skills other than hunting and raiding.

Throughout the campgrounds, a chorus of dogs began to bark but though his ragged ears went up, Ke-'jaa did not bark. While he might snarl, he never barked. A barking dog endangered its master.

The strangely marked stallion whinnied at the

160

racket made by hundreds of howling dogs and pulled restlessly at its picket pin.

Cholla looked up at the beautiful black and white paint and reassured him. "It's all right, boy."

"I never did hear how you came by that horse," Tom said.

"See the Medicine Hat coloring?" Cholla gestured. "That coloring is thought lucky by many tribes. My friends, the Randolph family out at the Wolf's Den ranch, raise these horses and they gave me this one. His ancestor was a wild Medicine Hat stallion called Sky Climber that roamed the hills of Nevada for many years."

The stallion's coloring is unusual, Tom thought. The large spot on its chest truly looked like a war shield, and the top of its head was black, making it seem as if the horse wore a black cap.

They bedded down for the night. If Tom had known what Colonel Wade's secret orders were, he would have warned Cholla; he would have warned all the scouts so they could escape.

Tom was a battle-hardened veteran, but he was horrified on that hot September day when the soldiers were ordered to force all the Apaches onto the trains.

"Sir, what about their things?" Tom had protested to Lieutenant Gillen. "What about their blankets and all that stuff? What about their horses and dogs?"

Gillen grinned and popped a peppermint in his mouth. "Blast it! Our orders are to load Apaches, nothing else. Be reasonable, Sergeant, you don't really think we could ship all that stuff across the country, especially all those damned dogs? Where they're going, they don't need horses."

Cholla shook his head. "You may throw me out of the Army or shoot me, Lieutenant, but I want no part of this. There's not enough room, and the windows are nailed shut."

"We can hardly have the red bastards escaping now, can we, scout?"

"But it's going to be sweltering, Lieutenant, and some of these people have never even seen a train before. They'll be terrified."

Gillen's face flushed an angry red. "These savages have tortured and killed white people. My buddy is rotting in a shallow grave because of these bloodthirsty bastards! You think I care what happens to them?"

Mooney glanced around. Even as the three argued, black soldiers began loading the Indians on the train. They and their white officers had their orders.

Ironic, Tom thought in that split second, the blacks, who have just been freed from slavery, are taking part in enslaving the red people.

When women hesitated, soldiers yanked children from their arms, threw them on the train. The women followed their youngsters onto the cars, sobbing. Old people had their few precious possessions pulled from their arms and dumped next to the track as the soldiers used rifles butts to herd them, like cattle, into the cars.

Hundreds of dogs ran about in the confusion, yelping and howling, trying to follow their Apache masters into the cars, only to be chased away by soldiers.

162

Surrounded by the weeping of children and the howling of dogs, Tom looked around in sudden dismay. More soldiers had appeared. They were jerking the Indian scouts off their ponies, dragging them onto the trains.

"No!" Tom shouted. "These are friendly braves — see the red headbands? These are the scouts who helped us! There must be some mistake!"

"See the colonel! We got our orders!" the soldiers shouted back.

"Cholla, I'll find the colonel, see if I can find out what's going on!" Tom dismounted, pushed through the crowd.

His blue uniform seemed plastered to his body by sweat and dust as he searched frantically for the officer in charge. Everyone kept directing him to someone else. Behind him, the soldiers had disarmed most of the scouts and were loading them bodily onto trains. It took four men to pull the big scout, Cholla, off the rearing stallion. Tom looked back as he ran through the jostling crowd. Ke'jaa snarled and snapped at the soldiers, trying to protect his master as they dragged Cholla off the horse, chained him.

Mooney turned and ran back through the crowd toward the train. Most of the Indians were aboard now; he could see their frightened faces through the dirty windows that wouldn't open to allow a breath of air in this September heat. The stench and the noise and the dust seemed to swirl around him. "Stop! You can't do this! This man is a government scout! There's been a mistake!"

But Gillen signaled the soldiers to drag Cholla on

163

board. The dog tried to bite him, and he kicked at it and swore. "Sergeant! Stop interfering with our orders or I'll have your stripes!"

"But, Lieutenant—"

"If you don't like it, find the colonel and file a complaint."

"*Sikis* . . . brother," Cholla shouted at him, "get to Crook—he'll help us. Save my dog and my horse—"

Gillen clubbed him down then, and the soldiers dragged him into the car.

This couldn't be happening. Sergeant Mooney stood on the platform, trying to hold onto the frantic dog as it struggled to follow its master on board. The engine blew a warning, and then its wheels began to turn. Smoke billowed from the stack as the engineer signaled his crew.

Screams echoed from the train. Then it shuddered and jerked, started to move. Mooney looked back at the brown, frightened faces pressed against the glass. Some of these people had never even seen a train before and were terrified of the noise and movement.

It was all Mooney could do to hold on to the frantic dog as the train moved slowly out of the station. Hundreds of dogs set up a hellish racket as if they realized they were being left behind. Dozens of the animals ran alongside the cars, barking and trying to board. Big dogs, small dogs, half-wild, some a mix of coyote or wolf.

"Holy Saint Patrick!" Tom whispered under his breath, in horror. General Crook. Yes, he must reach Crook. Tom would tell Gatewood what had happened, and Gatewood would contact Crook. Even as he stood

164

on the platform looking after the train, it cleared the station and began to pull away, the frantic dogs running after it, not understanding why they had been left behind.

Ke'jaa turned his muzzle suddenly and bit Tom's hand. "Sonovagun! You ornery—!" But the dog was off and chasing after the train.

Mooney ran back to the horses. They were milling about, some of them dragging their reins. Blankets and bundles of food lay in the dust, where the Indians had dropped them in the shuffle. He mounted his horse, took off after the train at a gallop. Tom had promised his friend, his brother, he would save his dog.

The train gained speed as it headed east. At Albuquerque, it would turn north along the mountains toward Colorado. Black smoke hung on the air behind it. Dozens of frantic dogs, their tongues hanging out from exhaustion, still ran alongside or behind the train, barking as if asking why they had been left behind, who was to look after them.

One after another, they tired and dropped back, lay panting along the track. Mooney kept riding. In the distance, he saw Ke'jaa still loping alongside the train as it picked up speed. To reach Cholla, the dog would run itself to death.

Mooney finally caught up with Ke'jaa as the dog slowed. By now his horse was lathered and snorting. How many miles? Five? Ten? The train had turned into a black spot on the horizon and was finally swallowed up all together.

"Ke'jaa, you sonovagun! Come back here!"

The dog hesitated at the sound of its name, almost staggering with weariness. Its red ribbon of tongue hung out over great fangs, and its chest heaved so that Mooney could see its ribs as it breathed.

"Ke'jaa, come to me, boy. Come to me!" He dismounted, yelled and whistled at the big mongrel.

The dog turned and stared at him, looked after the train and tried to take another step. Then it collapsed and lay in the rough brush as if dead.

Holy Saint Patrick. Mooney cursed as he reached for his canteen. He had to save the dog. Cholla would be back when this mess was straightened out. Tom bent and poured a little water over the dog's muzzle. Then he took off his bandanna, wet it and wiped the dog down while the nearly dead animal snarled at him. "I know, you lop-eared cur, but I promised!"

The dog was too large to lift. It took Tom awhile to get the dog back on its feet so it could follow him to the station on uncertain legs. It kept looking back toward the horizon that had swallowed the train that bore his master away. Tom would have tried to throw it across his saddle and carry it, but he knew Ke'jaa wouldn't let him do that, even if he could lift him. He felt as angry and confused as the dog, but there was nothing he could do until he went through the chain of command.

Tom Mooney remembered all that now as he paused before the office door, rapped sharply.

"Come in."

He entered, forgetting for a split second that the dog was with him. Ke'jaa came through the door too,

166

before he closed it and turned to salute Gatewood.

"At ease, Sergeant, glad to see you. I see you still have the scout's dog." The tall officer leaned back in his chair, rubbed his prominent nose.

"Yes, sir. Cholla was my friend. It was the least I could do."

"I wish I could do something more to help. . . ." The soft-spoken officer paused.

Too ethical to criticize the new leadership, Tom thought. He liked the gentle, brave Gatewood whom the Apaches called Bay-chen-daysen; Long Nose. He liked him much better than the favored Captain Lawton or the Army doctor, Leonard Wood, who seemed so ambitious to move up.

Gatewood frowned, looking down at the paper under his hand. "This came over the telegraph from Saint Louis; the brass has been trying to keep it quiet for several weeks, but it's leaked out."

"Sir?"

"Cholla managed to get off that train somewhere east of the Mississippi."

"Holy Saint Patrick!" It took everything in him not to throw his hat in the air and cheer. Then Tom remembered himself and came to attention.

"He hasn't got a chance; we both know that." Gatewood unfolded his lanky frame, rising from his chair. He put his hands behind his back and paced up and down. "Lieutenant Gillen's in charge of recapturing the fugitive."

Tom's heart sank. "He'll kill him, given the chance."

"I know." Gatewood rubbed the bridge of his nose. "There's a 'dead or alive' order out on the scout."

This time, Tom couldn't suppress a groan. The dog looked up at the sound.

"Since you two were close friends, I thought I'd let you know." Gatewood gave him a long, searching look. Doubtless he had heard the rumors about what had happened at the ambush site from Gillen, but no one could prove anything without a witness and the other three soldiers had backed Mooney and Cholla.

"I'm much obliged, sir. If there's any news . . ."

"I will. You're dismissed, Sergeant."

Mooney saluted smartly, turned, and went out, the dog pushing ahead of him. Outside, Tom turned and looked toward the east. Fifteen hundred miles. *Too far. Too damned far.* But Cholla was a man who lived on the edge, accepted risks every day. He was not going to conform, he would rebel.

The scout had been treated dishonorably, chained and thrown on that train like a criminal when he had done nothing to merit such a terrible injustice. Tom knew his Apache brother would rather die than to be sent to Florida. If he were alive, the big scout was already headed back across fifteen hundred miles to the land he loved.

The sunrise had never looked so beautiful to Tom before, all gold and purple and pink. He wasn't sure whether he felt a need to reassure the dog . . . or himself. "Ke'jaa, if anyone can do it, Cholla can."

For the first time in many years, Sergeant Tom Mooney bent his head reverently and said a prayer to Saint Christopher, patron saint of those who travel.

Chapter Nine

When Sierra awakened before dawn, Cholla was staring down into her eyes. She wished she knew what went on behind that stoic face. Then she remembered last night, and her own face burned. How could she have behaved like such a wanton?

But of course it's all part of my plan, she told herself as she got up without speaking, bustled about fixing them a bit of food. Since she had let him make love to her, no doubt he would let his guard down. Maybe she would yet have a chance to use those scissors.

Cholla frowned and rubbed the back of his neck as he finished his coffee. "If that *hombre* did go for help, there may be someone on our trail. We'd be wise to abandon the wagon, just take what we can carry in backpacks and use some isolated trails, stay off the roads."

The scissors. They would be left in the abandoned trunk. "If we do that," she said, "we'll have to leave a lot of things behind. The traveling won't be nearly as comfortable."

He gave her a wry look as he stood up. "I've got the whole U.S. Cavalry and armed citizens looking for me and you talk about 'comfort'?" Then he seemed to reconsider. "Oh, of course. I should have realized you'd have attachments to some of your personal things. Very well, Dark Eyes, we'll keep the wagon at least another day, but with all these hills, we would be better off to take to the foot trails."

Sierra waited for him to make some snide, crude comment about how much she had pleasured him, but he only looked at her a long moment. Had she pleasured him? Maybe he had had other women who'd given him more enjoyment. Hadn't Robert often taunted her with how awkward and unlearned she was at making love?

As the Apache packed up the camp, Sierra took her long hair down, brushed it. When she looked up, he was watching her. "Leave it down," he said. "I like it that way; sort of wild- and abandoned-looking, the kind of hair a man wants to tangle his hands in."

Very pointedly, she ignored him, put her hair back up in a prim bun at the back of her neck. Maybe last night she had been the kind of woman the scout spoke of, but that wasn't the real Sierra. The real Mrs. Robert Forester was prim, restrained, conforming.

"Sierra, you defy me?"

For a moment, she almost backed down, then realized that might be admiration in his dark eyes. He must like women with a bit of flint to them. Flint and steel create sparks, she thought, remembering their wild, tempestuous coupling on the creek bank. Her face burned with the memory, but she only raised her chin. "It's my hair; I'll wear it as I please!"

He didn't answer as they broke camp. They pushed forward hard all day, putting many miles behind them. They were deep into wooded hills now, pine and blackjack, scrubby pin oak and wild bois d'arc with its bright green seed pods as big as apples.

Cholla grunted with satisfaction when he found a bois d'arc sapling. "I hear this is what the Plains tribes call Osage orange and make bows from. I don't have many cartridges for this rifle, I'd better plan on making myself a bow."

Taking out the butcher knife, he hacked off several branches, threw them in the wagon.

They traveled until dark, when they pulled off at a fresh water spring and camped. He sat by the fire working on the bow while Sierra cooked a rabbit he had snared.

"Tomorrow," he said, "we'll go on afoot. I think we're on the northeastern edge of the Indian Territory, maybe."

More Indians. "Will those Indians take you in and help you?"

He laughed. "Hardly! The tribes there are not friends of the Apaches, but then, I doubt they are too happy with whites right now. Gossip around the fort said the government in Washington was thinking about taking some of the land away from the Indians and giving it to white farmers."

"I thought Indian Territory belonged to the tribes as long as the grass grew and the rivers ran?"

He gave her a long look. "Whites have a habit of making promises they don't keep. That's why I was on my way to Florida, chained up like an animal."

He is a proud man, she thought. Perhaps the loss of pride and dignity meant even more to him than the loss of freedom.

Once they got deep into Indian Territory, who knew what might happen to her? And if they were going to abandon the wagon tomorrow, she'd better take her chances on killing him tonight. How would be the best way to do that? Keen as his senses were, she could hardly slip up on him in the dark. And if she wasn't careful and only wounded him rather than killing him, there was no telling what terrible retribution he'd inflict. She thought of all the stories she had heard about Indian torture and shuddered.

"What's the matter?"

She glanced up, saw him staring at her. "Nothing. Nothing at all."

"I saw you shiver. Are you cold?"

"Maybe I am at that. I'll get an extra blanket from the wagon." *What a perfect excuse!* Sierra went to the wagon, climbed in, dug out another blanket. Under it, she carried the pair of scissors hidden in the folds of her skirt. She spread the blanket near the fire. "I suppose I am a little chilly. The nights are getting a bit cold as autumn comes on."

"Soon we'll be farther south and maybe we'll outrun the weather."

"How do you intend to do that?" She lay down on the blanket, the scissors hidden by her side.

He rubbed the back of his neck thoughtfully. "There's bound to be a train through Indian Territory—maybe a freight train. If we could catch a ride

172

in a boxcar, we could go a long way in a short time."

Sierra shivered again. "I really am a little cold. We might as well conserve the heat and share blankets."

"You sure?"

She couldn't meet his penetrating gaze. "After last night, it's not as if we were on formal terms."

"I didn't force myself on you," he reminded her softly.

"All right, so I behaved like a mare in heat." Her face turned bright red.

"I didn't say that." He brought his blanket, spread it next to hers. "If you're regretting it—"

"I'm your captive and you'll do with me what you wish," Sierra snapped. "Don't lie to me."

"Go to sleep. We've got a lot of traveling tomorrow." He closed his eyes.

She had expected him to demand her body, and she'd planned to stab him during the act when he least expected it. She felt the scissors cold and hard under her hand. Did she dare try to stab him in the chest?

No, alert as he was, he'd come awake as her hand came down, grab her wrist. She had to get him on top of her so she could put those scissors deep in his back.

Sierra turned over on her side, toward him. She pressed her breasts up against him. Then, almost as if she made the gesture in her sleep, she threw an arm across his body. In his sleep, he turned toward her, pulled her against the heat of him. She waited for something to happen, but he really did seem to be sleeping. Maybe it was like Robert said, maybe she wasn't very desirable. Should she risk stabbing him? She was afraid to take the chance.

173

Sierra rubbed her breasts against his arm, tilted her pelvis so that her body touched his all the way down. He was awake now. She felt him come alert, the maleness of him harden.

"Sierra?"

She didn't answer, pretended to be asleep, but she rubbed against him again. His mouth found hers and she relaxed her lips, let him probe inside with the tip of his tongue, then gradually sucked his tongue deep into her mouth as her hand slipped inside his shirt to stroke his nipples. His hand, fumbling with the bodice of her dress, felt hot as it cupped her breast.

Sierra gasped at the sensation. She had forgotten how good his hands felt as he tantalized her nipples. Then he pushed up her skirts. She wasn't wearing any underthings.

His palm felt hot on her bare thigh. She opened his pants. His manhood was hard and hot and throbbing in her grasp. He undid the front of her bodice. With his teeth nibbling around her teats, Sierra forgot about her plan—about anything but the ache thudding in her belly. She pressed her breasts against his lips, wanting him to take them deep in his mouth, suck them raw until she couldn't stand the sensation one more instant. She dug her nails into his wide shoulders.

She wanted him. That surprised her after all the times she had lain on her back, cold, unresponsive, letting Robert use her while she thought of other things.

Sierra pulled him on top of her, her heart thudding so hard, he must feel it under his mouth.

174

"You surprise me," Cholla whispered.

"I surprise myself," she answered truthfully and opened her thighs for his thrusting. He was built big, and she felt every inch of him as he thrust in her, faster and harder each time.

Her hand went to find the scissors. She kept her mind on what she intended to do as his passion built. At the moment he reached the zenith of his pleasure, she grasped the scissors, hesitated a split second as she brought them down.

Out of the corner of his eye, he must have seen the movement, because he dodged ever so slightly and the sharp blades cut his shoulder a glancing blow.

"You white bitch! Try to kill me, will you?" He slapped her. Scarlet dripped down his arm and chest. "You want blood? You got blood!" He wiped his blood across her breasts and rolled off her. Then he grabbed the scissors, threw them into the brush.

Too terrified to move, Sierra lay there, breathing hard, her ears ringing, his warm, scarlet blood smeared across her naked breasts. Merciful heavens, now he will kill me, she thought, since I failed to kill him.

But he was too intent on his injury to notice her. Swearing mightily, Cholla tore away part of her skirt, wrapped it around his arm. "I should have known better! I should have known it was an act! You lie just like the other whites!"

"What did you expect?" she stormed back at him. "You kidnap me, drag me across Missouri, scared for my life—"

175

"By Usen, I'll know better next time!" he raged. "And to think I was beginning to—"

"Beginning to what?"

"Nothing, Mrs. Forester! Nothing!"

"How do you know my name?" She was on her feet now, half-naked, smeared with his blood and shouting. Her nerves had been stretched too taut by everything that had happened over the past few days. She didn't care anymore if he killed her. She expected that sooner or later anyway, and she was weary of the tension.

"You told me," he said. "Remember?" He looked up from his bandaging.

Had she? She couldn't remember. Should she try to run for the woods again? He was swift as a bobcat and had the stamina of a mountain goat. He'd only hunt her down. She stood, watching him finish the bandaging, waiting.

He got up, grabbed her arm, twisted her hands behind her. "I'll know better next time."

"Next time?" She almost spat the words at him. "Go ahead and kill me. I expect it!"

"And waste a good hostage?" His mouth twisted into a hard, mirthless grin. "I need you, Sierra, in case I get trapped somewhere. I don't think white soldiers will shoot at a human shield, especially a pretty one like you."

She struggled, but he tied her up anyhow. This is what I get for taking chances, Sierra thought miserably as she lay down on the grass and watched Cholla spread out blankets by the fire. If she'd been obedient and done exactly as she was told, he might have freed her by now. Grandfather had warned her about having

176

the attitude of her mother. She vowed right then and there that if she escaped this ordeal alive, she would take a job somewhere and blend into the masses, conform as Grandfather had urged.

Cholla slept peacefully enough it seemed, but Sierra didn't get much rest. The next morning, he dug through their things, made two backpacks of the barest kind of necessities, and turned the old mule loose in the lush, wild grasslands nearby. As he had already pointed out, the mule needed a good rest before it could go any farther, and old as it was, it deserved its freedom.

He dug through the trunks. "I guess we have everything we can use." He picked up the photo of Robert. "Don't you want this?"

So he had seen the photo. She thought about his question a minute, shook her head. She was tired of being a hypocrite, even though she still hated the Indians for widowing her and leaving her defenseless in the world. "He never even bought me a wedding ring; that's how little he cared."

He gave her a long, searching look. "All right then, come on." He jerked his head toward the south. "We'll hike through the hills, and maybe somewhere along the way, we'll find a train or maybe a good horse."

"You don't have anything to trade those Indians for a good horse."

He looked her up and down. "Don't I?"

She trembled at the thought. "Aren't you going to

177

untie me?"

"And risk getting killed again? You can walk with your hands tied behind you." His tone was curt as he pushed her ahead of him on the trail.

There was nothing to do but start walking. With her hands tied behind her, however, her balance wasn't very good. And when a fly lit on her nose, she couldn't brush it off. Besides that, as the day progressed, her arms began to ache from being tied. But Sierra decided she could be as stubborn as he was. If he expected her to beg, he was going to be very disappointed. All day they traveled toward the south, through oaks and walnuts that were already turning flame red and gold and russet with the coming autumn.

Twice she stumbled and fell, and strong hands reached out, hauled her to her feet, pushed her forward. Along about dark, she began to balk. "I can't walk much farther." She sank to the trail, but his big hand yanked her upright. "You *will* walk."

His voice had such a hard edge that it scared her. Whatever softness toward her she had sensed in this man was gone now.

"If I reach the point where I just can't go any farther, are you going to put a bullet between my eyes and leave my body where it falls?"

A look of anguish came to his rugged features for a split second, and then his face became inscrutable again. She wondered about it a moment, then decided she had been mistaken. There was nothing weak or sensitive about this man — not now, not ever. She had begun to think of him as a human being. Well, she had been a fool. He was nothing but a fierce, heartless savage.

Heavens, suppose she was even now carrying his child? What does it matter? she chided herself as she stumbled forward. He's not going to let you live long enough for him to know or care.

She fell again, sank to her knees.

"Get up or you'll die right here."

"Whatever you do to me, I . . . I can't walk any more." She looked over her shoulder at him. The bloodstained bandage on his arm reminded her that she had failed, but she was glad she had tried. If only she hadn't hesitated at the very last second, those steel blades would have gone deep into his back, maybe into his heart, killing him instantly.

She closed her eyes, waiting for the gun against her forehead. Instead he swung her up in his arms, hung her over his shoulder and began to walk. She felt like a sack of potatoes. The Apache must need a hostage bad to go to all this trouble to keep her. She'd reached such a point of exhaustion that she didn't care whether she died, as long as she didn't have to keep walking.

A cool breeze came up suddenly and thunderheads built along the horizon in the pink and lavender dusk. From a long way off, thunder rumbled.

Cholla set her on her feet. "We may get a rain, and it's almost dark. We need to find shelter." He looked around, gestured to a hill ahead of them. "There might be a cave over there, or at least a ledge we can get under to wait this out."

The wind blew again, bringing with it the fresh scent of rain. Lightning cracked across the sky. Sierra needed no urging, she began to run toward the cliff ahead, Cholla right behind her. She stumbled and fell over a limb, and he pulled her to her feet and they kept running. Her face felt hot, was damp with perspiration, but the wind was cool on her skin. As she ran, the pins began to come out of her hair, and long locks blew free about her shoulders.

Cholla raced ahead of her, up into the rocks, looking around for shelter. The storm began as she ran toward him, a few drops at first, then more and more. The sky seemed to open up as she staggered onward, drenching her with wet, cold rain. She couldn't make it. But even as she hesitated, he came dashing back, scooped her up easily, ran with her through the rocks, and took her under an outcrop that formed a shallow cave back into the side of the hill.

Sierra sat shivering and miserable, watching it rain as her captor built a small fire from the bits of wood and pine cones that had lain under the rock overhang. Then he stripped off his clothes, draped them on rocks to dry. She averted her eyes, determined not to look at his perfect, virile body.

He came over, knelt, untied her, began unbuttoning her dress. "Get those wet things off," he ordered.

She slapped his hands away, then opened her backpack and discovered that in her haste, she hadn't packed an extra dress. Undaunted, she went behind a rock, stripped off her wet things, laid them over the rock, and wrapped herself in her blanket before returning to sit by the fire.

He glanced up at her, didn't say anything as he roasted the rabbit he had killed with the bow late in the afternoon. He had even salvaged the coffee and the little pot. When he held out a cup of the steaming brew to her, she took it in both hands and savored its warmth gratefully. "So now what happens?"

"Just like I said, Dark Eyes," he tore off part of the crispy meat and handed to her, "I thought I heard a train whistle this afternoon, or maybe I only imagined it, but that would be the fastest way to travel."

Sierra ate her meat and looked out at the pouring rain. "You really think you can do this, don't you?"

"Do what?"

"Make it all the way back to Arizona Territory."

"Maybe not, but I have to try. I'm not one to give up and be pushed along with the herd."

If anyone can make it, he can, she thought, or he'll die trying. Or kill anyone who gets between him and his goal.

When she looked up, he was staring at her. "I've had time to think," he said, and touched his bandaged arm gingerly. "You hesitated at the last minute with those scissors—why?"

For some reason, the question angered her. "I've got bad aim. Believe me, I meant to bury them in your back!"

"Maybe so." He stared at her a long moment, not saying anything. She wished she knew what he was thinking. "You're a cold one, Dark Eyes, like a black widow spider, plotting to kill the male even as he mates with her. I thought you said you never took chances, that you always conformed?"

"Desperate circumstances call for desperate measures," she retorted.

He raised one eyebrow at her. "You're not such a mouse as you pretend to be. There's a little flint to you after all."

She was suddenly weary of being baited, of wondering whether he was going to kill her or just put her through such misery she would wish she were dead. Without another word, she stretched out on the dry pine needles and leaves.

"Don't you want to come over here by the fire?"

"No, I'm doing fine back here."

"You know, with autumn coming on, snakes are denning up for the winter — maybe even in the back of this cave."

Sierra sat bolt upright. "Snakes hibernate?"

He nodded, then yawned and stretched before spreading his blanket by the fire. "You're welcome to come over here."

She got up, still holding her blanket tightly around herself, went over and sat down on a rock. Outside lightning still crackled and rain poured down, a sweet, clean scent blowing in to mix with the pungent smell of the burning pine cones. When she looked over at him, he had drifted peacefully off to sleep, but the weapons were under his arm so she couldn't possibly get any of them without waking him.

Damn him anyhow. At least he hadn't tied her up again. It occurred to Sierra that she could slip out of the cave and run. Where? It was dark out there and pouring rain. He had the weapons and the food. Even her ragged dress was hanging up to dry, and she didn't know where in hell she was except somewhere in northeastern Indian Territory . . . maybe. She wasn't even sure of that. Tonight wasn't the time to try another escape. Cold and cramped, Sierra lay down on the ground near the cave entrance and dropped off to sleep.

All too soon, it was dawn and she didn't feel like moving, even though Cholla was up and dressed. "Sleep well?" he asked.

"You know I didn't." Her tone was pointed and sarcastic.

He seemed to ignore it. "I've been outside looking around," he said as he poured her a cup of coffee. "The rain's stopped, and I swear I heard a train whistle in the night. I think we'll try to find the tracks, maybe catch a ride on a boxcar."

She sipped her coffee and stared at him. "Haven't you heard any of those stories about men trying to catch rides on freight trains. You can fall under them and lose a leg."

"The other choice is to keep walking south."

Sierra thought about it a long moment, looked down at her sore, blistered feet. "Let's try for the train."

"Here, I've been working on something for you. Remember that deer I killed a few days ago?"

Sierra nodded, wondering. Then he handed her a pair of butter-soft moccasins and a deerskin dress. Her clothes and shoes were ragged. She looked from the outfit, back to him. "Why, thank you."

"It's not much." He looked a little chagrined. "I'm

not used to doing woman's work, but your feet looked sore."

Even though she wouldn't have admitted it for the world, she was touched that he had noticed. For a savage, he was showing a sensitive side she hadn't realized he possessed. But then, she reminded herself fiercely, I wouldn't be in this godforsaken place, footsore and ragged, if he hadn't kidnapped me weeks ago.

Sierra went behind a rock, changed into the new, butter-soft things. Then she braided her hair rather than put it up in its usual bun.

He looked at her approvingly. "You look like an Indian girl now; you're dark as one, too, what with the sun."

The thought infuriated her and she would have unbraided her hair and taken off the deerskin dress, but he was hurrying her and she was afraid of his anger. Sierra packed their backpacks while he put out the fire. Then they started walking.

It must be at least October, she thought as they walked through the bright gold and orange of the trees. Gray fox squirrels chattered at her from the limbs of oak trees; redheaded woodpeckers hammered away on branches. And, from patches of sumac turning blood red in the chilly morning, shy deer peeked at her. If there was a prettier place than Indian Territory in the autumn, she wondered where it might be and said so without thinking.

Cholla nodded. "To me, there's a prettier place; the Sierra Madre and the lonesome stretches of the Apache country. I miss it already; air so clear, water so cold. Game is plentiful. With a little salt and meal and coffee, a man could live there a long time without having any contact at all with civilization."

He sounded so poignant, so wistful, her heart almost went out to him, but then she remembered that he was her enemy, her captor, and maybe in the long run her killer.

They kept walking. At midday he let her rest a minute while they ate some berries and a squirrel he'd brought down with his bow. Then they began walking again in the direction he indicated.

Her feet hurt and every muscle in her body ached, but she was determined not to whine about it. If he thought her a weak, whimpering mouse, she'd show him!

It was late afternoon when Cholla finally paused, his head cocked. "Listen."

She paused, but all she heard was her own weary breathing and a crow's coarse call somewhere nearby.

"A train whistle," he said, "don't you hear it? It's coming this way."

Sierra strained to hear, wishing she had his keen ears. Then she heard it too, echoing through the wooded hills. It sounded miles away.

"Come on," Cholla ordered. "I think it's heading this way."

He threw aside the axe, grabbed her hand and forced her to run. Once she fell and he caught her hand, pulled her to her feet, and they ran on. But she was already tired, and after a few minutes, her lungs seemed on fire. "Go on!" she gasped. "I can't make it, just leave me and go on!"

He turned and looked to the north anxiously. The thin puff of smoke from the engine drifted over the crest of the horizon. "If I leave you, you'll never find you way out of here, and I've got the weapons and food. Come on!"

She staggered and almost fell. "I'd just as soon sit down and die rather than try to catch that train."

He grabbed her hand and dragged her along with him, "No, we're both getting on it. I need you too much to lose you now!"

With him pulling her, she could either run or be dragged. Her feet began to move forward again, her heart pounding hard, her breath coming in gasps. She didn't say anything, didn't argue, that took too much energy. With his strong hand clasping hers, she couldn't stop unless she fell, and she didn't want to be dragged. Sierra kept running.

Cholla gave a triumphant cry and pointed. Coming over the crest of the hill like a long black snake, the freight train inched along the track, blowing steam and smoke. Sierra measured the distance with her eyes as they ran. They couldn't make it. They might come close, but the train would be gone before they could reach the tracks.

"It's no use," she shouted, but Cholla seemed to pay her no heed and because he held on to her, there was no way she could stop running. They were close enough now to see the engine passing and some of the cars. It was a long train. Cattle cars with mooing steers rattled along the track as the two ran toward them.

The train was passing now, the cars whizzing by.

We will come close, but we won't make it, Sierra thought. She didn't stop running. Cholla stumbled, dropped the rifle, but he didn't break stride to retrieve it.

The rifle. We need that rifle, Sierra thought, how can we manage with nothing but a bow and a butcher knife? But she didn't slow down. Her attention, like his, was focused on that all-important train.

Cholla gave a glad cry, looked over his shoulder, gesturing. She saw the cause of his excitement; an empty cattle car, its big door ajar, almost at the end of the train. If we manage to get aboard, we won't have to walk for a long time, Sierra thought, and her speed picked up as they ran alongside the train. Gravel crunched under her feet, cinders blew back at them, along with the smell and smoke of the engine. The noise was deafening.

The Indian was ahead of her, running strongly with long, powerful legs. Then one of his big arms reached out, caught the side of the empty car, and he swung himself up. For a split second, he hung in the air, and Sierra wondered if he would end up falling under the thundering train; then he was in the door of the car, reaching back for her.

"I can't make it!" she screamed at him but the noise drowned her out. He shook his head and leaned far out of the car, reaching for her hand as she ran alongside. If he isn't careful, he's going to lose his balance and fall under those giant steel wheels that will cut him in half, Sierra thought. Abruptly she saw herself being left behind to fend for herself in this untracked wilderness, and she was more afraid of that than she was of him.

His hand caught hers, locked around her wrist. Then he lifted her. For a heart-stopping second, she hung between heaven and earth, the ground whizzing past. She grabbed his muscular arm with her other hand, knowing that if he couldn't lift her she would be pulling him to his death under the roaring wheels. He seemed to realized it, too, because sweat broke out on his bronzed face as he held her. Then, with sheer, brute strength, he lifted, and her feet felt the sudden safety of the wooden floor of the cattle car.

"Safe!" she gasped as she clung to him, and both turned toward the darkened interior of the car with its scent of hay. "We've made it and we're safe!"

"I wouldn't bet on that, sweet thing!" said a drunken voice.

Sierra turned slowly. Two cowboys lolled on bales of hay in the corner, one had a pistol; the other a half-empty bottle of whiskey.

Chapter Ten

Sierra stared at the two men sprawled in the shadows of the boxcar. A tall, lean one with ice blue eyes, a shorter, more powerful one. Unshaven and tough-looking, they reeked of whiskey.

She glanced out the open door of the boxcar. The train now being on the straightaway, jumping was a good way to get killed. She looked up at Cholla, he gave her just the barest shake of his head.

"Hey, Slim," the short one said, "lookie here! Two Injuns! And one of them a purty squaw."

The taller, lean one grinned at her. He looked mean as a bobcat with a sore foot. These are not ordinary cowpokes, Sierra thought, with a prickle of fear.

"Hey, sweet thing," Slim drawled, and he gestured. "Come on over here and I'll give you a drink of my whiskey."

Sierra didn't move. She shook her head slightly, backed up against Cholla's big body.

"Pete, you was wrong about our bad luck." Slim grinned and took another drink. "Losing our pokes and horses in that card game in Coffeyville was bad, but if we hadn't hitched a free ride on the train, we wouldn't have come across these two."

Pete frowned, put his hand on his pistol. "I don't know about the buck. He don't look like he intends to share her."

Slim stood up, held out the bottle. " 'Course he will. Pete, you just don't know nothin' about Injun bucks." He motioned to Cholla. "You, Injun. You got heap nice squaw. Me'n Pete use her a little, you know?" He winked. "I give you heap big drink firewater."

Sierra backed against Cholla, shaking her head. "I . . . I'm not Indian," she said. "The law is looking for me, and—"

"Sure me trade," Cholla broke in, as if he suddenly realized both men were well armed and could help her if they understood her story. "Me trade time between woman's legs for big gulp whiskey—both you, two drinks whiskey." He held up two fingers as he echoed the drunken gunslinger's pidgin English.

Sierra whirled on him, surprised and angry. "Now wait just a darned minute, I have some say in this, and—"

"Squaw, hush." Cholla grabbed her roughly, pushed her toward the men. "Do as I tell you." Then, to the men, he said, "For whole bottle, you can have squaw until you get off train."

Slim laughed, and his tense frame relaxed. "Sounds okay by me, Injun. I better warn you it's quite a few miles, we don't get off 'til the nearest station to Younger's Bend."

Sierra stood there, frozen with horror, as Cholla accepted the bottle, pushed her toward them. "Make white men happy, woman, while I drink firewater."

Protesting and struggling, Sierra was dragged over to the corner while Cholla stood in the middle of the car, gulping whiskey, letting it drip down his chin.

Pete looked at him, scowling. "Disgusting!" he growled. "Damned disgusting the way them Injuns lap up booze."

Slim struggled with Sierra. "Forget the buck," he growled under his breath. "After he's drunk, we'll kill him and take whatever's in the bedrolls, plus keep the squaw."

"No!" Sierra fought him. "No, I'm a white woman, I tell you; the law's looking for me!"

"For us, too, sweet thing!" Slim laughed and dragged her up against him, kissing her, forcing her mouth open. His breath reeked of sour, cheap whiskey.

Pete said, "I don't know about this, Slim the boss won't like us bein' seen in Coffeyville, and then draggin' home some female—"

"I expect to have my fill of this one before we get back to the hideout," Slim snarled, struggling with Sierra. "Then we can throw her off the train, too."

Sierra screamed, but the whistle of the train drowned her out, and anyway, Cholla appeared to be staggering drunk now as he lurched about, turning up the bottle and letting whiskey run down his chin.

"At least we don't have to worry about him," Pete said, turning his full attention to the girl. "He's so drunk, he won't know or care what happens."

Sierra fought the pair with all her might, but the two were strong. Both had laid aside their weapons as they struggled to force her down on her back in the straw. Cholla slumped in a corner of the car, drinking whiskey, ignoring her screams as the men gradually pushed her to the boxcar floor. In the desperate struggle, Sierra's shift fell off one shoulder, revealing the swell of soft breasts even as her skirt inched up her thighs.

Slim's eyes looked hard as pale blue glass as he stared down at her. "Who gets her first, Pete? You or me?"

"Hit don't make me no never mind," Pete hiccoughed, his eyes fixed on Sierra's body as he helped Slim hold her down. "As long as I get her several times before we reach Younger's Bend."

"Well, it matters to me," Slim grinned without mirth as Sierra writhed and struggled to get away. "I never got me no whore before I lost all my money at cards, so I feel hard enough to ram it through a fence post."

Sierra managed to turn her head and bite his wrist.

"Injun bitch!" Slim struck her hard across the face. "Now you lay still and let us do it, you hear? Maybe if you make us both heap happy, we'll see you get whiskey, too."

"Lordie" — Pete had his hands on her legs — "did you ever see a body like hers? Lookie at the color of that skin, Slim. Maybe she is white."

"Then she's a whore nobody cares about nohow," Slim snarled. "No white woman travels with an Injun buck. She deserves this if she's been lettin' him top her."

Both stared down at her half-naked, writhing, struggling body. Only Sierra, looking up as she fought, saw Cholla looming behind the pair.

"What the—?" At the look in her eyes, Pete half turned, reaching for his pistol, but he had taken it off and laid it aside.

"Get your dirty hands off her, you white bastard!" Cholla grabbed him, slammed him against the wall. Both gunfighters dove for their weapons, but Sierra caught Slim's arm, held onto it as he struggled to get his gun. He cursed and slammed her up against the wall, but she hung on like a small snapping turtle as Cholla and Pete fought.

Pete looked powerful, like a seasoned saloon brawler. But the gunslinger was no match for the giant Apache who lifted him up over his head, slammed him against the wall of the swaying boxcar, then crashed down on him.

Pete managed to crawl to his gun, pull it from its holster, even as Cholla fought him for it. Sierra hung onto Slim's arm for dear life, sinking her teeth into his hand as he slammed her around, trying to shake free to go to Pete's aid. Despite Sierra, he did manage to grab his own pistol.

The Apache and the white man were fighting in the doorway of the moving, swaying boxcar now. Any wrong move and both would go out. Cholla managed to wrench the pistol from Pete's hand even as Pete stood up, ready to charge again. The gun roared amid the smell of burnt powder. Pete clasped his chest, and staggered backward, fell out the door.

Cholla shouted, "Get out of the way, Sierra!"

But Slim had her up against him, using her for a shield. "Throw the pistol out of the boxcar, Injun, or

193

I'll blow a hole in her back!"

Sierra had never been so scared as she was now, feeling the cold steel of the gun barrel in her back. Slim's other arm was around her, his flesh burning through her shift. He held her against him so tightly, she felt the buttons of his shirt against her back, the bulge of his manhood against her hips.

Cholla hesitated.

"Do it, Injun," Slim growled. "I've killed before, I don't have no regrets about doin' it again!"

Very slowly, the big Injun walked across the swaying floor, tossed the pistol out the door.

"Now you jump out after it."

"It'll kill him!" Sierra protested.

"So?" Slim's voice sounded as cold as his ice blue eyes.

Cholla hesitated in the door of the car.

"Jump, Injun, or watch me blow your woman's guts out and then get you next."

She saw the indecision on the rugged, dark face. "How do I know you won't kill her anyway?"

"Kill her?" Slim laughed softly against her hair. "Waste what this sweet thing has to offer a man? Maybe later . . ."

If she had to choose between the two men, Sierra would rather be Cholla's captive. Emotion overcame her good sense, and she shoved her elbow back, catching Slim under the ribs.

With a groan, he let go of her, doubling over as she managed to break free.

"Get out of the way, Sierra!" Cholla dove for the man and caught him around the legs. As Slim went

194

down, the pistol tumbled from his hand and slid across the jolting floor.

While Cholla and Slim struggled, Sierra grabbed for the gun. She had it. The two men rolled over and over in the hay as they fought. She pointed the pistol at them, unsure what to do. If she pulled the trigger, she might hit either one. "Stop it! Stop it, you two! Get your hands up!"

Because of the roar of the clacking wheels or because they were too intent on their life-and-death battle, they didn't stop or look up as they fought. They rolled near the open door of the boxcar.

It occurred to Sierra as she pulled the hammer back that she ought to shoot them both, push the bodies out the door, and telegraph for help at the next station.

While she hesitated, the two men struggled in the door of the boxcar. If it swayed suddenly, one or both of them would go out. The fall might or might not kill them, depending on where they landed alongside the tracks.

Sierra saw the glint of steel, saw that Slim had Cholla's big knife. She had only a split second to act as the blade flashed down, and she pulled the trigger without taking time to aim.

The kick of the Colt knocked her backward. Choking on the acrid scent of gunpowder, she fell, but she saw Slim clutch his shoulder, drop the knife, stagger backward. Cholla slammed into him, knocked him out the door of the boxcar, staggered, almost went out himself.

Sierra still had time to pull the trigger, kill the big

scout. She'd be free at last. But she hesitated, and Cholla staggered across the boxcar, took the pistol from her, then flopped down beside her, breathing hard. "Much obliged, Dark Eyes."

How stupid I was, Sierra thought with a sigh. He has the gun now, and things are back as they were. "I didn't do it to help you." She leaned against the hay bale and closed her eyes. "I did it to keep from being raped."

"I didn't intend to let the bastards rape you." His eyes flashed with anger as he looked toward the open door.

"You couldn't prove it by me," she snapped. "The way you were guzzling that whiskey."

"Do I look drunk to you?"

It dawned on her suddenly that it had been a trick. Up against two men with guns, he could only use deception to get the upper hand. "You think they're dead?"

Cholla shrugged, put the knife in his belt, and lay down on the hay next to her. "Who knows? I think I got Pete, but if Slim lit in a soft place, he might live to stop a sheriff's bullet."

"Let's see if they had any food." Sierra dug through the cowboys' things, found some dried jerky and some bread. They still had the one pistol, but both men had been wearing their gun belts, so there were no extra cartridges. Cholla had lost the axe and the rifle getting on the train, and she had dropped the bow.

"Great!" Cholla said. "All we've got is one pistol with its five shots and the knife."

"We're still alive," she said, "and I didn't get raped.

I'd call it a fair day's work."

Cholla looked at her and grinned. "Maybe I misjudged you when I thought you were such a shy mouse. I think Tom would call you 'sassy.' "

"Who?"

"My friend, Tom Mooney."

Sassy or not, I'm no better off, Sierra thought. She was still the Apache's prisoner. She should have shot him when he stood in the doorway of the boxcar, but she just didn't have the guts for killing. Then she remembered that she had pulled the trigger on Slim with no hesitation. Maybe at the next railroad station, she could manage to escape from Cholla or signal a railyard worker.

It began to rain again. Cholla got the cowboys' blankets and wrapped them both around her when she began shivering. Then he handed her the bottle of whiskey. "This should warm you a little."

"Aren't you cold?" she asked.

"No." However, she noticed he hunched up a little in the straw and wrapped his arms around himself. "The weather's beginning to turn bad," he muttered. "If we don't get farther south — and soon — we're going to be caught in some snow, or at least sleet and a cold wind blowing down from the north."

She didn't even know what month it was for certain, much less which day. It had been several weeks, maybe more, since this whole ordeal began, but the constant traveling, and everything else that had happened, had made time unimportant.

Sierra smiled suddenly and took a sip of the whiskey, handed him the bottle. "It's bound to be October.

197

They're dedicating the Statue of Liberty this month."

He looked at her blankly and took a drink.

"One of our countrymen, Jozsef Politzer, who started out with the St. Louis newspaper, was a major fund raiser for the pedestal for the statue. I understand it's going to have some poem on it about: 'Give me your tired, your poor, your huddled masses yearning to breathe free. . . .' "

"Does that apply to Indians?" He glared at her and handed the bottle back. "What is this thing? This statue?"

"Everyone's talking about it." Sierra tried to explain. "It's a statue of a lady holding a light to guide immigrants to freedom in America."

"So they can build houses on Indian land?" He raised one eyebrow. "Doesn't it strike you as ironic and dishonest that at the very time they're putting up this statue dedicated to freedom, your government is throwing Indians in prison in Florida and stealing their land?"

She had never thought about it before, and she didn't like the uneasy feeling it gave her. "On the other hand," she said boldly and took a long drink, "what about all those people starving in Europe or crowded into filthy tenements in big Eastern cities? Is it right for them to suffer while the Indians have millions of acres and only use the land to roam on?"

He frowned, then conceded that perhaps she might have a small point. "I suppose in the long run the Indians will either conform or be caged or killed."

She looked at him. Was there any black or white to this? She couldn't see someone like Cholla being a faceless part of the masses. He was too much a rugged individualist. The times were going to change whether people like the Indians suffered or not. "White women aren't treated any better in our society than red men," she said.

He rubbed the back of his neck. "Maybe that doesn't say much for the society. You'd make a good lawyer, Sierra—if you were a man."

"A hundred years from now, I might get a chance to be a lawyer. By then, they may even let women vote."

"Maybe by then Indians can vote and be lawyers too," he said. "I hope my people aren't still being mistreated a hundred years from now."

"Mistreated! Your people have been scalping white children! Indians need to become civilized, make some progress."

"Conform, you mean?" he almost snarled it at her. "When we tried, we were tricked. There isn't much progress to be made sitting in a stone cell or running from the cavalry."

"Cholla, in the long run the only way women or your people are going to come out ahead is to rear up on their hind legs and say, 'I'm as good as any *white man* and I'm not going to take this anymore!' Once we get the education, we can force them to recognize us, but we've got to beat them at their own game. We've got to be better than they are at business and law and medicine."

"I thought your slogan was: 'The nail that sticks up will be hammered down.' "

Had she ever really believed that? She had too much of her mother's blood after all. "That was my

199

grandfather's slogan. He and his countrymen had suffered terribly in the Old Country."

"So now all of them crowd on ships and come over here and my people suffer; all the Indians suffer."

"And there's no help for it." She shook her head. "Nothing either of us can do about it. Maybe someday one of us will have children who will help change things, or grandchildren or even great-grandchildren."

Her voice trailed off and she glanced up to catch him watching her thoughtfully. Maybe she imagined it, but she didn't see so much hatred in his eyes as she had before. "What happens tomorrow?"

He looked out at the night coming on in the chill rain as the train moved through woods and hills, headed south. "I don't know."

For the first time since she had seen him, he looked weary, almost defeated. She didn't want to pity him, feel for him. But he was only a man after all, not a screaming, red-skinned savage like those in the dime novels. He had fears and hopes and loves. She thought about the dead Apache girl and wondered what had happened to her?

"Do you have any idea where this train goes?" The whiskey was beginning to warm her insides as she lay back on the hay beside him.

"No." He shook his head, rubbed the back of his neck. "As long as it's heading south or west, that's all that matters. If I'm going to be killed, and I intend to be rather than be captured, I want to die as close to home as possible."

It occurred to her then that he was resigned to his own death. He'd rather die than be looked at through bars by curious whites, as if he were an animal.

"Give me your tired, your poor, your huddled masses yearning to breathe free"—but not American Indians, she thought suddenly, seeing things from his point of view. She felt chagrined and embarrassed for the whites.

It dawned on her that she must not feel this way. After all, these savages had killed her husband as well as dozens of settlers who just wanted a few acres to live on. She turned it all over in her mind, confused now as to what she had once thought was right and wrong. Sierra felt him shiver next to her, remembered she had both blankets. "You cold?"

"No, of course not."

Why had she asked? Did she think he would admit to it? He had given her both blankets, had fought a life and death battle to keep those men from raping her. In some ways, he was more chivalrous and caring than her husband had been.

"I'm a little warm," she lied, and tossed one of the blankets to him. In the darkness, he took it. Now she was cold. She snuggled down in the hay as the train rattled its way through the darkness. The *clickety-clack* lulled her to sleep.

Somewhere in the middle of the night, she found herself drawn closer to his warmth. She felt his arm go around her and pull her up against him. His virile body seemed to radiate heat. She went back to sleep wrapped in his arms, her head on his shoulder.

When she half awakened sometime later, he was kissing her face, half-asleep himself. Without even re- alizing she did so, she slipped her arms under his shirt, pressing her breasts against him. Outside, as the train swayed along into the darkness, cold rain continued to fall.

"Sierra?" he whispered.

She didn't answer, knowing he asked permission. It isn't like him to ask, she thought. He was a man who took what he wanted, and besides, she wasn't certain what her answer should be.

His lips brushed along her jawbone, his breath almost featherlike on her skin. "Sierra? Are you awake?"

She closed her eyes, pretending to be asleep. Her pulse began to race, but she decided she must not let this man have her body. She must not give him permission. She must not . . . It was hard to remember why she must not when her emotions raced and the scent of his male skin was so close to her face. His hands were callused as they stroked her breasts. I cannot lie here, pretending to be asleep, she thought, as he ran the tip of his finger around her breast and then down to stroke her navel.

She didn't open her eyes, but she gasped at the sensation of his hand on her skin.

"Just as I thought," he murmured. "You are not asleep." And his mouth came down to cover hers very gently.

She tried to remember that she must not let herself enjoy this newfound sensuality. She must resist or lose her dignity. Still, she let his probing tongue open her lips as his hand slid down between her thighs. Didn't she want to stop him? Of course I do, she thought indignantly, but she couldn't keep from spreading her thighs so his fingers could stroke and tease her body.

Her pulse seemed to be thundering in her ears.

"Kiss me, Sierra," he whispered. "You're my captive, please me . . . I want my captive's caresses."

She should fight him off and protest, but she couldn't seem to bring herself to do so.

"I'm going to put my child in your belly, Sierra, and even if you bear it without me, when it moves in your womb, when your breasts swell with milk for it, you won't forget me. Someday maybe the grandson of my loins or my great-grandson will do all those things you talked about, lead my people, help my people."

"No, I won't be used like this."

He pushed her shift up, then rolled over on his back, positioning her above him. His big hands clasped her breasts, pulled them down to his hungry mouth. Where her thighs joined, she felt the erect, throbbing heat of him against her.

"Ride me, Sierra," he whispered urgently. "Beg me for it. You want me inside you, I know you do. . . ." His hand now went to her small waist holding her against him while his tongue worked its way across the skin of her breasts until he found first one nipple, then the other.

An ache began to build deep inside her as he sucked hard, making her nipples raw and tender. She couldn't stop herself from pressing her breast against his mouth, wanting him to take as much as possible of it in. The scent of him was all over her, and it excited her. His maleness was a molten chunk of steel between her thighs.

He was steel, and she was flint. Sparks and fire. Rubbing against him only built the flames of passion between them. At any moment now, Sierra thought dazedly, he's going to flip me over on my back and I won't have to make a choice. He will mate with me whether I want it or not.

His almost feverish hands pawed under her buckskin shift; she wore no underthings. He molded her hips against his loins, pressured her body against his until his manhood rubbed against her.

The aching void in her was growing, becoming unbearable. She had to have it filled, to have him penetrate her quivering, silken depths. Flint and steel make a fire that can only be cooled one way. Without even realizing she did so, Sierra rose up and came down on him hard, feeling that fiery heat go all the way into her depths.

"Ahhh!"

She didn't know if he made the sound of pleasure or if she did. And it didn't matter. Nothing mattered but riding him, using his hard male body to pleasure herself. His hands were on her waist, guiding her, raising her slightly, bringing her back down on him while his mouth teased and caressed her nipples.

"Kiss me, Sierra."

What could she do but obey her captor? As the train rocked on gently through the rainy night, she leaned on her elbows so he could still stroke her breasts, took his rugged face between her two hands and ran her tongue along his lips.

His mouth opened and she probed inside with her tongue, her excitement building. She teased the interior of his mouth and then he held her close and sucked her tongue deep into his throat.

His hot maleness seemed to be throbbing almost uncontrollably deep within her, and then she realized it was her own body, going into spasms she could not stop, instinctively wanting to squeeze the life-making seed from him and keep it in her belly.

He bucked under her, grabbing her waist, lifting her, bringing her down hard, impaling her on him.

When he began to give up his seed, she was barely aware of it because spasms swept over her. Flint and steel . . . Sparks and fire . . .

When she awakened with a sudden start, she realized it was almost daylight outside and the train had stopped moving. She didn't have time to think about last night, she wasn't even sure she hadn't dreamed it. But Cholla was up on one elbow and he looked worried.

"What is it?"

"We've stopped at a station. I see people around." He had his face against the cracks, staring out.

But even as it occurred to her this would be a good time to yell for help and get the renegade captured, he clamped a hand over her mouth. "Keep quiet, Sierra. Remember, you look like a squaw in that getup, and there're a lot of renegades and outlaws in Indian Territory. They might not believe you're a white girl when you tell them."

As if she could make that decision anyway, with his hand across her mouth. She looked down and realized her nipples were red and swollen. She flushed at the thought of how she had behaved last night.

Cholla was right about one thing; in this getup and with her black hair in long braids, she looked Indian. He still might trade her off to some passing male for a good horse or some supplies, and who would believe she was the missing white widow? She'd be some buck or half-breed's prisoner and no better off than she was now.

He made a disgusted noise as he looked out. "I think we've got trouble. A couple of railroad men got aboard. If we could just get off—"

The train let out gusts of noisy steam, rattled a little, whistled, began to move.

Very slowly he took his hand off her mouth. "I had thought about getting off here, but I'm not sure where we are and the tribes of the Territory don't like Apaches."

The train began to pick up speed, chugging and hissing. Could she pull away from him, jump out of the boxcar before it began to move any faster? There was bound to be a telegraph office right here at the railroad.

He caught her wrist. "I know what you're thinking, Dark Eyes. I don't intend to let you go yet. I still need you."

The train began to move away from the yard. It had only been a place to load water and wood for the engine, after all.

"You realize," Sierra said, "that they might be looking for me? Why don't you jump off the train? You can be long gone by the time the train crew finds me."

"Because I need you, Sierra. I need you to warm my blankets, to be my hole card in case I get trapped.

206

As long as I've got a use for you, I don't intend to let you go."

"When?" she insisted, angry with herself as well as with him. What kind of slut was she to let herself be used to pleasure her captor? A prisoner who wanted to stay alive—and her body was something that he seemed to enjoy.

His attention was elsewhere. "A couple of tough-looking railroad men got on this train, detectives or yard guards most likely."

"For what reason?"

He shrugged. "Maybe nothing. Maybe looking for us. Maybe checking the train once in a while for tramps or stray cowboys riding for free."

If they found her, she was saved . . . unless, as Cholla had suggested, she looked so Indian herself, the railroad men wouldn't listen to her and would throw her off the train as a free-riding squaw.

For an hour or so, nothing happened. The sun had come out and the day warmed. Then Cholla, looking through the end of the boxcar, stiffened. "They're in the next car, Sierra, they'll be able to see us in here."

The concern in his voice was evident.

"Even if we hide behind something?"

"The hay isn't enough. Maybe if we climb up on top of the car and lie flat—"

"Get on top of a moving train? Are you loco? No, thanks." She folded her arms and sat down. "I'll just wait until they get here and explain I've been kidnapped. You can do what you please."

"All right. If they think you're just some squaw

catching a ride across the Territory, that's your problem. Try to land soft when they throw you off the train." He put on his backpack, stuck the pistol and knife in his waistband, and started through the small escape door at the end of the car.

"Wait, I . . . I think I'll come with you." She grabbed up her bedroll.

"Be careful," he warned, as they climbed the ladder at the end of the swaying car, "one slip and the last thing you'll see are those big wheels coming at you."

Here she was risking her life again because her captor had put her in a life-threatening situation. Sierra got madder as she thought about it, but she hung on desperately as she climbed to the top of the car. She crawled along the top, trying to cling to the swaying train. She'd show him! Damn him, she wanted the satisfaction of living long enough to testify against him. Maybe she could get him hanged rather than sent to prison.

The car lurched and Sierra flattened herself, hanging on tightly. She didn't have time to think about weighty matters right now, like the satisfaction of watching him hang. She was too busy just trying to stay alive. The noise, the smoke, and the cinders blew past her while the car clattered and swayed under her. It seemed a long way to the ground, and the train was moving fast on this straightaway. I wouldn't have to fall under the wheels to die, she thought in terror. At this speed falling from the top of the train would be fatal.

"Hang on, Dark Eyes," Cholla shouted, and he crawled over next to her, put his big arm across her back.

Immediately she felt safe, remembering the strength of the man. With him hanging on to her, protecting her, she wouldn't fall. Then she had mixed emotions as she reminded herself that if it weren't for the Apache, she wouldn't be in this mess.

The landscape whizzed by in a dizzy panorama of green trees, gold and scarlet leaves, and bright red sumac bushes. Up ahead she could see the twisting, snakelike path of a river. At the same time, she saw two heads as the railroad bulls climbed the ladder at the end of the car ahead, gestured and shouted.

The roaring train swept their words away, but their angry frowns left no doubt the two men were coming after them. They not only had pistols, they had billy clubs. They climbed to the top of the swaying car and, obviously used to walking on the roof of one, started toward the couple.

They would be crossing the river bridge in another half-minute. If the men threw them off, would she die when she hit the water?

Her heart was pounding like a hammer. She turned her head to Cholla. "What now?"

"Right now," he shouted in her ear, "they think we're just hitching a ride. If I shoot one of them, the telegraph system will have the whole railroad looking for us. Besides, they're armed."

Sierra glanced at the two men balancing on the top of the next car as they gradually worked their way along it. The train was almost at the river bridge now. South Canadian River, the sign on the bridge read.

"Sierra," Cholla shouted in her ear, "I think we'd

better take our chances and jump!"

"Jump?" Maybe she hadn't heard him right. She looked from the water running below her over to Cholla. "Are you crazy?"

But he was already standing up, reaching for her hand.

"No! I'm not going to jump!"

He pulled her to her feet, and she fought to keep her balance atop the swaying car. She looked at him, at the men coming toward her, the black water running below her.

"Better to jump than get thrown!" he shouted. "This is no place to fight two men! Come on!"

She shook her head at him. He could be a rugged individualist if he wanted, but she'd stay and try to reason with the railroad bulls.

"No!" She shook her head again.

Cholla had hold of her wrist. "Jump wide," he shouted, "or you won't clear the bridge!"

Sierra fought to get out of his grasp, but his expression told her he meant to take her with him, even if they both died.

"Damn you!" She shouted as she struggled to break free, saw his muscles tensing for the jump, heard the sudden crack as one of the railroad men took a shot at them.

"Wait!" she screamed at the men. "There's a mistake! You don't know who I am!" The roaring of the train carried her words away as the men raised the pistol again.

The river or a bullet. Even as Cholla tensed, she knew he was taking her with him whether she wanted to go

210

or not. In that moment, Sierra jumped, putting all her strength into it, hoping in that split second when she began to fall that she had jumped far enough to clear the bridge.

Chapter Eleven

It seemed forever she fell screaming toward the fast-rushing river swollen by all the rains. Her skirt was up around her waist as she descended, and she remembered that she wore no underwear. The water wasn't pretty and blue; it was dark like coffee. She hoped Cholla would drown. As she hit the water and it closed over her head, she suddenly remembered she couldn't swim.

Merciful heavens. She was going down and down in the water, holding her breath automatically. It was dark and muddy and cold, so Sierra vaguely realized it couldn't be heaven or hell. She felt herself being swept along by the current and wondered if it would hurt to drown?

Drown? She didn't intend to die in some cold river below a railroad bridge in Indian Territory. Not unless she got to see her abductor die first!

Sierra fought and struggled toward the surface, her lungs on fire. *The light.* She must make it up to the light. She had to take a breath, and when she did, all she got was a mouthful of water. Panicked now, she began to fight her way to the surface, choking and coughing.

Hands were reaching for her, big, strong hands. Cholla. She saw his face in the water. He was trying to finish her off. *Damn*. She began to fight him.

He shouted something, but she couldn't hear him. She didn't know whether the roaring in her ears was due to fading consciousness, the rushing river, or the train above. She struggled to get away from him and went under again. Around her, branches and leaves floated by, frothy foam lay like brownish cream on the coffee-dark surface.

Then a hand clipped her across the jaw and she stopped fighting because she couldn't seem to move and the light grew dim. The river bank looks so far away, she thought, and then his arm went around her and he swam strongly through the water.

She was on her back, looking up at the sky and thinking how blue it was and how interesting it was that the smoke from the train still hung in the air over the bridge even though the train now crawled, like a black snake, over a distant rise.

Then Cholla stopped swimming, stood up as he touched bottom. He swung her into his arms, carried her to the river bank, set her on a dry place on the ground, then flopped down beside her, choking and coughing. "Sierra, are you all right?"

She wasn't dead, but she was soaking wet and cold. "I . . . I think so." She managed to raise herself on one elbow. "You did this! You pulled me!"

"Oh, shut up!" he snapped as he sat up. "You're alive, aren't you? I could have let you drown!"

"Not as long as you need a hostage!" She screamed it

213

at him. "Not as long as you can find a use for me! Give me that pistol. I'm going to kill you!"

He glared at her. "Sierra, the pistol was lost in the river, so were the bedrolls. All we've got is the knife, not even any matches."

"Wonderful! I don't have to drown, now I can starve or freeze."

"If it makes you feel any better"—he frowned and flopped back down—"just remember I'm going to freeze and starve, too."

"That might make it worthwhile. I hope those railroad men come looking for us."

"Don't count on it," Cholla said. "They probably just saw us as a couple of Injuns, not worth the bother."

She was already beginning to shiver in the cool afternoon air. "I'm going to live," she said through gritted teeth. "I'm going to live so I can see you hang!"

Lieutenant Quimby Gillen hunched his shoulders against the cold wind, then looked out across the barren Kansas plains and back to the small railroad station. "Blast!" He slammed a fist into a palm so hard that Corporal Finney jumped. "Blast that sonovabitch! We've been all up and down the track, almost to Albuquerque and back, checking all along the way. Where in the hell do you suppose he is?"

The corporal cleared his throat. "Who knows, sir? Maybe you should ask General Miles about forgetting this assignment—"

"Hell, no!" Gill roared. "This is a personal thing, too! When Lieutenant Forester was killed under such mysterious . . . Never mind."

Finney stared out across the frosty prairie. "The Apache may not even be alive anymore, sir. We haven't run across anyone who's seen him or heard anything of him since he killed that banker."

"If he's dead, I want to see the body. I want to see his red carcass crawling with flies, you hear me?"

"Yes, sir."

"Besides he had a hostage—Mrs. Forester. It burns me to think what acts of violence that damned savage has done by now—raped and scalped her, most likely. If you hadn't been such a dunce back there at the bridge . . ."

The boy didn't say anything. It occurred to Gillen that Finney might be thinking if his superior officer had been on duty where he belonged instead of lying between a whore's legs, Cholla wouldn't have gotten past them in that wagon. But of course the freckled-faced corporal didn't say that, he wouldn't dare.

The question was what to do now? The brass was already wanting him to give up the search and go back to the fort. He'd probably face a demotion and a transfer for letting the prisoner escape. So far, a major who owed him a favor for introducing him to Trixie had kept the Army off his back, but that couldn't last much longer. If he didn't come up with something soon, his Army career was finished.

He reached for his bag of candy, crunched a lemon drop between his teeth, and put the sack back in his jacket without offering the boy a candy. "Maybe we should go back to Saint Looie and start over again."

"You really think there's any point in that, sir?"

"You questioning my judgment, Corporal?"

"No, sir, but we've checked all the railyards and even

215

along the Mississippi, just in case he drove the wagon off into the water before he caught a train."

Gill looked beyond the windswept tracks, out across the prairie. Blast it all, he really didn't know what to do next. He'd stalled Trixie about going to Arizona with him. In truth, he was beginning to regret his involvement with the little tramp. She always smelled like stale smoke and medicine. Anyway, smoking was for men, and women ought to stay in their places and not try to take over men's rights.

A bushy, dried weed blew past them, so round, it rolled over and over, like a ball, across the prairie. "What is that blasted thing?"

"A tumbleweed, sir."

"A what?"

"A tumbleweed," Finney explained patiently. "The German immigrants from Russia accidently brought them in."

Gill watched the thing bounce along the barbed-wire fence. "Germans don't come from Russia, they come from Prussia or some such place."

"These do." The corporal warmed to his story. "Seems these Germans have been raising wheat in Russia for years and years. But the new czar decided to run them out, so they emigrated to here and Nebraska, looking for a likely place to grow wheat."

"So get to the point," Gill growled.

"The German women sneaked their best Russian red wheat seed into this country sewed into their petticoat hems, or so the story goes. Mixed in with that seed was the seed of the Russian thistle, we Americans have taken to calling it tumbleweed."

"Which is one more thing I hate about Kansas!" Gill

216

turned back toward the railroad station, reaching for his bag of hard candy. "At least we can get in out of this damned cold wind."

The gray sky spat snow as they walked across the platform. The old telegrapher ran out of the station, waving a paper. "Lieutenant, a message just came through for you."

"Gimme that!" Gill jerked it out of the old man's hand, stared at it. " 'Apache and captive reported near Missouri Ozarks. Stop. Proceed to following location. Stop. See a man named Tiny Hankins. Stop.' "

Gill reread it several times. "Well, I'll be damned. Cholla headed south instead of trying to follow the train tracks back the way he came. Round up the patrol, Corporal. We'll catch a train east and then ride one down to see this hillbilly."

"But, sir," Finney protested, scratching a freckled ear, "Cholla could have traveled a long ways by now, depending on how long it took this Hankins to decide to go for the law."

"At least we'll be out of Kansas," Gill barked. He turned to the telegrapher, waved the paper. "Can we get a train directly to this location?"

The elderly man pushed back his green eyeshade, shook his head. "Nope. You'll have to wait for a train heading east, then catch another south."

Gill grumbled under his breath about the delay, then headed back toward the warm shelter of the railroad office. "At least I'll have seen the last of Kansas and its bare plains and blowing tumbleweeds!"

Trixie stared out the window at the snow falling on

the street below. She'd been waiting for word from Gill for several weeks now but hadn't heard anything. She'd even bedded that Army major he'd sent to her just to keep the brass from yanking his lieutenant's bars over his mistake.

"Maybe I owed the bum that," she said doubtfully to her reflection in the dirty window glass as she pulled the soiled green satin robe closer around her. "Yeah, I'm a talented singer, not a whore," she reassured herself. "All these guys promise everything, then don't give a girl nothing but a hard time. Maybe I should have stayed at Miss Fancy's or the Gilded Lily, but I was meant for the big time."

At the Gilded Lily, she had starred as the naked girl in the punch bowl when the rich gents were throwing a party. She'd sit in the bowl and let them pour champagne all over her as they filled it. Like naughty little boys, the men seemed to get a kick out of dipping their punch cups in the bowl. "I got talent," she told herself. "I look just like the Cameo girl, and I can sing, too."

She cranked up her phonograph and sang a few bars of "Beautiful Dreamer" as she went over to the table, took a big swig of patent medicine. Almost immediately, she began to feel better. That cocaine stuff was the latest craze, and Trixie preferred it to booze. People were already starting to talk about cocaine being dangerous, but everyone was using it. Now if it was bad for you, would they be allowed to sell the stuff? She took another long drink, walked uncertainly over to pick up her pack of Cameos and a silver matchbox, struck a light against the bottom of the table. "No, I'm prettier than the Cameo girl." But older — much older, her mind said.

Trixie took her cigarette and ashtray, walked unsteadily to the sofa, flopped down. "Yeah, I'm a real talented performer," she told herself, and giggled a little. Who would believe she'd first begun her career singing in the choir at the church where her stern father was pastor? "Pa, you said I was going to end up in a den of iniquity, a Sodom or Gomorrah." She giggled. "I wouldn't mind if money and glamor and excitement went with it, but East Saint Louis has to be the dullest, most backward place in the world. Where I want to go is 'Frisco or New York."

She took a deep puff and blew a smoke ring, watched the smoke drift. The wind rattled the window. Trixie was running low on money and had gone back to her old pursuits temporarily to get enough to travel on. She had told her lover about Otto Toombs accidental death, knowing in advance that no one at the big mansion would shed a tear.

Julia Griswold Toombs was swathed in black widow's weeds when she went out driving with her father and brothers in the family carriage. All three men had a discreet taste for fast women, cards, gambling. Otto had told her he thought that was why the old man had pressed Julia to marry. In a banker's family, there must be no hint of scandal, and evidently there were some whispers about Julia. But they were only gossip after all, Otto had said with a sigh of disappointment. Fashion and jewels were the only weaknesses the beauty had, as far as he could see. The Griswold men were discreet in their sinning. Was that why the servant girls at the mansion were unusually pretty?

Trixie smiled to herself and puffed on her cigarette. If only Otto had known he wasn't the only occupant of that big mansion Trixie was accommodating in return for expensive items like jewelry and gold. Now, with even that source of income ending, she would have to move on, whether she wanted to or not. Maybe she could go to Tombstone, where it was supposed to be warm, then later on to 'Frisco. There was a well-known saloon in Tombstone, the Birdcage Theater. Maybe they could use a singing star.

The elegant and secretly sinful Griswolds. Trixie had known her lover would tire of her sooner or later, and the family was so powerful, she was afraid to try blackmail. She might end up dead in the river. Maybe some folks would think what her lover wanted was unusual, but it didn't matter to Trixie. She had done and seen everything in the past few years since leaving Texas, and nothing surprised her anymore.

Still, her pride was hurt at being replaced. She reached over, picked the crumpled note up off the floor, reread it as if doing so would change the content.

My dearest, I am going to have to end our relationship and our little afternoon meetings. But I will come see you one more time. I wouldn't want you to be replaced without some suitable reward. . . .

Replaced. That hurt Trixie's pride. She took a deep drag on the cigarette, enjoying the taste of the tobacco, and read another line.

That little French maid Otto hired just before he died has been so satisfactory, with her working here, there'll be no chance of my indiscretions being noticed as I've always feared with you.

The note ended with the hope that Trixie hadn't been
hurt and the promise that there was going to be money
for her in any case.

Her pride was what was hurt. *A French maid.* She wondered if the woman knew all the things that would be expected of her by the residents of that fine house besides
looking after the aristocratic Julia's clothes?

Trixie balled the letter up again, threw it on the floor.
The small clock on the mantel chimed the hour. It was
time. Would her lover come as promised?

Trixie got up, crushed out her cigarette, went to the
window. The elegant Griswold carriage with its pair of
matched black horses was just pulling up out front. She
watched the cloaked figure get out, brave the wind to
run for the doorway.

Aw, she didn't care about the French maid; she didn't
care about anything as long as she had her medicine
and her Cameos — and a chance to get out of this cold,
go where it was warm and then on to 'Frisco.

Trixie heard footsteps coming down the hall, went to
the door, listened for the rapping. "Yes?"

"Love, you know who it is." The voice was low,
breathy.

"Just slip the money under the door and go back to
your damned French maid," Trixie said.

"She's been sick, too sick to pleasure anyone. I
thought, just for old times' sake, we could . . . well, you
know. . . ."

The rich, rotten Griswolds, Trixie thought in
disgust. Like Otto, the son-in-law, the whole
family thought money could buy anything. "I'll expect a

221

little extra," she whispered against the door.

"Anything you want, love. Just let me in."

I'm really a talented artist, a great singer, Trixie told herself as she unbolted the lock, but sometimes a girl has to make a few sacrifices to arrive at stardom. "Come in, but you can't stay long." She opened the door.

"Wouldn't it have been a joke on Otto if he had known?" Julia Griswold Toombs smiled as she threw back the hood of her ebony velvet cloak, and swept into the room.

Tom Mooney couldn't sleep. He stared at the adobe walls of his quarters, listening to the wind rattle the windows. Bad winter coming fast, the sergeant thought, and wondered about Cholla, where his friend was at this moment and if he were even alive? Nothing had been heard since Lieutenant Gatewood had last called him in to tell him Cholla had escaped from the train and had kidnapped Mrs. Robert Forester.

Tom speculated on whether Mrs. Forester was still with him. Cholla might have killed her. He wasn't the type to hurt a woman, but knowing the lieutenant had raped and killed Delzhinne, he might have made an exception of Forester's woman. At the very least, on this long journey, the virile Apache would use her.

Tom twisted restlessly in bed, trying not to think of the woman in the photo, the girl with the beautiful dark eyes, spread out on a blanket under the Apache's hard, brown body. She might even be carrying Cholla's son by now.

The dog raised its head and regarded him solemnly.

222

"Ke'jaa, I wonder where he is at this moment, if he's still alive?" When Tom realized he was almost waiting for the dog to answer, he flushed with embarrassment, glad there was no one around to hear him conversing with a beast. "You've been alone too long," he whispered, "and your friend has the woman you want."

He listened to the wind moaning around the buildings of the fort, like an Indian spirit wailing to get inside. Did he want Cholla to make it back to Arizona? Holy Saint Patrick, that wasn't possible, was it? And if Cholla did, the Army would only kill him for his trouble or gather him up again and ship him back to Florida. Word had come that the Apaches were beginning to die in the humid, steamy coastal swamp. The children were being separated from their parents and sent to Carlisle, Pennsylvania, to an old Army camp that was being converted into a school to "civilize" them.

Suppose they found Mrs. Forester and she had no place to go and her belly was big with an Apache bastard? No one would want her. But Mooney would. He liked babies, any kind or color. Maybe if she had no one else to turn to and was expecting a child, she might, she just might, consider a middle-aged trooper who hadn't much to offer but a small farm that needed a lot of work and improvements. He didn't have the money for that. He could stay in the Army, but an officer's widow wouldn't be interested in a sergeant. He could offer her his love.

Tom blushed, trying to imagine saying sweet words to a woman. She would probably laugh at his clumsy attempts to say anything romantic. He would read her some poetry, and maybe she would be impressed. One thing was certain, he could offer a woman steadfast love and a devotion she wouldn't find in most men. And maybe, somewhere down the line, after they had lived together awhile, she might finally learn to love him, too.

He reached out for the photo in the pocket of his jacket, which hung over the chair next to his bed, held it, listening to the wind and the dog's soft breathing.

When he closed his eyes, the girl in the photo came into his arms and smiled.

"You're just the kind of man I've always wanted, Tom, a shy, but sincere one who would take care of me. I don't care that you're not young and good-looking."

"All my life, I've looked for a woman, a soft, kind woman who understood me and didn't laugh when I read poetry aloud. If you've got a child, I don't mind at all, bless the saints, no. We'll raise it along with our own. I just wish I had a little money to fix up the farm."

"The money doesn't matter, Tom. We care about each other and we need each other. That's all that counts, you know." She would reach for the book. "Ah, you like poetry, I see. So do I. Read me that poem about: 'I could not love thee, Dear, so much, loved I not honour more.' "

She settled herself in his lap in front of the fire and he read to her while her dark hair spilled across his shoulder. Together, they were one against the world. When the wind rattled the shutters, he wasn't alone anymore.

The sound of the bugle blowing reveille brought him up out of bed with a start. For the first time in many years, Tom had overslept.

224

The Publishers of Zebra Books Make This Special Offer to Zebra Romance Readers...

AFTER YOU HAVE READ THIS BOOK WE'D LIKE TO SEND YOU 4 MORE FOR *FREE* AN $18.00 VALUE

NO OBLIGATION!

ONLY ZEBRA HISTORICAL ROMANCES "BURN WITH THE FIRE OF HISTORY" (SEE INSIDE FOR MONEY SAVING DETAILS.)

MORE PASSION AND ADVENTURE AWAIT... YOUR TRIP TO A BIG ADVENTUROUS WORLD BEGINS WHEN YOU ACCEPT YOUR FIRST 4 NOVELS ABSOLUTELY *FREE*
(AN $18.00 VALUE)

Accept your Free gift and start to experience more of the passion and adventure you like in a historical romance novel. Each Zebra novel is filled with proud men, spirited women and tempestuous love that you'll remember long after you turn the last page.

Zebra Historical Romances are the finest novels of their kind. They are written by authors who really know how to weave tales of romance and adventure in the historical settings you love. You'll feel like you've actually gone back in time with the thrilling stories that each Zebra novel offers.

GET YOUR FREE GIFT WITH THE START OF YOUR HOME SUBSCRIPTION

Our readers tell us that these books sell out very fast in book stores and often they miss the newest titles. So Zebra has made arrangements for you to receive the four newest novels published each month.

You'll be guaranteed that you'll never miss a title, and home delivery is so convenient. And to show you just how easy it is to get Zebra Historical Romances, we'll send you your first 4 books absolutely FREE! Our gift to you just for trying our home subscription service.

BIG SAVINGS AND FREE HOME DELIVERY

Each month, you'll receive the four newest titles as soon as they are published. You'll probably receive them even before the bookstores do. What's more, you may preview these exciting novels free for 10 days. If you like them as much as we think you will, just pay the low preferred subscriber's price of just $3.75 each. *You'll save $3.00 each month off the publisher's price.* AND, your savings are even greater because there are never any shipping, handling or other hidden charges—FREE Home Delivery. Of course you can return any shipment within 10 days for full credit, no questions asked. There is no minimum number of books you must buy.

4 FREE BOOKS

TO GET YOUR 4 FREE BOOKS WORTH $18.00 — MAIL IN THE FREE BOOK CERTIFICATE T O D A Y

Fill in the Free Book Certificate below, and we'll send your FREE BOOKS to you as soon as we receive it.

If the certificate is missing below, write to: Zebra Home Subscription Service, Inc., P.O. Box 5214, 120 Brighton Road, Clifton, New Jersey 07015-5214.

FREE BOOK CERTIFICATE

4 FREE BOOKS

ZEBRA HOME SUBSCRIPTION SERVICE, INC.

YES! Please start my subscription to Zebra Historical Romances and send me my first 4 books absolutely FREE. I understand that each month I may preview four new Zebra Historical Romances free for 10 days. If I'm not satisfied with them, I may return the four books within 10 days and owe nothing. Otherwise, I will pay the low preferred subscriber's price of just $3.75 each; a total of $15.00, *a savings off the publisher's price of $3.00*. I may return any shipment and I may cancel this subscription at any time. There is no obligation to buy any shipment and there are no shipping, handling or other hidden charges. Regardless of what I decide, the four free books are mine to keep.

NAME

ADDRESS _____ APT _____

CITY _____ STATE _____ ZIP _____

TELEPHONE ( )

SIGNATURE _____ (If under 18, parent or guardian must sign)

Terms, offer and prices subject to change without notice. Subscription subject to acceptance by Zebra Books. Zebra Books reserves the right to reject any order or cancel any subscription.

GET
FOUR
FREE
BOOKS
(AN $18.00 VALUE)

ZEBRA HOME SUBSCRIPTION
SERVICE, INC.
P.O. Box 5214
120 BRIGHTON ROAD
CLIFTON, NEW JERSEY 07015-5214

AFFIX
STAMP
HERE

He dressed quickly and went about his duties, the dog trotting ahead of him as he crossed the parade ground. Schultz came around the corner, saluted. "Lieutenant Gatewood wants to see you, Sergeant."

"There's news?"

"They don't tell me things like that. When you find out, me and Taylor and Allen would like to know. Cholla's our friend, too." The corporal put a cigar between his stained teeth.

Tom nodded and took off at a brisk pace for the officers' quarters, the dog running ahead of him. He was almost afraid of what the news might be; probably that the Army had finally cornered and killed the Apache scout.

He knocked and entered, snapped the slender officer a salute. Gatewood returned it, wrinkling his nose thoughtfully as he stared at the message before him. "Someone has finally spotted them."

Them. The woman whose picture he carried in his jacket and the best friend he had. He must wait for Gatewood to continue, but the officer was staring out the window. He, too, has been in Arizona a long time, Tom thought. Half a dozen years ago, Gatewood had been one of those involved in tracking down Victorio when that Apache was raiding.

Gatewood looked up suddenly as if he had forgotten the sergeant was present. "Some fellow in Missouri named Hankins spotted the pair of them. Says he and two friends were out hunting somewhere in the hills and this Apache just jumped them, killed his friends and wounded him. Supposedly, he was lucky to escape with his life."

"Begging your pardon, sir, attacking peaceful citizens for no reason doesn't sound like Cholla."

"Neither does stabbing the vice president of a bank with a letter opener," Gatewood said.

Tom shook his head, tight-lipped. "Cholla? Never! He's being blamed for things he wouldn't do. Is this Hankins sure it was Cholla?" Tom argued, "maybe he's mistaken—"

"And just how many big Indian braves do you suppose there are running about in Missouri?"

Tom grudgingly conceded the point. "And the woman?"

"She's with him, but it seems she was trying to escape. According to this Tiny Hankins, he and his friends were trying to assist the lady in her escape when the Apache turned up, killed the other two, damn near killed him. Hankins got away and walked several days to reach a telegraph station. He says the Indian carried the woman off again."

Tom didn't know whether to be happy or sad. His friend was still alive, but the Army was closer to catching him now. And the woman was with him.

"Sit down, Tom," the lieutenant said softly.

Tom sank down into a chair.

"The colonel has asked me to talk to you." There was reluctance in Gatewood's eyes.

"Sir?"

"Gillen's not doing all that well tracking him."

"He isn't the brightest officer in the Army. I always thought he couldn't find his way to the latrine and back, and his candy chomping gets on everyone's nerves." Tom grinned and ran stubby, freckled fingers through his thinning hair. A suspicion began to build in his mind. When he looked up, something about Gatewood's manner told him he was probably right. Charles Gatewood was an honorable man, a gentleman. That was why he was still a lieutenant and probably would be when he died.

"Sergeant, I have been ordered to tell you that since you know Cholla, know him well enough to understand how he thinks, you could be valuable in this hunt."

Tom just stared at him, unblinking.

Gatewood looked away and rubbed the bridge of his prominent nose, turning the pen over and over in his hands. "Besides they think you could talk him into surrendering if they get him cornered. No one else could."

Tom swore softly under his breath. "The sonovabitches want me to help them capture or kill my friend?"

Gatewood turned the pen over and over in nervous fingers. "There's a promotion for you — and the reward if they get him."

Tom stared at the wide pine planks of the floor. It was worn white from cavalry boots. The dog lay looking at him almost gravely as if it wondered what his answer would be.

"The colonel could order you to do it," Gatewood said.

"Sir, you've been in the Army long enough to know this ain't the kind of duty you can order a man to do. There's too many ways he can mess up if he doesn't want to do it."

The officer grunted agreement, turning the pen over and over in his hands, while Tom stared at the worn floor boards, thinking.

Would the woman be so grateful if he helped rescue her that she would consider him? Would any man besides himself want her after she'd been used by the Apache scout? Could he have her if he betrayed his friend? *"I could not love thee, Dear, so much, loved I not honour more."*

Tom chewed his lip. "The promotion doesn't mean much, Lieutenant. I'm thinking of retiring at the end of this hitch, however, there's one question about the reward."

Gatewood looked as if he did not quite believe the sergeant was asking about the reward. He seemed disappointed, sad. "What about it?"

Tom looked him in the eye and grinned. "First, find out if it's thirty pieces of silver. Then tell the colonel the Irish sergeant said the Army could stick its reward up its—"

"I don't believe I'd better tell him that." Gatewood threw back his head and laughed. He looked relieved. "I'll just tell him you are needed here and too damned old to do much more than putter around the post anyhow."

"There you have it. Is that all, sir?"

Gatewood nodded. As Tom stood, the dog got up off the floor. When Tom turned to go, Gatewood came around his desk, held out his hand. "Thank you, Mooney, you have renewed my faith in my fellow man. There aren't many who'd turn down a chance at a promotion and a reward."

Tom thought of the woman as he shook hands with the officer. Maybe by not helping in the capture he was throwing away his chance to meet her. "I wish the reward and promotion were all that was at stake here, sir."

"Oh?" Gatewood waited, but Tom couldn't bring himself to say any more. He figured the lieutenant would probably tell him he'd been alone too long and ought to go down to the *cantina* and get himself a woman. But that wasn't the kind of woman he wanted.

Tom paused with his hand on the doorknob. "You'll let me know if there's any news?"

Gatewood nodded. They exchanged looks without saying anything. Neither of them really expected the Apache to make it all the way back. It was just impossible, even for a rugged individualist like Cholla. The next news we'll hear, Tom thought, is that troops have surrounded Cholla and he has died in a blaze of gunfire rather than be captured.

He thought about the woman again and of long, cold nights spent before the fireplace on the old farm back in Michigan. "Sir, I . . . I know this is a strange question, but has anyone heard if Mrs. Forester reads poetry?"

Gatewood looked absolutely blank. "What?"

"Never mind. It was a foolish question." Tom turned quickly and went out, afraid of looking foolish. The lieutenant might read between the lines and understand too much. Besides being a lonely man, Tom Mooney was a very private one.

Outside, the chill wind blew against his face as he and the dog stared off toward the northeast. The Apache had managed to cross several hundred miles, if this Tiny Hankins was to be believed. By now, if he were alive, Cholla might be somewhere in Indian Territory on this crisp autumn morning.

Tom took out the photograph and stared at it, wondering if he had done the right thing. Would Cholla hurt Sierra Forester because her husband had murdered and raped the Apache girl? How, by all the saints, had Cholla found her? Could it be coincidence?

The odds were against it. Had the Holy Mother herself stepped in on this one? What kind of miracle was a kidnapping, maybe even a rape and murder?

He stared off into the distance, wondered where the pair was and if they knew Gillen was closing in on them? At least this time Tom Mooney had no blood on his hands. . . .

Sierra sat by the fire Cholla had started by rubbing two dry sticks together in a small bit of moss. It had been a long night and a cold one, with both of them huddled up together, trying to stay warm without blankets, trying to forget their hunger. In the morning Cholla had finally gotten a fire going, and he had cut another branch of Osage orange to make a new bow. But first he had made a snare from the dried grape vines that grew wild in the area, had caught a rabbit and cooked it.

Sierra ate all he gave her of the roasted meat and licked her fingers. As she finished, she realized he had taken only a very small piece for himself. "You didn't get enough."

He shrugged and worked on the bow. "I wasn't hungry."

"I don't believe that."

He raised one eyebrow, then returned to his work. "A few weeks ago, you were a timid mouse, now you argue with me and speak your mind continually. I think I like you better the other way."

"I just decided I didn't have to put up with being one of the mindless masses, that I could make my own destiny if I put my mind to it."

"Put your mind to finding things washed up along the river, things we might be able to use. Like some rope or cans we can cook in—or maybe even our bedrolls. We could dry them out."

"Those are long gone down river," Sierra said. "Maybe we could make some fishhooks and catch a few fish."

"Fish?"

She frowned at him. "Fish are usually found in rivers. We could roast them on sticks."

"No." His voice was firm as he shook his head. "You sound like the government. I think one of the reasons they decided to put the Apaches in Florida was that they thought we could cut expenses by catching a lot of fish to eat."

"So? Sounds reasonable."

"The Apache do not eat anything that swims."

She looked at him and frowned as she unbraided her hair, shook it out to dry. "That's silly."

"Is it?" He paused in his bow-making. "Some Apaches have developed a taste for Army mules. It's good, fat meat. They don't understand why the whites don't eat them."

Sierra made a face. "Merciful heavens!"

Cholla laughed. "Same difference. The whites have no respect for Indian taboos. I'll starve before I start catching fish."

"And what about me? Am I supposed to starve, too?"

He looked at her a moment, then sighed. "For you, I might do it. I wouldn't want my hostage to die on me."

"What are we going to do now?"

"I don't know." He seemed tired and even a little defeated as he looked around. "This Indian summer can't last forever. We've got to be out of this country before winter begins in earnest. Somehow, my instinct tells me this is going to be an unusually bad season."

She gave some thought to the train again. Sierra had no idea how often one came through. She wondered if there was a town or a ranch or any place they could walk to to get food. "If we run across a town or something, are you going to turn me loose?" She had finished combing her hair with her fingers and started braiding it again.

"I haven't decided. Don't worry me about it." He sounded annoyed and out of sorts.

"Well, at least we're alive," she said.

He smiled wryly. "You never did thank me for saving your life by pulling you out of the river."

"Why, you —! I wouldn't have been in the river if it weren't for you, or even on that train." She reminded herself of all the things she'd been through because of him, and she promised herself she would be there to enjoy it when the Army hanged him or loaded him back on a Florida-bound prison train.

"At least we're alive."

"Alive?" Sierra fumed. "We're out here with no supplies, no food. We don't know where we are. It couldn't get any worse than this."

Cholla's head came up suddenly and he froze. "Oh, yes, it could. Don't move, Sierra."

His tone and the way he clasped the butcher knife as he stared past her shoulder caused Sierra to turn around. A white woman wearing an elegant black velvet riding habit, two fancy pistols in her belt, rode out of the nearby woods, leading a group of mounted men.

"White people. I'm saved!" Sierra stood up even as

232

Cholla grabbed for her. She eluded him, went running to meet the riders. "I'm here! Hey, here I am!"

The woman might have been pretty in her younger days, but she was nearing forty and her face was weathered and plain. She looked startled, held up a hand to halt the men riding with her. Sierra glanced over her shoulder, but Cholla had disappeared into the woods.

Well, maybe they won't capture the Apache, but at least I'm safe, Sierra told herself. She ran toward the riders, waving her arm. "I sure am glad to see you! I need help."

She came to a sudden halt, staring up at one of the men, recognizing him. The memory of ice blue eyes burned into her brain.

He grinned and leaned on his saddle horn. "You sure do, sweet thing. I ain't forgot you."

It was Slim.

Chapter Twelve

Sierra wasn't quite sure what to do. She glanced over her shoulder. Cholla had disappeared into the brush. It suddenly dawned on her that she was free, even if she had to deal with Slim.

She managed to smile, then stepped forward and addressed the woman rider. "I'm Sierra Forester. The law is looking for me. I'm so glad to see you."

"Sweet thing," Slim drawled, "the law is lookin' for a lot of us. Ain't that right, Belle?"

"Shut your mouth, Slim," the woman snapped, she fixed her cold, dark gaze on Sierra. "Are you the one that shot Slim?"

What could she say with Slim leaning on his saddle horn, grinning down at her, a bandage around one arm. "I sure did. He and Pete tried to rape me."

"I thought as much. It seems he forgot to tell me that." The woman turned and glared at Slim, then smiled at Sierra. "Pete wasn't worth the bullet it took to kill him nohow. I'm Belle Starr from over at Younger's Bend. You heard of me?"

Her expression indicated she expected Sierra to say

yes, so Sierra obliged. "Why, of course. Everyone's heard of you. I'm honored to make your acquaintance."

The woman beamed at the men in her party, her plain face lighting up. "You see? Those dime novels about me are getting around." To Sierra, she said, "You appear to be in dire straits, miss. If you'd care to accompany us back to my place, maybe I can find some clothes to fit you, although you wear a larger size than I do."

That certainly isn't true, Sierra thought, but she sensed this older woman had a great sense of self-importance. Why else would she wear such an elegant velvet riding outfit and have two fine pistols stuck in her waistband? "I'd be happy to accompany you, Miss Starr."

"It's *Mrs*. Starr," Belle said frostily.

Slim snickered. "Belle's been married so many times, she keeps a preacher on call. How many times is it, Belle, four?"

The woman fixed him with a withering gaze, and then her quirt snapped suddenly. The short whip caught Slim across the face.

"God damn, Belle, I was only jokin'!" Slim snarled, and the other men in the party looked away uneasily.

"Slim," Belle said coldly, "when Jim and my son get back from Fort Smith, I think we need to have us a little talk. My latchkey is always out to hard cases, but I think you've done wore your welcome out."

"I didn't mean no harm, Belle." Slim rubbed the red weal on his face. "I'm much obliged for everything you've done for me."

235

"Then you ought to remember that Hanging Judge Parker over at Fort Smith would dearly love to know where to find you."

"I said I begged yore pardon, Belle," Slim grumbled. "You want I should get down and crawl on my belly like a damned dog?"

Sierra began to feel uneasy. She had evidently been forgotten during this quibbling. "Mrs. Starr, if you'd take me someplace where I can get a message to the Army or the law, they're looking for me."

"They're looking for me, too," Belle smiled a little proudly. "Only the fact that I help Judge Parker run down an *hombre* now and then here in the Nations keeps him off my back." She turned to one of the other men. "Joe, get the lady a horse."

The unshaven hombre brought around one of the fine pair of unsaddled palominos he'd been leading, and Sierra managed to get up on the beast. It wore a Running B brand on its hip. B for Belle, she thought as she looked over the glowering men and decided to ride up next to the woman. When she glanced at Slim, he ran his tongue along his lips in an almost obscene manner. He mouthed the words at her, Just wait!

Sierra shuddered. She might not be any safer riding with this rowdy-looking bunch than she had been with Cholla, but if she could get a message to the authorities, she'd be out of here in a day or two.

Belle looked over at her as they rode along. "What happened to the big Indian Slim says was on that train with you?"

"He kidnapped me to use as a hostage," Sierra said,

236

"but when Pete and Slim tried to rape me, he got Pete."

"Sounds like quite a man," Belle said as they rode along. "I like Indian bucks; been married to two of them."

Sierra frowned. "I think he was just trying to hang on to me in case he needed a human shield if he tangled with a posse."

"What happened to him?"

"He turned tail and ran like a rabbit when you rode up," Sierra snapped. She was a little surprised to find that Cholla's desertion annoyed her. Out of the corner of her eye, she saw Slim watching her. Had she gotten out of the frying pan and into the fire?

They rode to Belle's cabin on the bend of the South Canadian River, to the east of where Sierra and Cholla had jumped off the train. Sierra got the feeling that Belle might be little more than a den mother to every two-bit outlaw in the Indian Nations. Once she was cleaned up and wearing one of Belle's old dresses, though, the woman acted annoyed because at supper the men watched Sierra and ignored her.

When they finished eating, they went into the parlor and Belle sat down at the piano. "Do you play?"

"No, but I'd love to hear you," Sierra said politely.

Belle immediately preened a little, both delighted and relieved that she had found something at which she could best the younger woman. "I was good enough. I played at theaters some, and I always dreamed of being on the stage. I was hoping my daughter, Pearl, would follow in my footsteps, but she doesn't seem to have much talent in that direction."

237

"Oh, I'd be pleased to meet Pearl—and the rest of your family, too."

Belle stiffened. "Jim and my son, Eddie, are gone on business, and Pearl . . . well, Pearl's gone to visit her aunt in Missouri."

Slim snickered, and Belle fixed him with a black look. "Is there something terribly funny, Slim?"

He coughed, got up, and poured himself a whiskey. "No, ma'am."

"I think," Belle said icily, "tomorrow you'd better ride on, Slim."

Sierra caught the tension as the other men exchanged glances. She was only glad the older woman didn't have her quirt at hand. The way Belle was glaring at Slim, the gunfighter would have had more red welts across his face.

Belle began to play the piano. She played "Buffalo Gals," "Listen to the Mocking Bird," and that Civil War favorite, "Lorena."

Sierra was so tired, she could hardly sit up, but she applauded politely as did the men. Whatever else Belle Starr was, she was a talented performer. She wasn't all that pretty, though. She looked every day of her forty years, and her face was hard, the face of a woman who had survived the Civil War and a lot of personal adversity.

Slim caught Sierra's arm. "Hey, sweet thing, how about a dance?"

She tried to protest, but Slim swept her into his arms, holding her tightly as he danced her across the plank floor. His body rubbed against hers, and the lust in his eyes was unmistakable. Sierra complained about a hurt ankle, pulled away from him, went back to the piano.

Belle played a couple more songs, then looked bored and stood up, frowned at Sierra. "You can have Pearl's room at the end of the hall."

"Thank you," Sierra said, "and tomorrow you'll try to get a message to Fort Smith, or maybe give me an escort there?"

"We'll see," Belle answered with a shrug. Sierra realized immediately that she was expected to keep her mouth shut and let Belle make the decisions. Certainly the older, plain-faced woman did not seem to like other women. Maybe she saw them all as enemies, especially younger, prettier ones.

Sierra said her good nights and retired, making sure she locked her door behind her. Had she fallen into a nest of outlaws and robbers? She might not be a bit better off than when she'd been a captive of the Apache.

Cholla. His face came to her mind, and she finally faced the fact that she was annoyed with him, no, angry with him for deserting her the minute the group had ridden up. By now he was probably headed southwest, Sierra already forgotten in his all-consuming passion to return to his own land. She just hoped he didn't take another hostage along the way.

What was she to do now that she was rid of him? She thought about it as she got ready for bed. When she got to Fort Smith, she might go back to St. Louis. Why? She didn't know anyone there who would help her.

It occurred to her that Robert had relatives in Austin, although she had never met them. She had written a

239

note to Robert's mother at his death, but had never gotten an answer. Her husband had said his mother had disinherited him. Perhaps grief might have softened his mother's heart, and Sierra would be welcomed into the family fold. She hadn't realized how much she missed Zanna and Grandfather and how alone she was. Any family was better than none at all.

Sierra got into bed and blew out the lamp, wondering where Belle's daughter was? Slim's snicker hinted of scandal. Well, it was hardly Sierra's business. She lay back on the pillow with a sigh, and dropped off to sleep.

Cholla watched from the brush as Sierra climbed up on the palomino and rode away, bareback, with the older woman and the men. He had to fight an urge to run after them, stop her. But he stayed put. Armed with only a butcher knife, he could hardly take on half a dozen outlaws. He had recognized Slim when the group first rode out of the trees.

Sierra should have obeyed when he'd told her to run, but the stubborn girl wouldn't listen. Cholla wasn't close enough to hear the conversation, but the riders' expressions told him Sierra might have gotten herself into more trouble than she realized.

That wasn't his problem anymore. He turned toward the southwest and started walking. Within hours, Sierra might have a posse or the soldiers looking for him, so he intended to get out of the Territory as fast as he could. If she ended up being the entertainment for a bunch of white outlaws, that wasn't his concern. But his steps slowed after a few hundred yards.

Sierra wouldn't be in this mess if it weren't for him. On the other hand, it was all she deserved for being Robert Forester's woman. He hoped those *hombres* enjoyed her as much as he had. Then he remembered her in his arms, writhing under him as her own passion built, and rage swept over him at thinking the white men might make use of her beautiful body. Sierra belonged to him.

He rubbed the back of his neck, undecided. Finally, cursing himself for a fool, Cholla set off after the group. Keeping out of sight and checking hoof marks, he followed the riders to a big cabin on the bend of the river. It was nestled in a grove of trees.

By Usen, why did he bother? She didn't want to go with him, and he could find a new hostage down the line if he needed one. Dragging a captive along only slowed him down and complicated things. Of course, *I didn't come just for Sierra,* he thought as darkness came on and he crept to the cabin window to look in. He would just check to make sure they were all occupied, then he'd steal a horse and maybe some supplies from this nest of white outlaws, and be on his way. He heard music. White man's music.

They were all gathered around a piano, and the older woman played. Cholla took a long look at Sierra. Washed and combed and in a clean outfit, she was breathtakingly beautiful. From outside the window, he watched Slim look at her, lust in his pale, ice blue eyes, then sweep her into a dance.

Sierra held herself rigid as if she weren't enjoying herself at all, but Slim only held her tighter, rubbing

241

his body against hers.

It serves the little chit right, Cholla thought, but he was annoyed with the man nonetheless. Sierra was Cholla's captive, and he'd begun to think of her as his personal possession. He didn't like to see Slim rubbing his chest up against her breasts. Maybe if I take her away with me, the older woman will shrug off the whole incident and forget about it, he told himself. After all why should she help a younger, prettier woman when her expressions reveal she is jealous of Sierra?

The older woman stopped playing. They were going to bed now. Cholla watched them leave. The men went out the back door to a bunkhouse. When he looked around, both women had disappeared into a hall. What should he do?

Good sense told him to wait until everyone was asleep, climb through the window and steal some of the guns in the rack over the stone fireplace, take some food from the kitchen, grab a horse, and be on his way southwest. Horse stealing could get a man hanged faster than murder in the West, Cholla remembered. But the group had some good mounts. He recalled the pair of palominos one of them had been leading, unusual coloring and top quality.

It was cold outside, frost gradually settling on the dead grass and making it crunch beneath his moccasins. The lights went out in all the buildings. Cholla crept around to the wing where the hall led, tried to decide which window was Sierra's. There was really no way to tell.

He chose one, pushed the window up slowly,

242

climbed over the sill. A woman's form lay under the blankets, barely visible in the shadows, dark hair spread loose over the pillow. He tiptoed over, leaned closer. With no moon, it was as dark as the inside of a cave in there. He leaned over clapped a hand over the woman's mouth and held onto her as she came awake, struggling. "It's okay," he assured her softly. "It's me. I came back for you."

Immediately, the woman stopped struggling and relaxed. Cholla heaved a sigh of relief. Was she happy he was there, or was it a trick? When he removed his hand, was she going to scream and bring everyone running?

Without taking his hand from her mouth, he lay down on the bed beside her. She reached out to pull him close, stroke his chest, run her hand down his thighs. The implications were obvious. She wanted him; was glad to see him. Maybe the little fool had realized she was in deep trouble here with all these *hombres* eyeing her—a fawn in a coyote's den.

He slipped his fingers off her mouth as he covered it with his own, her tongue went between his lips, her hand reached to unbutton his shirt.

Her skin didn't feel as satiny smooth as before. Nor did her breasts seem as large as he remembered, and they sagged a little in his hand. A horrible thought crossed his mind. Cholla pulled back and took a good look at the woman who was already reaching to unbutton his pants.

"Don't stop, you big brown stud," she whispered. "If this is a dream, I'm enjoying it."

He was in that older woman's bed. What was he to

do now? She had her hands all over him, was trying to kiss him again. If he told her he'd come for Sierra, she was going to be very insulted.

Knowing he must stall for time, Cholla whispered, "I liked what I saw back at the river, decided to follow you."

"Jim won't be back for several days. Maybe you could stay and become part of this bunch."

"What would Jim say?"

"Who the hell cares? He's not much older than my son; not a man like you. You seem to be all man." She ran her hands over his big body.

But all Cholla could think of was Sierra. He couldn't make love to this woman, yet he didn't dare insult her by refusing. What would he do if she yelled for her gunmen? No matter, his body didn't want anyone but Sierra. Cholla pulled away from her.

"What's the matter, Injun?" She tried to kiss him, but he turned his head.

"I . . . I, nothing. I can't—"

A scream suddenly echoed down the hall.

"All right, where is she?" Cholla's feet hit the floor.

The woman sat straight up in bed. "Who? That girl—"

But Cholla was already out the door and running down the hall toward the sound.

Sierra had awakened suddenly as a hand clamped down on her mouth. She came up out of bed fighting, bit down hard on the hand.

The man swore and struck her, but she managed to scream once before he got his hand back over her mouth, muffling her cries. "Damn you, sweet thing, shut up!" he whispered tersely as he wrestled her back down on the bed. "Now just lay still and you won't get hurt!"

Slim. How had he managed to get into her room? Had anyone heard her cry for help? She was dizzy from the blow and had the warm, coppery taste of blood in her mouth as they struggled in the dark. In the background, she heard a big body crash against her locked door, the splintering of wood. Then the door was flung open and she saw the silhouette of a man. Heavens, there were two of them.

The man who'd broken in lunged, swearing as he grabbed Slim and slammed him against the wall, so hard a picture came crashing down amid the tinkle of glass.

"Cholla!" She'd never thought she would be so glad to see anyone. He didn't answer but fought Slim, crashing into the furniture. All she could do was watch from the bed.

A light came down the hall. "What's going on? Stop it! You hear? Stop it?"

But the two men continued to fight as Belle came into the bedroom carrying a coal-oil lamp, followed by the rest of the men, half-dressed and yawning.

Cholla slammed Slim up against the wall and looked around at Sierra, then toward the open window as if trying to decide whether the two of them could get out quickly enough. Slim slid down the wall and lay slumped on the floor.

Belle held her lamp high, and the glow took in the wrecked room, the bloody combatants. "What happened here?"

"I woke up with Slim trying to get in bed with me," Sierra gasped. It dawned on her suddenly that though the window was open, Cholla hadn't come from that direction. He had come through the hall door, and his shirt and pants were unbuttoned.

Belle set the lamp on the table and glared at all of them. "Slim, I thought I told you to leave her alone."

The man stumbled to his feet, wiping blood off his mouth. "Now, Belle, it isn't as if that sweet thing hasn't been givin' that Injun all he wants. She could favor a white man with a little bit of that honey."

Belle brought her other hand up slowly. It held the quirt. "This ain't about the girl, Slim. It's about disobeying me. Any man rides with me, he does what I say!"

Slim backed away, shaking his head. "You damned old, used-up bitch! You ain't gonna whip me no more! By God, you ain't gonna whip me like I was a bad colt!"

Belle stepped forward quickly, brought her arm back. Slim threw his hands up to protect his face, but she brought the lash down hard. It sang through the air, slashed him across the neck and shoulders, and he cried out in pain. "You old, dried-out whore, someday somebody'll kill you!"

The quirt cracked, catching Slim across the face. "Somebody may," Belle shouted, "you sorry sonovabitch, but it won't be a yeller dog like you! Now crawl outa here the same way you got in!" She hit him again. "Crawl! You hear me?" She struck him again and again. Slim went to his knees, trying to protect himself from the sharp sting of the lash. He scrambled to the window, dove through it.

"That'll larn him," Belle said with satisfaction as she slapped the quirt against her leg.

Sierra realized suddenly that she had been holding her breath. She let it out sharply. She also realized that the rest of the men, including Cholla, were now staring at her, that her nightdress was torn. Even Belle must have realized it. She frowned and gestured. "All right, the show's over! Everybody get back to bed."

The sleepy crowd of men faded away, leaving the three of them standing there. Without a word, Cholla strode to the window, looked out, then closed it. "This lock is broken."

"I don't doubt it." Belle seemed to have forgotten Sierra was in the room. She picked up the lamp, smiled coquettishly at Cholla. "We can go back to bed now and finish what we were just starting."

Cholla went over, took her hand, kissed the fingers. "I'd like that, but I'm afraid Slim might come back, so I suppose I'll have to say no this time. Maybe another time."

The woman turned and glared at Sierra, then looked back at Cholla and smiled. "You take my fancy, Injun. I have a weakness for young Injun bucks, and Jim July would never know the difference. If you want to change your mind . . ." Her voice trailed off as she looked up at him.

"We have to think of your reputation. No man worth his salt, not even an Injun, would dishonor a woman like you." Cholla gave her a charming smile.

"Maybe we'll talk about it later."

Almost reluctantly it seemed, Belle paused in the doorway with the lamp. "If you get tired of this inexperienced little chit," she said to Cholla, "and decide you want a *real* woman, you know which room is mine." She glared one last time at Sierra and left.

Cholla closed the door and looked at the damage he'd done. Then he dragged a chest in front of the entrance to the room. "I don't think we'll have any more trouble tonight."

Sierra was incredulous. "You intend to sleep with me?"

"I could go back to Belle's bed if you want. I've had an invitation."

She was furious. "I'd say you've had more than an invitation, I'd say you've already had a sample."

He looked down as if he'd just realized his clothing was unbuttoned, disarrayed. "I got into her room accidently, looking for you. Then I had to pretend it wasn't an accident, so I wouldn't get killed."

"You're just like a bull, aren't you?" Sierra pulled her torn gown up on her shoulder. "Just climb any heifer that's handy."

Cholla came over to the bed. "An old cow is a better description," he said. "She reminds me of what the cavalry says about a sorry-looking horse; she looks like she's been rode hard and put up wet."

He sat down on the bed.

"Get off my bed."

"Don't order me about, Sierra." His voice was cold. "I'm not Slim, to be whipped like a cur. You're my captive, remember? I give the orders now."

This is crazy, Sierra thought. She had escaped from her captor, but now he was back in control and no one around here was willing to stand up to him. Her heart sank. She wasn't safe after all. "I don't have to stay in this room. I'll go into the parlor and spend the night on the sofa." She got up, went to the door.

"You just do that, Dark Eyes," Cholla challenged. "Who knows which of those men will sneak into the parlor if they find out you're there?"

She paused uncertainly, her gown falling off her shoulder, her breasts revealed in the moonlight that now shone through the window. "If one of them tries anything, he'll have to answer to Belle and her quirt."

Cholla got up off the bed, came to the door, whirled her around. "Every man among 'em would figure five minutes between your thighs was worth being whipped half to death."

"Is it?" She hadn't meant to say that.

"To me, it is." Before she could say anything else, his mouth came down on hers, his hands went to her shoulders. She tried to pull away from him, angry that he had been in Belle's bed and was now wanting to use her to satisfy the lust the outlaw queen had built in him.

She managed to turn her face away. "No!"

But his mouth found hers again, his hands inside the torn gown now, thumbs stroking across her nipples. "I just whipped a man to keep him from touching you. When two stallions fight over a mare, the winner gets to mount her."

She tried to pull away, but he tangled his hand in her long hair, holding her face so she couldn't move away as his mouth ravaged hers. His body pressed against her, and she felt his heart pounding against her breast, his manhood, throbbing, hard, against her body.

He picked her up as they struggled, holding her easily as she fought him. She dared not scream, sure now that Belle wouldn't bother to come. He carried her to the bed, set her upon it and, with one hard yank, tore her nightdress away. "I've had you before, Sierra. Why are you resisting me now?"

I am trying to resist my own traitorous body, she thought as she pressed back against the headboard, watched him pull off his shirt, step out of his pants. She would not give him the satisfaction of letting him drive her so wild with desire that she would claw his back and whimper. Not when he had just come from another woman's bed.

She made a dive, trying to get off the bed. "Damn you! Let me go!"

In answer, he pushed her over onto her back, fell on top of her. "You want to play it this way? Want me to beg your forgiveness? Beg to be allowed the privilege?" he said against her lips. "I'm a man, Sierra. A *real* man. I don't beg, but I'll wager I can make you beg for it!"

"Damn you!" She tried to twist out of his hands, but his mouth was ravaging hers, sucking her tongue deep into his throat, and his hands were all over her. When she fought him, he caught both her small wrists in one big hand, brought her hands down to his manhood.

"This is what you want, Sierra. Tell me."

"No!"

"No, you won't tell me, or no, you don't want it?"

He was hot and throbbing under her fingers. She arched up against his lips, trying to remember what he had asked. "No . . ." she whispered again, "Don't . . . don't stop."

She was only vaguely aware that he had turned loose of her wrists and that she was pulling at him, wanting him between her thighs, digging her nails into his wide shoulders and lean hips.

"I won't stop," he whispered. "I'm going to brand every inch of you." He came into her with one hard, long stroke, his lips on hers, so that when she felt him ram deep, her cry went into his mouth and she didn't know whether it was a sound of pain or pleasure. She only knew that she couldn't let him go until she had reached whatever zenith of feeling her body was rising to. Nothing mattered but this sensation of him inside her, the ecstasy of her body locking onto his.

He was still in her as they both dropped off to sleep.

The next morning early, as they drank coffee at Belle's table, Cholla told the older woman they were going to leave.

Belle glared at Sierra. "You goin' with this Injun?"

Sierra considered the question. Not willingly, she thought. But if she stayed, she'd be in danger the first time Belle turned her back. Being Cholla's hostage was better than that. She thought about asking Belle for help in contacting the authorities, decided she would be wasting her time. Belle was a bandit. She wouldn't contact the law.

"Well?" Belle demanded.

"I . . . I think I'll go with him," Sierra stammered.

Belle gave her a black look. "Now if you ain't sure—"

"No, I'll go with him."

With a glum shake of her head, Belle stood up. "In that case, I'll have someone pack you some supplies, give you a couple of horses."

Sierra and Cholla looked at each other in surprise.

"Why not?" Belle shrugged. "I have a reputation for hospitality. Just don't tell anyone I did this, okay? If anyone asks where you got the stuff, say you found the horses or something like that?"

They nodded.

She went to the door, yelled. "Hey, Joe! Slim ever turn up?"

"No, he's hightailed it for someplace else, I reckon."

"This pair is leaving." Belle looked back over her shoulder at them. "Saddle up those two palominos and pack some grub."

"The palominos, boss? But—"

"No 'buts,' Joe; just do like I tell you."

Sierra could hardly believe her eyes when they went outside into the cold, crisp dawn. "These are two of the finest horses I've ever seen." She traced the Running B brand on the mare's rump, "They are worth a lot of money. I can't believe you'd be so generous."

Belle smiled thinly. "I can afford it, and Belle Starr

252

has a reputation in these parts for being generous."

Cholla gave her a grateful nod, then helped Sierra into the saddle and swung up onto the other horse. "Thanks, Belle."

For just a moment, Sierra thought she saw jealous rage cross Belle's face, and then it faded. Of course she could be mistaken about the woman. If Belle was angry about Cholla ending up in Sierra's bed, this was a strange way to show her displeasure.

Cholla said, "We don't know the country, Belle, which way is best?"

Belle hesitated, then pointed. "If you'll ride in that direction, you'll do just fine."

They thanked her again, turned the horses, and rode out.

Belle stood looking after them a long time, until they were only small dots on the far horizon.

Joe stood with her, scratched his head. "Belle, I don't understand you. The directions you gave them, they'll be damned lucky if they don't end up riding into Sundance, and that's one tough town."

"Ain't it, though!" She stared after the pair, still angered because the man she'd tried to seduce was interested only in the younger woman. "Joe," she said, "get over to Fort Smith. See if Judge Parker is looking for an Injun named Cholla or a woman named Sierra Forester. If so, let the law know which way they headed, just in case they don't ride into Sundance."

His weather-beaten face furrowed in surprise. "You turning them in?"

"Not if no one's looking for them." She felt tired, defeated, and betrayed. In spite of everything, her

253

own half-grown son hated her for her stern discipline with the quirt. Her daughter had gotten pregnant, and was even now at an aunt's home in Missouri, hiding and in disgrace. Belle didn't have to ask why the lock on that bedroom window of Pearl's was broken; probably Pearl had broken it herself so her lover could get in at night. Belle just hoped it hadn't been that worthless Slim.

"But, Belle, those horses," Joe said.

"What about them?" She glared in the direction the pair had ridden on the fine palominos. Joe was right; if they kept on in that same direction, they were going to end up near the edge of Sundance.

"You know what they'll do to that pair if they get caught with them horses from the Berrigan Ranch?"

Belle smiled and nodded. She would have her revenge on the virile brave who had dared spurn the Bandit Queen of the dime novels. "Sure, I know. But then, in the West they always lynch horse thieves!"

Chapter Thirteen

Sierra heaved a sigh of relief as she and Cholla rode away from Younger's Bend. Though she was still a hostage, she'd rather not risk staying at Belle Starr's place until she could get a message to the Army or the law. She'd take her chances with the Indian.

At least they had fresh clothes, two good horses, and supplies, including a saddle gun. Belle had given Sierra a buckskin-fringed outfit and a pair of soft, rawhide boots. Now they rode southwest through the cool autumn day.

Cholla glanced over at her. "With your hair in braids, you look like a local Indian. It should be easy for us to pass ourselves off as Cherokees, and it's probably safer."

"Suppose we run into some *real* Cherokees?" she challenged.

"Don't borrow trouble. We'll worry about that if it happens."

Now that they were safely away from the outlaw hideout, Sierra wondered if there was a settlement in the area and whether she could figure out a way to escape from Cholla if they found one.

They rode several miles. The sun was out, burning away the frost from the flaming red sumac and yellow-leafed cottonwood trees.

Cholla glanced abruptly toward a small rise. "Get down!"

"What?"

Before she could move or react, he dived for her knocking her off her horse. They both hit the dirt heavily as a rifle shot whined past them, echoing and reechoing.

She lay on the soft dirt, the breath knocked out of her, breathing heavily and looking up at him as he shielded her with his body. The horses whinnied and reared, galloped off. "What . . . what happened?"

He grabbed her by the collar, dragged her behind a rock as the rifle cracked again. Cholla swore softly under his breath. "I happened to look up, saw the reflection off the gun barrel. Someone's trying to kill us!"

Her heart pounded with apprehension. They were at a disadvantage since the carbine was in the rifle boot on Cholla's palomino. "Why—?"

"Shh." He held his finger to his lips for silence. "All we've got is my knife," he whispered. "If he decides to come after us, we've no chance against a rifle. I'm going to try crawling around behind him. In a few minutes, maybe after he fires again, you cry out or do something to hold his attention."

She grabbed his arm as he crept away. "Suppose you don't come back?"

He grinned at her. "Then you'll have to try to cut your own deal with the dry-gulcher. It shouldn't be hard . . . with that body." He crawled away.

Her mouth felt so dry, she couldn't swallow. Somewhere close beside her, a redheaded woodpecker beat a *rat-a-tat-tat* on a dead tree. Suppose the unseen assassin isn't a man, she thought, suddenly remembering the way Belle Starr had looked at her. Or maybe the sharpshooter wasn't after her at all; maybe he was part of a posse or an Army patrol looking for the Apache. If she stood up, threw up her hands and surrendered, warned them, would they get Cholla and free her? A shot cracked past her, splintering a nearby oak tree and sending a squirrel racing away, chattering indignantly.

Maybe she should just stay down and wait, see what would happen. No, she had to know if that was the Army or a posse.

She made her decision. "Don't shoot!" she shouted and gradually stood up, hands in the air. "Don't shoot! That last shot got him. I'm not armed!"

For a long moment she just stood there in the stillness, listening. At any second, she expected a bullet to take her life. Would she feel any pain? The silence was unbearable. "Don't shoot!" she screamed again. "I'm not armed!"

Very slowly, a man stuck his head out from behind a rock in the distance, his rifle barrel glinting in his hands. "No tricks now!"

She held her hands high, shook her head frantically. "No tricks! I'm keeping my hands where you can see them!"

He stood up, grinning, his rifle still trained on her. He was lean and broad-shouldered, and he had ice blue eyes. "Well, sweet thing, it seems we meet again."

Slim. Not again. Where was Cholla? It occurred to her that given the odds, the Apache might elect to steal Slim's horse and take off at a gallop. The palominos had probably run a short distance and stopped to graze.

Her mouth seemed frozen with fear, but she forced her lips to form a smile. "Well, hello, Slim, I was hoping to run across you again."

He waved the gun at her. "Come out where I can see you, gal. Is the Injun really dead?"

She saw Cholla loom up behind him, slash at him with the big knife.

Slim tried to scream, but the sound became a bubbling gurgle as scarlet blood splashed the front of his shirt.

When Slim fell, abruptly, Sierra's legs would support her no longer. She leaned against a boulder and shook all over as Cholla took Slim's rifle, then wiped his knife on the dead man's shirt and put it in his belt. He came through the brush to her. "Are you all right?"

"I . . . I . . ." She finally managed to nod. "I never saw a man get his throat cut before."

He looked almost sympathetic. "You've been through a lot of things you never experienced before you met me."

She stared at him. He wasn't a man; he was a cold, killing machine. How could she have felt drawn to him? "How many men have you killed?"

Cholla sighed. "Too many. If I could find some little corner of the world and live in peace without anyone trying to kill me or lock me up, I'd be glad not to ever have to do it again." He took her arm, gently stood her on her feet. "Let's see if we can catch the horses."

They caught Slim's bay and one of the palominos. Unfortunately, it was hers, not the one with the saddle gun, but now Cholla had Slim's fancy rifle. The palomino they caught had thrown a shoe.

She looked toward the dead man. "Aren't we going to bury him or something?"

Cholla shook his head as he put his big hands on her waist, helped her mount the palomino, and swung up on the bay himself.

"That other palomino will head back to his own barn. That may bring riders backtracking him to this place. Even Belle might not take kindly to my cutting Slim's throat. For all we know, she sent him out here to ambush us; I don't trust her. Let's clear out in case anyone shows up."

"What about this palomino's shoe?"

They started out at a walk.

"Maybe it'll be all right for a while, until we can find a blacksmith," Cholla said. "I just hope he doesn't come up lame." He looked at the rifle in his hands, whistled low. "This is fancy—cost a lot. I'm afraid to guess how Slim came by a rifle like this; looks almost one of a kind."

Sierra looked up at the sky. Late morning. She wondered what day of the week it was? What month even? Probably the middle of October or even later,

259

she thought, looking at the golden leaves swirling from the trees. They blew in small drifts and made dry, crackling sounds as the horses rode through them.

Within a couple of hours, the palomino came up lame. Cholla dismounted, examined the hoof, shook his head. "I was afraid of this; bruised the frog of its hoof in that headlong gallop when Slim spooked them."

"So now what?" She looked over at him as he swung back up in the saddle, the leather creaking beneath his big body. He fingered the rifle absently. It is unusual, Sierra thought, gazing at the fancy etched brass on the stock. But then gunslingers liked fine guns and spent a lot of money on the tools of their trade.

"I don't know. We'll keep riding to the southwest. Maybe we'll run across a ranch where we can trade horses, or even a blacksmith."

If we find some law-abiding people, I'll have a chance to escape, Sierra thought.

They rode the better part of an hour before Cholla's keen eyes noted a couple of wisps of smoke drifting on the horizon. He pointed them out. "Maybe a ranch, let's go."

She tried to act indifferent, though her heart was beating hard with excitement. At last they might run across some law-abiding people who would help her.

Finally they topped a rise and saw a small settlement below. It isn't much, Sierra thought with disappointment, a store or two, a few ragged cabins, maybe a livery stable. There were a surprising number of people on the streets, a few horses tied up at

260

hitching rails, a couple of buggies and wagons.

"Sierra," he said, "you behave yourself when we ride in there."

"I don't know what you mean."

He reached over, caught her arm, turned her to look at him. "Yes, you do." His voice was low and cold. "I don't want to have to kill anyone, but I will if you give out any signals that might cause me trouble. As far as these people are concerned, we're Cherokees just passing through. With your hair braided and that buckskin outfit you've got on, you could pass for an Indian."

They rode in, Sierra trying to decide what to do next. She knew Cholla was good with a rifle. He hadn't survived this long without being able to protect himself. If he was cornered, she didn't doubt that he might try to shoot his way out. Innocent people would be killed, and it would be her fault. She'd have to think of a plan.

Cholla looked up and down the street, ignoring the barking dogs and curious stares. "Let's go in this general store and see what they can tell us about a blacksmith."

If she could get out of his sight, she'd ask for help. "Why don't you go in? I'll watch the horses."

He grinned at her, then shook his head. "Me no stupid Injun. Come, squaw. You come in too, not talk to strangers."

Reluctantly, she dismounted. They tied their horses to the hitching rail and went in, Cholla carrying the fancy rifle.

A fat man with three chins stood behind the

counter, thumbs tucked in his dirty white apron. They waited for him to finish weighing and bagging some nails for a cowboy, who gave the pair a long look as he went out.

Sierra said, "Does the cowboy know how much of your thumb he just paid for?"

The fat man turned an ugly red, and his three chins quivered. "I ain't used to smart talk from blanket butts like you, Injun gal. My scales are honest."

Cholla grabbed her arm, glared at her. "Is there a blacksmith in town?"

The storekeeper's small eyes seemed fascinated by the rifle. "Usually there is, but he's gone out to shoe old man Berrigan's cow ponies."

Sierra and Cholla exchanged glances, and she managed to keep from smiling at her piece of luck. The longer they had to stay in town, the better her chances were of sneaking a message to someone without Cholla knowing about it.

"Injun, you want to trade that rifle?"

Cholla shook his head. "We'll just be going on then."

"Mighty fine rifle for an Injun," the storekeeper rocked back on his heels. "I'd give you heap firewater, candy, and ribbons for your squaw for it."

Cholla shook his head again, fell into the pidgin English. "Me no want sell. Come, squaw."

But as he started to turn, the fat man reached out and caught Sierra's arm. "Then how about another little trade? I'd give you a heap of stuff to take your woman in the back room for a few minutes."

"You load of guts," Cholla snarled, "get your hands off her!"

The fat man blinked and slowly removed his hand. "I ain't used to being talked to like that by an Injun."

"This Indian Territory," Cholla said. "What's white man doing here anyway?"

"I'm married to a squaw, just like most of the white men around here. That gives us some land rights." He glared at Cholla. "I'm an important man, Injun. I wouldn't cross John Koger if I was you."

Cholla stood his ground. "Don't want any trouble. I just want to find blacksmith."

The storekeeper leaned on the counter, looked at Sierra with hungry eyes. "Why don't you let the squaw make up her own mind? Hey, you." He made obscene gestures to Sierra. "Little of your time. I give you pretty cloth, ribbons, beads."

Cholla leaned across the counter, grabbed the fat man so hard he tore his shirt. "Maybe you no hear good, white man. Squaw mine. Nobody touches but me!"

For once, Sierra kept silent and began to retreat behind Cholla's big frame. She'd find someone else in this settlement to help her.

As they turned to leave, another cowboy entered. "Say, Koger, who's ridin' that palomino tied to the rail?"

Cholla glared at the man. "Who wants to know?"

The man appeared to back away. "The boys is talkin' out front. Where'd you get that horse, Injun?"

It occurred to Sierra that Belle hadn't given them

263

any papers. Maybe they wouldn't challenge a woman. "It's my horse," she said.

Now it was the cowboy's turn to look her over, to take in the rifle Cholla carried. "Koger, ain't that Lem Jenks's fancy rifle?"

Koger rocked back on his heels. "I just asked him about that?"

"I bought gun," Cholla said.

The two white men looked at him with renewed interest, veiled hostility.

What next? Sierra thought. What kind of settlement had they ridden into? She was beginning to have terrible feelings about all these questions.

The cowboy cleared his throat, looked away. "Well, I suppose that's all the questions I needed to ask. Be seein' ya, Koger."

He turned and went out. Sierra breathed a sigh of relief, but Cholla's scowl remained. He caught Sierra's elbow. "Squaw, we go."

He propelled her outside and right into the bunch of armed men waiting for them, along with the man who had been in the store earlier. "Get your hands up, Injun!"

Cholla looked as if he might fight, but he seemed to realize there were women and children around who might get hurt. While he hesitated, the cowboy jerked the gun from his hand and someone else took the knife out of his belt. The men then overpowered him, twisted his arms behind him, and bound his wrists. When he still struggled, the cowboy hit him across the temple with the barrel of his revolver, and Cholla fell unconscious.

Sierra didn't look at him. She must think about herself. After all, he was a fugitive. "Thanks!" she said. "This man kidnapped me weeks ago, and I've been forced to travel with him ever since!"

The expressions on the men's faces showed doubt. The fat man came out of the store behind them. "A likely story! Don't pay her no nevermind, boys. That squaw is just tryin' to slip out of trouble her own self."

"No." Sierra shook her head, "No, it's true. If you don't believe me, contact the Army; see if they aren't looking for an escaped Apache and a kidnapped woman named Sierra Forester. There's a reward."

The men looked skeptical, but the last word put a gleam in a few eyes.

Koger kicked at Cholla. "That right, Injun? Is she your squaw, or did you kidnap her?"

Cholla's eyes flickered open. He glared around the circle, looked up into Sierra's eyes and said nothing.

Damn him anyway. Sierra tried again. "Look, someone telegraph the Army. You've got a telegraph at the train station, don't you? You can all divide the reward."

Koger grabbed her arm. "Squaw, I think you're just trying to wriggle out of this. If we turn our backs, you'll be hightailing it out of town."

"Besides," one of the others said, "she says that's her palomino. Ain't that a Running B brand on it?"

Sierra looked from one to the other. "That stands for 'Belle.' Belle Starr gave it to me."

Someone in the gathering crowd guffawed. "We like Belle around here, gal. And we don't like it when someone's always tryin' to blame her for somethin'."

265

Koger scratched his fat belly. "Sam, you go telegraph. See what you can find out about this pair. Jack, I think somebody better ride out to the Berrigan place, see if they've had any palominos go missing."

Someone in the crowd said, "Mayor Koger, shouldn't we be sending to Fort Smith to find out what we should do with this pair?"

"Parker's court only deals with white folks that he sends U.S. Deputy Marshals in to get, and I'd bet my mama's Bible that these is Injuns," Koger answered.

Another man pushed his hat back thoughtfully. "Injuns is supposed to deal with Injuns. Ain't we supposed to call in the Injun police and let them handle this?"

"I think not, if they ain't local Injuns." Koger tucked his thumbs in his apron again, puffed up with his own importance. "What we'll do is put chains on them, lock them up in my storeroom until we find out just what we are supposed to do."

The cowboy shook his head. "It's Saturday, Mayor."

"So?"

"So there'll be a big crowd in town this evening. When the men get to drinkin,' there could be some real trouble."

"Aw, we'll see about that," Koger scoffed. Then he winked at Sierra. "Besides, as mayor, if we was to have a lynchin', it would just save the taxpayers, and maybe the Army or Hanging Judge Parker, a lot of trouble."

This talk scared Sierra. "Look," she said, "if someone knows this Lem Jenks, why doesn't someone go

266

get him? If he'll tell how he sold that fancy rifle to . . . Never mind."

She stopped in midsentence, suddenly aware that even if she got the man to swear he sold the rifle to Slim, they might have to explain what had happened to the gunslinger, and for all she knew, the blue-eyed desperado might be related to Koger or someone else in town.

Koger nodded, and his three chins shook. "A couple of you boys ride out to Lem's place. See what you can find out."

"But, Mayor, it's a long ride," someone in the crowd protested.

"Wal, we got lots of time." The mayor smiled and rocked back on his heels. "Not much excitin' happens hereabouts, we can stretch this out and make it last. When we get all the facts, we'll do something."

Sierra looked at Cholla lying on the ground. He was beginning to come around. She forced herself not to feel sorry for him. "You can't take the law into your own hands," she argued. "You'd better call in the Army or the marshal."

Koger kicked the Apache in the belly. "Some of you drag this bastard over to my storeroom, Squaw, you come along, too, until we get this all sorted out about how you two come to have this horse and rifle."

Sierra was mad, but she was also scared. There weren't many women around, only a couple who'd poked their heads out of a nearby cabin that might be a bordello or a saloon. She didn't think anyone was allowed to sell whiskey to Indians, but the settlement of Sundance looked like one of those isolated places where everyone winked at the law. No doubt strangers seldom came here, and no one asked nosy questions.

Cholla fought the men as they dragged him toward the general store, which only annoyed them, Sierra noted. With Koger's fat fingers digging into her arm, there wasn't anything she could do but go with them.

The men dragged Cholla through the store, into the storage room, and chained him to an iron anvil in the middle of the floor. It was a large room, and the short chain made it impossible for Cholla to reach any of the four walls.

Koger grinned as he held on to Sierra's arm. "Okay, boys, everyone out. We'll let you know what we find out this evening or tomorrow morning."

There was some grumbling. "Aw, Mayor, we was hopin' to have a little court trial, you know, maybe even get to hang him our ownselves."

Sierra felt fear as she looked around. These hard cases weren't joking. But the way they were looking at her scared her even more.

"Hey, Mayor, what are you gonna do with the squaw?"

He laughed. "I got me some ideas."

"Sadie's place could use a new gal," one of the men piped up. "Those two or three old whores ain't enough for all of us on a Saturday night—"

"No!" Cholla charged them, and when he hit the end of the chain, it rattled as it cut into his wrists. "No, don't any of you touch her!"

The men all laughed and backed out of his reach. The mayor didn't let go of Sierra's arm. He looked at the crowd of gawkers. "Hey, fellas, why don't you all go have a drink? It's gonna be a long time before we know anything about this pair."

"Aw, Mayor, we might miss something."

"The drinks are on me," the mayor said.

Immediately the crowd headed out the door. That left the three of them in the store room. Sierra was scared now. She could tell by his eyes that Koger didn't believe her. "Hey, gal," he said softly, "you wanta end up in our local whorehouse?"

Cholla hit the end of the chain, and it rattled and rang but was too heavy to break. "Get your fat, dirty hand off her arm."

"All right." Koger took his hand off her arm, then leered as Sierra heaved a sigh of relief. "That's not what I want to handle anyway."

Before Sierra could react, the fat man grabbed her, pulling her to him, running his hands up and down her body, pawing her breasts.

"You pig!" Sierra went at him with all her strength, clawing his face with her fingernails.

He turned loose of her, and she ran into Cholla's protective embrace.

The Apache glowered at Koger as he drew her trembling body close. "If I get a chance, you fat bastard, I'm gonna kill you for touching her. She was telling you the truth out there. Her name is Sierra Forester, and I kidnapped her near Saint Louis. When the Army hears from you, they'll come quick. They're looking for me."

The fat man stuck his thumbs in his grimy apron, stayed just out of Cholla's reach. "You're just like a mad dog on a chain, Injun. On a Saturday night

269

with whiskey flowing, it wouldn't take much to get this pack of 'breeds, renegades, and outlaws to have a lynching just for the fun of it. And this little gal might just disappear into Sadie's Place, but nobody would say anything about any of it outside this settlement."

Sierra blanched. "You can't do that."

"Can't I? I'm the mayor, and I got the support of some of the more important 'breeds and white men who've married Injun women. I pretty much do as I damned well please." He looked Sierra up and down in a way that made her shiver. "They might even decide to lynch you, gal, if they get enough whiskey in them."

"No." Cholla shook his head. "I tell you, I'm the one the law's looking for. Let her go!"

Koger looked Sierra up and down again. "I'm getting tired of the squaw I got. If'n you was interested, gal, and looking for a new man, I might be able to keep the men from lynching you or puttin' you over at Sadie's place."

She glared at him and shuddered. "I'd rather bed a pig."

His face turned an angry red. "Gal, you may not be so pert later tonight when that crowd gets a little whiskey in them. This fat man may begin to look good to you when the boys get out of hand. If you change your mind, just yell."

Sierra spat at him from the safety of Cholla's arms.

"Gal, you shouldn't have done that," the storekeeper said very slowly. "I'll remember that."

He turned and went out. She listened, heard him

lock the door from the outside. Then she looked up at Cholla. "It looks like we're both in trouble now."

"If that fat pig tries anything with you, he'll never mount another woman."

His arms seemed a haven of security and safety to her, even though he was unarmed and chained. She laid her cheek against his big chest and reminded herself that he had brought all this trouble on her. If she were back in St. Louis, where she belonged, she wouldn't be facing a lynching, or becoming a whore at Sadie's or, worse yet, the mistress of a fat, dirty pig of a man. When she pictured what Koger must look like naked, she winced, mentally comparing his form to the Apache's muscular, brown body.

"I . . . I'm sorry I got you into this," he said against her hair. "I'll try again later to convince them you're just an innocent hostage. If they'll wait to hear from the law or the Army—"

"What about Belle?"

Cholla cursed and let go of her, sat down on the anvil. "That old bitch! Probably those horses were stolen. Who will believe she gave them to us?"

She slumped to the floor next to him, leaned against his knee. "The whites have a saying; 'hell hath no fury like a woman scorned.' "

"Which means?" His hand absently stroked her hair.

"It means our bandit queen wanted you in her bed, and she doesn't like being upstaged by a younger woman." She thought a long moment and came up with another chilling thought. "Cholla . . . about the fancy rifle."

271

"What about it?" he asked absently as he stroked her hair, his mind obviously working on a solution to their problems.

"Suppose Slim stole that rifle or killed someone to get it?"

He sighed audibly, his chains rattling as he rubbed the back of his neck. "By Usen, you're right. An *hombre* like Slim doesn't pay for something like that."

"And if we tell them about Slim, he may be a local and they'll get us for killing him."

"Can't win for losing," Cholla said. "Maybe if I take all the blame, they'll listen to reason when I explain your situation again."

"Did you see that look in Koger's eyes?" She looked up at him. "All that swine can think of is getting me down on my back. He isn't going to listen to anyone. But thanks, anyway."

She noted his wrists were raw from fighting against the chains in his attempts to protect her. Somehow it was hard to hate him anymore. She was beginning to know him too well. Even though he had kept her hostage and dragged her with him all over the country, she had come to think of him as a man, not just an Indian. Maybe his people had killed Robert, but she couldn't hold Cholla responsible for that, could she? After all, he had been an Army scout. She was tempted to ask him if he had been at the arroyo when Robert was killed, then decided not to. The cavalry was large, the odds were against it. Besides, though she wouldn't admit it even to herself, she was afraid he might tell her some things about Robert she didn't really want to know, for deep in her heart she suspected her husband wasn't the hero the commendation made him out to be.

The day dragged on into dusk. There was a small window in the storeroom, and Cholla held Sierra up so she could see outside. What she saw made her apprehensive.

"Well?" Cholla asked.

"There're many men on the street, lots of noise and activity from over at Sadie's place. The men are standing around in groups, talking, and they keep looking toward the store."

"Doesn't sound very good," Cholla grumbled, setting her down.

She stood looking up at him, feeling his hands on her small waist. A sense of electricity seemed to pass between them, and she swayed toward him. For a split second, she thought he would bend his head and kiss her. Then she pulled away.

Outside, there seemed to be some commotion.

"Let me look again," Sierra said.

He lifted her easily.

There's a bunch of men riding into town, several of them mounted on fine palominos. Those cowboys look mad."

"Wonder if it's the Running B outfit? I should have known those horses were stolen." He set her on her feet.

"What do you suppose they'll do?" Sierra sat on the floor, leaned her head on her knees.

"Depends on how much they drink, what happens

273

when they track the owner of that fancy rifle down, and whether the Army or a U.S. Deputy Marshal gets here in time."

She looked up at him, alarmed. "You don't really think they'd lynch us, do you?"

"Not you—me." He paced the length of his short chain, and it rattled against the floor. "Of course what that fat pig has planned for you, you might prefer to be lynched. I wish I could get a message to Lieutenant Gillen. He was a friend of your husband's, he'd try to help you . . . I think."

She looked up at him not quite sure what emotion she felt. "How do you know that?"

She saw a look cross his rugged face, a look that said he had revealed more than he'd meant to; then it was hidden behind the stoic eyes. "I . . . I knew your husband."

Would he tell her? It seemed important somehow that she find out Robert wasn't what she had perceived him to be. "Cholla. I have to find out. I didn't know Robert very long before we married, and a woman always wants to know later what others thought of her husband. Was he brave and well liked?"

"Of course," the Apache said, but he didn't look at her. "All the men thought well of the lieutenant, expected him to be promoted to captain because of his bravery, but then he was killed in action."

He wasn't telling her everything he knew, but she wasn't sure she wanted to press him further. If he was lying about her husband, did she really want to know the truth? "Thank you for that," she said softly.

He half reached out to her as if to touch her face, seemed to think better of it, sat down on the anvil with a sigh. "I'm sorry it came to this, Sierra."

"It's okay. I was beginning to hope you'd make it all the way back. In spite of everything, people can't help pulling for an underdog. I had even finally decided to help you. When you left me at the fort . . . well, I wasn't sure what I'd do then, but I wouldn't be any worse off at Fort Bowie than I was back home."

"Don't you have anyone anywhere?"

She shook her head. "Robert had family at Austin, Texas. He said they have money and social position. I'd thought they might welcome a dead son's widow, even if he had been a black sheep as I suspect he was."

"You don't know that for sure."

"It's kind of you to try to make me think well of him." Sierra smiled ruefully. "I don't really quite understand you, Cholla."

"Sometimes I don't understand myself." He sounded angry and annoyed as he stood up, the chains rattling. She wondered then what he was thinking.

It had grown dark outside, but there was a full moon on this crisp autumn night and its glow shone through the tiny window. No one bothered to bring them any food, but there was a bucket of water and a dipper in the room.

Outside, the noise increased as men came to town for a Saturday night of drinking and gambling—or maybe riders had carried word out to outlying ranches and settlements about what was going on in

Sundance and the curious had ridden into town. There isn't much entertainment around here, Sierra thought, so the prospect of a necktie party might sound interesting.

Hours passed, and the rowdy crowd seemed to be growing, or to be getting drunker and noisier when Cholla held Sierra up to the window again so she could see out.

This time, he lowered her slowly, letting her body slide down the length of his. He didn't let go of her but held her tightly against him.

Without meaning to, she pressed her face against his chest. "I'm scared."

"I know." He slipped his arms around her shoulders and held her as if she were a frightened child. "If they come after me, Sierra, I'll try to create a ruckus, a big fight. Maybe, with the commotion you can get away."

"That won't do you any good."

"I never expected to come out of this alive, but I want to die with dignity. A rope around the neck is no death for a warrior. If you do manage to escape, contact my friend at Fort Bowie, Sergeant Tom Mooney. We've saved each other's lives a couple of times. He's almost a *sikis*, a brother to me. He'll help you."

They heard the rattle of a key in the lock, and then Koger stuck his fat face in the door. The smell of him and the ruddy color of his face as he peered in, holding a coal-oil lamp, told them he had been drinking as much as the others. "I got someone here who wants to see you."

276

The other man came in, staying carefully out of Cholla's reach. Sierra immediately recognized the lieutenant as the man she had seen near the East St. Louis bridge.

She glanced up, saw the hatred and bitter anger on Cholla's face. "So, Gillen, you finally caught up with me."

Chapter Fourteen

Sierra looked from one to the other.

The officer smiled and pulled out a paper bag, popped a peppermint in his mouth, crunched it noisily. "Well, Cholla, I understand you may be lynched later tonight. It couldn't happen to a more deserving Injun." He looked curiously at Sierra.

"I'm Mrs. Robert Forester," she said, going over to him.

He took off his hat, made a courtly bow. "Mrs. Forester. Forgive me for not recognizing you, but with you dressed as an Injun—"

"Just get her out of here," Cholla snarled, "before that mob gets any more liquor in them."

She was safe. At long last, she was safe. She heaved a sigh of relief. "Oh, Lieutenant, I'm so glad you came."

He offered her his arm, and she took it. "Ma'am, let's go somewhere where we can talk, out of the earshot of this . . . this . . ." He seemed to realize he was in the presence of a lady. "Forgive me, Mrs. Forester, we've been so worried about you. After all, your husband was my dearest friend."

He escorted her out of the storeroom, and the fat man padlocked the door again. The officer turned to Koger. "Is there somewhere the lady and I can converse privately?"

The storekeeper seemed dumbfounded. He scratched his triple chin and nodded. "My cabin, right behind the store. Honest, Lieutenant, we didn't know she was white. She looks purty Injun with that dark skin and her hair done up in braids. I'll see there's food and stuff."

He hustled out the back way. Sierra smiled at Gillen. "Merciful heavens, I'm so glad you got here, Lieutenant."

"There, there." Gillen patted the arm that was linked through his. "Blast it all! I know this whole ordeal has been a terrible nightmare for you. And that drunken crowd out there is getting uncontrollable."

A bottle smashed against the front of the store, as if to confirm the mob's mood.

They walked out the back door to the cabin. "Lieutenant Gillen, you're an answer to my prayers. I'm so glad you and your men have arrived in time to save us."

"*Us?* Dear lady, I came to rescue *you*." He fumbled in his jacket for the little sack of hard candy, offered her some. Sierra shook her head, but he crunched a lemon drop with relish. "Mrs. Forester, I only have one other man with me, and Corporal Finney's over at the railroad station. As time passed and the trail grew cold, the others were called back to duty. I'm not at all sure the two of us can do anything about

279

that mob if they decide they want to hang that blood-thirsty savage."

They paused in the door of the cabin. Sierra looked at him, unbelieving. "Does that mean you don't even intend to try?"

He seemed to be weighing his words; then he patted her arm again in a condescending manner. "I realize you are exhausted and maybe a little hysterical. Any woman would be under these circumstances—"

"I am not hysterical."

He was beginning to sound just like Robert. It dawned on her suddenly that in the past few weeks she had changed. No longer was she afraid to stand up for herself. Was it her mother's blood, or had the Apache's attitude rubbed off on her?

She could tell by his suddenly pursed mouth that the lieutenant was displeased and not quite sure how to proceed. "Mrs. Forester—Sierra—why don't we eat a bite and talk? I intend to get you on a train as soon as possible."

Out in the street, the noise seemed to be increasing. The sounds of men laughing, of bottles breaking, drifted back to the cabin. Was Cholla in any real danger? Did she give a damn? My! She had changed. The prim trodden-on Mrs. Robert Forester would never have cursed.

They went inside, and Koger's squaw hurried about, fixing them food. Then she slipped out a side door, and Koger decided to go back to the store. "That crowd's getting out of hand," he complained. "I don't want them to break my windows or destroy anything."

Sierra excused herself, went into the back room. She washed her face and unbraided her hair before she came back to the table.

"Well, now." The officer smiled, evidently interested in her. "I hadn't realized you were so pretty, ma'am. Robert had said . . ."

His voice trailed off in confusion, and she knew that whatever her husband had said, it wasn't complimentary.

"I think even poor Robert would have to admit I've changed a lot, if he were alive. Nothing improves a woman's appearance like self-confidence." She began to eat. The meat and bread were hot and delicious, and she wondered suddenly if anyone had taken a plate to the Apache. Why the hell should she care? For kidnapping her, he deserved whatever he suffered.

"Somehow, Mrs. Forester"—Gillen smiled as he ate—"I expected to find you a total wreck after what that savage must have put you through."

His voice trailed off again, and it occurred to her that he was curious as to whether Cholla had slept with her. She decided to appear totally ignorant of that. "I'm not sure I know what you mean, Lieutenant."

"Well, yes, of course." He cleared his throat in confusion and went on eating.

"I understand there's a reward on the Apache's head. Don't you need to protect the scout from that mob."

"The reward will be paid whether he's dead or alive," Gillen said pointedly. "You know, he's wanted

281

for murdering that banker in East Saint Louis."

She paused, her fork in midair. "What banker?"

"Why, the one who held the mortgage on your farm, dear lady. Otto Toombs was found stabbed with a letter opener."

Sierra shuddered at the thought, but shook her head. "The scout's innocent of that. He's been with me ever since he abducted me."

Gillen almost glared at her. "Would you swear to that in court?"

"I certainly would! I want to see the Apache get what's coming to him, but I also believe in justice. Cholla and I both saw Otto alive the day he came to the farm to foreclose." Gillen was trying to hang this murder on Cholla, and she wondered why. She looked straight at him. "Are you afraid of the scout for any reason, Lieutenant Gillen?"

His face flushed. "Of course not."

"I can see that you might be." She smiled a little too sweetly as she drank her coffee. "I understand you had him chained and were beating him half to death when he managed to overpower you and get off that train."

He looked furious and seemed to be fighting for control of his temper. "You are baiting me, Mrs. Forester, and I do not understand why. I am here to rescue you, and after all, I was your husband's friend."

"Were you there when Robert died?" She was a little angry at herself. He had come to save her, and now she felt driven to annoy him.

"I don't know what that savage told you about that day at the arroyo or what happened—"

"The Apache was on that patrol with Robert?"

"He didn't tell you?" Now it was Gillen's turn to be glib. "Cholla was Robert's scout. Somehow the patrol ended up riding into an ambush. When my patrol heard the noise and came as fast as we could, there were five of them left alive, Cholla, that Sergeant Mooney, Corporal Schultz, and two others. I got there just as they were burying poor Robert."

An uneasy doubt gnawed at Sierra's mind. "They seemed to have been in an awful hurry to get him under ground. Wouldn't it have been more likely that they would have taken the body back to the fort cemetery?"

He hesitated and finally said, "Mrs. Forester, Robert was my friend, and I would like to be yours."

"There's something you're not telling me." She put down her cup, stared at him. "Lieutenant, what actually happened out there that day?"

"I wish to hell I knew!" He slammed down his fork, stood up, his chair going over backward with a clatter. Then he turned away for a long moment. "What I can't figure out is why they would all lie and make him out to be a hero when they all hated him so much!"

She felt shattered. Was it because she was finding out what she had feared to be the truth about Robert, or because the Apache had lied to her? And if he had, why?

Outside the drunken shouting had increased. On a nearby shelf, a clock ticked. It was after eleven, late for such noise in a small town, even on a Saturday night.

She licked dry lips. "Are you . . . are you telling me that Robert didn't deserve those medals, that he was a coward?"

"I didn't say that."

"You hinted at it!" She stood, her voice rising in anger.

"Mrs. Forester"—he used that soothing tone again—"I realize you're tired and distraught—"

"Damn it, Lieutenant, don't patronize me! I am tired of being treated in such a condescending fashion by the men in my world! *Every* woman is tired of it!"

He turned livid as he popped a piece of candy in his mouth, crunched it hard. "Very well. I've been trying to treat you like a lady, but I find you aren't one. Small wonder, considering you've survived all these weeks with that savage. I presume you let him do anything he wanted with you rather than kill yourself to keep from being disgraced."

She must not lose her temper with him. He had information that, for her own peace of mind, she needed. She would try a different tack. "Lieutenant Gillen," she said softly and went over to put her hand on his arm, "forgive me. As you said, I have been under a lot of stress. I am completely alone in the world, with no man to protect me." She pressed herself against his arm. "Since you were my husband's friend, perhaps I could count on you?"

He looked at her a long moment, visibly stirred by her proximity. "Robert was wrong about you," he whispered. "Maybe he was just the wrong man."

"And maybe you're the *right* one?" She almost cooed

as she looked up at him, and then she reached up and kissed him.

She felt his sudden movement of surprise, and then he grabbed her, pulled her up against him, and kissed her with abandon. "Robert was a fool," he muttered, and his mouth ravaged hers. "A fool . . ."

She forced herself not to pull back from his wet mouth that still tasted of peppermint. "Was he a coward as well?"

"I don't know," he answered almost absently as if he couldn't remember. He held her tightly now, his manhood hard and throbbing against her. "He had to be, I guess. Running from the enemy when he was killed . . ."

Of course she had suspected that all along, but how did Gillen know Robert had turned to flee the battle? She let him fumble with the top of her dress, let his hand close over a breast. *He does this so clumsily,* she thought with distaste, and was surprised to realize her thoughts were on the big Apache, on his skillful, supple hands and muscular body.

"Lieutenant, what was that patrol doing in the arroyo that day?"

He kissed her eyelids, wetly, as his hands fumbled with her breasts. "Don't know . . . guess Robert thought there was gold there. . . . The Injun warned him it was hostile territory."

Gold. Of course Robert would be looking for gold. Wasn't that why he had married her? For the very first time, she faced the truth. But there were other mysteries she wanted answers to. Why would Cholla and the troopers lie, make Robert appear heroic, when they hated him? To *coverup* something. Of course this was some kind of cover-up. But of what?

Gillen held her tightly, rubbing himself against her. "You hot little chit. There's a bed back there."

The thought made her gag. She wondered if he took a sack of candy to bed? Maybe she was opening up a Pandora's box, but she suspected there was something else he hadn't told her. "Of course," she murmured. "Sure."

She let him lead her to the back, sat on the edge of the bed and watched him peel his clothes off. He wasn't built nearly as well as Cholla.

He looked down at her. "Aren't you going to get undressed?"

Sierra looked around. There was an empty oil lamp on the bedside table. A big, heavy lamp. She gave Gillen her most provocative smile. "I thought you might enjoy undressing me, Gill."

"Blast it all! Lady, your husband was sure wrong about you!" He flopped down on the bed, reached for her.

She leaned over and kissed him teasingly. There was bound to be more to all this than she knew, and she felt she would never rest until she found out. She told herself it was because it had to do with her opinion of Robert, but it dawned on her abruptly that it had more to do with what she thought about Cholla and about why he might have lied to her. "Gill, why did you and Robert hate the scout so?"

"Don't want to talk about him, or that Apache girl." He had his hot, sweaty hands on her thighs, was pushing her dress up.

286

She felt a chill go down her back. "Tell me about her."

He was too busy trying to get Sierra's dress open. "We didn't mean to," he muttered. "We was drunk, and Delzhinne fought us. We only meant to enjoy her a little."

Even though she didn't want to, Sierra suddenly pictured the scene: the Indian girl fighting them off as they raped her. Her own husband. Her heroic husband.

She reached quietly for the empty lamp as Gill pawed at her, as his wet mouth nuzzled her neck. She brought the lamp crashing down on Gill's head.

Had she killed him? Her heart seemed to be pounding in her throat. No, he was breathing, lying sprawled across the bed. She shuddered at the memory of his wet mouth and of his sweaty hands on her thighs. Then she slid out from under him and stood up. Now what?

She tiptoed softly out the door and into the cold night. A pair of horses was tied up near the back door of the store, Gillen's most likely and the one he had thoughtfully brought for her to ride to the train station. She saw the glare of torches out front, smelled smoke. The mob roaming the street looked very drunk and rowdy. In fact, as Sierra untied one of the horses she wondered if they might not torch the store and half the buildings once they got started, just for the fun of watching them burn.

A rider galloped down the main street as she swung up into the saddle. "Hey!" he shouted. "They found Lem Jenks! That Injun killed him to get his rifle, all right!"

"Lynch him!" the mob roared. "Let's lynch that Injun!"

Sierra hesitated, listening.

"Now boys!" She recognized Koger's voice. "Be careful with those torches now. You wait out here, and I'll bring him out! No use damaging my place!"

"Get him out here, Mayor, or by God, we'll burn it down!"

The crowd roared their approval.

Sierra paused. They were going to hang Cholla. Well, he deserved it after what he had put her through. Koger would be headed in there now to drag him out. Then he'd be strung up from the nearest tree with no more dignity than a stray dog was killed. Even an enemy deserved better than that. Something else. Gillen's revelations had raised more questions than they'd answered. He hadn't been there the moment Robert had died. Cholla had. If Cholla was hanged, some questions would be forever unanswered. That is the only reason I am doing what I'm doing, Sierra told herself as she tied the horse, ran in the back door of the store.

Koger had just unlocked the door to the storeroom. He was halfway in as Sierra came up to him. "What do you want, gal?"

She caught his fat hand and smiled at him in the moonlight. "The lieutenant had to go on. I decided I liked you . . . if you still need a woman."

He shook his head. "I got no time for you now, maybe later. We got to hang this Injun." He jerked his head toward Cholla who was standing quietly in the background.

"But maybe afterward?" She leaned into his embrace, unbalancing him a little.

He took a step backward, scratched his head. "Gal, if you don't beat all."

She pressed up against him. "After you hang the Injun, I got ways to reward you for keeping the others away."

"I'll just bet you do." His small eyes gleamed in the moonlight, and he took another step backward as she pressed against him, completely oblivious to the silent man in chains behind him.

If she had calculated the length of Cholla's chain just right . . . Sierra went into the fat man's embrace pushing him another couple of inches backward.

By now, all Koger seemed to be thinking of was the woman in his arms. She was rubbing herself against him like a bitch in heat.

It was just close enough. There was only the slightest clink of metal as Cholla moved fast as a rattlesnake. He grabbed the fat man from behind, clapping a hand over Koger's mouth. Keys flew from a pudgy hand, landing over near the door. The fat man struggled, but he was no match for the Apache. With one mighty jerk, the scout threw Koger across his knee, broke his back; and dropped him on the floor. "Sierra, the key! Get the key!"

She stood there just out of Cholla's reach, saw him pulling against the chain, knew the keys were just a few inches too far away for him to grasp.

Out front, she heard a man shout, "Koger, damn

it! Don't get to thinking about law and order! Come out with that Injun or we'll burn the place down with both of you in it!"

Cholla stood there looking at her. He didn't beg or threaten. He just looked. "Sierra?"

If she didn't save him from the mob, she would never have all the answers she needed for her own peace of mind. Something too terrible to discuss, something secret, had occurred out in the lonely desert on that hot July day. If the two officers had raped and killed the girl he loved, could Cholla have used the ambush to his own advantage? *Murder.* Had Cholla . . . ? Could Sierra have let her own husband's killer make love to her? She wanted to know if Cholla really cared for her or he'd only been extracting a bitter vengeance. If he died at the hands of this mob, she would never get the answers to the questions that plagued her.

She picked up the keys, but her hands were shaking so badly Cholla had to take them from her and unlock the chains. He grabbed her arm, half led, half dragged her out the back door into the night. "Where's Gill?"

"I struck him on the head with a lamp. There're two horses out back!"

Even in the moonlight, she saw the gleam of white teeth. "By Usen, you do surprise me! I apologize for ever calling you a mouse."

Too late they noted there were no guns on the saddles, but it was too risky to go back. They mounted up and rode out quietly to avoid being noticed. When they reached a rise, they paused and looked back. The store was in flames.

Cholla said, "That'll give us a couple of hours. By the time the mob waits for the fire to cool and then discovers there's only one body in it, we can be miles away. Thanks for coming back to help me."

She forced herself to smile at him. "I couldn't let them murder you," she said. "I'll help you get as far as Fort Bowie, if we can make it that far. After that, you're on your own, all right?"

"It's a bargain."

They turned their horses and galloped away toward the southwest. Later, when the time was right, she would try to get answers. Right now more than the cold air chilled her. Had she just saved the life of her husband's killer? And had Robert and Gillen really raped and murdered the Apache's woman? If not, why had he and the other men on the patrol lied about what had happened out there to make Robert look good? Were they trying to protect Robert . . . or someone else?

She couldn't bring herself to question him as they rode on for the next several days. They slept in a barn one night, took some horse blankets from there to use as coverings for the next few days. They didn't have any weapons, not even Cholla's knife, but he managed to make a snare from wild grapevines and caught a rabbit. Sierra knew he lied when he told her he wasn't very hungry and insisted she eat the major part of it.

Several times as they rode south, she looked over

and caught him staring at her. She wished she knew what he was thinking. Once he said, "You could have gotten away without me. Why did you come back?"

She hesitated, not quite sure herself. "I owed you one," she murmured. "After all, you saved me from the moonshiners and from drowning in the river."

He raised one eyebrow at her. "It's kind of you not to point out that you wouldn't have been in either spot if it hadn't been for my kidnapping you."

"I just didn't like the idea of them lynching you," she snapped and avoided his gaze. It was more than that, more than what had happened at the arroyo. She wouldn't let herself think she might be beginning to care for this Apache who could be using her to revenge what her husband had done to his woman.

She didn't want to think too much the reasons behind her behavior. "You've managed to get this far, maybe I can help you make it as far as the fort. After that, I'll start a new life with a clear conscience, and you can slip across the border. It isn't far to Mexico from there, is it?"

He shook his head. "Maybe fifty or sixty miles."

"I wish we were in Arizona now." She was cold and hungry, and the wind blew from the north in earnest. They'd be lucky if they didn't get caught in a blizzard. "Where do you think we are?"

"With the clouds building and the sky so overcast the last couple of days, I don't know any more than you do."

She was horrified. "You mean we're lost?"

"Maybe. The farther south we get, the better chance we have of getting away from this cold weather. I just hope we don't wander into Kiowa-Comanche country. Those two tribes aren't on the best of terms with Apaches."

She hunched her shoulders and kept riding. At this moment, she didn't know if she'd rather be captured by hostile Indians or freeze to death out in the southern section of Indian Territory.

Although they slept curled up together to conserve body heat, she was determined not to let him touch her, use her. But when his lips brushed hers, she couldn't keep her treacherous body from clinging to him, wanting what he offered. Her body didn't care that his embrace, his kiss, was only a bitter vengeance for the wrong her husband had done him.

Had she no pride? She should at least ask the questions that came to her, see if he could resolve all her fears. But when the tip of his tongue brushed across her lips and his fingers stroked her nipples into two hot points of sensation, nothing else seemed to matter to her except getting him between her thighs, imprisoning him there with her captive caress until he gave her what she hungered for. Then later, lying in his arms, she hated herself for wanting him so badly that she didn't question him because he might give her the answers she feared.

Sergeant Mooney. It would be a relief to finally get to talk to the sergeant at Fort Bowie. Maybe he would hold the pieces to the puzzle that Cholla held back.

For several more days they rode south through the blowing snow. Sierra lost all track of time. She looked over at Cholla, cold and miserable. "It can't get any worse than this."

"It just did." Cholla suddenly reined up, looking off in the distance.

Her gaze followed his. A group of Indians rode toward them. Her heart almost stopped. "Should we run?"

"Yes, but it's too late, they've seen us."

She watched the dark, sullen faces as the men rode closer. "Are they — ?"

Cholla nodded. "Comanches."

Sierra made a little sound of dismay. "Merciful heavens! What'll we do?"

"We can't show any fear. Like all Indians, the Comanche respect bravery."

Bravery. Had Cholla killed Robert? And if so, was it because her husband was a coward or because of Delzhinne? *Has he only made love to me for vengeance, laughing secretly at my passion as he used he?* She winced at the thought as she watched the Indians ride closer. Now she would never find out.

"We might as well bluff," Cholla said without turning his head. "Maybe I can think of some reason for us to be trespassing on their land. If I can convince them I've come to bring their chief a present —"

"You don't have anything of value to give him; our horses aren't worth much."

He looked at her, and a chill went down her back. She knew by his expression what he was thinking. Yes, Cholla might be able to save himself if he had a good gift for the chief.

He had one all right, a white squaw.

Chapter Fifteen

Cholla was more afraid for Sierra than he was for himself. He sat his horse, watching the Comanches approach. Ever since he had been forced onto the train at Holbrook, he had been prepared to die, had even expected to die. Yet at this moment, life seemed very sweet and he wasn't ready to give it up easily.

He watched the silent warriors approach. He might buy his life by giving them the white woman. Her expression betrayed that was what she expected him to do. Certainly it was a fitting revenge against Robert Forester. But his very being rebelled at the idea.

The men rode close, reined in. Cholla recognized that most were Comanche, a couple were Kiowa. He held up his hand in greeting. A Kiowa immediately began sign language, but Cholla shook his head, indicating that he understood little of that. The greatest allies of the Comanche, the Kiowa were wily traders with other tribes and knew sign language better than most.

But Cholla had an idea. From the Mexicans

around Arizona, he had learned some Spanish. He figured the Comanche and Kiowa had, too.

Buenos días," he began. He told them in Spanish that he and his woman were lost, then asked about their chief and where their people were camped.

The men looked at him for some moments, seemed to be appraising Sierra. Finally one of them said, "Quanah Parker" and pointed west.

In rapid border Spanish, the brave told Cholla that the party was out hunting and that their half-breed chief, Quanah Parker, was camped a few miles away.

Cholla gave them his most fierce look, to discourage their undisguised admiration of Sierra. *"Hombres,* take me to Quanah."

A hook-nosed Comanche glared back and asked him what tribe he was.

"Apache." Apache. Enemy. It was a name the Zuni had given his tribe. They called themselves the Dine'. The braves exchanged looks. He touched his broad chest. "Cholla."

"Like the cactus one does not dare touch?"

"Sí." He nodded.

To his surprise, several braves' stern faces broke into smiles, and a chatter of Comanche and Kiowa went through the party, each head nodding and pointing at the pair.

Sierra looked over at Cholla, evidently encouraged by the smiling faces. "What's happened?"

Cholla shrugged. "I'm not sure I know. They seem to recognize my name. Only thing I can figure, they must have me confused with someone. They want us to go with them back to Quanah Parker's camp."

She mentally counted the number of braves. "Do we have any choice?"

"Not really. I told them you were my woman."

She looked as if she might protest, so Cholla said under his breath, "Indians are big on hospitality. If you are a captive and not my woman, they might expect me to share you, and they'd pass you around like they would tobacco, or maybe make a gift of you to one of their warriors."

"Hospitality has to end somewhere," Sierra said tight-lipped as they set off in the midst of the hunting party. "Are we going to come out of this alive?"

Cholla looked straight ahead as they rode. "I don't have any idea. That depends on their chief's whim."

"But they've been conquered," Sierra whispered to him. "He can't do anything to a United States citizen."

"Who's to stop him? Would you like to wire President Cleveland to protest?"

"Don't be sarcastic," she said huffily.

"I'm just pointing out the facts."

"Will it do me any good to tell them who I really am?"

He frowned at her. "If you want to tell them you're the widow of a Cavalry officer who was killed fighting Indians, go right ahead. Do I need to tell you the soldiers put Quanah and his people on the reservation back in seventy-five?"

Her face paled as if she'd abruptly realized that, illegal or not, their fates were now in the hands of the half-breed chief and his people.

* * *

It was a long way through blowing snow west to the warriors' camp, and the pair had soon lapsed into silence. Cholla was more worried than he wanted Sierra to know, but there was no point in upsetting her. He had made his decision when he'd looked over at her and seen she was more frightened than she admitted and was depending on him to protect her. He would endure torture or whatever the Comanche and Kiowa wanted to put him through if they would set Sierra free. The thought surprised him, and he again reminded himself that she was his enemy's woman. Then he stopped lying to himself and knew deep in his soul that somewhere along the way his feelings for her had changed.

They reached Quanah's hunting camp after a couple of hours. By then they were both chilled and hungry. In fact, with the weather worsening, Cholla wondered as they dismounted whether the two of them could have survived the night with no more food and clothing than they had.

They stood in the center of the encampment, and Sierra looked up at him as an Indian woman came and took her by the hand. "Go on," he urged. "She'll take you into a *tipi*, get you some food. I'll meet with Quanah, see what's going on."

"Can't I go with you?"

He shook his head. "Women don't come along when men parlay. I'll be there later."

She walked away reluctantly, looking back over her shoulder at him.

He watched her, wanting to shelter her in his arms, to tell her everything would be all right. Instead, he

298

drew himself up to his full height and squared his shoulders proudly, ignoring the people who had come out of the shelters to stare curiously at the strangers.

A warrior came out of a *tipi* and stood looking at Cholla, his arms folded across his chest. Quanah Parker, Cholla thought in awe as he stared back at the legendary half-breed. He saw a tall man perhaps in his late thirties, with only a few gray hairs in his long braids. But it was the chief's eyes that caught Cholla's attention; they were a deep blue-gray.

Cholla walked over, faced him. *"Buenos días."*

"I speak English, do you?"

Cholla nodded.

"Then speak it," Quanah said dryly. "Someday all must learn it. The day may come when neither my nor your grandchildren or great-grandchildren will even remember their own language." He gestured toward his *tipi*, and they entered.

Quanah sat down cross-legged before the fire, gesturing to indicate his guest should sit to his right. The heat felt good to Cholla's half-frozen body. Gratefully, the scout sank down, too.

When he looked up, the blue-gray eyes were studying him. "We will smoke and talk," the Comanche announced grandly.

"I am honored to be the guest of the great Quanah."

"You have heard of me?"

"I have heard the bluecoats talk of the brave chief who fought at Adobe Walls and the Palo Duro Canyon of Texas."

"All so long ago." The half-breed seemed almost

wistful as he reached for some tobacco and papers, handed some to Cholla, rolled himself a cigarette. "As I remember, the Apache do not smoke the ceremonial pipe, and besides"—he smiled wryly—"some of the things civilization has given my people are better than what we had—but not much."

Cholla rolled himself a smoke, lit it with a burning stick from the fire. It tasted good. His body was beginning to warm. "The great chief is out hunting?"

Quanah nodded and puffed on his cigarette, staring into the fire. "Mostly I eat agency beef, but now and then, I take my braves and we go off and camp, shoot a few rabbits and deer, pretend that things are as they were when I was young and we and our allies controlled the Plains. In those days, the buffalo were many; so many that for miles, when the herds moved, the Plains were a brown sea of fur. When the soldiers deliver the cattle now, the young men chase the beef down and shoot them with arrows." He made a derisive noise. "Some of them have never seen a buffalo. I am glad my father, the great chief Peta Nocona, did not live to see the day Comanche warriors chased tame cows and played at hunting."

Cholla shook his head. "It is no better for my people."

Quanah stared at him. "I saw your woman. Is she Indian or white?"

What should he answer? This stoic chief did not look like a man to be lied to. "She is white. I stole her. She was an enemy's wife."

Quanah nodded in understanding. "So it was with my father. My mother was a blue-eyed white girl stolen in a Texas raid. The whites came one day and stole her back."

For a moment, he said no more, and there were no sounds but the crackling of the fire and the howling of the wind. Cholla watched him, wondering what thoughts crossed Quanah's mind.

"My mother and baby sister are buried in Texas," the Comanche said. "Someday I hope to move their bodies so I may be buried next to them. The whites will take your woman away from you, too, as they took my mother."

"I have promised her I will return her to her people at the end of our journey in exchange for her help."

Quanah looked at him in surprise. "You would give up a woman like that? She is pretty, would bear you fine sons and warm your blankets on lonely nights. My father would never have given up his white woman. The Texians took her away by force while he was gone."

"I . . . I have given my word to her." He did not want to think about losing Sierra.

"A man does not make promises to women. Such oaths are for warriors. Put a son in her belly and keep her. When its tiny mouth sucks at her breast and she is warm and safe in your lodge, she will forget about wanting to return to the white civilization."

That was not a decision Cholla wanted to deal with right then. "I will think on this," he said somberly, wondering when Quanah would get to the point.

"There is talk that the White Father in Washington will soon allow white farmers to come in, take the rest of our Indian lands, and plow it up for farms."

Cholla nodded. "I have heard these rumors. No doubt the whites will pay you for the land."

"Pay!" Quanah snorted in derision. "You think we will have any choice but to accept what they offer? If we say we do not wish to sell, they will take the land anyway. So when they offer, all the tribes will take the money. A hundred years from now the whites will say they didn't *steal* Indian Territory, they *paid* us for it."

Cholla smoked and listened to the chief's grumbling in polite silence. Perhaps the half-breed was lonely and wished to talk to someone who had been lately in battle. It had been a dozen years since the Comanche had fought.

"You are indeed the Apache called Cholla?" The light eyes seemed to stare into his soul.

Cholla was disconcerted, but he nodded. "The great Comanche chief surely has not heard of me?"

"Ah, but we have!" Quanah's handsome face broke into a grin. "Those who hang around Fort Sill near my house say messages come and go among the soldiers. It seems you have caused them much loss of face to have slipped through their fingers and headed home. All the tribes are glad to see the soldiers look so foolish!"

So that was it. The news that he had escaped the train and dodged the Army had traveled through the tribes, and they were all enjoying this minor triumph he had brought all Indians. "It is a little thing that I do." Cholla ducked his head modestly. "No doubt you could have done better."

"You are a proper warrior, even though you have scouted for the bluecoats." Quanah grunted his approval and puffed on his cigarette. "I would not call traveling hundreds of miles and stealing one of their women a small feat. A hundred years from now, I think you will be a legend."

"Quanah Parker will be a legend with his great exploits; few will remember the Apache who escaped a train to try to return to his homeland." Cholla again ducked his head.

Quanah chuckled. "I would not be too sure. The Comanche would like to be a part of this great thing you do. I will see that you are fed, supplied, and, after a day or two of rest, sent on your way."

Cholla heaved a sigh of relief and threw his cigarette into the fire. "I am planning to try for the freedom across the border. Come with me."

The half-breed's blue-gray eyes gleamed with hope and interest for a moment; then the light died and he shook his head regretfully. "I am chief now, the last chief of the Comanche. As such I have responsibilities to my people. I cannot slip a whole tribe through the bluecoats. So I will hunt for a few days, then return to the reservation near Fort Sill."

"You will not even consider it?"

Quanah shook his head and threw his cigarette into the fire, staring into the flames. "But know that my heart and thoughts go with you, free as the eagle flying. You may be forgotten by the whites, but Indians of every tribe will remember you and tell your tale many times by their campfires and say, 'Here was a man who would not bend, who would not accept his fate without a fight. Here was a brave man."

He stood up slowly, and Cholla did also, knowing

the interview was ended. They went outside. The chill wind howled like a ghost spirit, blowing snow across the ground.

Quanah looked to the north, his face solemn. "They say at the fort the winter is one of the worst in memory. On the Great Plains to the north, the snow piles in deep drifts and kills the ranchers' cattle by the thousands."

"I am headed across the border into Mexico where it is cold only sometimes in the mountains of the Sierra Madre. A man can live there in peace, I think, and ignore the civilization that smothers him."

The Comanche looked at him almost wistfully, the wind blowing his gray-streaked hair. "You could ride straight south now, and be in Mexico."

Cholla shook his head. "That is not the part I know; the place that the Apache have roamed for generations is south of the Apache stronghold. Besides, if I can manage it, I have a white friend at the fort I would like to send a final good-bye."

"Do you not fear this white will betray you?"

"No, he is my *sikis*, my brother." Cholla shook his head, "I have killed to save his life, he has killed to save mine. That alone, had I no other reason, would make me trust him without question."

Quanah gestured toward a *tipi*. "You will find a warm fire and food in there with your woman. Rest a day or two with the Comanche. I have a half-Cheyenne rancher friend to the south I will send you to. Maybe he can find a way to get you to your own country."

"*Gracias*." Cholla watched the chief turn and go to

304

his own lodge. Darkness fell slowly across the deserted camp as he entered the lodge Quanah had indicated.

Sierra looked up from the fireside, stood. Without even seeming to think about it, she came into the circle of his arms. "When you didn't come, I was worried."

Not for me, Cholla thought, but for fear of what might happen to you if the Comanches killed me. He said, "I think everything will be fine. The chief is amused that I have made fools of the whites. The story of my escape has spread through many tribes over the past few weeks."

She pulled him down before the fire, handed him a tin plate of roast meat. "They'll let us go?"

The meat was hot and juicy and Cholla ate with relish. "More than that. Quanah promises aid. He has a friend to the south in Texas he thinks will help us."

She heaved a sigh of relief and leaned back on her elbows, watching him eat. "Then maybe in a few weeks, I will be safe at Fort Bowie and you'll be across the border?"

"There's still a long way to go," he cautioned, avoiding the question.

"We've made it this far, though I didn't think we would; I don't see why we shouldn't make it the rest of the way."

He merely grunted and finished his food. It was warm and cozy in there by the fire, even though the snow blew outside. He rolled himself a cigarette from the stock Quanah had given him, lit it from the fire. "Come here," he ordered without thinking.

She moved over, leaned against his knee, and he stroked her hair as he smoked. "With your hair down, you remind me of an Apache girl," he said softly, "wild and free and primitive, not civilized like you were with your hair all done up in a little knot on the back of your head."

She looked at him, saying nothing, and he wondered about her thoughts, wondered if she could possibly have guessed how her husband had died? Somehow her opinion of him was beginning to matter very much. But no matter, he must not tell her the secret.

What man gives his word to a woman? Such oaths are only given to other warriors. Put a son in her belly. When the tiny mouth pulls at her breast, she will forget that you told her you would free her. She will warm your blankets on lonely nights.

"A penny for your thoughts." She smiled at him.

It unnerved him and he started. "What?"

"It's just something whites say."

If she only knew what I am thinking . . . She must not find out because then she wouldn't help him, and he might need her cooperation to make it through the rest of the trip. He threw his cigarette into the fire, reached out to pull her to him.

She stiffened only a moment and then relaxed. *A penny for your thoughts.* He dared not ask what she was thinking. He might not want to know. Besides, he trusted no white but Tom Mooney. Sooner or later, Sierra would again attempt to betray him. He still wasn't sure why she had elected to rescue him from the mob in Sundance. Maybe she'd thought being the temporary bedmate of an Apache was better than being put in a whorehouse for use by that white mob.

He kissed her. She resisted momentarily and then responded, and he slipped his tongue between her lips and squeezed her breast. He imagined them swollen with rich milk for his son. When she had nursed the child and it slept, Cholla would draw her to him and put his own mouth on her nipples.

Her small hands slipped inside his shirt, and she trailed her nails across his chest. He gasped with pleasure at the sensation and ran a hand up her bare thigh. Then he leaned on one elbow while she put her head in his lap, and he stroked and teased her velvet place with his fingers. She was wet and hot and silky. He ran his lips along her thigh even as he felt her open his pants. Her breath was warm on his throbbing manhood. *Would she . . . ?*

He couldn't hold back a gasp of ecstasy as she made the ultimate gesture.

"No," he whispered, but her tongue was moving over the rigid staff of his maleness and he found himself putting his hand on the back of her neck, tangling his fingers in her wild mane of dark hair, pushing deep into the soft heat of lips that pulled at his very being.

Her skin felt damp with the heat of her passion, her whole body was throbbing, her need intense and demanding. He quit fighting and gave in to the pleasure her lips created even as he began to kiss along her hot inner thigh, caressing his captive with his mouth.

He teased the ridge of her femininity with his tongue, felt her go tense and quiver from the need of

307

him as she demanded more with her lips. Cholla let her take what she wanted from him even as his tongue stroked her into spasms, and they could not get enough of each other.

Afterward, they lay entwined, staring into the fire, and as he did not dare ask her thoughts, she did not dare ask his. But he was virile, needing more of a woman than most men and giving more. He took her three more times that night, and each time he penetrated deep into her, determined to leave his seed in her womb.

Quanah is right, Cholla decided as he moved inside his woman and felt her clasp him tightly. He need not ask himself whether he cared for Sierra or what he had promised her. After all, she was just a female to be used to produce sons, to warm his blankets and cook for him. It would be lonely in Mexico. But Cholla would not be alone now. He would not tell her where they were headed, and if she trusted him, she would not realize where she was until it was too late. Then what could she do but sob and scream futilely? Eventually she would submit to his dominance. He would not ask; he would take. Whether she wanted it or not, Sierra would go to Mexico to stay with him forever!

Chapter Sixteen

Sierra wondered what the Apache was thinking as she let him take her over and over again the next several days. But she did not ask. What was it that Gillen had hinted at? When she thought of the possibility that Cholla might have killed her husband, her mind had rebelled at his touch. But her body wanted his, and she couldn't seem to help herself. I should have left him back at Sundance to hang, she thought as she surrendered to his kisses.

She would not admit even to herself that when he kissed her or stroked her skin, her emotions prevailed over her mind and she didn't care about anything except feeling his arms around her, the hot steel of him penetrating her to the very core. It occurred to her that if she weren't more cautious he might get her with child, and then what would happen to her when she was finally free? There weren't many white men who would take a woman carrying a savage's child.

But he was not to be denied, and when he touched her with his hands and mouth, held her

309

against him, she forgot everything but the pleasure of coupling with him. It almost seemed to her that he was trying to breed her. The thought both excited and shocked her.

Day blended into night in the warmth of the *tipi* while the cold wind howled outside. She had not known a man could be so virile as Cholla proved to be, that a man could build a fire that consumed her.

Finally the weather cleared and the snow had a crust that made it passable. Quanah gave them warm furs and supplies, fresh horses, and a pair of braves to guide them south. As they mounted up, the chief came out to see them off.

"My braves will lead you to the Triple D ranch in the Texian Hill Country," Quanah said. "My friend, Trace Durango, is half-Cheyenne, and since the Cheyenne have long been allies of the Comanche and Kiowa, he will help you."

Cholla frowned. "The Cheyenne and the Apache are not friends. Perhaps he will not want to help."

"In this case, I think he will." Quanah smiled. "It is not often anymore that warriors win against the soldiers."

They thanked him profusely. Cholla said. "Are your braves allowed off the reservation? Will there be trouble if they lead us?"

"What the whites don't know won't hurt anyone," the chief said with a wry smile. "Now go, with my

310

thoughts giving wings to your horses' hooves." He looked at Sierra a long moment. "Apache," Quanah added, "remember what I told you about Mexico."

"I remember and agree."

They rode out, headed south, the horses' hooves crunching the frozen snow.

Sierra turned the words over in her mind. "What did Quanah mean?"

"Nothing." He shook his head. "Since you are just a woman, you would not understand men's thinking."

Sierra started to protest, then decided it wasn't important. What did she care what Cholla did when he got to Mexico as long as she was safe and secure back in white civilization?

For countless days they rode south, the weather warming a little as they moved deeper into Texas. They used up their supplies and then lived off the land, but they had plenty of ammunition and none of the four went hungry. The braves said almost nothing to them, merely did the task they had been sent to do.

With whatever privacy they could manage, Sierra and Cholla curled up together and kept each other warm each night. Often he would awaken her, wanting her and doing things to her body that made her want him. As she dug her nails into his back and arched herself under him in heated passion, she almost smiled as she thought of Robert's barbed comments on her coldness.

Her white life seemed like a distant bad dream, she so seldom thought of her dead husband anymore. But for some reason she couldn't understand, she wouldn't let herself think of the future, though she knew she ought to be looking forward to reaching Fort Bowie.

Finally the Comanches indicated they had almost reached their destination. It is warmer here, Sierra thought. Water ran clear and cold through limestone. The gentle hills were green with cedar trees. The two warriors rode with them to a rise. Over on another hill, lay a white, sprawling *ranchero* that looked almost like a big castle.

One of the braves pointed to the adobe buildings. "Trace Durango," he grunted. Then he and his partner turned their paint ponies and headed away at a gallop even as Sierra and Cholla attempted to thank them.

It occurred to her as they rode into the courtyard that she could ask for help in escaping Cholla here, but she decided that would be futile. Trace Durango was a half-breed himself, and a friend of Quanah's, so he wouldn't aid her. Besides she had told Cholla she would help him reach freedom, and she felt inclined to keep her word. She tried to remind herself that she should hate him, but sometimes she had a difficult time remembering why and had to search her memory. She told herself the feeling the scout evoked in her was admiration for his bravery and daring—or even raw lust—nothing more.

They reined their tired horses up in front of the grand hacienda. The place was breathtaking, giant oleander bushes everywhere, a bubbling fountain in the center of the small pool in the courtyard, a few doves cooing and dipping their pink bills in the water for a drink.

A little Mexican boy came out the French doors to one side of the courtyard, followed by a yapping, tiny brown dog.

Cholla cleared his throat. "We are here to see Señor Trace Durango."

"Señor Durango? *Ah, sí, señor.*" The little boy took their horses' reins and turned to point to the grand house.

Cholla dismounted, came around to help Sierra down, and they walked across the patio, the tiny dog yapping their arrival to the world. An elderly Mexican servant woman with gray hair and a plump body opened the door, escorted them into the big hall.

"Señor Trace," Cholla said to the old woman. She nodded and beckoned them to follow her.

The place took Sierra's breath away. It was the most grand manor she had ever seen, with rich Spanish-style furnishings, paintings, and fine rugs. Whoever the Durangos were, they were people of power and wealth.

Cholla looked around, his face showing that he had never seen anything like this either.

The old woman led them down the hall and into a room Sierra recognized as a fine library. Shelves of books lined the walls, guns hung in racks on one, and hunting trophies—deer antlers and bobcat heads—were displayed amidst the books. It was a truly masculine retreat, with its dark wood desk and the leather sofa before the giant stone fireplace. French doors looked out onto the courtyard. Cholla walked to the fire, warmed his hands.

Sierra glanced up. "Look!" She gestured to the big painting over the fireplace. It seemed to dominate the room. The woman depicted in it was a beauty, dark-eyed, with wild hair blowing around her shoulders; hair the color of honey. "I wonder who she is."

"That's Cimarron." The voice came from behind her. "The most beautiful woman who ever lived, except for my mother."

She whirled to face a tall, dark, and brooding man. His Spanish and Indian blood showed in his handsome face. The sprinkle of gray in his black hair told her he must be in his middle or late forties.

"I'm Trace Durango," he said, and came into the room, his hand outstretched. She let him take her hand and kiss it in a courtly gesture; then he turned and shook hands with Cholla. "May I get you a drink?" Without waiting for an answer, he went to the desk on which several expensive crystal decanters stood. "Sherry for you, *señora?*" Sierra nodded. "Whiskey or tequila?" he asked the Apache.

"Whiskey."

"Prefer tequila myself with a little salt and a twist of lime," Trace said and brought the drinks over.

Sierra looked at the portrait again. "Cimarron . . . what does it mean?"

"It's Spanish, it means Wild One." He sipped his

drink and smiled gently as if remembering. "It's a very long and romantic story."

"I would like to meet her," Sierra said.

"Oh, she's gone to San Antonio with the children for holiday shopping. I'm supposed to take the buggy tomorrow and drive down to join them for some of the festivities."

For the first time, Sierra looked around and saw the decorations, realized that it must be near Christmas.

Without thinking, she blurted out, "Señor Durango, how far is it to Austin?"

Cholla frowned at her.

Trace shrugged. "Oh, less than fifty miles. Why, do you know someone there, *señora?*"

"Do you by any chance know the Forester family?"

He frowned. "Everyone in Texas knows the Foresters. They are very rich and powerful and . . ." His voice trailed off, and she had the sudden feeling that Trace Durango did not think much of that family and was too polite to say so. *If I could reach Robert's mother, would she take her son's widow in?*

Cholla glared at her and cleared his throat. She had a feeling that if she brought up Austin again, he would quickly change the subject. "Quanah sent us," he said. "We need your help."

Immediately, Trace's handsome face sobered. "Tell me all about it."

Sierra curled up on the leather sofa before the fire, sipping the delicious sherry and staring at the portrait while the men talked. The woman in the painting almost seemed alive. Her face was radiant,

315

and in her eyes was an expression only love could have put there.

When Sierra drifted off to sleep, curled up on the sofa, the men were still talking. She remembered someone covering her with a blanket, and when her eyes flickered open, she smiled up at Cholla as he brushed the hair away from her face.

She dreamed of Austin and the fine home Robert's family would have. If they took her in, she would never have to worry about anything again. Once the security would have appealed to her, but now when she thought of wearing a tight corset and attending social functions as a proper widow swathed in black, she felt stifled by the conformity of the conventional life. In fact, Sierra had grown so used to sleeping wrapped in furs and cooking over a campfire that she wasn't even sure living inside four walls appealed to her anymore.

She was only vaguely aware that Cholla lifted her from the sofa, swung her up in his powerful arms. She nestled her cheek against his broad chest.

She heard Trace's voice. "You can have the guest room upstairs. Maria will show you. There will be food left out, wine; and if you need anything else, just pull the bell cord. At any hour a servant will respond."

She didn't even bother to open her eyes as the man held her close and carried her upstairs. She felt him set her on a bed, and she opened her eyes sleepily to watch him close the door, begin to undress. He is going to make love to her again she thought with a contented smile, and snuggled deeper

316

into the bed. She felt him undress her, kiss her breasts until the nipples swelled against his mouth, wanting more. Sleepily, she reached out to pull him down on her, feeling the heat of him penetrating her as he thrust again and again.

She kissed the corners of his mouth, dug her nails into his shoulders and imprisoned his straining body by locking her legs around his hard, muscular hips. When he came inside her, throbbing as he spilled his seed, she went into spasms of passion, dropped back off to sleep with him still imprisoned in her body.

In the middle of the night, they sneaked downstairs like two naughty children and found a delicious outlay of food and wines left for them as Trace had promised.

When they returned upstairs, Cholla took her again with such renewed virility that she could only wonder at his ability to satisfy her body. Somehow the way he made love to her had changed from those early days right after he had kidnapped her. Now he was more gentle, almost as if he might care for her. But of course, that is nonsense, Sierra reminded herself. She was a woman with a ripe body who just happened to be convenient for his use. Still, he had created such a hunger in her that she didn't care what the circumstances were; she had to admit she couldn't get enough of him. There was no love involved; it was lust between two healthy young animals, no more than that.

The next morning, they cleaned up, breakfasted with Trace in the big dining room. "I've decided the easiest thing to do is put you on the train at San Antonio. You'll arrive in Arizona Territory in style."

Cholla looked at him in alarm. "But the whites will arrest us—"

"No, they won't." Trace said with easy confidence, "You'll be dressed in the finest of clothes, you'll have money in your pockets and a compartment; no riding in the day coach for you. I'll even give you a couple of fine horses, ship them in the baggage car. No one will dare question you. They'll think you're a rich Spanish couple on a holiday."

It began to dawn on Sierra that it might work. In just a few days, she might be at Fort Bowie, planning the New Year. "But I don't have any nice clothes."

"You're about Cimarron's size; she has closets and closets full. Let's get moving. We've got to get to San Antonio."

In a little more than an hour, they were climbing into the buggy, both well dressed, complete with baggage. Over Cholla's protests, Trace had insisted the Apache's hair be cut like a white man's. The little Mexican boy came out of the nearby barn, leading two very fine horses; one black gelding and a strangely marked paint mare.

Cholla's face lit up. "Why, that's a Medicine Hat mare. My friend in Arizona raises them. Quint gave me a stallion."

318

"You don't say?" Trace grinned. "You know Quint Randolph of the Wolf's Den Ranch?"

Cholla nodded.

"Small world," Trace said. "Quint's a relative by marriage. When you see him **again**, tell him the family sends regards. By the way, if you have any trouble on this trip, I have an adopted younger brother in west Texas, Maverick Durango of the Lazy M spread."

The men fell into excited conversation as the small boy with the barking little dog at his heels tied the horses to the back of the buggy and waved good-bye.

They were still deep in conversation as Trace slapped the reins and the buggy began to move. Sierra wondered if she was doing the right thing? What if she suddenly jumped on one saddle horse, spooked the other, and took off? Could she find her way to Austin, and would Robert's mother welcome her into the fold?

Harriet Forester sat in her elegant carriage and made her assessment of the man sitting across from her. Lieutenant Quimby Gillen was what Texans called "lowdown," the kind of man who would do anything to advance himself, maybe even raise sheep. His worst mistake was in underestimating her. His expression said he dismissed Harriet Forester as a doddering old woman whom he could fool with his oily charm. Just the kind of friend Robert would have chosen.

He offered her his sack of candy, and she shook

her head, folded her hands in the lap of her expensive black dress. Gillen popped a lemon drop in his mouth, crunched it with a loud, irritating sound much like the crushing of rock in a quarry.

"Good-bye, Lieutenant, so nice of you to come."

"Good-bye, Mrs. Forester. I am sorry about your son." He picked up his valise, stepped from the fine carriage out onto the Austin railway platform. "Remember, if Robert's widow tries to contact you—"

"I don't need to be instructed like a stupid schoolgirl," she snapped. "I'll be only too happy to let the Army know at once. No strumpet will get her hands on any part of the Forester estate."

Gill ran his tongue across his teeth, tasting the last tartness of the candy and studying the woman across from him. The Iron Lady. A servant had told him the citizens of Austin called Harriet Forester that behind her back. No one would dare say any such thing to her face. While the gray-haired woman with the almost turquoise-colored eyes was no great beauty, she still had a presence that money and power could give a matriarch.

He took her hand, kissed it. "Good-bye, dear lady, and should you ever have a need, think of me as another son." Especially when it comes to disposing of your money, he thought as he smiled at her.

"I have other children, Lieutenant," she said coldly, withdrawing her hand from his, "although Robert was one of my favorites, I'll admit that. He was spoiled and headstrong. I'll always regret disowning him too hastily."

"I'm sure you felt you had good reason, dear lady," Gill murmured soothingly.

"All my children do as I tell them," Harriet Forester said, "or at least, they *used* to. Robert had never had to earn a dime in his life, and he really didn't know how. I suppose he thought he had no option but to join the Army. I had hoped it would make a man of him; I never dreamed he might marry some low immigrant chit, then get killed."

The train blew a warning whistle, and Gill picked up his bag, leaned in the window. "If Sierra should contact you, let me know immediately. The Army intends to capture that savage she's traveling with."

Harriet Forester shuddered. "Indians! I hate them. You saw my daughter, Emily. Her mind has never been the same since she was carried off and we had to pay a ransom to get her back. Sometimes I wish those Comancheros had killed her." Tears came to her eyes. "She'd be better off dead than crazed as she is now."

He tried to pat her hand again, but she pulled away and he had a sudden feeling there was more to this stern woman than he gave her credit for.

"Yes, Lieutenant," she said, "you can be sure if this Sierra person should contact me, I'll let you know immediately. Do you really think they might get this far?"

The train whistled, and Gill looked toward the cars waiting in the station, then back to Robert's mother and nodded. "That girl tried to kill me back at Sundance, and I was only trying to rescue her. She's just a shameless hussy, not worthy of your proud name."

"All aboard!" yelled the conductor.

Gill turned away from the elegant carriage.

"Lieutenant, how will I reach you if I hear from her?"

"You know where I change trains. You could wire the station there, I suppose, or wire any station along the way and they'll get the message to me. Good-bye, dear lady. You remind me of my own dear departed mother." He touched his hat, held on to his bag, ran for the train as it began to move.

The rich old bitch, he thought with a sneer as he swung aboard, turned, and waved to the elderly woman in the fine carriage. She did remind him of his mother—the same kind of sour-faced old hag, angry because her favorite son had died. She wished it had been Quimby and said so. Like her husband, she resented his taking one peppermint for himself.

Gill went down the aisle of the swaying train, hanging onto the backs of seats to balance himself. As he walked, he congratulated himself on his cleverness. "Gill, blast it all, you've certainly thought of everything."

He smiled with satisfaction as he put his bag in the overhead rack, sank onto one of the horsehair seats. If Cholla somehow made it all the way back to Arizona, Gill intended to be waiting for him there, to kill him or turn him around and put him back on the train to the Florida prison. And the girl. He touched his head where Sierra had struck him with the lamp. Maybe he would offer not to press charges in exchange for sexual favors.

A railroad conductor came down the aisle, and Gill grabbed his arm. "Hey, this train on time?"

"A little behind, sir, but we'll make connections all right if we don't pick up too many folks at all the stops between here and there." He looked at the ticket Gill held out. "Yas, sir, you shouldn't have no trouble makin' your connection on west to Arizona."

Gill pocketed his ticket, leaned back, and stared boredly at the other passengers, considered how many little whistle-stops there were in that hundred-mile stretch between Austin and the bustling city where he would change trains. Idly he reached for his sack of hard candy and wondered if the San Antonio station would be crowded with holiday travelers.

Chapter Seventeen

Sergeant Tom Mooney paused in front of the stable door, stroking the big Medicine Hat stallion. "Sure, and I miss Cholla, too. The Lord only knows where he is."

The yellow dog lying at his feet whined softly. Here he was with the Apache scout's animals, wondering just where his friend might be right now with winter sweeping across the country.

Lieutenant Gatewood's tall, slender frame came around the corner. "Ah, Sergeant, I've been looking for you."

"Sir?" Mooney saluted, almost afraid to hear whatever news the lieutenant might bring.

"There was a breakdown in the telegraph wires farther north, ice on them and all that. But we finally heard from Gillen."

"And?"

Gatewood rubbed the bridge of his nose. "He actually made contact with Cholla and the hostage in some little Indian Territory settlement called Sundance."

Tom's heart seemed to skip, and he flexed and un-flexed freckled fingers, afraid the next words would be of Cholla's death. And what had become of Sierra Forester?

"Strange," Gatewood mused as he leaned against the stall, patted the horse. "Gillen says the woman hit him in the head, nearly killed him. Then she helped the Apache escape a lynch mob."

"Holy Saint Patrick!" Mooney didn't know what to think. "Is Lieutenant Gillen sure the woman was Mrs. Forester?"

Gatewood nodded. "Yes, he spoke with her, offered to help her, so the wire says. She fled town with Cholla."

She's fallen in love with him, Tom thought with sinking heart. The photo in his jacket seemed to burn into his wiry body. The best friend he had in the world and the woman whose photo he had fallen in love with. "Did you say they got away, sir?"

"According to Gillen. He's convinced Cholla will try to make it back here. Surely he isn't loco enough to do that."

Mooney shrugged and drummed his fingers against the stall door. "He's probably the only man I know who could, sir." Of course he will come back, Tom thought. Cholla loves and knows this country, all the way down into Mexico, better than a man knows the body of his own woman.

"Gillen was going to search that area, then go on down to Austin. He has some idea that Sierra Forester might try to make contact with Robert's family and, if so, then he'd at least have some clue as to their whereabouts."

"He thinks Cholla is headed south again?"

"The tracks headed south before he lost them. Of course Cholla might end up in Comanche country along the Red River, and that tribe isn't friendly to Apaches."

"If I remember right, Quanah Parker is chief there and half-white. There's no second-guessing what that crafty fox will do. He might help Cholla just for the hell of it."

"Could be." Gatewood turned and looked toward the northeast. "There's a terrible blizzard going on farther upcountry in the high plains, snow in big drifts, cattle dying by the thousands. Some say it's going to be the worst winter on record. Yes, if I were Cholla, I'd be headed south and then west as fast as possible."

Tom turned and looked in the same direction as the lieutenant, wondering if the woman was safe, where his friend might be at this very minute. "If Cholla makes it into south Texas, sir, he'll be out of that terrible cold."

"Gillen is being called back. The brass have decided not to waste any more time on this chase. Besides, if the Apache is headed to Arizona, they think they can nab him right here."

Tom chewed his lip and thought about his moral dilemma. If he were in a situation where he had to betray his friend but it gave him a chance to have the woman, what would he do? What would *any* man do?

"Gillen was going on down to San Anton' after he left Austin," Gatewood said, "then catching a train west. Don't know exactly when he'll show up here, maybe in time for Christmas." He turned to leave,

326

then paused and came back. "Oh, I knew there was something else, Sergeant. Your enlistment is up at the end of the month. Have you decided whether to reenlist or head back to Michigan?"

Mooney hadn't decided. Nothing had seemed important these last few weeks but Cholla and Sierra Forester. Today he felt old and tired. "I'm still thinking about it, sir. My elderly parents live on a farm there. I thought by being thrifty, maybe I could make a go of the old place."

"Would you mind escorting a lady back to Michigan?"

"Sir?"

Gatewood frowned. "Sad story. Young schoolteacher from up there. Came down last year to teach ranchers' children here, even got engaged."

"Then why's she going back?"

"Well, it seems, in the very last of all that Indian trouble, she was raped."

Tom winced. He could almost guess the rest. "And now the young man doesn't want to marry her."

"Worse than that. She's with child from the attack. I suppose she's tried to hide it all these months, not knowing what to do. You can hardly blame the young rancher."

"I can blame him," Tom said fiercely, suddenly very protective of the sad little schoolteacher. "It isn't her fault, and a child's a child."

Gatewood patted his shoulder. "That's what I like about you, Tom. You've got the softest, most fiercely loyal heart of any man I ever met. I thought you might escort the girl back."

"She got folks there?"

"I don't think she's got much of anything." Gatewood shook his head. "But since she's a Michigan girl, she's going up there to try to make a life for herself."

"Poor little thing," Tom murmured. Being Irish, he had a natural sympathy for the underdog, and when it was a helpless woman — and a baby . . .

"You wouldn't mind escorting her if you don't re-up?"

"Of course not. When's the lass coming?" The sergeant stroked the horse thoughtfully.

"Right at the end of the month. There's snow in the high country, so she can't get in right now."

"I hope I'm gone before Cholla gets here," Tom blurted out. "I'd be torn between loyalties." And love, he thought, thinking of Sierra Forester.

"I understand, Sergeant. I like the Apache, too. But I know you, Tom. You'll do what's right, no matter what."

Mooney wasn't so sure of that. Were right and justice the same? Did a man have a higher allegiance to the country he'd sworn an oath to or to what was morally right? He nodded absently, his mind busy with his dilemma. "Thank you for your confidence, sir."

Cholla. He may be my problem and it may be my decision, Tom thought. If the scout makes it across Texas, he'll come here and turn south toward Mexico because he knows the terrain. It's all sort of like a play, he reflected, each player awaiting his or her turn to come on the stage. With any luck, Thomas Connor Mooney would be on his way to Michigan escorting the pitiful little schoolteacher before Cholla got

328

this far. Lieutenant Gatewood was a man of principle. What the hell would Gatewood do if he had to handle this dilemma?

Trixie La Femme leaned on the bar at the Birdcage Theater and lit a cigarette. Tombstone. What a dirty, flea-bitten town it was. It might have been something once, but with the mines falling off in production, she could forsee it becoming almost a ghost town in a few years. Well, it deserved to die as far as she was concerned.

Humming a little of "I'll Take You Home Again, Kathleen," she looked around at the nearly empty saloon, took out her medicine bottle, gulped a long drink. Here she'd come all the way from East St. Louie, thinking this might be a step up to a great career, and they'd put her in the chorus. Most of the time, she was flat on her back upstairs under some cowboy or miner. And one of them had given her a disease that would eventually prove fatal.

Trixie hadn't told anyone, especially the boss. When the Birdcage found out, she'd be fired, and she didn't have enough money to make it to San Francisco yet.

Well, these damned cowboys deserved it if she gave them the unexpected gift of a killing disease. Trixie was no prude and would do anything for a little extra money, but some of these Westerners had fantasies that shocked even her. More than once she'd entertained a naked cowboy wearing only boots and spurs, or she'd had to cater to unusual desires involving whips and pistols.

She hadn't even heard from Gill, and he was the reason she'd come here in the first place. "If I don't hear nothing in a few more days, I'm gonna go up to Fort Bowie myself and see if they've heard from him. It ain't that far," she muttered.

She wouldn't put it past him to forget about her completely. Maybe she'd stumble on to some rich old coot, or a rancher with a few bucks, and wouldn't need Gill.

The evening was beginning to pick up, now that it was getting dark. Another man came into the Birdcage. Just a young cowboy, Trixie thought and took a deep drag on her cigarette. Then she took another look. No, not a cowboy, a prosperous rancher. She'd learned how to spot an expensive Stetson, fine, handmade boots. And he wasn't bad looking.

Immediately Trixie turned, took a deep breath so that her breasts jutted out. "Hey, mister, you lookin' for a little fun?"

"You look like you could give a man some fun." He grinned as he came over, leaned on the bar, signaled the bartender to bring him a drink.

"I'm not really one of the regulars," Trixie hastened to say. "I'm a singer, headed for 'Frisco; got big plans when I get a good break. Everyone tells me I look like the Cameo girl. Just got stranded here by a fella."

His expression told her the Cameo girl meant nothing to this dumb hick. "We got something in common then, I reckon. I'm stranded here myself. Got into town on business a couple of days ago, and now there's snow in the high country. Might as well stay in Tombstone a few days."

She snuffed her cigarette out, put her hand on his

330

arm familiarly. "Maybe I can help make that time pass."

"You gonna sing to me?" He snickered, shifted his weight so that his sleeve brushed her breasts.

"If you want. I know how to do a lot more things than the girls around here." She moved so that her breast pressed against his arm. Trixie smiled when she heard his sharp intake of breath. "You got a wife and kids that'll be disappointed if you don't get back for the holidays?"

"I had me a gal, but I broke it off. What do you think of a schoolteacher who'd let herself get raped by an Injun and then not do what any respectable woman would—kill herself?"

Respectable woman. Trixie wondered suddenly if that weak, whimpering little Sierra Forester had ever escaped from the Apache. She hoped the scout had made Mrs. Forester beg for mercy, then batted her eyelashes at the rancher. "No white man would take an Injun's leavin's, would he? I mean, if that girl ain't pure, you don't want her."

The bartender brought the drink, went away.

"Worse yet," the man said confidentially as he sipped the whiskey, "she's gonna have an Injun brat because of it."

"No!" Trixie exclaimed. "So of course you broke the engagement?"

"Wouldn't any man? I mean, she tried to hide it for months, but when her belly began to swell and I cornered her, made her admit it, she had the nerve to cry and say she hoped I'd be sympathetic and marry her anyways."

"But like most men, you won't?" She reached out,

fiddled with his shirt collar so she could stroke his chest.

"Of course not." The rancher pushed his hat back. "I mean, a man expects to get out and sow a few wild oats, but when he marries, he don't want used goods; especially if she comes with a half-breed brat. She's goin' back to Michigan, and I hope I never see the tramp again."

Trixie winked at him. "So how about sowing a few wild oats with me?" She took his hand, looked toward the stairs.

He finished his drink, put his other hand on her bottom, stroked it. "Baby, I hoped I'd find a little fun when I came in here, and I reckon I'm lucky you were the first one I spotted."

"Don't it beat all, though? Maybe it was just meant to be." She led him toward the stairs.

"I figure a man who's been through what I been through, having to realize the girl he was set to marry is used goods, that entitles him to a good time, sort of to kill my sorrow, so to speak."

She went ahead of him up the stairs, undulating her hips so he could see them move in the tight green satin dress. Looking back over her shoulder she smiled at him. "Honey, I'm gonna do more than 'kill your sorrow.' I'm about to give you something you never expected to get in your whole life!" She smiled to herself at the irony of it all as she took his arm and they went down the hall to her room.

Sierra sighed with relief as she and Cholla settled themselves in an expensive compartment on the westbound train and waved good-bye to Trace Durango. They would be forever grateful to him, she thought as she turned away from the window. She looked down at the expensive blue velvet dress she wore. Trace had costumed them, given them money, and paid for the compartment so they wouldn't have to ride in a day coach and mix with passengers who might ask questions. More than that, he had loaded two fine horses in the baggage car, the good black gelding for Cholla, the fine Medicine Hat mare for Sierra.

She looked out at Trace one more time. The handsome rancher stood on the platform. His lips formed the words; Vaya con Dios. Go with God. Then he turned and was gone.

Cholla sat down on one of the overstuffed chairs and looked around the compartment. "Do you think we'll have any trouble?"

"We've got lots of food in the picnic basket, so we shouldn't have to leave the compartment. All we've got to do is sit back and ride from San Antonio northwest and then through New Mexico and Arizona Territories."

"If there're any problems," Cholla said, "will you deal with the conductor? I might be able to pass myself off as a rich Spanish gentleman, but I'd rather not take the chance."

Sierra nodded, lost in her own thoughts. In a few days, she would be at Fort Bowie and Cholla would be gone from her life forever. Why did she feel sad instead of relieved?

Minutes passed, but the train did not leave the station. Cholla became restless. "Something's gone wrong," he murmured. "Do you suppose there's any

333

chance the Army's found out I'm on this train?" He had not dared get aboard carrying weapons, so if there was any trouble, he was defenseless.

"Let me go find out," Sierra said, rising. "I'll ask the conductor."

As she started out of the compartment, Cholla caught her arm. "After all we've been through, you wouldn't betray me?"

"No." She shook her head. "You know better than that. You gave me your word you'd free me if I helped you get back to Arizona, so I gave you my word I'd help you get there. I won't break it."

Cholla looked away at hearing her words, and she wondered about that, but she shrugged it off as she went in search of the conductor.

"Is there a problem?"

The whiskery old man touched his cap with respect as he looked over her expensive dress. "No, ma'am. The connection coming from Austin was a little bit late, and we held up for them — holidays and all, you know. They're in the station now and loading. We'll be moving in just a minute or two."

Sierra nodded with relief and turned to go back to her compartment. Through the dirty window of the car, she thought she saw a cavalry officer on the platform. The man looked vaguely familiar, but she shook her head and dismissed the thought.

On reentering the compartment, she explained the delay to Cholla. Still, he did not visibly relax until the westbound train finally whistled a warning, then began to puff and chug out of the station.

* * *

They didn't leave their compartment as the train traveled west. The Texas Hill Country view gradually gave way to the flat, barren plains of West Texas where only lately Comanches had roamed. It was somewhere in New Mexico Territory that the pair finally exhausted the contents of their huge picnic basket.

Cholla said, "What should we do? I have gone hungry many times as a scout, but I don't want you to."

Sierra shrugged. "Trace gave us plenty of money and there's always food available at the stations. I'll just get off at the next stop, get whatever's available, and bring it back with me."

He looked worried. "Suppose some soldier sees you and recognizes you?"

"Now who would know me? Besides, I'm a wealthy Spanish *señora* traveling to Tucson for the holidays. No one would dare question me, I'm too rich and powerful!"

The both laughed, and Cholla reached out, pulled her to him, kissed her forehead gently.

"I'm going to miss you when we finally get there." Sierra sighed.

He looked away without answering.

He's not going to miss me, she thought. He's going to be glad to be rid of me. I suppose I've been nothing but trouble and a hindrance to him. When he needs a woman, he'll find an Indian or Mexican girl to share his exile.

At the next station, Sierra got off and went into the grimy little dining area. The food looked bad, but then passengers didn't expect any better. Maybe someday those Harvey House Restaurants would reach this line, or the trains might actually have dining cars where people could eat as they traveled. But for now, Sierra would just have to buy what she could and take it back on the train for the two of them.

A great many passengers had pushed their way into the crowded little eating area. Sierra played her role of elegant Spanish *señora* and was waited on quickly. The tortillas and barbecue she chose appeared to be of better quality than what the other passengers were being served. She filled her basket, added some expensive fresh fruit. Finally she started out of the smoky, crowded building.

Somewhere near the counter, she heard the rattle of a paper bag and an annoying crunch.

"Blast it all! Hurry up with that new bag of candy. My train won't wait forever!"

Sierra looked up. A cavalry lieutenant was berating the help and creating a scene. *Quimby Gillen.* Sierra's heart skipped a beat and she almost dropped her basket. What on earth was he doing here? Then she remembered looking out the train window in San Antonio and seeing a cavalry officer with a familiar face. Why hadn't she recognized the lieutenant? They were obviously riding the same train west! Merciful heavens, what was she to do?

He turned his head, looking her direction, chomping the hard candy. She wasn't sure whether he saw her. Was he alone or was there a whole patrol on the train? As calmly as she could, Sierra left the building, hurried across the platform, carried the basket into the compartment.

336

"Have any trouble?" Cholla took the food from her.

"No, of course not." She didn't look at him. He might see her apprehension, and there was no use worrying him when he couldn't do anything about the situation.

She went to the window of the compartment as Cholla dug into the basket, pulled out some barbecue.

"All aboard!" the conductor shouted.

Sierra watched the passengers rush from the adobe building, get back on the train. Sunlight reflected off the silver bars on his bright blue uniform as Gillen strode across the platform, swung up on the car ahead of theirs.

"Sierra, what's wrong?" Cholla momentarily stopped eating.

"Nothing." What could they do? If they tried to get off here, Gillen would surely see them from the window. There were a number of soldiers standing around on the platform, some idlers watching the train pull out. All Gillen would have to do was shout to those men and they would overpower Cholla.

The train began to move out slowly, chugging as it pulled away from the squalid adobe station. *Should I tell him?* She decided against that momentarily. He would want to fight his way off the train, and unless they could get the horses off, too, they'd be afoot. She couldn't remember how many men she'd seen among the passengers. Only a couple of soldiers. But the male passengers might be counted on if Gillen needed them. It occurred to her abruptly that she could betray Cholla, go up into the forward car and alert Gillen. At the next station, there'd be a telegraph office where the lieutenant could send out a call for help, armed soldiers waiting at some station down the way. No, she wouldn't do that. Cholla had given her his word and she intended to help him get away.

Cholla watched Sierra and wondered. Her mood had changed since she had gotten off the train to bring back the food. The very fact that she wouldn't look at him when he questioned her alerted him that she wasn't telling the truth. Something had happened back at the station, and Sierra was lying about it. Had she betrayed him? There would be a telegraph office at that station. Had Sierra sent a message ahead so an Army patrol would be waiting to board the train and arrest him farther west?

He studied her, and when she looked up and met his gaze, Sierra glanced away. *She knows,* he thought abruptly. Somehow she had figured out that Cholla meant to break his word about freeing her. She knew that he was determined to take her across the border whether she wanted to go or not. And maybe, if she'd guessed that he didn't intend to keep his word, she would not keep hers either. Had she also found out the other secret—about how her husband had died?

There was no way to know for sure, nothing to do but wait. Now that the train was moving again, he didn't see any way to stop it and get the horses off. It was no good being stranded afoot and without weapons in this hostile country. One thing was certain, he didn't intend to be captured or to give up his hostage without a fight.

* * *

With indigestion plaguing him, Lieutenant Quimby Gillen leaned back against the uncomfortable horsehair seat as the train pulled out. The food along the route was almost impossible to eat, and his teeth were bothering him again. I ought to give up sweets, he told himself, then rattled the paper bag absently as he crunched a hard candy while other passengers turned to glare.

The woman. Who had she been? Gill had seen just the elegant beauty's back as she'd hurried out of the station. Had she gotten on the train? He had lost sight of her in the crowd. If she had been on this train since he'd got on at Austin, why hadn't he seen her? Gill had been through all the day coaches. Why had she looked so familiar to him?

The train picked up speed as it left the station, and Gill was too preoccupied with his aching teeth to think about much else for a while.

It was a couple of hours later that he suddenly sat bolt upright and slammed his fist into his hand in a fury, startling the drowsy passengers around him. Blast! Of course she looked familiar to him. *Sierra Forester.* Was she on this train and was that Injun with her? More than that, where were they now? He got up and worked his way through his car toward the front. It was hard to keep his balance in the swaying, dirty car. He entered the next car, looking at every face. The train was crowded with holiday travelers and poor immigrants headed west. He searched every car to no avail as the minutes passed.

Maybe he had been mistaken. Maybe he was becoming so obsessed with this chase, he was beginning to see his quarry everywhere. Gill leaned over and looked out the window at the barren landscape. It was almost dusk. What should he do? He was traveling alone to Fort Bowie in virtual disgrace; his patrol had been sent to another assignment. If that big Apache was on this train, Gill didn't want to face him in a showdown alone, even though, as a soldier, Gill carried a sidearm. Looking around, he decided there weren't enough men traveling on this train to organize any kind of a force. Besides, Gill himself was probably the only one carrying a weapon.

He sought out the whiskered conductor. "How many cars on this train?"

"Seven." The conductor pushed his cap back. "Then there's the caboose and the baggage car. Oh, and of course the compartments."

Compartments. Those are for the wealthy, Gill thought, so they don't have to mix with the ordinary people, so they can be comfortable. But where would the Apache and Sierra get the money for a compartment?

"Conductor, I thought I saw a lady I used to know on this train, but then I couldn't find her — attractive, wearing an expensive blue dress."

The old man's pink face lit up, and he nodded. "Ah, yes, the señora and her husband. They have a compartment, of course."

"Of course." Gill thought a minute, uncertain of what to do. He didn't want to confront Cholla alone; he knew the Apache's bravery and fighting skill too well. He wanted a bunch of armed soldiers backing him up if and when he took that Injun bastard off this train. That the pair was riding in a compartment made no sense, but none of that mattered right now.

All Gill could do was go back to his seat and wait. He turned to the conductor. "How far to the next station?"

The old man took off his cap, scratched his head, "Oh, an hour. Why?"

"Something important has come up." Gill thought about it, decided against sharing his knowledge. While he didn't care too much if passengers got hurt in the capture, that might upset the brass and get him in trouble. Besides, Gill didn't want to risk anyone on this train trying to cut himself in on the reward. "Alert me when we're getting close to the station. I must get off there and send a message ahead."

"Sure thing, Lieutenant."

Gill went back to his seat. Yep, he'd send a wire. It would take a little time, but farther on the Army would have an armed patrol waiting to take Cholla off the train. All Gill could do now was wait. He wondered if Sierra Forester knew he was aboard. Of course she didn't, or she and the Injun would have gotten off somewhere along the line.

He laughed to himself now as he stared out at the pale lavender and gray dusk, popped another peppermint in his mouth. Blast it all! He could hardly wait to see that pair's surprised faces when the soldiers boarded and searched them out. It was going to be so ironic. Gill would put chains on the Apache, take him on to Bowie Station and get orders to ship him right back out to Florida. If Sierra would be friendly, maybe Gill would change his testimony and say he'd been mistaken, that she hadn't helped Cholla escape

341

back at Sundance, that she'd been forced to leave with the savage. For not sending her to prison, Gill expected her to be very grateful. Maybe it was going to be a good holiday after all.

His spirits light, Gill hummed a few bars of "Jingle Bells" under his breath, rolled the candy around in his mouth, and settled back to wait for the next station.

Nevada pushed his hat back on his black hair, looked at the train track from where he and his gang hid in the cottonwoods on the small creek. "Ben, you sure about that train?"

The grizzled old Confederate veteran nodded. "Sure, Nevada. We heard there's a gold shipment coming through."

"What do you mean, *heard?* I got a price on my head, and can't afford to take chances. Oh, well, what the hell? I don't expect to live long anyway."

Nevada was philosophical about it. Times were changing, but he could not, or would not, change. He would be twenty-six on his next birthday, but to-night he felt fifty. The days of riding with Billy the Kid in the Lincoln County Wars were gone forever. He looked down at the gold signet ring he wore, thought of his heritage. He would not go back to that fine home, and maybe now he wasn't welcome anyway.

"Nevada," Charlie said. He looked lean and weathered as old leather. "You suppose the train'll see those rocks piled on the track in time to stop?"

Rod snarled, "Who the hell cares? I'd like to watch it derail, see folks die!"

Nevada glared at the outlaw, wishing he hadn't allowed Rod to join them. Five was the magic number of Nevada's father's people and the new man made six. "Rod, if you don't beat all! Remember, we don't hurt innocent people, and we only rob the train, not the passengers."

"I don't mind hurtin' folks," Rod said, and spat to one side. "And it appears to me takin' nothin' but railroad gold is foolish."

"I'm still runnin' things, Rod, unless you think you can outdraw me," Nevada said as he stroked the neck of his strangely marked black and white stallion.

There was even a reason for his choice of railroads. A long time ago, there had been a rich, elegant beauty who had spurned him because of the scandal of his bloodlines. The beauty's family was the major stockholder of this railroad.

Nevada didn't want to think about her because he still loved her. "Jack, you and Charlie build up the fire in front of that barricade a little. We want to give the engineer plenty of time to stop; no use derailin' it and hurtin' anyone."

The Whitley brothers rode off to do his bidding, and Nevada looked around at the others in his gang. Hard cases and losers, most of them, who had outlived their time. Nevada, he thought ironically. But he had been born and raised in Arizona Territory. Only old Ben knew his real name; the prominent name Nevada had cast aside.

Nevada deftly rolled a cigarette, lit it. Mex leaned over for a light and Nevada lit his cigar, but when Rod leaned forward, Nevada shook his head, blew the match out.

Mex said, "Not three on a match, Rod. The boss is superstitious."

Rod grumbled to himself, got out his own matches. "Hell of a way to spend the holidays. I wanted to be back in Tombstone for Christmas."

Christmas. Waves of nostalgia swept over Nevada as he smoked and remembered happier times. But he couldn't return to the family he had turned his back on.

"It don't make sense," Rod grumbled, rubbing his unshaven chin, "not to rob the passengers if there ain't no payroll."

Nevada shook his head, and a lock of jet black hair fell from under his Stetson across his dark face. "Rod, I won't tell you again, we don't rob passengers, we only take the railroad's money."

Ben nodded in agreement, and Mex shifted his weight in the saddle as the two Whitley brothers rode back to join them.

"Listen," Ben said.

They all strained their ears.

Faintly, as if from a distance, Nevada heard the echo of a train whistle, then the distant rumble of wheels coming from the east. His Medicine Hat stallion moved restlessly under him, as if knowing they were about to ride into action.

Without thinking, Nevada crossed himself. He knew it was superstitious, but it was part of him. His beautiful mother was Spanish and Cheyenne; his father . . .

He wouldn't think about that right now. There was too much pain in the memories of what had driven him away from a fine home and onto the outlaw trail.

In the dusk, the fire on the tracks flickered like a ghostly light or maybe a candle lit for the dead. In the distance now, he saw the black locomotive coming toward them from the east. It would have to top a rise to see the fire and the pile of rocks on the tracks; there would be enough time to stop but not enough time for the engineer to react before the outlaws were climbing aboard the cars.

Only a few more minutes, Nevada thought, throwing his cigarette away. He checked his ivory-handled pistol again. "Ready, boys? Any minute now the engineer's gonna see that pile of rocks and the fire, and he'll start hittin' those brakes!"

Chapter Eighteen

Sierra had just started to move across the compartment when the engineer braked. The wheels seemed to lock, steel scraping against steel as tons of iron slid along the track. She was thrown off balance, into Cholla's arms. Terrified, she screamed, "For God's sake, what's happening?"

He grabbed onto a wall to steady them, then shook his head, his face tense and nervous as he sat her down on a chair. "I don't know. The train's stopped."

She felt a chill. Quimby Gillen had managed to reach the authorities somehow, and the troops had ridden out to stop the train.

"Dark Eyes, what is it?" He touched her shoulder.

"I . . . I didn't know how to tell you. I couldn't decide what to do about it."

"What?"

She realized suddenly what his expression meant. "No." She shook her head. "I haven't betrayed you."

"What, then?"

"When I got off the train for food, I saw him."

"Saw who? Tell me, damn it!"

He had both big hands on her shoulders, and she realized how strong he was, how dangerous he could be; but she wasn't afraid he would use his strength against her. "Lieutenant Gillen is on this train."

"What? How long—?"

"I don't have any idea." Sierra pulled away from him, peered anxiously out the window into the coming night. *Riders.* She saw riders coming out of the cottonwood trees toward the train.

Cholla looked out, too, began to swear. "He's managed to wire ahead for a patrol."

"I wasn't sure he saw me." She turned toward him, wondering how to assure him she hadn't betrayed him. Somehow that seemed so terribly important to her. "And then I didn't know what to do."

The both looked out at the riders coming toward the train, guns blazing. The train had come to a complete halt, and smoke from the engine drifted past the window. So this is how it ends, she thought, a shootout in the barren reaches of New Mexico Territory. She wasn't even afraid, she realized with surprise. Only sad that Cholla hadn't made it across the border. Somehow it had become terribly important to her that he make it to freedom.

"Sierra"—he shook his head as he peered out the window into the growing darkness—"those aren't soldiers."

"What? Who are they?"

He laughed under his breath. "I'm not sure you're ready for this, but I think the train's being held up!"

She blinked, staring out at the six men who had ridden up to the train, were swinging aboard the coaches. The leader was tall and dressed much like a

Mexican *vaquero*. She saw silver flashing on his clothes, on his horse's bridle. "Mexican bandits." She drew away from the window in horror.

"No." Cholla shook his head. "They look like white men except for the leader; I'd say he's Spanish and Indian. This might be a lucky break, but I'm going to hide you 'til I'm sure."

"But what—?"

"Get down!" He pushed her gently to the floor. "I'm going to see if I can join up with them, at least temporarily."

She suddenly felt bereft at the thought. Within a few minutes, he might be gone, leaving her on the train. "What about me?"

He looked at her a long moment, regret in his eyes. "So you go free sooner than you expected."

"What about Gillen?"

"Tell him you were forced to help me back in Sundance. If you can get to Fort Bowie, my friend, Tom Mooney, will help you. Demand your share of the reward if they get me."

"No! I—"

"Don't argue with me; there isn't time! Crawl under that table and stay there 'til it's over."

His tone left no room for argument. With a sigh, she looked at the skirted table. "All right, whatever you say."

"Oh, Sierra"—he turned around—"give Tom a message for me, will you?"

She nodded, still unable to believe he was really leaving her.

"Tell him I'm sending him that gift I promised him. You got that?"

"A gift? What—?"

"Just tell him, all right?"

She nodded. In a few minutes, he might be gone with those outlaws. She should be thrilled. Why, then, did she feel so sad? "You're sending that gift you promised."

He seemed to think a long time. "Something else. Tell him: Usen's own. Ke'jaa's den."

" 'Usen's own; Ke'jaa's den.' That doesn't make any sense."

"It doesn't to you, but it will to Tom—after he thinks about it awhile. Good-bye, Sierra. I'm sorry about all the trouble I've caused you." He pulled her to him and kissed her as if he never wanted to let her go.

Then he turned to leave and, abruptly, she didn't want to be left behind. "Wait! I want to go with you!" She grabbed his sleeve.

"No!" He pushed her away from the compartment door. "You'll be safe on the train. Gillen may be mad, but there's really nothing he can do to you, not when I forced you to help me escape. You got that? You were afraid of me, had to obey me."

"Let me go with you!" She caught Cholla's arm.

He tried to shake her hand off. "No. Gillen can't hurt you; ask the conductor for help. You've got money enough to go on to Fort Bowie—"

A sharp rap on the door. "Open up!"

"Sierra," Cholla snapped, "get under that table! You want to get raped by this bunch?"

Someone was slamming against the locked door now. "Come out! Come out with your hands up!"

"Sierra, hide."

Reluctantly, she let go of his arm, crawled under the table, to be completely concealed by its long white cloth just as the door splintered. She heard jingling spurs as someone entered.

"Get your hands up, *señor.*"

"Easy, *hombres,*" Cholla said in a soothing tone, "I'm not giving any trouble, see? I've got my hands up. I want to go with you."

"What?" The voice had a decided Southern drawl. "You must be loco. Jack, get Nevada."

"Sure, Ben. Where is he?"

"Helping Mex and Rod break into the baggage car."

She heard the man leave, but she could still see two pairs of boots besides Cholla's. Now she was afraid. She didn't want to be raped by a bunch of outlaws, but she was afraid for Cholla. Suppose they decided to kill him and leave him lying in a pool of blood?

She heard someone else come in, wearing a pair of boots with spurs that jingled — a man who walked with an easy grace. Under the edge of the tablecloth, she saw fine, handmade black boots with fancy silver spurs. He had small feet for a man. "What's the trouble, Ben?"

"Nevada, this *hombre* wants to go with us."

"Now why the hell would a wealthy Spaniard want to leave with us?" Nevada sounded like a Westerner.

"I'm not all Spanish, any more than you are, despite your clothes."

Sierra gasped at Cholla's daring, but Nevada must have thrown back his head and laughed. "I like your guts, pard, but you still haven't answered my question."

350

"Let's just say you're not the only one the law is looking for. I've got a horse in the baggage car."

"Mister, there's two fine horses in the baggage car, and I recognize the brand. How did you come by stock from the Triple D and how come there's two?"

"I bought them."

Nevada swore. "I know Trace Durango from a long time back. He might give some of his best stock to a friend, but he wouldn't sell it!"

"Does being a friend of the Durangos help or hinder my chances of going with you?"

The sound of boots coming in, and another voice. "Nevada, we got all the gold from that strong box. What's holdin' us up? We could be robbin' passengers."

"Rod, this *hombre* wants to go with us."

"Some greaser gent wants to play outlaw? Hell, no!"

"I give the orders here, and I told you we only steal from the railroad." Nevada's voice sounded cold, dangerous.

"Listen you two," the Southerner drawled, "we can't stand here jawin' all night! When this train don't make it into the next station on time, they might begin to wonder."

"You're right, Ben. Stranger, if Trace Durango thinks you're all right—"

"Aw, Nevada," Rod growled, "why don't you just let me kill him? I ain't killed nobody in a long time—"

"And won't, Rod, unless there's good reason, not as long as you ride with me. Stranger, I'm still wonderin' how you came by those horses?"

"Maybe I killed Trace and stole them."

351

"Even more unlikely!" Nevada laughed. "I've seen Trace Durango handle a gun. Are you a friend of his, *señor?*"

"Is it going to cause him trouble if I am?"

Nevada shifted his weight. "That's what I like, loyalty. You're all right."

"Hey, what's this?" She recognized the voice of the man called Rod. "I see some blue velvet under that table."

Sierra's heart froze.

"Leave her alone!" Cholla shouted, but already Sierra saw the outlaw's hand reaching to pull her out.

"Get your hands off me!" She struggled, but he dragged her out from under the table, a grin on his unshaven face.

"Leave her alone!" Cholla tried to come to her aid, but the handsome, dark one with the silver spurs held him at bay with a pearl-handled pistol.

"So the gent was hiding something more valuable than gold. I don't blame you, *señor.* A woman like this one, I'd hide her, too." This handsome, dark rascal had the voice of Nevada. He touched the brim of his Stetson politely, and his ring reflected the lamplight; an unusual gold ring with a wolf's-head design.

Rod looked her up and down slowly, rubbed his unshaven chin, and leered. "Let's take the gal, leave the man."

She stared at all of them. Besides Nevada and Rod, the third man looked like an older Southerner.

A fourth man, a swarthy Mexican, stuck his head in the compartment. "What the hell's keepin' you *hombres?* We need to clear out *muy pronto.* . . ." His voice trailed off as he saw Sierra.

Rod said, "How many's in favor of killin' the sonovabitch and takin' the girl for ourselves?"

The others looked at Nevada.

He glared at Rod, then looked at Sierra. "A woman along is bad luck. You two really want to go with us?"

"No," Cholla said. "I go; she doesn't."

"Don't I get any say in this?" Sierra stuck her chin out stubbornly.

"Hell! I don't have time to sort this out." Nevada grinned. "Both of you come along, we'll figure it out later!"

"No," Cholla protested.

She heard the clicks as the hammers on all the pistols were pulled back.

"I give the orders, *señor*," Nevada said. "Ben, get those two horses out of the baggage car. I don't know who the hell this pair is, or how they came by those horses, but I intend to find out what they're doin' with Triple D stock."

Ben turned and left.

The handsome outlaw leader gestured with his pistol. "Okay, you two. Walk ahead of me into the forward passenger car."

Sierra hesitated. Lieutenant Gillen was in that car.

"Get movin', lady!" Rod snarled.

"Watch it, Rod," Nevada said softly. "I don't hold with scaring a lady."

"What would you know about *real* ladies?" Rod sneered.

"More than you would," Nevada replied, and his face grew sad, thoughtful.

There was nothing Sierra could do but hang on to

Cholla's arm, walk ahead of the outlaws at gunpoint through the next car. When she passed Lieutenant Gillen, she saw the fury in his eyes, the sweat of fear on his face.

At the end of the car, Nevada turned around and waved his pistol at the passengers. "Everyone just keep their places; no one'll get hurt. I'm taking these two with me."

Gill seemed to forget himself and came halfway up out of his seat. "You can't do that! This man is wanted for everything from murder to assault!"

Nevada looked him over coolly. "Would you like to make a little wager, Lieutenant?"

Gill hesitated.

Old Ben stuck his head in. "Nevada, we got that pair of horses unloaded, the gold, too."

Nevada's white teeth shone in his dark face as he grinned. He turned to the conductor. "Tell the president of the railroad I send regards again to his beautiful daughter." He tipped his hat in an almost arrogant salute. To Sierra and Cholla, he said, "Move! We're getting off this train!"

I might be better off dealing with Gillen than these outlaws, Sierra thought with a sinking feeling. But she wasn't getting any choice.

She and Cholla stepped out onto the platform and then went down the steps into the darkness. Another man came galloping from the direction of the baggage car, and he had Sierra's horse and Cholla's by their bridles.

"Mount up," Nevada ordered.

She looked over at Cholla.

"Do as he says, Sierra."

"Sierra?" Rod leered at her as they all mounted up. "Pretty name for a pretty girl."

Cholla swore under his breath. "Don't you even think about touching her, you bastard."

"You'll answer for that later, *hombre.*"

"Shut up and let's get out of here!" Nevada ordered. He spurred his horse forward. As the light from the train window caught the sleek, spotted hide of his unusually marked horse, Sierra saw that the handsome outlaw rode a Medicine Hat stallion.

The group galloped away from the train, Sierra fearing they might be in more danger from the outlaws than they had been from Lieutenant Gillen. But it was too late for regrets, and besides, there was nothing she could do. She and Cholla had temporarily escaped from the Army only to be riding with six of the toughest-looking gunslingers who ever held up a train.

They rode for hours through the darkness, stopping only long enough to cool the horses. Where they were headed, Sierra could only guess except that she was certain they might have gone off in one direction, then turned in another to fool anyone who might try to follow them. Toward morning, when she thought she couldn't sit the saddle another minute, they rode into a box canyon in some low-lying hills and reined up in front of a cabin so hidden in the mesquite that she didn't see it until they were upon it. A lucky horse shoe hung over the door.

She whispered to Cholla, "Have any idea where we are?"

355

He shook his head as he dismounted, came around to help her down. "Only that we changed directions in case anyone was trying to follow us, then turned back west. We're somewhere in western New Mexico Territory, is all I know."

"You two shut up," Rod growled, gesturing with his pistol, "unless you want to talk loud enough for the rest of us to hear."

Nevada looked back over his shoulder as he handed his reins to one of the others. "Take it easy, Rod."

Rod looked as if he might say something, then seemed to think better of it. "I was just afraid they were plottin' something."

"So let them!" The leader took off his Stetson, slapped it against his leg, dust flying. "Frankly, Rod, when you were off in Tombstone a few days, I enjoyed the quiet. You find a doctor there?"

"He was out of town," Rod said as he gestured, indicating the pair of captives should go ahead of him, "but I did find a cutie at the Birdcage Theater. She wants to be a singer."

Even in the moonlight, Sierra saw a dark frown cross Nevada's rugged features, and he swore under his breath. "With what you got, you take up with a woman? That's rotten, mister."

"Aw, I probably didn't give her what I got. Besides, it cost me enough. I had to listen to her sing, and she sounded like a squallin' cat."

Sierra was scared. She held onto Cholla's arm as they all went into the cabin, leaving Ben to put away the horses.

The darkly handsome leader looked her up and down. "Can you cook, ma'am?"

Rod snorted with amusement. "I got better ideas for her than cookin', Nevada."

Cholla bristled, pushed Sierra behind him. "Don't touch her."

"I plan to do more than touch her." Rod laughed.

"Why you — !"

But even as Cholla went for the sneering outlaw, the leader stepped between them. "Easy, *señor.*" He isn't gonna touch her."

"Who says?" Rod squared his shoulders. "If she's gonna be here awhile, we got a right to expect a little entertainment from her."

"*I say,* Rod, at least until someone comes along who can outdraw me, and I don't think you're that man."

"Someday we'll see about that."

Cholla broke in. "Nevada, you don't have to fight my battles for me."

"So who asked you?" The dark eyes were cold. "This has nothing to do with you or your woman — it has *everything* to do with who leads this gang."

The others stood around, patiently rolling cigarettes. "Rod, we're with Nevada," Jack said. "Me and my brother Charlie joined him when he saved us from a lynch mob. So if you're lookin' for someone to back your play, don't count on us."

"Same here," the swarthy Mexican grunted.

Sierra hurried to the fireplace. "I'll fix some food." The tension dissolved immediately, and the men settled themselves around on chairs. Ben came in and built up the fire for Sierra. She watched them all out of the corner of her eye as she looked for flour and lard, began to make biscuits. The Whitleys lit cigarettes, Ben got out a bottle and glasses.

"Now"—Nevada grinned at Cholla with even white teeth—"tell us just why the law's after you, *señor.*"

The scout hesitated. "It's a long story."

"We got time." Rod grinned malevolently.

"Shut up," Nevada said to him; then he turned to Cholla. "*Señor,* why is the Army on your trail, what did you do?"

Sierra cooked and listened as Cholla told what had happened from the time he jumped off the train near her farm. When he'd brought them up to date, Nevada leaned back in his chair and laughed. "Well, I'll be damned! So you're that Apache! Half the country is looking for you. We've heard about you in every *cantina.* Maybe you'll bring us luck after all."

Rod's yellow eyes gleamed. "Nevada, if there's a big reward, we ought to hand him over to the Army."

But the *pistolero* shook his head, sipped his drink. "We aren't bounty hunters, Rod."

"But he's just an Injun—"

"I'm Injun, too," Nevada said, "or have you forgotten? Spanish and Indian. Besides, we've got no friends in the Army. Why should we do them a favor?"

"I was thinking of the money," Rod grumbled.

"Well, stop thinking about the money." Nevada threw his *cigarillo* into the fireplace and sipped his whiskey. "We made a good haul from the railroad this time. Besides, any man who can lead the Army on a merry chase like he's done, and make them look like a bunch of fools, is all right with me."

"But Nevada—"

"You heard me!"

His voice carried the authority of a whip crack.

No wonder he's the leader of this cutthroat crew, Sierra thought.

Cholla sipped his drink. "I don't know anything about you," he said to the other man.

Nevada shrugged wide shoulders. "I lead this gang; that's all you need to know. The past is best left buried."

Sierra glanced over at him. He looked sad, almost tragic. He ran one hand through his black hair, and she saw the fine ring gleam on his hand. This is no ordinary outlaw, she decided as she fried bacon. Everything about him showed class and education. She wondered suddenly who he really was?

Nevada sipped his drink, looked at Cholla. "You want to ride with us, you're welcome to join up; share and share alike."

"I'll think about it." Cholla looked over at Sierra. "I was on my way to the Sierra Madre."

"That's a pretty lonely life," Nevada said.

Rod laughed and gulped his drink. "Not if you got a little hot tamale like that one to take with you."

Cholla gave him a look that would freeze hot water. "If you go anywhere near her, I'll cut you like a steer!"

Nevada looked at him keenly, then turned and looked Sierra over. "Is she your woman? I thought she was a hostage."

Sierra went brick red and busied herself with the biscuits.

"She's mine," Cholla said with finality. "And I don't share."

Nevada sighed almost regretfully. "There was once a girl . . . never mind. If Sierra were mine, I wouldn't share either."

359

Rod slammed his glass down on the table with a ringing sound. "Now wait just a damned minute! It ain't fair that we all got to do without while he gets her all to himself. He ought to be made to share."

Cholla's voice was cold. "Any *hombre* here thinks he's big enough to walk across me to get to her—"

"You heard the man, Rod." Nevada grinned.

"But he's just a damned Injun bastard, and—"

"Enough!" Nevada's chair came down on all fours with a bang that rattled the windows. "Enough!"

Rod's face went pale. "I . . . I beg your pardon Nevada. I plumb forgot about your . . ."

Sierra looked at him. Rod's voice trailed off weakly. He had obviously brought up something forbidden. She wondered even more about the handsome, mixed-blood outlaw with the wolf's-head ring.

She was scared, but she was also mad. "It looks like you galoots might think about consulting me, while everyone talks about sharing me around!"

Nevada threw back his head and laughed, but his dark eyes were full of admiration as he looked her over. "Spirit! I like that in horses and women!"

"But, Nevada," Rod argued, "that ain't fair. We out number him. Why don't we just take her?"

The leader gave Sierra a charming wink. "I think we had better consult the lady; I was raised a gentle man."

"I'm with Cholla," she said, stepping to his side.

Rod's face broke into an ugly sneer. "You'd take that savage over a—"

Cholla hit him then, charging into him, knocking

360

him backward. They crashed into a table; it splintered under their weight and they went crashing to the floor.

Ben watched, but the other three moved as if to interfere. Nevada held up his hand. "Let them fight," he ordered. "Rod's been askin' for trouble a long time; he's overdue to have his plow cleaned."

Sierra stared, horror-stricken, as the two men fought, rolling about hitting each other, slamming into furniture. A picture came down with a clatter and tinkle of broken glass.

"You bastard!" Rod swore as they struggled. He snatched up a piece of the broken glass, slashed at Cholla, cut his cheek, and scarlet blood smeared them both.

Sierra smelled the warm, coppery scent of it, felt sick; but there was nothing she could do. In that instant, Cholla slammed Rod up against a wall, and Rod reached for the pistol in his holster. Nevada's Colt blazed suddenly, the noise like thunder, the acrid smell of gunpowder filling the room.

Rod clutched his chest, staring in openmouthed horror as blood seeped through his fingers. Then he crashed to the floor.

Nevada crossed himself, blew the smoke from the pearl-handled pistol barrel, reholstered his gun. "I don't hold with letting a man gun an unarmed one down."

Cholla strode to Sierra's side, put his arm around her, looked at Nevada.

The handsome outlaw shrugged. "Rod was overdue for a hanging anyhow. He'd been on the prod for weeks. Besides, now I'm back to my magic number of

361

five again. Jack and Charlie, get that body out of here."

The men all relaxed, and the two brothers went over, picked up the body, carried it outside. Evidently no one had liked the dead outlaw.

Cholla knew at that moment that he loved Sierra. He didn't want or need her; he loved her. Of course she didn't care about him. Gently he put his arm around her shaking shoulders, shook his head. "Thanks, Nevada."

"Don't mention it. My father . . ."—he hesitated—"my stepfather was a Kentuckian, so I was brought up in the old-fashioned Southern tradition. Ladies are meant to be protected." Nevada began to roll a cigarette.

"If you'll give us permission to leave, we're headed for Arizona," Cholla said.

"Arizona. Lots of memories there. . . ." Nevada's voice trailed off. He lit his cigarette. "And then what?"

Cholla looked down into Sierra's eyes and made his decision. He loved her, but he hadn't been straight with her; he had intended to force her to go with him, no matter what he had promised. Now because he loved her, he would do what was right, no matter how much of a sacrifice it was, how much it hurt him. "I'm headed south of the border," he said softly, "but I promised Sierra I'd leave her at Fort Bowie. I have to keep my word because she trusts me."

He waited then, hoping against hope that she would say, I've changed my mind, I want to go with

362

you, be with you for all time. Take me across the border with you.

Of course she didn't, and he couldn't bring himself to tell her that he cared. He was a proud man, one who wouldn't bend to anyone, not the whole U.S. Army, not incredible odds, and certainly not to a woman. No, she isn't just a woman, he admitted silently. Sierra is *ishton, the* woman, best loved of all the women who ever shared my embrace. But he was too proud to tell her that.

Nevada shrugged and smoked, staring into the fire. "One time there was a girl . . ." he said softly, almost as if he were voicing his thoughts to himself. He shrugged and looked at them. "Very well. You two stay a day or two and rest up; then, barring bad luck, we'll get you headed on those last few miles to Arizona." He reached over and knocked on the wooden table.

Cholla thought about Gill. "There might be an Army patrol looking for us. I don't want to bring you our trouble."

Nevada stood up. "Kind of you to tell us, but we aren't worried. In fact, we might enjoy leading the Army around in circles for a few days until they get tired of it all, realize they've been fooled, and go away. Is that food ready, ma'am?"

Sierra nodded.

"Then let's eat."

So Cholla and Sierra stayed with the outlaws for a couple of days. During that time, he made love to her with a passion that was bittersweet because they were so soon to part. While he wanted her, he would not force her to accompany him across the border. He would not even lower himself to ask. She didn't really care about him, and the life he faced was a hard, lonely one full of danger. When he took her in his arms and made love to her in the darkness of their small room in the outlaws' cabin, it was a bittersweet experience because in only a few more days, they were going to be separated forever.

Chapter Nineteen

Nevada tried to get the couple to stay on until after Christmas, but they declined.

"The Army's looking for us in this area," Cholla said. "And I promised Sierra I would get her to Fort Bowie, so we're going on."

Sierra had mixed feelings about the approaching end of the whole adventure. A new year ahead of me, she thought, I'll be starting a whole new life. But I'll be doing it alone.

Cholla changed into Western clothes, and she put on a fringed, buckskin dress and the boots Trace had given her. They waved good-bye to the outlaws and rode out.

"What're you thinking?" Cholla asked after they had ridden west for a while.

"About what I'm going to do in the coming months."

He didn't look at her. "Will you be going back to East Saint Louis?"

"I . . . I don't know." She shook her head. "My mother always wanted to go West; maybe it was my desire, too. I didn't dream it could be so wild and beautiful."

"Sierra," he mused, so softly that he seemed to be speaking to himself, "wild and beautiful and untamed."

"Maybe I'll stay." She waited for him to say he wished she'd go with him, but he only looked straight ahead and kept silent as they rode through the barren stretches of mesquite and cactus toward Arizona Territory.

How foolish of me, she thought. He wouldn't want to be burdened with me any longer. Besides, if he did ask, she wasn't sure what her answer would be. Life with him would be full of danger and hardship. It would mean turning her back on everything she had known. Maybe she wasn't such a rugged individualist as she'd thought.

But then, it didn't matter because he didn't ask. In fact, as the days passed and they rode west, he became moody and withdrawn. She lost track of the days, was aware Christmas had surely come and gone, but what did it matter to two fugitives in western New Mexico Territory?

Trixie looked out the upstairs window at the activity on the street below her room at the Birdcage. With Christmas over, a temporary lull hung over the town of Tombstone. Things wouldn't pick up until New Year's Eve. Not that it mattered. Her boss had found out she was diseased, and she'd been fired. That very afternoon.

Now what the hell was she to do? She pulled her soiled green satin robe around her and reached for the bottle of medicine, took a big swig. After a few minutes, that nice glow came over her and things didn't look so bleak anymore.

San Francisco. She had been headed for San Francisco. Of course that was where someone of her talents belonged. Trouble was, she didn't really have much money, what with the cost of her medicine—and she needed more and more of that as time passed.

Trixie pulled out her pack of cigarettes, stared at the Cameo girl. Of course I look just like her, she reassured herself, though not quite as young. And I'm not getting any younger. As for the disease, well, everyone has to die of something eventually.

What to do? The management had told her to clear out by tomorrow. Where to go?

"San Francisco, of course." She said it aloud. She wasn't sure if the police in East St. Louis had found out she'd been in Otto Toombs's office when he'd died, but she was afraid to go back and find out.

"How, Trixie?" She stared moodily into space. "You got no money." Quimby Gillen. She wondered if he had made it back to Fort Bowie? That was only a few miles to the north of Tombstone, and she had a little money. Maybe she should go up there, see if Gill would buy her a train ticket.

"He ain't one to give somethin' for nothin.'" Trixie grinned. He'd get something for his money, all right; the "social" disease she'd given that young rancher. "Yeah, there's poetic justice in that, ain't there?"

Humming a little of "I'll Take You Home Again, Kathleen," Trixie began to make her plans.

Out in New Mexico terrain, Lieutenant Quimby Gillen was in a decided fury. He reined his lathered horse in, slammed a fist in his palm. "Blast it all! It's like looking for two grains of sand in all these miles of the stuff!"

He twisted in his saddle, staring at the weary patrol with him, stuffed a lemon drop in his mouth, crumpled the empty sack, and threw it on the ground. "I thought we'd be able to follow the tracks when they left the train."

The bald old sergeant took off his hat, wiped his face. "Beggin' your pardon, sir, the men are tired, and we've even spent Christmas roamin' around searchin.' "

"Don't you think I know that?" Gill fairly seethed with frustration and anger. Here he'd had a patrol sent over from the nearest fort, thinking it couldn't be that long now before he ran Cholla and Sierra down, and they'd disappeared again. Besides, his teeth were hurting. Maybe he should try some of Trixie's medicine. That stupid, no talent bitch had disappeared from East St. Louis. He hoped she was out of his life for good.

"Sir," the sergeant said again, "take it from one who knows this area, there's lots of places they could hide. If they have someone with them like that bandit called Nevada, we might never see them again. Nobody knows the whole Southwest as well as Nevada does."

Gill heaved a sigh, his shoulders slumping as he leaned on his saddle horn. Maybe the pair weren't even in the area anymore. Wouldn't it be a joke on him if, while he was on a wild-goose chase in New Mexico, Cholla and Sierra Forester had escaped into Arizona? He had no doubt that was where Cholla was headed.

Would the Apache try to get to Fort Bowie? Surely he wouldn't have that kind of gall. "On the other hand, I wouldn't put anything past that crafty fox," Gillen said aloud.

"Sir?"

"Never mind. Blast it, never mind!" It suddenly dawned on him that Cholla had a friend at Fort Bowie, Sergeant Tom Mooney, and the Medicine Hat stallion was there. He might try to reclaim it. Besides, he might intend to leave the woman off there, making it his last stop before he turned straight south and rode the fifty or so miles to the border and the freedom beyond.

"Sergeant, we're quitting," Gillen snapped. "You and the patrol can go back to your fort."

"And you, sir?"

"That damned Injun probably thinks he's got me fooled into spending weeks and weeks roaming around this bleak country looking for him, but I'm gonna outsmart him. I'm gonna go back to the nearest station, catch that train west. With any luck, maybe I'll get to Fort Bowie before Cholla does!"

Tom Mooney sat on his bunk, a worn book of

poems in his callused, freckled hands. But his mind was too busy for him to enjoy reading. "Aye, Tom, ye old Irishman, now that Christmas is gone, you've only a couple of days to make your decision."

The dog raised its great head and looked at him gravely.

"And you, Ke'jaa, do you think you'd mind livin' on a Michigan farm?" He paused and looked out the window to the east, wondering where the dog's master was at this moment?

The woman was still with Cholla; that much was clear. Only a couple of days ago, there'd been a wire from Gillen saying he'd actually been on the same train as the pair without realizing it and they'd gotten away right under his nose by escaping during train robbery. Right now the lieutenant was combing western New Mexico Territory for Cholla, but if Gillen didn't find any trace of him soon, he'd been coming on in to the fort to see if the Apache turned up there.

Tom sighed, put down the book. Maybe Cholla would come here to try to get his horse and say goodbye to his old friend. Tom hoped he wouldn't. As a sergeant of the U.S. Cavalry, Mooney didn't want to be torn between duty and his deep friendship for the Indian.

The woman. He stroked the worn book cover and thought about her. Gillen's wire sounded as if he weren't sure whether Sierra Forester had, indeed, been forced off that train or had left of her own free will. Perhaps she didn't care about the Apache; perhaps she had been under extreme duress all this time. He took the photograph out and looked at it, wonder-

370

ing if any woman could learn to care for a wiry, middle-aged Irishman with no money.

The reward. If Tom helped capture Cholla, there'd be a reward — and a promotion if he decided to stay in the Army. With those changes in his situation, would Sierra be interested in him? Could he betray his friend if there was any possibility of having the woman? Love makes a man do strange things, he thought. When it came to a showdown, Tom wasn't sure what decision he'd make. He hoped to God he didn't have to make any — and he wouldn't, if Cholla stayed out of the area.

Tomorrow night was New Year's Eve. Most of the men at the fort would be partying; some would be on leave. Not much happening now that the Apaches had been shipped away. Next week, Tom could be on a train headed home, escorting the pitiful little schoolteacher. But right now he didn't want to think about making any kind of decision or even of whether he was going to leave the Army. He bowed his head and prayed that if faced with a choice, he would do what was morally, if not legally, right.

Sierra and Cholla rode west until they were in low mountains covered with spruce and cedar.

She looked over at him. "Where are we?"

"The Chiricahua Mountains," he answered, looking west. "By tomorrow afternoon, late, you'll be at Fort Bowie."

"And you will be safe over the border in Mexico," she said, not sure how she felt about that. Once she had been astounded that a primitive Indian had made a decision to travel fifteen hundred miles to freedom. Then, after she had gotten to know Cholla, it had seemed reasonable enough that he would do it. She tried to sort out her feelings as they spurred their horses and rode on.

Not so long ago she had hoped to see Cholla dead. Then she had grown to respect his daring and courage and, through him, the Apache people she had once thought of as cruel savages. Finally, though she didn't want to think about it or admit it, even to herself, she began to feel more than respect for him.

Not that it matters, she thought as they rode through the mountains. To him, she was nothing but a hostage, although at times she sensed she might be more than that to him. Of course that was ridiculous. She glanced over at his proud, cold expression, wishing she knew what he was thinking. What difference did it make anyway? Her own thoughts and feelings weren't clear to her. If he did ask her to turn her back on civilization and ride away with him, could she, would she?

What foolishness, she thought, watching him, this man doesn't need you. He doesn't need anyone. He is completely self-sufficient. You can stop wondering what you would do because he doesn't want you, doesn't need you. When he feels an urge for a woman, no doubt many an Indian girl would be pleased to be carried off by him for his temporary use.

They rode until dark and then camped.

Sierra stared into the fire after they had eaten. "You didn't want to ride on in tonight?"

"And get shot by a guard? Besides, I'm not riding in—you are."

"What about your stallion?"

He settled down next to her on the blanket, smoking a hand-rolled cigarette, and shook his head. "I'd never be able to get the Medicine Hat out of the stable, and I wouldn't want to put Tom Mooney in a bad spot. Besides, Gillen may have caught a train and beat us there. He may be waiting for me to show up."

She leaned against his shoulder, thinking how much she had come to rely on him. "I'll wager the lieutenant is still riding around New Mexico, looking for us."

Cholla blew smoke into the air. "Don't underestimate him, Sierra. He's smart enough to be a worthy enemy, if not a brave one."

"Yes, of course."

"This is our last night together." He threw the cigarette into the fire. "Tomorrow, I'll guide you to within a few miles of the fort and let you go on alone."

Go on alone. Yes, I'll be all alone. But she wasn't upset. She had learned a lot about herself. Never again would she be afraid to follow her own star, no matter what others did.

The nail that stands up will be hammered down. No, Grandfather, she thought with stubborn conviction, sometimes the nail is made of such steel, it breaks the hammer. Without thinking, she put her small hand on his big one.

He turned his hand over so that hers lay in his wide palm. "Our last night," he whispered.

He reached for her, and she went instinctively into his embrace. Tomorrow they would part, but they had this one night together. Whether it meant anything to him or not, she would savor it forever.

He made love to her very slowly and gently. To Sierra it seemed he was loath to see their time end. *Perhaps that is only my imagination,* she thought as she cradled his dark face against her white breasts.

Their lovemaking was tender, sensitive, as if both were saying good-bye to something they never expected to experience again. It crossed Sierra's mind as they lay in each other's arms that she might now bear a child. Once she would have been horrified by the thought, wondering how she would survive, what people would say. Now she wanted his child. Their love story could have no happy ending—there had been too much tragedy for Cholla's people and hers already—but she would welcome their child and would manage to rear it somehow.

His lips traveled along her neck to her ear, his breath sending delicious shudders of sensation through her. "What are you thinking?"

Would he laugh if he knew what she had really been thinking? "Oh, just how nice it will be to get back to civilization and a real bathtub instead of washing in a creek."

"I made love to you the very first time in a creek, remember?"

Nothing, not age or time could ever make her forget that earth-shattering experience, but she only nodded.

The memory they shared seemed to heat their blood, and he slipped his tongue between her lips, caressing the insides of her mouth until she was arching her body toward his, wanting him to suck on her nipples, wanting his hard manhood throbbing inside her. He tilted her hips up with his hands, plunging into her warm depths, and they meshed, giving and taking until finally, totally spent, they slept in each other's arms.

The next day, she found herself stalling until Cholla said, "If you don't hurry, you won't make it to the fort by dark. I'll ride with you a ways."

She chided herself and then mounted up. They rode in silence.

She couldn't stand the quiet after a while. "What will you do after you leave me?"

"I'll go back to our campsite and wait until night," Cholla answered. "After dark, when there's less chance of being spotted, I'll follow my favorite trail to the border. With any luck, I'll be in the Sierra Madre by morning."

Without me, Sierra thought, but she said nothing.

It was late afternoon when Cholla reined in and pointed. "The fort's only a couple of miles farther on; you won't have any trouble finding it."

Don't ride away without me! her heart cried out, but she wasn't going to tell him how she felt, not when he would only laugh at her.

"Do you remember my message to Tom Mooney?"

"Yes, I . . . I remember. I'm to remind him about the gift." She paused. "But, Cholla, you haven't given me anything to present to him."

"Don't ask any questions," he ordered, grim-faced, "just tell him that. What about the rest of the message?"

Sierra swallowed hard. "Usen's own, Ke'jaa's den." It still didn't make any sense to her, but evidently it would to Tom Mooney.

"Well, good-bye." He seemed awkward and hesitant as if not quite sure how to end this.

She decided to make it easy for him by pretending to be relieved and lighthearted. "Good-bye and good luck."

Then, not having intended to, she leaned across and kissed him. He clung to her as if he would never let her go, his mouth hot on hers, both their pulses pounding. She thought she felt him tremble, but decided it must be her own body shaking. A kiss to last us both forever, she thought, and blinked back tears as she finally pulled back from his embrace. Never in all these weeks had she seen him look so grave as he did now, but he said nothing.

She forced her lips to curve into a smile. "Well, good-bye and good luck," she said again.

He started to say something, nodded curtly.

Sierra turned her mare, rode away toward the fort. It was good that she did not hesitate, because tears were overflowing her eyes. She didn't look back.

Cholla watched her ride off, just sitting his mount as the small figure on the spotted horse grew smaller and smaller. It took all of his will to keep him from riding after her, forcing her to go with him as he had once planned to do. He loved this woman, he knew that now. Loved her enough to do what was best for her — give her the freedom she wanted. But, ironically, she had made a captive of his heart.

At least she would be well taken care of; he had seen to that. He was sending her, and maybe the child she carried, as a gift to Tom Mooney. His friend would look after her, maybe even marry her. When Tom figured out the message about all those nuggets in the cave where Cholla had first found the puppy, he and Sierra would be able to live richly on the treasure forbidden to the Apache — the gold Robert Forester had hunted so long. Was it justice that Forester's woman end up with it? Maybe so.

And what of Gillen? Cholla could do nothing about the lieutenant. But with Tom's enlistment almost up, and the sergeant now a rich man, Gillen would be slamming his fist into his palm a thousand times in helpless frustration, knowing Cholla had outfoxed him again.

Finally Sierra disappeared over the horizon. Cholla looked after her a moment longer, his vision suddenly blurred. Then he blinked and cursed the dust that must have brought tears to his eyes.

With a heavy heart, he turned his black gelding and rode back to his campsite to rest and wait. When darkness fell, he would ride for the border and turn his back forever on Arizona

Territory and the woman he loved.

Cholla watered his horse, hobbled the black gelding, and left it to graze. Then he lay down in the shade of a big boulder overlooking the breathtaking view to the south. He would rest until dark, then ride for the border under cover of night. Gradually he dropped off into a deep, troubled sleep.

Cholla moved restlessly, lost in the nightmare that came sometimes. Once again he scouted for Lieutenant Forester's patrol, through the mesquite and the cactus, the dust and the relentless heat rising up in little waves from the scorched land. Forester, searching for gold, had insisted on riding into that arroyo despite Cholla's warning that it was a good place to get trapped and wiped out by any stray hostiles in the border area. The blond Texan wouldn't even listen to his seasoned old sergeant. Forester was looking for treasure, and he'd seen sunlight glint off distant rocks.

The reflections turned out to be coming from spent cartridges from an old battle, not nuggets, and within minutes, they were surrounded and cut off, trapped in the arroyo by hostile Apaches sniping from the hills around it. Cholla smelled the sticky sweet blood, the gunsmoke drifting in choking clouds. All around them, shots rang out, echoed and reechoed with the hostiles' shrieks.

He was prepared to die; a warrior expected to be killed in battle. Certainly Mooney and Schultz and the other two troopers still living were stoic as they returned the withering fire. Cholla could smell the white officer's fear sweat on the hot summer air.

"You did this," Forester babbled, waving his pistol. "You found out, brought me out here to get me killed!" Cholla didn't know what he was talking about. Most of the patrol was already dead, and the survivors were almost out of shells and water.

The lieutenant was so crazy with fear, he was raving. "You did this, you damned Injun, because of her. You got me out here to kill me!"

Cholla tried to calm him, tried to remind him that his own greed had brought them into this steep gully despite the scout's warning.

But Forester was past reason. Sheer terror and madness shone in his pale turquoise eyes. "You damned Injun, so we enjoyed her a little; that's what squaws are for! I'm sick of you following me around. Sick of waiting for you to take your revenge, you hear?"

Cholla began to get a sick feeling in his stomach. The men left in the patrol—Sergeant Mooney, Corporal Schultz, Taylor, and Allen—had turned to listen to the hysterical babbling. Cholla hadn't known; he'd suspected Geronimo's renegades. But he knew now.

We. Who was "we"?

He managed to control his fury. As scout, his first responsibility was to lead this patrol to safety. "Lieutenant, we'll settle our personal differences later. Right now, we've got to stay alive until someone hears the firing, sends another patrol."

"No, by God, we'll settle them now! Now, do you hear? I'm gonna kill you, Injun, before you kill me.

All these others are white men; they'll swear you led us into this trap. I'll see that they do. There won't even be an investigation."

Cholla looked past him at Sergeant Mooney, but nothing Tom could say would get through to the crazed officer.

Forester waved his pistol and screamed, "Throw your rifle down, Injun! I'm gonna end this once and for all!"

Cholla did throw the rifle down, and he backed away, feeling cold sweat run down his back as Robert Forester cursed and screamed and waved the pistol at him.

July. The heat rose up in little waves off the rocks; weapons were too hot to touch. The fine dust clung to their sweating bodies. *Water.* He'd give a year of his life for just a mouthful of tepid alkali water. Cholla looked from the ranting, crazed officer down to the rifle at his feet. Beyond Forester, Mooney seemed paralyzed.

The hostiles were mounting another attack now, and somewhere in the distance, Cholla heard the echo of a cavalry bugle sounding a charge. *Noise.* Screams and gunshots and horses rearing and neighing. A cavalry bugle again, still a long way off. His own breathing and the blond Texan's swearing and sobbing.

"I'll kill you, you Injun bastard . . . tired of waiting for you to come after me . . . kill you . . . kill you. . . ."

If I could just reach that rifle at his feet, Cholla thought. He looked around frantically as the officer

screamed and ranted. He didn't care about the consequences of shooting an officer; at the moment he only
cared about staying alive.

"Don't even think about it, Injun!" Forester shouted
and pulled back the hammer. "Right between the
eyes, just like Delzhinne got hers! Right between the
eyes—"

Cholla woke with a gasp and sat bolt upright, looking around. He was asleep by a boulder. He'd been
waiting for darkness, so he could slip across the border. He wiped the sweat from his brow. If he had broken the vow, told Sierra the truth, the nightmare
might have gone away. But he was bound by that
oath. They all were—the survivors of the massacre.
Because of that, he could never tell her what had really happened. He wished somehow that she knew.

He leaned against the rock, sighed, and thought
about his four loyal friends—loyal to him, loyal to
each other. The vow had been Cholla's idea, but it
was Schultz who had suggested they bury the young
officer as fast as possible, so no one would ever know
what had happened. Gillen had showed up with his
patrol just as they were burying Forester. Had the
lieutenant ever put all the pieces of the puzzle together? Allen and Taylor had suggested that Forester
be recommended for a medal and a commendation.
Only that veteran soldier, Mooney, had wanted to tell
the truth, but the others had demanded he take the
vow and keep silent.

Like the rest, Cholla expected to take the secret to
his grave. It was the honorable thing to do. He
couldn't tell Sierra, even if knowing the truth about

381

her husband's death might have changed things between them. He had a feeling that she suspected he had killed her husband.

It was almost dusk. He shot a rabbit and roasted it over his campfire, thinking about how lonely he was going to be without Sierra. As soon as night came, he would be heading for the border. Though he was leaving his heart behind, his course was set and he didn't intend to look back.

Chapter Twenty

Sierra kept her eyes on the distant horizon as she rode away, forcing herself not to look back at Cholla. If she did, she might not be able to stop herself from wheeling the mare about and returning to beg to go with him.

He doesn't want me, she thought regretfully, so there is no reason to throw away my pride. Sierra had served his purpose as a hostage, and she had warmed his blankets for many weeks. He had no further need of her. While he had made love to her lately as if he really cared, perhaps she had only believed that to be so.

For a few minutes, as she rode, Sierra listened for the sound of hoof beats coming from behind. She even reined in, but heard only a hawk winging across the sky and a small lizard slithering through the dry brush.

She chided herself and turned once again toward the fort. What was she hoping for? For him to come after her. *This is reality, Sierra, not a storybook. He won't come.*

She touched her lips with her fingertips, savoring the memory of that final kiss. Then she took a deep breath and nudged her mare into a slow canter. The wind picked up, blowing sand across her tracks. No soldier would be able to find his way to Cholla's camp because of her horse's hoof prints, Sierra thought with satisfaction, leaning into the wind.

What did the future hold for her? Well, whatever it was, she would go forward with the confidence and fearlessness she had learned from the Apache. She was certain his story would grow and grow until it became part of Western legend. One man had defied the civilization that tried to tame him, one man had defeated the most powerful country in the world, had made a laughing stock of a whole Army. No doubt someone's head would roll over this. She hoped it was Lieutenant Gillen's.

The sun was low on the horizon when Sierra reined in and saw the adobe walls of the fort. Soon it would be dark and Cholla would be leaving for the border. Should she wait until then to ride in? She thought for a moment, then shook her head. If she approached the fort after dark, some trigger-happy guard might shoot her. Besides, she didn't intend to tell them Cholla's whereabouts, not even if they threatened her, threw her into the guardhouse. She nudged the mare forward.

The fort seemed to be slumbering as she rode in. Hardly anyone was in sight, and the wind blew swirls of dust across a deserted parade ground. A corporal, hurrying past, stopped, came over. He took a cigar from between stained teeth.

"Ma'am, may I help you?" He stared up at her, polite curiosity on his face, as if he wondered why a tanned and weary woman was riding in alone in such hostile country.

"Yes, I'm looking for Sergeant Tom Mooney. Do you know him?"

"Yes, ma'am." The corporal touched his cap politely. "I'll take you to him." His eyes were bright with curiosity, but she sensed he was too polite to question her. A lone, unknown woman riding down out of the hills would be unusual anywhere.

Sierra dismounted, not offering any explanation. She wouldn't trust anyone until she was certain Cholla had reached his goal.

"This way, ma'am." The corporal threw away his cigar and nodded toward the row of adobe buildings.

She led her horse and looked around as she followed him. "Where is everyone?"

"It's New Year's Eve, ma'am, and since there's not much danger anymore, most of the men are off duty, having a few drinks at the *cantina* or even over in Tombstone."

"I see."

New Year's Eve. Well, maybe this was a portent of things to come, good tidings and good luck for herself and for Cholla.

The wind let up some as he led her to a building, gallantly tied her horse to the hitching rail, and rapped on the door.

"Yes?"

"Sergeant Mooney, it's Schultz. There's someone here to see you."

The past was over. A new year was beginning. Yet Sierra felt that everything important to her was ending.

A rather short but wiry middle-aged man opened the door, a sergeant with thinning, sandy hair, warm eyes, and freckled hands. So this was Cholla's friend. He looked dependable, trustworthy.

"Sergeant Mooney? I'm Sierra Forester."

He blinked as if waking from a dream. "Sierra Forester? Excuse me, ma'am, I . . . I'm so surprised to see you, I've forgotten my manners. Come in." Turning to the corporal, he said, "That'll be all, Schultz, I'll call you if I need you."

Sierra entered, looked around.

"This is Lieutenant Gatewood's office," the sergeant said by way of explanation. "He's ill and another lieutenant is due in on the train tonight, so I'm helping with the filing and paperwork. Do sit down, Mrs. Forester."

She took a chair, looking the Irishman over critically, liking what she saw. There was something good and moral and solid about this plain, hard-working trooper.

And Mooney looked at her, almost as if he couldn't believe his eyes. "You're more beautiful than your picture," he blurted out and then reddened.

"You saw the photo my husband had?"

"Of course. The . . . the lieutenant carried it with him and often spoke of his love for you."

386

Sergeant Mooney might be a gentle man, a caring man, but he was as poor a liar as Cholla. Obviously neither had had much experience at it.

"I knew my husband better than that," Sierra said softly, "but thank you for trying to spare my feelings."

He fumbled with a book on the desk, looking both awkward and foolish. "Is Cholla all right?"

At the sound of the Apache's name, a big yellow dog that looked more like a coyote rose up from behind the desk, sniffed the air curiously.

"Is that his dog? Oh, I'm so glad it's alive!" Sierra clasped her hands. "Cholla thinks the soldiers shot him."

"I managed to save him. I thought it was the least I could do for a friend."

She held out her hand to the dog. "Ke'jaa?"

"Beggin' your pardon, Mrs. Forester, but I wouldn't touch that dog if I were you. He doesn't take to strangers."

The dog stopped sniffing the air, walked silently over to Sierra, sat down in front of her and laid its huge head on her knee.

Sergeant Mooney's mouth dropped open. "Holy Saint Patrick! Ma'am, this is a shock. That's a one-man dog. Ke'jaa never even took up with Delzhinne."

Cholla's woman. Sierra had wanted to be his woman. But one woman was the same as another to that proud, remote man. She stroked the dog's head absently, saw the curiosity in the Irishman's eyes. "Cholla's all right, Sergeant. He'll be headed for the border once it gets dark."

Tom Mooney sat down on a corner of the desk,

drew a visible sigh of relief. "Thank the saints. Then he'll be safe by morning."

"This dog is thin, Sergeant," Sierra ran her hand over the dog's ribs and looked at the sergeant reproachfully.

"He's grievin' himself to death, no matter what I do. Life doesn't seem to mean nothing to him without Cholla."

She knew just how the dog felt. Funny, she should be celebrating her safe arrival at the fort, her future in this new year that would dawn tomorrow. But like the dog, all she could think of was a bronzed man and how much she missed him already.

She must have looked forlorn and sad, because the man stood up, came over, stood before her hesitantly. "Mrs. Forester, I . . . I want to tell you that I'm at your disposal. Anything I can do to help you, I'll do and gladly."

She looked up at him, watching him clench and unclench his freckled hands in an agony of embarrassment. It's almost as if he's in love with me, she thought in amazement as Tom Mooney blushed like a schoolboy. She wondered suddenly if Cholla had any inkling of this.

"Sergeant . . . Tom." She reached out, put her hand on his arm, feeling she could trust him, as Cholla trusted him. "Thank you for caring and offering to help. He did tell me to give you a message."

"A message?" He half turned away as if already regretting his impulsive words.

"He told me to tell you he was sending you that gift he promised."

Mooney turned and looked directly at her. "Do you have any idea what he meant?"

She shook her head, but the expression on his weathered face told her that he did and was shaken by it.

"There was more — something about Usen's own and Ke'jaa's den."

Now it was Tom Mooney's turn to shake his head. "I'm afraid that means nothing to me."

"Me either, but he said to think on it and you'd know."

Mooney looked baffled. "Maybe it wasn't important."

"Cholla acted as if it were. He made me repeat it several times. Don't you have any idea of what he's telling you?"

"I'll give it some thought." The sergeant looked down at her hand on his arm, blushed again, and suddenly very conscious of the way he looked at her, she dropped her hand to her lap. She now understood the first part of the message. *She* was the gift. Cholla was sending his woman and the child she might be carrying to the only white man he trusted to take her in and look after her. Was he doing it for her or for his friend?

Ke'jaa whined softly, and she looked at the dog, thinking how lonely Cholla was going to be. The dog would be company for him, maybe even some help to him. "I want to get Ke'jaa to him. If I leave right now —"

"Mrs. Forester, Sierra, be sensible." Mooney shook his head. "Lieutenant Gillen is due here about dark;

389

he's coming in on the train. I'll do anything I can to delay him. I just hope his train is late — too late for him to organize a patrol and try to ambush Cholla at that little arroyo near the border."

"Is that the one where my husband was killed?"

Tom looked startled, then seemed to avoid her gaze. "Yes, ma'am, the lieutenant is buried near there, a fine and brave man he was, too."

"You don't need to try to spare my feelings, Sergeant," she said and stood up. "I knew him better than you did."

He turned brick red and cleared his throat. "I . . . I'm not sure what you mean, Mrs. Forester."

There were a couple of things she had to know. They would haunt her unless she did. "Sergeant Mooney, do you know anything about the death of Cholla's woman?"

"Cholla's woman?" He looked baffled.

"Delzhinne." She was impatient with him.

He blinked and shook his head. "Delzhinne was Cholla's younger sister, ma'am."

"Sister? But I thought —"

"Mrs. Forester, Cholla never took a wife — too choosy and too proud. Oh, he's had many woman, all right, but none he cared enough to call *ishton,* most beloved, the one and only woman in his life. I always figured when he found the woman he wanted, she'd be something very special." His eyes were full of questions that he was too polite to ask.

Sierra tried to hide her state of confusion. A sister. His *sister,* not his woman. That didn't eliminate the next question she must ask. "I see. Sergeant, be honest with me. I want to know how the girl died."

He didn't meet her eyes. "Maybe it was Geronimo's renegades who did it. She was . . . well, you know." He blushed uneasily. "Then she was shot between the eyes. I just found her, that's all."

"Tom, I think you know more than you're telling." Sierra watched his face, not even sure what it was she probed for. There was just this uneasy feeling in her heart.

"Now, don't jump to conclusions. There's no evidence that your husband or Lieutenant Gillen . . ." His voice trailed off.

She had wondered about a Pandora's box, and now her questions had brought all sorts of horrible, dark things winging out of one, things that were worse than those in her nightmares. "I never mentioned either Robert or Gillen; *you* did. You have reason to think they did, don't you? From the beginning I've sensed a cover-up concerning this whole thing."

"I . . . I . . . It might have been anyone—probably was renegade Apaches."

A clock ticked loudly on the wall. She knew now that Cholla hadn't selected her by coincidence; he had plotted and planned his revenge. "Cholla knew that Robert did it, didn't he?"

"Not until Lieutenant Forester blurted out—" Mooney stopped, in an agony of confusion now, and turned away, flexing and unflexing his fingers.

And then somehow other pieces of the puzzle dropped into place. "The arroyo. It came to a showdown in the arroyo, didn't it?"

He turned his back and didn't answer, but she saw his wide shoulders tremble.

Whatever had happened out there, she knew abruptly that she didn't want to hear about it. "Never mind. I . . . I'm sorry I asked."

He turned around, seemed to be going through an agony of indecision. "You love Cholla, don't you?"

Sierra bit her lip and faced her own truth. She had to swallow hard to be able to get the words out. "Now that you ask, I . . . I suppose I do."

"And you're afraid he might have—?"

"No! I don't want to hear it!" She put her hands over both ears. "Whatever you're about to tell me, don't! Even though my marriage was a sham, I'm not sure I could bear to hear—"

"If it were just me, I'd tell the authorities." Mooney almost whispered it. "But besides Cholla, there are three soldiers who might be liable for prosecution for conspiring to withhold the truth."

Slowly she took her hands away from her ears and found that she was trembling.

The clock ticked . . . and ticked . . . and ticked.

"Mrs. Forester, do you read much poetry?" He went over, picked up a worn book from the desk, handling it almost with reverence, opened it.

Merciful heavens, what a strange question to ask at this critical point, she thought. He's been at this solitary place too long. It has affected his sanity.

She swallowed hard. "A little. My mother loved it."

"Do you know a poem by Richard Lovelace—it dates back to the 1600's—'To Lucasta, on Going to the Wars'?"

392

She couldn't believe the turn of the conversation. Then it dawned on her that maybe he was trying to tell her something, about Cholla. She thought for a long moment. " 'I . . . I could not love thee, Dear, so much, Loved I not Honour more. . . .' "

The rest of it escaped her, and abruptly she felt terribly annoyed. He was trying to get her off the subject of the incident in the arroyo. "I don't see that this has any bearing—"

"Sierra, if there was ever a man who exemplified that poem, it's Cholla." The sergeant stared at the print on the page. "We . . . we swore an oath of secrecy out there that day. I thought it wrong, but Cholla insisted."

"I see." She didn't really see at all, but whatever had happened to Robert, it was terrible enough that the survivors had plotted together to cover it up. She wasn't sure she wanted to know any more, but she couldn't stop herself from asking. "Then Cholla's guilty as I feared."

"Sierra"—Tom shook his head—"he's guilty of being so honorable that he would lose you rather than smear his honor by breaking his oath and endangering his friend and those who conspired to keep the secret."

"Please don't say more." Her tone made it clear that she had heard enough. He is protecting Cholla, she thought with a rush of empathy. Knowing she cared for the scout, Mooney was attempting to do the honorable thing himself—take the blame. The clock on the wall ticked silently in the growing dusk.

He seemed to be weighing something heavily in his

393

own mind. "Sierra, please don't think badly of Cholla. Maybe I should tell you—"

"Never mind. I don't want to hear anything else." She shook her head when he tried to continue. Of course Tom Mooney was lying, but at what cost to himself, knowing by his expression that he wanted her?

"Sergeant Mooney, have you withheld other things, too?"

He stiffened, instantly on his guard. "What do you mean?"

His guarded tone and uneasiness immediately told her that he had.

"Sergeant"—she bit her lip—"I think you have real reason to believe Robert was responsible for what happened to Cholla's sister. But you never told Cholla, did you?"

He actually wrung his hands, paced the floor. "How could I? I knew Cholla would kill him for it. Cholla's my friend; I was trying to protect him. Instead, keeping quiet brought about what happened that day. That makes me guilty, don't you see?"

No, she thought, Robert was guilty of rape and murder, and Cholla took revenge. She faced the realization that the scout meant more to her than what had happened that hot, summer day.

"I'm going to ride out, see if I can intercept Cholla before he breaks camp, take him his dog."

"I don't think that's a good idea, Sierra."

She ignored him. "Is there any way I can get his horse to him, too?"

The sergeant ran a hand through his thinning hair.

"I doubt it. Everyone recognizes the stallion and knows Lieutenant Gillen bought and paid for it. No one would care about the dog. If you'll tell me where Cholla is, maybe I can get Ke'jaa to him."

"Sergeant, if you get caught helping a fugitive, it would mean big trouble for you."

"Cholla is my *sikis,* my brother," Tom said. "He saved my life once, and I saved his. Me or any of my men would do whatever it took to help him."

She wasn't sure what the Army would do to a cavalry sergeant who aided a fugitive. Throw him in prison, probably. Besides, Tom Mooney didn't know exactly where Cholla was camped. She thought she could find her way back to the spot, but she wasn't sure she could tell Mooney how to get to it. And if she got caught, what could the Army do to a woman? Anyway that didn't matter anymore.

There was a knock on the door. Both started, and Sierra looked at the sergeant. *Could it be Gillen already?*

Schultz opened the door, moved his cigar from one side of his mouth to the other. "Sarge, can I see you a minute? Taylor's reported."

Tom Mooney hesitated. "Will you excuse me a minute, Mrs. Forester?"

She nodded. The two men went out, and Sierra fidgeted, trying to decide what to do. It was almost dark outside now. If she didn't hurry, Cholla would be gone and she wouldn't get his dog to him. Somehow that seemed terribly important to her . . . or was it only that she wanted one last chance to see him?

She stood up. She ought to go but she didn't want to leave without hearing whether the corporal brought bad news. Was Gillen on the post already? Or had Cholla been hunted down and killed? The dog watched her silently, alertly, as if it didn't intend to let her out of its sight until she led it to its master.

A rap at the door.

"Come in," Sierra said.

The door opened and a woman barged into the room, a woman wearing a big hat and a bright purple dress. "I'm lookin' for Lieutenant Gillen. Where the hell is everyone?"

Trixie. Sierra could only gape at her. What on earth was she doing here?

The colorfully dressed woman seemed to take a good look at Sierra for the very first time. Then she leaned against the desk, lit a cigarette, and sneered defiantly. "Wasn't you Robert Forester's wife?"

"And weren't you Robert Forester's whore?" Sierra said coldly.

"Well, well!" Trixie blew smoke in the air and laughed. "You've certainly changed from the whimpering little mouse who once came to me, begging me to stay away from your husband."

"I'm sorry I wasted the effort; he wasn't worth it."

"You say that because he was goin' to leave you for me." Trixie gave her a smug smile.

Abruptly Sierra felt sorry for the woman. "I don't think he would have, Trixie. That's something women like you never learn. Married men may cheat with sluts, but they seldom marry them."

"You got your nerve, talkin' to me like that! I'm a star!"

"The only talent you've got, Trixie, is between your

legs, and no man values what he can get cheap!"

"You're such a know-it-all! Well, I know things, too," she crowed, "I'll bet I know several things about Robert that would surprise you."

Sierra sighed and looked toward the door. "I doubt there's a lot about Robert you can tell me that I don't already know."

"Such a loyal wife!" Trixie taunted, grinning cruelly. "Would you be so loyal if you knew he pushed your crazy old grandfather out of that loft?"

Sierra grabbed for the edge of the desk, tried to speak, couldn't. Grandfather had tried to tell her something as he'd died in her arms on the barn floor. Now she knew what it was. He would never have allowed Robert to mortgage the farm . . . if he had lived.

Her shock and unhappiness must have pleased and encouraged the other woman, because Trixie gloated, "I know something else you ain't gonna like—something Gill told me. Did ya know Robert was a yellow coward? He didn't really deserve no medals."

"I don't have to take this kind of abuse from you, Trixie." Sierra walked to the door. "Go crawl back in your cocaine bottle."

As Sierra reached for the doorknob, the other woman ran over, caught her arm. "You will listen to me! I want you to know about Robert, you with your marriage license, thinking you're so much better than me. He was a coward! Do you hear me? A coward!"

Sierra tried to pull away from her, but Trixie pressed right up to her.

"Your high-tone husband was just yellow, running

397

from the enemy. You know how I know? He was shot in the back, that's why! You hear me? I wanted you to know, you whimpering, weak little—"

Sierra slapped her then, slapped her so hard that Trixie's head snapped back and she dropped her cigarette, let go of Sierra's arm. The marks of five fingers showed redly on her painted face.

"Trixie, one thing I'll never be again is a whimpering, weak little anything!"

Sierra didn't want to even think of the implications of Trixie's revelation as she rushed out the door into the gray dusk of evening. The dog went with her.

. . . *shot in the back . . . shot in the back . . . the back . . . back . . . back . . .* But the words reverberated through her brain, echoing there like sounds in a canyon. Could this be true? One more piece of the puzzle dropped into place. Yes, it had to be. Sierra had sensed that everyone knew something about all this that she didn't. Suppose Robert hadn't been shot by a hostile? Could Cholla have—? She didn't even want to think about it, but she had to know. She swung up on her horse.

About that time, Tom Mooney and the corporal came around the corner. "Holy Saint Patrick! Where are you going?"

She was both angry and hurt. "Sergeant, look me in the eye and don't lie to me. I want some answers."

"I—"

"Was my husband shot in the back?"

He didn't have to speak. The stricken look on both men's faces gave her all the answers she needed. Sierra slashed the startled mare with her reins and took

398

off at a gallop, the big yellow dog running with her.

"Sierra, come back! Lieutenant Gillen is on his way from the station!"

She didn't even answer as she galloped away.

. . . *shot in the back . . . the back . . . the back* . . .
The words seemed to echo in her ears. Worse yet, Sierra realized she didn't care about what had happened to Robert. God forgive her, she only wanted to be assured that Cholla hadn't done such a cowardly thing. Maybe there were extenuating circumstances, she thought as she rode blindly toward his camp. So this was what the oath was covering up! There could be no legitimate reason for shooting a man in the back . . . could there?

Chapter Twenty-one

Lieutenant Quimby Gillen snapped the small whip over the horse and shifted his weight in the rented buggy. At least the wind had stopped blowing. Blast it all, why hadn't someone been at the station to meet him? The long train ride and, before that, the wild-goose chase around New Mexico Territory looking for that pair, had done nothing to improve Gill's mood.

In the silvery gray dusk of evening, the low adobe buildings of the fort looked deserted. Maybe that was why nobody had met him; they were all off getting drunk. It crossed his mind that maybe someone was trying to delay him. But why?

He pulled a small bag out of his jacket, popped a peppermint in his mouth, knowing his teeth would begin to hurt again. But every time he spent money on candy, he felt he was thumbing his nose at his cold, stingy parents.

As the buggy creaked down the road in the twilight, Gill realized just how quiet the fort was. In the barracks a few men must be playing cards or celebrating, he decided. With the Indian wars over and security lax, many were on leave or had deserted; others must be in the *cantinas* outside the fort, drinking and dancing.

If I don't get that damned Injun here, I can kiss my Army career good-bye, Gill thought. Not only was the American public beginning to pull for the underdog, the publicity of the escape, coupled with the fuss General Crook was making about shipping the Apaches to Florida, was becoming very embarrassing to the administration, and President Cleveland was furious.

"Blast it all anyway," he grumbled, and urged the horse to move a little faster. "What a hell of a way to spend New Year's Eve." Many soldiers had been at the little settlement at Bowie Station, getting an early start on the holiday. And how was Lieutenant Gillen going to spend his evening?

"At the fort," he groused, "makin' plans to try to intercept that damned Cholla."

Of course Cholla wouldn't be foolish enough to come here, he told himself as he drove on. If the Apache had any sense at all, he'd already crossed the border south of New Mexico Territory.

On the other hand, Cholla knew the terrain south of the Chiricahua Mountains and would favor it. Besides, he was just brazen enough to try to steal his stallion back.

The low adobe buildings loomed closer in the pale lavender dusk of evening. The lieutenant wondered about Sierra, where she was. If the scout didn't take her with him, Gillen wasn't sure what the Army could do to her for aiding and abetting the fugitive. Of course, if she got up in front of a judge as the wife of a dead hero, wept a little, and said she'd been forced to help her kidnapper, there wasn't a jury in the world who would convict her. Gill wondered if she realized that?

A movement on a distant ridge to the southeast caught his eye, and he blinked, looked again. For just a second in the growing darkness he'd thought he saw a woman on a paint horse, long hair flowing out behind her, a big yellow dog running alongside her mount. Then the figure had been swallowed up by the purple twilight.

"Blast, I must be losing my mind!" Of course no woman would be out riding alone and headed away from the fort when it was almost dark. With the Apaches corralled, there wasn't any Indian trouble, but there were bandits and rattlesnakes about. No, a woman just wouldn't do that.

He hadn't had anything to drink, so that couldn't be it. Gill stared at the empty horizon to the southeast again, not at all sure now that he hadn't imagined the hazy, mounted figure. A chill went down his back. He didn't believe in ghosts or in the spirits the old Apaches said haunted these mountains. Could he be losing his mind? The thought scared him. He'd known of men who were never quite the same after serving at some of these isolated posts. In fact, Forester had acted a bit crazed toward the end, just before he was killed in that ambush. Gill hurried his horse along, drove into the fort, and headed toward the stable.

Corporal Schultz and Sergeant Mooney looked up, dashed over, snapped to attention.

He gave them a halfhearted, sneering salute. "This is more like it. Why the hell didn't anyone meet me at the station?"

"Sir," Mooney responded, "there must have been a mix-up in communication."

"Blast it all, if I didn't know better, I'd think someone was tryin' to delay me."

"Oh no, sir."

Just then Gill noticed Taylor's bay gelding standing in the shadows of the stable, lathered and snorting. Had that bastard been watching for Gill? Instead of meeting him, had he galloped back to alert others of his arrival?

Gill crunched the candy between his teeth and decided not to make an issue of it, since he couldn't prove it and he might end up looking like a fool. He wasn't any more popular with the troops than Forester had been, he knew that. "Corporal, take this rented rig back to town later."

"Yes, sir." Schultz looked nervous as he took hold of the harness.

Gill swore and climbed down from the buggy. "Where is everyone?"

"Away from the post for the evening, sir," Mooney said, "and Lieutenant Gatewood's sick."

Gill merely grunted. He didn't like Gatewood anyway — too ethical. Ambitious officers like Lawton and

Wood were men he looked up to. He thought again of the mounted phantom.

Sergeant Mooney cleared his throat. "Beggin' your pardon sir, but there's a lady lookin' for you."

"A lady?" Gill brightened at once with the prospect of seeing Sierra Forester. Of course the shadowy figure on the horse had been only a product of his troubled mind.

"Yes, sir. She's in Lieutenant Gatewood's office."

Gill turned and strode away without stopping for any more conversation. His heart beat a little faster. A woman. Sierra Forester. Had Cholla already come and gone while Gill was en route? What rotten luck. Gill really needed permission from a higher-ranking officer before taking off on a patrol, but maybe on New Year's Eve, with so many officers off duty, he could bend the rules.

He thought of the specter he had just seen, the ghostlike woman on horseback, her black hair blowing out behind her. In the lavender and gray twilight, she had blended into the shadowy horizon and disappeared. He shivered a little. Would the recollection of that fateful night ever go away? Was he to be haunted forever by the memory of it?

If he and Forester hadn't been so drunk that they'd lost their judgment . . . But the Apache girl had looked so beautiful, so desirable, galloping through the hills on her pony. . . .

The two of them had chased her down as a lark, pulled her from her horse. First they'd just wanted to scare her a little, on the off chance that she knew

404

about the gold. In the struggle, the front of her dress was torn, and she'd had such beautiful breasts. Delzhinne had begged them not to shame her, but she was so pretty — and they were too drunk and aroused to think about her or the possible consequences of the act. Not until an hour later, when their lust was sated and they were sobering fast, did the two realize their careers were in danger if she reported them to their commanding officer. Worse yet, their lives, or at least their manhoods, were in immediate danger the moment Delzhinne's older brother found out what they had done to his beloved sister.

Even now, Gill winced as he remembered how Delzhinne had begged for her life when she'd understood they were discussing the best way to kill her. She swore she would not tell, got down on her knees to plead. Then, when she realized it would do no good, she fought them, trying to escape the inevitable. Forester had held her while Gill had put a bullet right between her eyes.

They were certain they hadn't left any clues, but later Robert had discovered a brass button missing from his coat. He'd been afraid to return to the death scene to retrieve it. They had bumped into Mooney later, back at the fort; but he hadn't seemed suspicious. Anyway, they'd figured the sergeant was just a dumb Mick, so they hadn't worried about his figuring out anything.

After that night, though, the two officers never had a moment's peace. Both feared that Cholla knew and was biding his time before extracting revenge in the most horrible way, or that if he didn't, somehow he would find out. Each day the lieutenants looked behind them. Their nights were sleepless; the slightest squeak of a board bringing them up out of bed, sure it was the Apache. Neither man could relax, for each was expecting Cholla to extract justice. Nerves frayed, both drank too much and became nervous wrecks in the weeks that followed.

Well, blast it all, Gillen thought, Robert had either turned yellow and tried to run from the hostiles out there in the arroyo or the big Apache had finally got his revenge. Damned if he's going to get Quimby Gillen. No, I'll see him imprisoned or, better yet, dead so I can finally sleep at night without listening for the quiet step of those moccasins.

He hurried to Gatewood's office, went inside. The woman had her back to him, but she wore a big hat and a gaudy purple dress. His heart fell as she turned around. "Trixie, what are you doin' here?"

She scowled. "Ya might at least act glad to see me." She sauntered over, got a big bottle of medicine from her purse, took a gulp. "Actually, I'm headed for 'Frisco."

"Good!" He dismissed her with a shrug. His teeth ached, and he felt depressed and angry because she hadn't turned out to be Sierra Forester. "Don't bother me anymore, Trixie, or I'll tell the law you stabbed that banker—"

"I didn't stab nobody! He fell—"

"Yeah, yeah." He made a gesture of dismissal. "Just get out of my life, you trampy, no-talent bitch!"

"Bastard!" She whirled on him, and for the first time, he noticed the handprint embedded in the makeup on her painted face.

"So who hit you?"

Her hand trembled when she lit a cigarette. She blew smoke rings in the air. "That Mrs. Forester was just here. She ain't the whimpering little mouse I remember. She slapped me and called me a slut!"

"Sierra Forester was here?" He grabbed her shoulders, shook her. "Tell me, how long ago?"

"A few minutes. Didn't you hear me? She called me a slut!"

"So she's a good judge of character. Where did she go?"

"How the hell should I know? But I got even with her." Trixie grinned. "I told her what you said about Robert bein' shot in the back!"

"Trixie, your mouth is the second biggest hole in your body and the least smart!"

"You got no right to talk to me like that!"

Gill shoved her. "Blast it all, shut up! I'm sick of you and your shriekin' voice. You sound like a coyote caught in a trap! I'm goin' after Sierra, and when I get back, I want you gone, you hear?"

She grabbed his arm. "But I came here to celebrate New Year's. I figured we could have our own little party. I was gonna make love to you."

Her hatred of him showed in her eyes. She was up to something, but he didn't have any interest in what

407

it was, not even in mounting her lush body for a few frenzied minutes. "Forget it, slut!" He slapped her hand away, went outside.

Sierra Forester was in the area, and Gill meant to have her, but he wanted that Injun dead first. He headed for the stable. Mooney and Schultz, Allen and Taylor were there. Their startled expressions told him he'd interrupted a meeting.

"Sergeant," he snapped, "was Sierra Forester on this post?"

There was a long pause. Even though the evening was cool, sweat broke out on the Irishman's face. "Holy Saint Patrick, I don't honestly remember."

Everyone was trying to stop him from doing his duty and getting that girl. "Damn it! Why is everyone lying to me, delaying me? I know she was here tonight, and that damned Injun is probably around, too."

Mooney took off his hat, ran a freckled hand through his thinning hair. "Now that you mention it, I believe she was here, but I think Mrs. Forester went back to Bowie Station to catch a train east."

"Mooney, you damned liar! If that was where she was headed, she would have passed me as I drove in. I'll bet she's gone out to meet that Apache."

"Now, now, sir." The sergeant made a soothing gesture. "There's no moon, and it's dark as the inside of a cow. We couldn't track them. And it's New Year's Eve, sir. Why don't you have a few drinks over at the *cantina* and, maybe tomorrow afternoon, take a patrol and ride out, have a look around?"

"Damn! You think I'm an idiot!" Gill slammed a fist into his palm. "By then, that Injun will be across the border and gone. I'm taking a patrol and goin' after him tonight!"

The men looked at each other, and the Irishman ran a finger around his collar as if he were choking. "Sir, with the holiday and so many men out, it'd be hard to round up enough sober soldiers to form a patrol. It might take me hours—"

"You four look sober, and I figure I can count on young Finney. Sergeant, I order you to round up a patrol, which I will lead. *Right* now! I want the men ready to move out in fifteen minutes. You hear me?"

"Yes, sir." Mooney looked grim as he snapped to attention.

"And another thing," Gill snarled, "take a pack mule loaded with ammunition and supplies. We're staying out until we run that red bastard to ground. Saddle up the Medicine Hat stallion for me. The irony of riding Cholla's own horse to hunt him down pleases me."

Sweat ran down the reddish face. "Yes, sir. It may take me awhile—"

"It better not!" Gill glowered at him. "You may not reenlist, but at this moment, you are still in the U.S. Cavalry. I could have you shot or imprisoned for deliberately impeding an officer in pursuit of his duty. Now, all of you, get moving!"

The troopers snapped salutes and left.

Gill laughed with delight, even though his teeth were aching again. In sheer defiance, he took out

409

the crumpled bag of candy, put a cinnamon drop in his mouth, crushed it noisily between his teeth. Only one thing hotter than cinnamon, he thought with relish, remembering the feel of Sierra's warm skin. He wondered if her insides were hot, too? He sure intended to find out. No matter how he got her, he wanted her ripe body under him at least once after he killed or captured that Apache.

The moon came out, big and yellow as gold—the Apache gold none of these damned savages would ever tell him or Robert about. They said their god, Usen, claimed it for his own and it was taboo for their people to dig for it.

Gill leaned against a post, munching candy and watching Sergeant Mooney assemble the patrol. On one thing, the Irishman had been right; some of the men had been celebrating early and looked a little the worse for wear. Most officers would wait under these circumstances, but if Gill held off until he had a full patrol of sober men, and official approval for what he was about to do, the Indian would be long gone.

He wondered again if Mooney knew what he and Robert had done to Cholla's sister. Mooney and the Apache were friends, and frankly, Gill would never feel really safe until both Cholla and Mooney were dead. Well, if the Apache was captured, he could always be shot "escaping" en route to the train station to be shipped to Florida. Gill would just have to make sure there were no witnesses.

As for the sergeant, this very patrol was going to

be his final assignment. Mooney would accidentally catch a stray bullet that would silence him forever, and it would be hard to prove that the Apache hadn't shot him or that his death hadn't been a tragic accident.

Mooney now had the patrol assembled. He led out the black and white paint stallion for Gill. Gill frowned as he looked over the hastily assembled group: Mooney, Schultz, Allen, Taylor, and Finney, and a few soldiers he didn't know. Young Finney looked a little drunk, but so did a couple of the nameless men sitting their horses. Gill suspected Mooney had dragged some of them away from an early celebration. "Sergeant, couldn't you find a full patrol of *sober* men?"

Mooney snapped to attention. "Like I told you before, sir, being's as how it's a holiday, I could give you a full patrol *or* a sober group, but not both."

"Blast it all!" Gill fumed, so angry his hands shook. "You're all trying to delay me; stop me from doing my duty. I ought to throw you all in the guardhouse. Order is what I want and can't get — order!"

"I'll have a beer." Finney hiccoughed and reeled in his saddle.

"Attention!" Gill shouted, and the patrol snapped up straight in the saddle. He'd ride that alcohol out of their systems. In a couple of hours, they'd all be cold sober, their heads pounding like horses' hooves on hard ground. They didn't like him. Like Pa, they didn't like him. He'd show them; he'd show them all.

411

Gill swung up on the Medicine Hat stallion. "All right, Sergeant."

As if Fate were trying to help Gill, the moon came out from behind the clouds, bathing the scene in light. The fresh hoof prints led out to the southeast.

Gill chortled. "Okay, there's her trail." He pointed, and they rode out, following the indentations made by the hooves of Sierra's horse. Gill glanced back at the patrol strung out behind him as they rode away from the fort. Nothing was going to stand in his way this time. He grinned as he imagined the look on Cholla's face when the patrol caught up with him. Pleased, he spurred the spirited stallion to a faster pace.

Sierra rode at a lope back toward Cholla's camp, Ke'jaa trotting along beside her Medicine Hat mare is if he knew she was returning him to his beloved master.

Her mood fluctuated between happiness and despair as she thought about seeing the Indian again. *Shot in the back.* She had sensed all along that Cholla knew something he wasn't telling, that he had some secret. So he had taken an oath to remain silent. She hoped that, if she confronted him, he would admit that Robert had, indeed, been a coward who had tried to run from the field of battle and had been picked off. The other possibility, that of a brother's revenge, she didn't even want to think about.

412

She would tell Cholla she had come to return his dog. If she got there in time. Sierra glanced up at the clear, cold night and shivered a little, even though the wind had died down. The moon was full, the stars sparkled in a black velvet sky. Cholla might already have left his camp, headed south. If she missed him, she didn't know how to find the trail he planned to take so she couldn't follow him. In that case, she might never know the answers to her questions. They would haunt her for the rest of her life.

Well, all she could do was hope she got there in time to confront him. The moon moved slowly across the night sky as she rode through the rugged hills. Somewhere a coyote howled, and the eerie sound echoed across the lonely landscape. When she took a breath, the smell of mesquite and cedar scented the air. Though it seemed like forever, it couldn't have been more than a couple of hours before she approached the area of the camp. As she rode closer, she saw no fire and her heart almost stopped. He had gone.

A rifle bullet sang past her, echoing in the night, causing her mare to rear, throw her to the ground.

"Cholla! Don't shoot! It's me, Sierra!"

He showed himself then, up in the rocks. "By Usen, I almost killed you!" He jumped down from the boulder as she scrambled to her feet.

"I . . . I brought your dog." She stood there awkwardly.

"My dog?" He looked at her in disbelief, then seemed to see the big, yellow animal for the first

413

time. "Ke'jaa!"

The dog ran to him, whining, laying its big head on Cholla's boot with a worshipful sigh.

Cholla knelt, threw his arms around Ke'jaa's neck. For a long moment, the only sound was the dog's whimpering as it licked its master's face.

The sight made Sierra glad that the pair was reunited. At least Cholla wouldn't be so alone in Mexico. "Sergeant Mooney managed to save him when the others were shot. I knew you'd want me to bring him."

"Thank you for that." He stood up slowly, looking at her. "Is Tom okay? Did you give him my message?"

Sierra nodded, wondering how she'd dare ask the questions that plagued her? "Lieutenant Gillen's due in at the fort tonight, but you'll be gone so it doesn't matter. In fact, I was surprised to find you."

He rubbed the back of his neck as if unsure what to say. "I was just a little slow in leaving." He nodded toward the dead ashes of his fire. "If you had gotten here five minutes later, I would have been gone."

She bit her lip, looking from the happy dog to the stoic expression of the man. . . . *shot in the back* . . . If Robert had been fleeing the scene, would Cholla or Tom Mooney have hesitated to tell her? Maybe, but she sensed something darker, more terrible.

To Sierra, it felt like they stared into each other's eyes forever. He seemed to be hesitating to leave, even though the longer he delayed, the more danger

414

he was in. And she could not bring herself to ask the questions that tormented her so. Did you murder my husband in such a cowardly way? Did you ever care one smidgen for me, or was I only part of your revenge, because of what happened to your sister?

"Well . . ." Sierra licked dry lips. "I . . . I guess I'd better be getting back. Good luck to you."

"Thank you for bringing my dog," he said. "And tell Sergeant Mooney I hope the gold gives him a comfortable old age."

Gold? She didn't know what he was talking about, but it didn't matter. *Take me with you,* her heart cried, but she didn't speak.

Tears blinding her, Sierra turned and walked toward her mare. She wanted to leave before she broke down. She had the rest of her life to weep.

Cholla stared after her, watching her walk toward her horse. She was going to ride away and leave him after all. In truth, he had delayed leaving the camp because he hoped she cared enough to come after him, to offer to share his dangerous life below the border. Then, when she had ridden in unexpectedly, he had almost shot her.

But she hadn't come here to go with him, only to return his dog. Still, he sensed something was wrong, that something had come between them.

Will she come with me if I beg her? He was a proud man, not used to pleading for anything. He considered taking her with him as a captive, as he had done when he'd first met her.

No. He shook his head as he watched Sierra adjust her bridle, making ready to leave. He didn't want her if she didn't care enough for him to accompany him of her own free will. To admit he needed her was more than he could bring himself to do, but there was more than pride involved here.

From the moment she had ridden in, he had felt a new, invisible wall between them. Had she found out the secret? Tom couldn't tell her, and Cholla wouldn't; not even if it cost him the woman he loved. There was honor involved, and a man without honor was no man at all.

Sierra was about to mount the mare. He had one moment to choose between his pride and the woman he loved. Suppose she laughed and said no. If he didn't ask, he would always wonder what her answer would have been.

He watched her swing up into the saddle, pick up the reins. He would regret this moment the rest of his life — the rest of his lonely life.

He suddenly knew that nothing mattered without her, not his life or his freedom, least of all his pride, and he ran toward her shouting, "Sierra! Don't go! Don't leave me!"

Surprised by his outcry, she turned in the saddle, saw him coming toward her, arms outstretched. "What did you say?"

"I said, *ishton*, don't go! I love you!"

God help her, she didn't care any more what had happened in that arroyo. Even if he had murdered Robert, she loved the Apache more than anything in the world, and nothing else mattered to her.

Sierra wasn't even conscious of doing so, but she slid off the horse and into his arms. "Oh, Cholla, dearest . . ." She could say no more because she was weeping and his dear lips were kissing the tears from her face as he pulled her hard against his chest and kissed her as if he would never let her go.

They were one against the world. They had each other, and nothing else counted. The danger, the lonely life, and the hardships they faced meant little as long as they could be together.

She slipped her arms around his sinewy neck and wept, only now she shed tears of relief and happiness. "Oh, Cholla, I came out here hoping you wanted me but thinking you didn't."

"I have no right to ask," he whispered. "We will have to live on the run. You will have to turn your back on civilization forever."

She looked up at him through tear-blurred eyes. "I don't care. I love you, Cholla, and if you love me, want me, nothing else matters! I don't care what happened that day! Do you hear? I don't care if you shot him in the back!"

She felt him stiffen, and he pulled away, looked at her a long moment. "Sierra, who told you that?"

"What difference does it make?" She looked up at him defiantly. "Nothing can change the way I feel about you. I love you, no matter what!"

He stared down at her. "You think I killed your husband and you'll go with me anyway?"

"I love you! I don't care about anything else!" She

417

began to weep, threw her arms around his neck.

"Oh, Sierra, I wish I could tell you . . ." He broke off, pulled her against his brawny chest, held her a long moment, close against his heart. She felt she could stay there forever, safe in his powerful arms, secure in his love.

Perhaps her mother had had some inkling of her daughter's future when she had named her. The West Zanna had longed for and never seen, the mountains she had only dreamed of, these were going to provide a refuge for her daughter.

"Never mind," Cholla whispered and kissed her forehead. "If you'll go with me, maybe I can learn to live with what you believe. We need to leave now, *ishton*, before Gillen tracks us down."

"I'm not afraid," she said, "I'll never be afraid again. The Army now has two nails that won't be hammered down." She looked up at him tenderly. She had not known love could be so wonderful.

The dog, resting at their feet, growled suddenly, and they both jerked around, startled. Ke'jaa cocked his head and stared toward the fort, ears alert, the hair on his back standing on end as he snarled again.

She felt Cholla tense. "What is it, boy? Is someone coming?"

In answer, the big yellow animal looked toward the fort, growling louder.

Sierra's heart seemed to stop. "Do you suppose someone followed me?"

"Maybe if we ride out right now—"

"Cholla!" The shout came from the other side of the rocks, Gillen's voice. "Cholla! We saw the horses. Come out with your hands up and no one will get hurt!"

Cholla yanked her down behind the shelter of the rocks, and the dog went with them. "Gillen! He's found us. I don't have much ammunition, Sierra." He looked down into her eyes, his face grim. "I don't intend to be taken alive. I'll die right here rather than be captured. But I'll send you out. You can count on Tom to take care of you." He put a hand to his mouth and shouted, "Gillen, hold your fire! I'm sending the girl out!"

"No!" She threw her arms around him. "I don't want to live without you! I won't go! Do you hear? I won't! If you're going to die here, I intend to die with you!"

"No"—he shook his head stubbornly—"you are the best part of me, Dark Eyes—the beat of my heart, the soul of me. I'll do whatever it takes to protect you."

She clung to him. "Never! I intend to stay right here and die with you, if need be. You're the best part of me, too. I never really lived, I only existed until you came along. I don't want to live without you."

In the moonlight, he looked grim as death as he handed her a pistol. "All right. We're in this together then."

She reached up and brushed his cheek with her lips as she took the gun. "I want you to know I

419

wouldn't trade a moment of the past several months. If I could choose to be anywhere in the world right now, it would still be here with you."

His eyes seemed to mist over as he cupped her small face in his big hand. "We're probably going to die here, Sierra."

"I don't care!" She grabbed his hand and kissed it. "We'll live life on our own terms or not at all. I wouldn't change a thing!"

He swallowed hard. "No regrets?"

"Only that I didn't meet you a long time ago, my dearest." Someday she was going to die, but she chose to do it here with her love. She kissed him one final time.

Chapter Twenty-two

My worst fear had been realized, Tom Mooney thought as he and Lieutenant Gillen, corporals Schultz and Finney, and troopers Taylor and Allen crouched behind the boulders and waited for Sierra Forester to be sent out.

Tom had delayed the patrol from leaving the fort as long as he could. He had even stopped on the trail twice to check his own mount for a loose shoe, with Gillen swearing at the delay and threatening to throw him in the guardhouse if he didn't get a move on.

Two of the men who had started out with them were too drunk to ride on and were sent back to the fort. Another soldier's horse threw a shoe and he had to return, so that left only six men to bring in Cholla, but it might be enough.

To make up for Tom's deliberate delays, Gillen had insisted they ride at a gallop until the horses were lathered and blowing. The scent of smoke from the dead campfire and the sight of two horses told Tom Cholla and Sierra hadn't yet left.

"Mrs. Forester!" Gillen shouted, "come out! Don't be afraid! See if you can get Cholla to surrender!" He laughed softly under his breath and said to the others, "if that Injun shows his head, blow him away!"

"But, Lieutenant," Tom protested, "there's a woman in those rocks with him! Maybe we can make a deal. If she comes out, in exchange, we'll let him go."

"Blast it all! You'd like that, wouldn't you? Let that Injun bastard escape!" Gillen turned toward the boulders. "Mrs. Forester, can you hear me? Come out now and you won't be hurt."

"Go to hell, Lieutenant!" Her voice rang from the rocks. "I'd rather die with Cholla than have you try to put your dirty hands on me again!"

Gill cursed while the soldiers around him laughed softly to themselves. He checked his rifle to make sure it was loaded. "Okay, the bitch has made her choice. If she gets killed, it wasn't because I didn't give her a chance."

"But, sir," Tom protested, "we can't fire, not knowing she's in there. Killing a woman is coward's work!"

"I'll take full responsibility," Gill snapped. "Remember, men, if we get this Injun, it'll be written up in the papers, and there'll be a reward to share, promotions and medals for everyone." With that, he raised up and fired two shots in rapid succession.

As the cracks of gunfire echoed through the hills,

Sierra's and Cholla's horses whinnied, reared, and bolted toward the patrol. The paint mare and the black gelding ran past the soldiers a few hundred yards, then stopped to graze near the cavalry horses.

Lieutenant Gillen grinned. "Ain't that a piece of luck? He didn't have their horses tied. Must have been gettin' ready to ride out." He cupped his mouth with his hands. "Okay, Cholla, we got you now! You don't have any horses; you're trapped. Give up and come out with your hands high, or we'll kill you!"

"I'd rather die here than be sent to Florida. Come and get me, Lieutenant!" The Indian rose up and his shot sang dangerously close, chipping away a piece of rock as it ricocheted near Gillen's head.

Gill crouched even lower, cursing Cholla's good aim. "That's okay," he said to Tom. "Time's on our side. We've got supplies, and we can get reinforcements." He turned to Finney. "Corporal, I trust you more than these others. I want you to ride back to the fort, bring us some help. I don't care if you have to go into the *cantina* and drag men out and put them on their horses. This Injun must not escape."

"Yes, sir!"

Finney was little more than a boy, and very drunk. Tom hoped he'd take forever to get to the fort. The Kansan stumbled to his horse, took off through the chill, dark night in a cloud of dust.

It's only a matter of time now, Tom thought. All they had to do was keep Cholla pinned down until help arrived. It was so unfair. All Cholla wanted to do was escape across the border and live the way his people had always lived, free of the restrictions of modern civilization.

"Sergeant," Gillen snapped, "you try to talk him out. You're his friend; he'll trust you to do right by him."

Friend, Tom's heart said, no, more than a friend. He is my *sikis,* my brother. Cholla had saved his life and Tom had saved Cholla's. Mooney was a good trooper, loyal to his country and honest, but this he could not do. "No," he said. "I won't do it. It's not honorable."

Gillen looked startled. "Maybe you didn't understand, Sergeant. That was an order!"

Tom looked at him a long moment. Gillen could ruin him, maybe have him shot for direct disobedience, at least take his stripes and throw him in the guardhouse. Instead of retirement, Tom might spend the next few years in prison at hard labor. But whatever it cost him, he was going to see that Cholla got justice. "No, *you* don't understand, Lieutenant. I won't do it. You can try to talk him out yourself, but I don't think he'll listen."

"Blast! I'm surrounded by traitors and ingrates!" Gillen was so angry he shook. He reached into his jacket, brought out the bag of candy he always caried. He munched a piece, sounding like a horse crunching corn.

Gill turned and ordered the other men to fan out into the surrounding rocks. "All right, Mooney, I'm going to crawl around behind him. Maybe it's only justice that the damned Injun is about to get shot in the back!"

Tom felt himself pale, but he looked the other man in the eye. "Don't talk about justice to me, Lieutenant. I still wonder if it was Forester or you who shot Delzhinne between the eyes after you two raped her!"

He saw the blow coming, threw up a hand to protect his head, but the last thing he remembered was the pain he felt as Gill's pistol butt caught him across the temple.

Gill looked at the unconscious sergeant, listened to the rifle fire around him. Blast it all! So Mooney knew. Well, hadn't he suspected as much? He'd make sure the Irishman didn't survive to tell. But those three troopers out there in the rocks were the sergeant's friends. Maybe Gill could find a way to finish the stubborn sergeant off without arousing their suspicions. He'd think about it. Maybe he could make Cholla look guilty.

In the meantime, Finney would bring help, no matter how slowly. Not that it mattered. Time was on the Army's side. By daylight, these hills would be swarming with soldiers, and Cholla wouldn't stand a chance. The patrol had plenty of supplies

on the pack mule, and the couple couldn't get awa[y]
without horses.

Cradling his rifle in his arms, Gill crawled quietl[y]
through the brush, up into the rocks behind the In[-]
dian. He saw the lovers in the moonlight, th[e]
woman close against Cholla's side. The big do[g]
crouched next to the couple. Sierra Forester coul[d]
just die with the damned savage. She was defian[t]
and stubborn. No one could be allowed to make [a]
laughingstock of the greatest army in the world, an[d]
no one had a right to live free anymore, certainl[y]
not anyone who would not conform to civilization['s]
restrictions.

His teeth were hurting him. Gill checked his rifl[e]
looked down at the pair. *Right in the back, yeah, ju[st]
the way my friend got it.* And he intended to kill th[at]
damned dog. He'd end up with the woman after al[l].

From where Gill lay, he could see that Cholla wa[s]
frantically looking around for shells. The Apach[e]
must be about out of ammunition while the soldier[s]
had plenty. And time was on the Army's side. [If]
Cholla didn't get away under cover of darkness, b[y]
morning the whole area would be swarming wit[h]
troops. The telegraph would pick up the story, an[d]
newsmen would be at the fort within hours. Lieu[-]
tenant Gillen would be a hero.

He heard occasionally random shooting fro[m]
Schultz, Allen, and Taylor. They weren't going t[o]
be responsible for killing an old comrade. Gill kne[w]
their excuse would be that their aim was poor. N[o]

426

Cholla's only real danger was from Gillen—or the troops that would arrive in a couple of hours.

He aimed the rifle, absently fumbled in his jacket for the sack of candy. Below him, Cholla and Sierra were arguing in the moonlight, and he wondered what it was they talked of in these last minutes of their lives.

Sierra looked at Cholla and shook her head stubbornly. "No, I won't do it!"

"Yes, you will!" Cholla's dark face was grim. "I won't have you killed. I'll yell at Gill, tell him to hold his fire 'til you come out. Whatever happens after that doesn't matter."

"It matters to me!" Sierra couldn't control herself. She began to cry and looked toward the south. If they had only had time to make it to the border. It was so near, yet so far away. It seemed terribly unfair that they had traveled all this way and had endured so much only to have it all end in tragedy and death when they were just short of their goal. "I won't do it!"

"Then I'll throw down my gun, walk out there, and surrender. I'm out of shells anyway. What about you?"

Sierra handed him her pistol. "I've only got one cartridge left. You know you can't trust Gill. He'll swear to anything, but when you step out there, he'll kill you."

427

Cholla sighed. "You're right. Gillen would rathe
kill me than capture me, and I don't know wha
Tom can do. He's being awfully quiet." He looke
at her for a long moment. "I love you, Sierra."

She clung to him, savoring the feel of him. Sh
knew already what he planned to do, and she coul
not fault him for it. No doubt he intended to goa
the lieutenant into killing him rather than be take
alive. "I'm glad we had this moment in time."

They clung together. The night was suddenly si
lent. Ke'jaa lifted his big head, sniffing the ai
Then he snarled, the hair on his back bristling
even as she heard the slightest sound in the stil
ness, a rattle of paper, a crunching noise as if
horse chewed corn. She screamed out a warning
but even as she did, Cholla whirled and pulled th
trigger.

A bullet whined down from behind them, rico
cheting off the boulder. In almost the same instant
Cholla's gun thundered next to her ear. The blue
clad man up in the rocks staggered, a rifle clutche
in his hands. The red, ragged hole between Gillen'
widened eyes spurted blood. The lieutenant stum
bled backward and went down, his rifle firing as hi
dead fingers jerked the trigger.

"Cholla, are you all right?" She saw a smear o
blood on his forehead and then realized a splinte
of rock, dislodged by Gillen's bullet, had graze
him. He drew her close. Now they could only wait
out of ammunition and not sure how many soldier

428

surrounded them. They had already done all they could, but it hadn't been enough. Sierra was prepared to die with Cholla, because she would not leave him and she knew he didn't intend to be taken alive.

Tom came to gradually. Head aching, he tried to remember what had happened. Lieutenant Gillen had struck him with the butt of a rifle. He had to do something to help Cholla. He had to . . .

The rifle shot cracked at the same instant Tom heard the woman shout a warning, and immediately after a pistol was fired. The sounds echoed and re-echoed through the wooded hills as Gillen stood, unsteadily, high in the rocks, the moonlight reflecting on his brass buttons. He looked surprised, there was a dark circle between his eyes. He toppled over.

Tom was almost too groggy to move, but Schultz crawled through the brush to his side, an unlit cigar clenched between stained teeth. "Sarge, with the lieutenant down, you're in charge. What do we do?"

Tom stood up slowly, his rifle hanging forgotten in his hand, his head caked with blood. He peered at the rocks.

Cholla, the girl, and the big dog looked back at him, in their eyes an unspoken plea. Blood smeared the Apache's face, but he had his arm around the woman, protectively.

Tom hesitated, looking at the pair only half-hidden by the boulder. Yes, it was his decision to make, wasn't it? If he killed the scout or captured him, he would receive a reward and a promotion. Nobody would believe the Apache if he told the truth about Lieutenant Forester's death, and with Cholla dead or in prison, Tom might be able to win Sierra's heart.

But Mooney was an honorable man. Staring at the helpless pair of lovers, he made his decision. There are people who are made of steel that won't bend, no matter how hard they are driven. And by the Mother of God, Tom was tired of being part of the hammer!

"Men," he said loudly, and turned away, "I think the hostile's been killed or we've lost him or maybe he's slipped across the border. Taylor, you and Allen throw the lieutenant's body across my horse, and let's head back to the fort to intercept that patrol."

Schultz stood up, lit the cigar clenched in his stained teeth. "Sarge, what about the Medicine Hat stallion the lieutenant was riding?"

Tom looked at the fine paint horse grazing quietly beside Sierra's mare. "I believe that pair of horses strayed, and we couldn't catch them." He pushed his hat back on his thinning hair. "Likewise the mule loaded with supplies. Do we understand each other, men?"

Taylor and Allen paused in loading the lieutenant's body across Mooney's horse, smiled. "Yes, sir."

Schultz blew a puff of smoke as he swung up on

430

his horse. "Rules and regulations don't matter as long as justice is done. We all felt that way at the arroyo, Sarge, we still do."

"Thanks, boys. Let's move out. My report will read that we believe the scout and his captive are probably both dead, no use in searching further."

"Shall we recommend Lieutenant Gillen for a commendation?" The corporal leaned on his saddle horn.

"I don't think he's got any relatives," Tom replied, "but it'll look good on Army records. God has a way of evening things out, after all. As I recall, medals and promotions were very important to Lieutenant Gillen. We'll do what we can."

"Oh, Sarge," Schultz said, "I think you should have the Indian's black gelding. It's a good horse, and you'll need one back in Michigan."

Tom thought about it. Was it right? Yes, Cholla would want him to have it. He swung up into the black's saddle.

Just before he rode away, Tom glanced back over his shoulder, saw the Apache look at him, mouth the words, *Gracias, sikis*. Thank you, brother.

Tom swallowed hard, touched his hat with his hand in a last salute to the pair. He was seeing them for the very last time; he knew that. It might have been possible to convince Sierra that Cholla had killed her husband, but much as Tom wanted her, he couldn't do that to his Indian brother.

For a split second, Tom was back in the arroyo

on that hot summer day, standing behind Robert
Forester as the crazed officer waved his pistol, planning to kill the unarmed Apache.

Tom hadn't even realized he'd fired until he felt
the recoil, smelled the burnt powder, heard the shot
ring out. The lieutenant half turned to look at Tom,
surprised and bewildered, one hand going back to
the scarlet stain spreading across the back of his
blue uniform. Slowly Forester dropped the pistol
and fell on his face. Tom's own gun fell from nerveless fingers as the enormity of what he'd done swept
over him.

Holy Saint Patrick. He had shot an officer in the
back to save the life of a friend. He could live with
that. Maybe it wasn't legal, but it was just.

And now the woman was leaving with that friend.
That was just, too. She loved the Apache, it had
shown in her eyes. Tom wished she knew that
Cholla was innocent, but he realized the Apache
would not break his vow. And if Sierra never found
out what had happened on that fateful summer day
it didn't matter, because she loved Cholla anyway.

Tom blinked away the tears that threatened to
blind him and turned to follow the patrol back to
the fort. Moonlight reflected off the metal on the
bridles of the horses ahead of him. It was a big
golden moon, bright as Usen's treasure.

Usen's own. Gold. Ke'jaa's den. It came to him in a
rush, the meaning of the message. There was gold
in the cave where Cholla had found the puppy

432

treasure forbidden to the Apache but not to a white friend. This was the last thing Cholla was doing for Tom Mooney.

Ahead of him, Schultz, Allen, and Taylor rode single-file, the last man leading the horse that carried Gillen's body. Those men were almost ready to retire, too, and their futures were bleak. Tom wondered what time it was? If it was after midnight, he was out of the Army and he had just decided he wasn't going to reenlist. There was a farm waiting for him, and a young schoolteacher needed an escort back to Michigan. He smiled to himself and wondered if she liked poetry and children.

He reined in and looked back one final time. In the moonlight, he saw two riders on Medicine Hat horses. Headed for the border, they were leading a pack mule. A big yellow dog loped alongside them. The woman's black hair blew out behind her as she rode south.

"Good-bye," Tom whispered. "Good-bye. 'May the road rise up to meet you, may the wind always be at your back, and may God hold you in the hollow of his hand forevermore.' "

He took the picture from his jacket then, took one last look at it. Then he let the wind take it from his fingers and blow it away toward the hills. He wondered suddenly what the little schoolteacher's name was?

"Is everything all right, Sergeant?" Schultz called.

"Yes. God is still in control, and things have a

way of working out as they should, Corporal." He watched the pair pause on a rise in the moonlight; then he turned the black gelding up the trail toward the fort.

Sierra glanced back only once and saw Tom Mooney looking after them. Cholla's friend, she thought. Tom could have told me Cholla killed my husband, and I might have stayed with him, not have come out here. The Irishman had been trying to tell her something, and she had been afraid to listen. What was it?

Abruptly, the words of the old poem came to her again, and she knew then what Tom had tried to tell her. Tears ran down her cheeks as she remembered the very last lines: "I could not love thee, Dear, so much, Loved I not honour more."

She looked over at Cholla. "You are the most honorable man I ever knew," she said. "You wouldn't break your vow and tell me Tom killed my husband to stop him from murdering you, not even if it meant losing me."

He looked thunderstruck. "Who told you what happened in the arroyo that day?"

"No one, my love." She smiled gently through her tears. "I suddenly understood the honor between friends, and I knew—I just knew. But Robert deserved to die, and justice has been done."

Now nothing mattered but her love for the big

man riding by her side. She shook her hair back and looked at him. "Can we make the border by daylight, my love?"

"If we ride hard." He smiled at her. "Are you ready?"

Sierra's heart was so full, for a moment she could not speak. She was turning her back on the world she knew, but whatever the sacrifice, Cholla's devotion made it worthwhile.

"Without knowing it, I have been ready always, just waiting for you to come into my life. Let's go," she said, and slapped her mare with the reins.

With Ke'jaa running ahead of them, the lovers galloped south toward the Sierra Madre mountains.

To My Readers

Yes, a brave did escape from a train carrying Apaches to Florida in September of 1886. Everyone agrees that his name was Massai, that he escaped in the vicinity of St. Louis, and that somehow he managed to return to his own land within a year. He was seen in Arizona by several witnesses who knew him. No one knows how he got there or what happened to him after that. The rest of his life, as with most legendary figures, is either unknown or is shrouded in controversy. Some say he was eventually hunted down and killed. Others say he disappeared across the border with a woman who loved him enough to give up everything to go with him. I'd like to believe that, wouldn't you?

Alberta Begay wrote in a *True West* article that Massai was her father and that he was a Chiricahua warrior who escaped from the train with another scout, a Tonkawa Indian, and returned to Arizona to take the Apache girl who became her mother across the border.

Jason Betzinez, in his book, *I Fought with Geron-*

imo, says Massai was a Warm Springs Apache scout for the Army.

Massai was also mentioned in General Miles's *Personal Recollections* and Frederick Remington's book, *Crooked Trails*.

Southeast of the ruins of old Fort Bowie, there's a high place with a breathtaking view known as Massai Point. Legend says he hid there, deep in the Chiricahua Mountains.

The Massai legend has inspired at least one other novel, a traditional Western, Paul Wellman's *Bronco Apache*, published in 1936. That novel became a movie entitled: *Apache*, starring Burt Lancaster. While that film shows Massai and Geronimo on the same train, actually they were sent on different trains from different stations. Geronimo and his men traveled through Texas, and ironic as it may seem, the Army band did play "Auld Lang Syne" as Geronimo's renegades were forced on board.

How many of the Army officers mentioned in this story were actual people? General Crook, General Miles, Lieutenant Gatewood, Captain Lawton, Lieutenant Colonel James Wade, and Dr. Leonard Wood.

As I indicated, Crook had made a pledge to the Apache so they would surrender. That pledge was promptly broken by the U.S. government. Crook resigned in protest and was immediately replaced by

General Miles a favorite of President Cleveland. Crook spent the next four years trying to right the wrong. When he died suddenly of a heart attack in 1890, there was no one of importance left to speak for the Apache.

Lieutenant Charles Gatewood, the slender, big-nosed officer who had risked his life going into Geronimo's stronghold to talk with him, was on the wrong side of the political fence because of his connections to Crook. Gatewood would later be sent to Wounded Knee and would be there at the time of the Indian massacre in 1890. He died in 1896, still an obscure lieutenant, virtually without honors and forgotten, and was buried in Arlington National Cemetery near his beloved commander. Ironically, Geronimo outlived them both and visited their graves while in Washington to ride in Teddy Roosevelt's inaugural parade.

What happened to the Apache? The Arizonians wanted to hang Geronimo and some other leaders of the Indian revolt, despite what Crook had promised. In fact, when the old Indian and his cohorts were shipped to Florida, President Cleveland ordered them to be taken off the train at San Antonio. The Apaches were held there more than a month while white authorities argued over whether they could legitimately be shipped back to Arizona for trial and possibly for hanging. Almost all the

Apaches were finally sent to Florida, where they remained for two years before being sent to Alabama. Many of the children were shipped to Carlisle, Pennsylvania to be educated. The Apache did not do well in any of those states. Fully twenty-five percent of them died during that time. Finally, in 1894, those who were still alive were sent to the Fort Sill area.

Geronimo died there on February 17, 1909, of pneumonia caused in part by lying unconscious in the rain all night after a bout with liquor. He is buried in the Apache cemetery under a pyramid of river stones topped with a concrete eagle.

In 1913, the Apache still alive were given a choice of staying in the Fort Sill area or of moving to the Mescalero reservation in New Mexico. None were allowed to return to Arizona. There were still people alive in that state who remembered the terrible tortures and killings committed by some of the warriors and feared they might occur again.

The few bands of Apache who stayed in the Fort Sill area are now known as the Fort Sill Apaches. You may see some of them do their fire dance if you ever attend the big annual Indian Pageant held during August of each year at Anadarko, Oklahoma, not far from Lawton. There are also several wonderful museums in the area, as well as the old fort; and buffalo and longhorn cattle can be seen at the nearby Wichita Wildlife Refuge. Quanah Parker, the half-breed, last chief of the Comanche, outlived

Geronimo by two years and six days, and he is buried at old Fort Sill, along with his baby sister and his famous mother, Cynthia Ann Parker.

Buried in eastern Oklahoma, southwest of the town of Porum, near the Eufaula Reservoir, is Belle Starr, the "beautiful Bandit Queen," of many novels. She wasn't beautiful or much of a bandit, but she did like Indian men. At least two of her four husbands were Native Americans. Belle lived at Younger's Bend on the South Canadian River in eastern Indian Territory. Like Geronimo and Quanah, Belle also died in February. She was ambushed and killed on February 3, 1889, two days before her forty-first birthday and a little more than two months before the Unassigned Lands were opened to settlement in the first and best-known of the Oklahoma land runs. Who killed her is still a mystery.

Belle's son, Eddie, died violently in 1896. Her daughter, Pearl, only twenty-one at the time of her mother's death, had no way to support herself and her illegitimate child, so she ran a bordello in Fort Smith, Arkansas, for a while. Legend says Pearl was fathered by notorious outlaw, Cole Younger, but my research unearthed information that disputes this popular belief. Belle had four grandchildren. One of Pearl's daughters, Jennette, was married briefly to Hugh Fair, an early member of the Sons of the Pioneers singing group.

* * *

There really was a railroad strike in the early spring of 1886. It led to confrontations, violence, and death in the town of East St. Louis. And the winter of 1886–87 is remembered as the year of the most terrible blizzards on record. Some ranches lost as much as eighty-five percent of their stock as hundreds of thousands of cattle froze to death.

I'm sorry to report that the Indians were actually loaded on a train on which the windows had been nailed shut, and they had to leave their belongings behind. The Army did auction their horses, but no one wanted the hundreds of abandoned Indian dogs left roaming the area. Because of the danger of rabies and stock killings, local cowboys, soldiers, and the residents of Holbrook shot most of the dogs.

If the name "Griswold" sounded familiar, remember that a distant cousin of Julia's, Melanie Griswold, married into this saga in *Nevada Nights* and was killed in a buggy wreck on her wedding day. I know some of you will really like the handsome train robber called Nevada and will ask about him. Yes, he'll turn up again later. Who is he? I won't tell yet, but if you've read *Nevada Nights,* I'll bet you can guess.

Some of you have written to say you didn't know this was a series and to ask why it is called Panorama of the Old West. I hate the word "series," probably for the same reason many of you do. In most series, if you miss a book, you can't figure out what's going on. A "panorama" is an all-encompassing picture, and I'm going to do just what the Cheyenne do here in Oklahoma, tie one tale to another, until I've painted a big picture of the history of the old West. I've tried to write each so that you can read only one without being confused. Of course, I hope you'll want to go back and read them all.

My editor has been forwarding a lot of mail. I *always* answer all of it, so if you didn't get a reply, remember that letters are sometimes lost in the forwarding process. I love to hear from readers. Please write c/o Zebra Books, 475 Park Avenue South, NY NY 10016. I'd appreciate your including a long, self-addressed, stamped envelope. Canadians, please remember I can't use Canadian stamps, so please purchase the appropriate exchange voucher at your post office. Why a long envelope? Because I'm going to send you a bookmark with a list of all my books on one side and a drawing of the most handsome Indian "hunk" you ever saw on the other, and I don't want to fold him in half.

Before you ask, I'll tell you that, yes, he is a real live guy who is part Apache, has blue eyes, and lifts weights for a hobby. *Romantic Times* magazine liked this bookmark so well, they gave it an award at their 1990 convention.

Someone asked if I would list all my books so far and specify when they came out. Well, here they are.

THE PANORAMA OF THE OLD WEST SERIES

Zebra Heartfires

CHEYENNE CAPTIVE February, 1987
  ISBN# 0-8217-1980-7
CHEYENNE PRINCESS September, 1987
  ISBN# 0-8217-2176-3

Zebra Hologram/Lovegrams

COMANCHE COWBOY September, 1988
  ISBN# 0-8217-2449-5
BANDIT'S EMBRACE March, 1989
  ISBN# 0-8217-2596-3
NEVADA NIGHTS July, 1989
  ISBN# 0-8217-2701-X
CHEYENNE CARESS January, 1990
  ISBN# 0-8217-2864-4
QUICKSILVER PASSION September, 1990
  ISBN# 0-8217-3117-3
APACHE CARESS October, 1991
  ISBN# 0-8217-3560-8

You should be able to order many of my past novels through your favorite bookstore or directly from Zebra.

Was Indian Territory as tough as writers tell you? You'd better believe it! One hundred three Deputy U.S. Marshals working for "Hanging Judge" Parker were killed during his twenty-one years as judge at Fort Smith, most of them in Indian Territory. There is no town in Oklahoma called Sundance, but we had plenty of towns just as tough, such as Ada.

My mother was born and reared in Pontotoc County. In the town of Ada, the county seat, on the night of April 19, 1909, two years after statehood, an armed mob took four men out of the jail where they were being held for committing murder during a ranchers' feud. All four were lynched.

A number of my correspondents want information on some particular tribe or how to track down Native American ancestors. Tracking down an ancestor is going to be very difficult unless you have some solid information and details. Your public library will help you with researching either of the above. I'm not very knowledgeable on any tribe that doesn't have some connection with my home state.

* * *

What am I going to write about next? In my research I have found stories of white men who turned their backs on their own civilization to ride with the Indians. Some of these men actually lived; others are only intriguing, mysterious legends.

In 1864, the frontier was being ravaged by the Plains tribes who took advantage of the fact that the white soldiers had all gone off to fight in the Civil War. But I told you about that in Trace Durango's story: *Cheyenne Princess.*

The Union was so desperate that an offer was made to release any Confederate soldier from a prison camp if he would sign up to join the Yankee Army and go West to fight Indians. These Southerners were known as "Galvanized Yankees." I mentioned them earlier in *Quicksilver Passion,* my version of Colorado's legendary gold-rush days.

Now suppose a rich, arrogant young Southern officer named Rand Erikson ended up in a hellhole of a Yankee prison? Suppose he was so desperate to get out, he joined the "Galvanized Yankees" and was sent to fight the Sioux? What if he was captured and turned over to a vengeful young Sioux woman whose warrior husband had just been killed by soldiers? Rand's very life may depend on whether he can charm this Indian girl into falling in love with him so he can escape. What will happen if he takes this Sioux girl back to the wealthy, aristocratic society and the elegant fiancée he left behind? Then a handsome, virile man is caught between two very different women and two different lifestyles.

Late at night here in Oklahoma, the warriors still gather in the glow of the powwow fires to tell the old medicine tales while the drums echo and the coyotes call. Like them, I have many, many stories to share. This is your personal invitation to join me in early 1992 as we return to the Sioux nation of 1864 and ride with the white warrior and his woman.

I'll save you a spot by the campfire. . . .

Georgina Gentry

READERS ARE IN LOVE WITH ZEBRA LOVEGRAMS

TEMPTING TEXAS TREASURE (3312, $4.50)
by Wanda Owen

With her dazzling beauty, Karita Montera aroused passion in every redblooded man who glanced her way. But the independent senorita had eyes only for Vincent Navarro, the wealthy cattle rancher she'd adored since childhood—who was also her family's sworn enemy. The Navarro and Montera clans had clashed for generations, but no past passions could compare with the fierce desire that swept through Vincent as he came across the near-naked Karita cooling herself beside the crystal waterfall on the riverbank. With just one scorching glance, he knew this raven-haired vixen must be his for eternity. After the first forbidden embrace, she had captured his heart—and enslaved his very soul!

MISSOURI FLAME (3314, $4.50)
by Gwen Cleary

Missouri-bound Bevin O'Dea never even met the farmer she was journeying to wed, but she believed a marriage based on practicality rather than passion would suit her just fine . . . until she encountered the smoldering charisma of the brash Will Shoemaker, who just happened to be her fiance's step-brother.

Will Shoemaker couldn't believe a woman like Bevin, so full of hidden passion, could agree to marry his step-brother—a cold fish of a man who wanted a housekeeper more than he wanted a wife. He knew he should stay away from Bevin, but the passions were building in both of them, and once those passions were released, they would explode into a red-hot *Missouri Flame*.

BAYOU BRIDE (3311, $4.50)
by Bobbi Smith

Wealthy Louisiana planter Dominic Kane was in a bind: according to his father's will, he must marry within six months or forfeit his inheritance. When he saw the beautiful bonded servant on the docks, he figured she'd do just fine. He would buy her papers and she would be his wife for six months—on paper, that is.

Spirited Jordan St. James hired on as an indenture servant in America because it was the best way to flee England. Her heart raced when she saw her handsome new master, and she swore she would do anything to become Dominic's bride. When his strong arms circled round her in a passionate embrace, she knew she would surrender to his thrilling kisses and lie in his arms for one long night of loving . . . no matter what the future might bring!

Available wherever paperbacks are sold, or order direct from the publisher. Send cover price plus 50¢ per copy for mailing and handling to Zebra Books, Dept. 3560, 475 Park Avenue South, New York, N.Y. 10016. Residents of New York, New Jersey and Pennsylvania must include sales tax. DO NOT SEND CASH.

HEART STOPPING ROMANCE BY ZEBRA BOOKS

MIDNIGHT BRIDE (3265, $4.50)
by Kathleen Drymon

With her youth, beauty, and sizable dowry, Kellie McBride had her share of ardent suitors, but the headstrong miss was bewitched by the mysterious man called The Falcon, a dashing highwayman who risked life and limb for the American Colonies. Twice the Falcon had saved her from the hands of the British, then set her blood afire with a moonlit kiss.

No one knew the dangerous life The Falcon led—or of his secret identity as a British lord with a vengeful score to settle with the Crown. There was no way Kellie would discover his deception, so he would woo her by day as the foppish Lord Blakely Savage . . . and ravish her by night as The Falcon! But each kiss made him want more, until he vowed to make her his *Midnight Bride*.

SOUTHERN SEDUCTION (3266, $4.50)
by Thea Devine

Cassandra knew her husband's will required her to hire a man to run her Georgia plantation, but the beautiful redhead was determined to handle her own affairs. To satisfy her lawyers, she invented Trane Taggart, her imaginary step-son. But her plans go awry when a handsome adventurer shows up and claims to *be* Trane Taggart!

After twenty years of roaming free, Trane was ready to come home and face the father who always treated him with such contempt. Instead he found a black wreath and a bewitching, sharp-tongued temptress trying to cheat him out of his inheritance. But he had no qualms about kissing that silken body into languid submission to get what he wanted. But he never dreamed that *he* would be the one to succumb to *her* charms.

SWEET OBSESSION (3233, $4.50)
by Kathy Jones

From the moment rancher Jack Corbett kept her from capturing the wild white stallion, Kayley Ryan detested the man. That animal had almost killed her father, and since the accident Kayley had been in charge of the ranch. But with the tall, lean Corbett, it seemed she was *never* the boss. He made her blood run cold with rage one minute, and hot with desire the next.

Jack Corbett had only one thing on his mind: revenge against the man who had stolen his freedom, his ranch, and almost his very life. And what better way to get revenge than to ruin his mortal enemy's fiery red-haired daughter. He never expected to be captured by her charms, to long for her silken caresses and to thirst for her never ending kisses.

Available wherever paperbacks are sold, or order direct from the Publisher. Send cover price plus 50¢ per copy for mailing and handling to Zebra Books, Dept. 3560, 475 Park Avenue South, New York, N.Y. 10016. Residents of New York, New Jersey and Pennsylvania must include sales tax. DO NOT SEND CASH.